SNATCHER'S RIDGE

THE ELIXIR SERIES
BOOK 2

JENNIFER DANIELS NEAL

SemiTone

BOOKS & MUSIC

I dedicate this work with love
to my fellow countrymen
of the United States of America
in the hope that we, with eyes wide open,
will learn and accept our history,
both the glory and disgrace.

May we carve what we pledge into reality,
a nation of liberty and justice for all.

So help us, God.

If you hear the dogs,
    Keep going.

If you see the torches in the woods,
    Keep going.

If there's shouting after you,
    Keep going.

Don't ever stop.
    Keep going.

If you want a taste of freedom,
    Keep going.

HARRIET TUBMAN

CONTENTS

Bear tends the fire until smoke rises through the tipi's flap, and flames illumine the buffalo skin on the floor. In the shifting light, the images painted there seem to dance.

This skin is the Tribe's history told in spiraling pictographs, and it has fallen to Bear to make sure no one forgets. He is Keeper of the Winter Count as his father was before him, and his grandfather before that.

The last time it was unrolled, Bear's father lay dying. While the Tribe dug the grave, Bear painted a replica—every symbol painstakingly precise in honor of the artist, the historian, the great storyteller who was his dad. The original was buried along with him.

Having just returned from the annual meeting, Bear kneels to consider how best to portray what the elders so quickly agreed upon, the defining event of the year. From the first snowfall, through all the seasons in turn, until the first snow fell again, nothing had been more remarkable than the celestial storm. For weeks, the stars fled across the sky in numbers, both thrilling and frightening, lighting up the night like a devouring fire. In the end, though, the stars that fled also vanished—snatched from the sky by some great, stellar net.

Bear's spine is straight, his expression solemn. On his chin, he rests the reed he'll use for a paintbrush. Finally, he flicks his braid behind himself and dips the reed into a small pot of black pigment. With one arc, he makes the moon, then switches reeds to use the red—the same red with which his father dotted human corpses the year smallpox took half the Tribe. He considers that before he presses the new reed to the old skin.

A knock against the tipi's entrance reveals a young woman smuggling a buffalo skin of her own. How she came upon such a treasure, he doesn't ask, but he's certain it was without fitting an arrow. She appraises Bear like she's in need of an accomplice, which makes him smile and shake his head. He doesn't bother rising to his feet.

"To what do I owe the pleasure, little fox? Have you no one else with whom to spar?" He shouldn't flirt with her. Definitely shouldn't invite her in. But in she comes, without so much as a greeting, and kneels to scrutinize his work.

Her black hair falls in straight lines. Her regal cheekbones beg to be drawn. "Why do you call me that?" she asks at length. For a moment, he has no idea what she means.

"Oh, *little fox?* To remind myself that you are as cunning as you are beautiful. I've seen you take things that don't belong to you. Things your victims don't even know they've given. Service. Insight. Buffalo skins?" He says the last as a question.

"Just how much of your time do you spend watching me?" she asks.

Laughing under his breath, Bear pretends to return to his work, but the truth is *a lot.* He watches her every chance he gets. Seeks her out when she's not around. Not that he'd admit to it. When she reaches toward his fresh illustration, he nabs her wrist. "It has to dry."

"I wasn't going to touch it." But she withdraws and sits back on her heels. "They weren't all snatched, you know."

Bear's brow begs the question.

"The stars. Some of them fell to Earth and rose where they landed, able to walk and talk as we do."

"Oh, where are they now, then?" he scoffs.

"They live as the igmuwatogla. They feel most at home among the lions."

Seconds pass. "You're playing with me," he says.

"I'm not. Did you see the way they came? From Oceti-Peta."

"The constellation?"

She nods. "Do you know what the Ojibwe call it? Gaadidnaway."

"The tail of the cougar," he interprets.

"And they're not the only ones. White people call it Leo. Do you know what that means?"

"Lion?"

"That's right. Many tribes see the constellation as a big cat. Even tribes across the great water."

"So, the stars fell from the sky to live with cats?"

"Well, that's not *why* they fell. They were smashed apart from the constellation. But yes. They trust the cats. Cats are reclusive. They're good at keeping secrets."

"And you know all this how?"

"Well, they don't keep secrets from *me*," she giggles, reminding him of the girl she used to be.

When Bear does nothing more than watch her, she takes it to mean he doesn't understand. "Bear, you know what I am, right? You must surely know what my grandmother was."

"I've heard you speaking to the horses," he recovers. "Heard them speaking to you."

"I do love the horses."

From the outskirts of camp, an animal screams, and Bear's eyes trail from the direction of the sound back to his visitor. "Where have you been this evening?" he asks with sudden suspicion. "Why weren't you at the meeting?"

"Oh, I was around."

He narrows his eyes. "Where have you been, little fox?"

"Can you not just call me by my name?"

The edge to her voice gives him pause. "What's the matter with you?"

"I need you to say it," she insists. "Because I need you to remember it."

Bear traces the pretty point of her ear where it protrudes from her hair. "Olowan." He concedes her name like a blessing. "Where have you been?"

Instead of answering, she unfolds her buffalo skin and spreads it beside his Winter Count. It's as blank as the last day the buffalo wore it.

She splays her fingers over it and says, "I've been praying. And I've been given a vision that needs to be recorded."

"*You.* Have been praying," he confirms.

"Is that so hard to believe?"

Bear shakes his head, but he's waiting for the punch line.

"Fine. I've been holed up in the mountain. There's an opening in one of the buttes, a cave in which I seek refuge from time to time. The vision *was* given to me. But by a crow." When he seems to accept her words as true, she says, "Will you do it? Will you fill this skin with lions and birds? So many birds, I..." She flicks her hand to indicate that no amount of counting could number the birds. Then she produces bright pigments that Bear has no access to—pots of yellow and turquoise. Shimmering silver.

His eyes go wide. "Where did you get these? Don't tell me the *star* people..."

The way she avoids his eyes shoots a pang of uneasiness through him. "Olowan, where did you get these? What are they made from?"

"Once you paint it," she hurries to say, "you'll have to keep it safe—just as you do the Winter Count. In fact, roll them up together. Or find another way. I don't want to know. I'm leaving, Bear. If I'm found, I'll be forced to—" She chokes on an unexpected sob, and before he knows what he's doing, he's pulling her into his arms.

"No one is going to force you to do *anything.*" He lifts her chin. "What do you mean you're leaving?"

"I have to go or great evil will come to the whole Tribe."

"No. You'll stay with me. You'll be my wife." He looks slightly surprised by his own words. "There. Now, you can add me to the ranks of those from whom you collect."

"I wish I could," she whispers. "But I'm not the only one in danger. The buffalo will go extinct. And in time, the honey bees, the lions. *You* —if I stay and he finds me."

"Who is *he?* That lion we just heard? I'll take care of him right now." Bear seizes his bow, but Olowan shakes her head and clutches his arm.

"Then who?" he persists. "One of the stars you spoke of?"

"No. But he is the reason they flee. Bear, I know you would fight for me. And I know you would die for me." She shakes her head to show that that's not an option. "*This* is what I need from you." She points to the blank buffalo skin. "This is greater than the Winter Count. Greater even than the Tribe itself. You have to find a way to keep it safe. And then you have to let me go."

"No," he protests. "I mean, yes, I'll paint it. I'll hide it away. But don't ask the rest."

For a moment, she is silent. But when another lion's cry goes up, she looks desperate.

"I'll keep it for you," he relents. "I'll do what you ask of me—except for let you go."

With a worried smile, she points to the images Bear has already painted. The arc of the moon. The fleeing stars. "Begin by drawing this again, but underneath, add a series of gates and an underground room where they empty. Add seven black feathers tied together, and use them as a divider between the gates and a meadow bordered by trees."

She proceeds to recount the vision. It continues with the birds. So many birds, Bear doesn't know how to convey the mass of them. There are starlings, swallows, magpies, crows. They swarm upon a lion in the middle of a spring-young forest. And there is a woman in a cage.

1

I FINALLY LEARN TO RUN

BEAM

How long have we been sitting at this stop sign? I haven't been paying attention because I've been reading texts from Chausie. Yes. Even though I just left his house.

My uncle is driving me home after a few weeks' adventure in which Chausie and I saved each other's lives. Repeatedly. Not to mention the lives of my mother and the wandering souls of my long-dead Indigenous ancestors. Native American. Indian. Oglala Lakota, to be precise. Look, I'm just now learning the most appropriate way to talk about the people with whom I share half of my genetic makeup.

Now that we're back in Atlanta, Chausie and I are just two high school seniors with graduation eight short weeks away. What will people think when we show up as a couple? The brainiac and the basketball player. I try not to smile. Will he hold my hand in front of everybody? Will he kiss me? He's exactly the kind of partner I never knew I wanted. I thought I'd end up with someone—I don't know—in a suit. Someone who follows rules. Someone tame.

I snort as the word comes to mind. Of all the things Chausie is, *tame* is not one of them. He's a mountain lion. Literally. He can shift in and out of lion form. I'm thinking about the way his tawny hair falls into his yellow eyes when I finally decide to look up—because Uncle Joel and I are *still* sitting at a stop sign. Over the trees, the red of sunset is fading to brown.

"Uncle Joel, have we lost our way?"

Uncle appears to be asleep at the wheel.

"Uncle Joel?"

"Yes. Lost my way," he mumbles. "Let me sleep. "

"But you're driving."

In the side mirror, I see a massive shadow ebbing in and out of itself as it overtakes the car. I don't mind admitting that in the last month, I have developed a severe traumatic response to nebulous things. Instinctively, I duck and cover. It's not until the shadow glides over us that I risk peeking through the sunroof. Happily, it is not a malicious entity bent on devouring the life light of humanity—like it was last week. This one is made up of birds. Hundreds. Thousands. Soon, my dread gives way to wonder.

"A murmuration of starlings!" I say and am pleasantly distracted.

(Among my many phases of scientific intrigue, was one in which I researched the collective nouns for types of birds. Did you know that a group of geese is named for what the birds are doing and not just for what they are? A gaggle if they're walking, a plump if they're swimming, and a wedge if they're flying?)

I roll down my window to hear the bird cries vacillate with their synchronized flight. "Listen to all that noise!" I say. It's an unnecessary cue. Over the steering wheel, Uncle Joel is fixed upon them. His lips are moving, but he's not speaking out loud.

"Have you ever seen so many?" I ask.

The starlings descend into the trees, over the ground, and onto the car! It's a little unnerving—the sheer number of them.

"They're not starlings," Uncle finally says. "They're magpies."

"Oh, then they're a conventicle!" I say with delight. I know. I distribute random facts like confetti.

Uncle doesn't share my excitement.

"A conventicle," I repeat. "That's what you call a group of—"

My uncle grows wild-eyed, like some of the homeless men I've seen downtown. He grips the wheel and floors the gas pedal while I yelp, and the tires squeal across the street, where we bump over the curb and onto the grass. A lot of birds take flight from the trees before us but re-alight just as quickly when Uncle skids to a stop.

"What has gotten into you?" I ask. He is often intense but seldom out of control. "Did you suffer some kind of a head— You did," I answer myself.

When Uncle came to our aid against an army that Chausie's stepmom had summoned, he was mercilessly attacked. Did something happen to him that the after-effects of my blood can't heal?

Uncle Joel is muttering about the birds and speaking so fast that it's all gibberish to me. He seems to be trying to get out of the car and—at the same time—to remain behind the wheel.

"Uncle, are you ill?" I ask.

One of his hands pries the door handle but the other is cuffing its wrist. He whips his head to me and practically shouts, "Who called a conventicle?!"

"You're scaring me," I tell him. "Should I get Dad?" I lift my phone. "Or 911?"

For a moment, Uncle Joel remains fixed upon me. Then he lunges and rips the phone from my grasp. The gesture is so shocking, that all I do is gape at him.

"I'm sorry," he rushes to say, but he tosses the phone in the back seat. "Let's keep driving. NO, LET'S NOT!"

The way he contradicts himself is beyond weird. He turns the key with such ferocity, that the starter makes a violent scratching noise.

That's enough for me. While my uncle struggles to get the car moving, I discretely unlatch my seatbelt and slide out the door. But he's on to me. He flails across the seat to grab me. At the very same time, he yells, "Beam, get out of here! Run away from me!"

I do. I flee into the woods where the birds create an opening and then close it back behind me like a curtain.

Now, you may be aware that running is not a gift of mine. Even as a kid, when it was supposed to feel natural, it did not. But I've had a lot of practice over the past few weeks, and you know what? Right now, I finally get why people enjoy it. It feels second nature. I think I could sprint a marathon. Bursting with speed, I leap over a fallen tree. I don't even stop to calculate how to do it. Then, I pounce up against a standing trunk—just for fun. This is awesome. Maybe I'm just made for *off*-road running! Something wilder and—*Umph!*

What's that thing *pride* goes before? Yeah, that's what happens to me. On the other side of one of those bold leaps, I tumble right over myself and am about to break my neck on the huge boulder in front of me when *nope!* Miraculously, I right myself and halt before impact. It's incredible how agile I am right now. It's—over. The ground beneath me gives way and I plummet into a hole, wildly, but uselessly, grappling as I slide about fifteen feet to the bottom.

I'm OK. I land on my feet.

It's not as dark down here as one might expect. I'm not sure why. There's no light except for what I can see of the late evening sky through the opening. I feel curious, which surprises me. You'd think that my first inclination would be to freak out, but instead, I look around. I'd like to know what caused the earth to sink in like this. I think this pit was dug on purpose.

As I explore the earthen walls, I notice that I'm seeing in shades of purple and blue. *Chausie?* I close my eyes to concentrate. *Are you with me?*

Back in South Dakota when I was physically separated from Chaus and desperate to find him, I was able to connect with him mentally. *Chausie, Uncle Joel isn't himself. I seem to have fallen into some sort of pit.*

For a moment, I take comfort that my catcher necklace makes me invisible to the worst of evil entities, but then I remember that the last time I wore it, it had been flung over a tower. I shiver to recall the look on Kanji's face—the man who stole it—as he flapped and fell to his death to retrieve it.

When I open my eyes, I still see the world in blue. I'm so certain that it is through *Chausie's* eyes, that I don't question the fact that I'm the one controlling the direction of his gaze or that the scene I'm observing is the one in front of my own face, the narrow walls of this pit in which I've landed.

My uncle's voice sounds from far away. He's telling me to come out so we can go home. Telling me he's back to himself now.

You know what I don't hear anymore? The birds. Where are all those birds? I look up through the opening to see some of them in the sky, undulating as one unified being. How odd that I can view them so clearly from such a distance.

That's when an old, wizened face looks down on me. His smile is more ambitious than kind. Not my uncle. "Aren't you a lovely thing?" he says and brandishes a small tube like a whistle. He puts it to his lips and blows, the sound of his breath puncturing my ears as a stinger punctures my throat.

2

A SMALL WOMAN IN A CAGE

CHAUSIE

I've barely said hello to my mom. I know she's dying to hear about my trip, and honestly, I'm looking forward to telling her. Right now, she's in the kitchen warming dinner for us. I was just supposed to throw my bag in my room and wash up. But then Dad called to let me know about the beaded pouch he'd stashed inside my bag.

I'm vaguely aware there is a rising commotion outside my bedroom window, but I am wholly focused on the contents of this pouch, now spread on my carpet—seven coal-black feathers strung together and Beam's catcher necklace—the same necklace she's supposed to wear because it protects her from evil. Oh, and let's not forget the cryptic note from her uncle that warns her not to be alone with him. Skipping the part about why someone would write such a note about themselves, it should be known that Beam *is* alone with him. Right now. And that she has stopped answering my texts.

When the outside commotion explodes into something too loud to ignore, I get to my feet to see what's going on. It's birds. There are so many, that I have to blink to ensure they're real. They're descending upon every inch of the front yard and smothering our two trees.

Thwack! I flinch as a feathered body slams against the window right in front of my face. The addled creature seems to mirror my surprise, falling away and then fluttering back into view to peck the glass. Does it want to get to me, or is it merely trying to escape the overpopulation of the yard? I lift the window, and in it hops. A crow dark enough to match the feathers that came from the purse. "I didn't pluck those," I tell it. "They were given to me." It doesn't seem to care. Its keen eyes search for something else.

"Can you speak?" I ask.

"*Caw.*"

"Can you speak in English?"

Suddenly, the crow emits a joyful little bark and hops onto the carpet to nab Beam's catcher.

"N-n-n-no," I tell it. But with its prize clutched in a talon, it jumps into flight and makes for the window.

"Stop!" I slam the window shut, and the crow veers to keep from colliding.

"*Caw.*" It flaps around and casts a sideways glance at me before it bounces the length of my bed toward the door.

"No!" I jump forward to knock the door closed. "It's not a toy. Beam needs it. Give it back or—I'll eat you."

I'm about to lion up to make good on the threat when my mom raps on the door. "Chausie? Everything OK in there?"

"*She needs it,*" the bird squawks. "*She needs it.*"

"Are you mocking me?" I ask the crow.

"What did you say?" comes Mom's muffled voice.

"*She needs it,*" the crow calls again. It half leaps, half flaps to my window sill, but it can't find purchase, so it stumbles onto my nightstand, sending the lamp clattering to the ground. "*She needs it. She needs it.*"

Its persistent declaration begins to panic me. "Is she in trouble?" I ask. "Can you get it to her?"

"*SHE NEEDS IT!*" it shouts.

With a frustrated grunt—and praying that my faith in this bird is not misplaced—I lift the window, and it soars out. Don't think I'm not right after it. I dive through myself, shifting into a mountain lion before I hit the ground. Out of the corner of my eye, I see Mom enter the room. "Chausie?" she calls. Her voice holds disappointment, tells me she thinks she's been duped, and it hurts me for her to believe I'm the same angry, resentful, impulsive boy I was a few weeks ago. But I can't do anything about that right now. I charge down the path as birds of all kinds screech and flap to get out of my way.

As the crow flies turns out not to be the straight line I was taught to believe. This stupid bird is doing S curves and I'm bounding after it like a spastic pet, careening around one thing and clearing another. My prey drive is so heightened, I have to keep squelching the urge to bat its feathered butt right out of the air.

We tromp through the front yards of every house between mine and the end of the neighborhood. I usually keep my lion form private. Mountain lions aren't supposed to live around here, and shifters just get abused. But there's nothing for it tonight, and all the noisy squawking brings at least two neighbors to their windows.

The end of my street butts up to something like three hundred acres of wooded hiking trails. Mom chose the place, knowing I'd need room to roam. She did a lot of things for me that I didn't appreciate at the time. Like leaving my dad—an act that, until recently, I only saw through the lens of my own loss.

The crow makes no distinction between neighborhood and reserved land, and it doesn't follow the hiking trails when we get there, but I don't either. In a few miles, we'll reach the river. How will I keep up with that bird, then? I can't ford it. If I try to swim, I'll end up downriver. No, I'll have to race to the bridge and double back on the other side. But I won't fall behind. I can't. I have to find Beam.

Who knows what her uncle's gotten himself into? It must have happened at the Vigilance. The last curator invited dark magic, and it's gonna take a boatload of sage to get rid of it before Beam assumes the post.

I think of her smiling through those big blue eyes when she told me she was going to take a gap year to immerse herself in her Tribal culture. A gap year—Beam—who would have been utterly *scandalized* to have entertained such an idea before she met me. I daresay I'm good for her.

My worries about the river are unfounded because the crow doesn't fly that way. Instead, it leads me into an unexpected meadow. We're talking tall grass and open sky. I don't recall this place. I've explored every inch of these woods.

The meadow is serene even though several kinds of birds are gathering in groups around the grass. The trees that border the meadow are far larger than in the rest of the forest. They must be hundreds of years old. Maybe this is a forgotten homestead whose house deteriorated while Atlanta grew up around it.

With a loud screech, the crow dives for a target. I can't tell what the target is. It's not Beam. Or if it is, I can't smell her yet. Even so, the crow lets loose its load, and I track it to the drop zone—where I stop dead. Beam's catcher has landed across the ornate bars of an old-fashioned birdcage—a bird *mansion* more like—and more out of place here than anything I can imagine. It looks better suited for the palace in *The Arabian Nights.*

Set in front of the cavernous hollow of one of those giant trees and made with a swing inside for a perch, the cage stands as tall as I in lion form, and its bars—if you can call them that—remind me of the frostwork gates in the In-Between. They seem to radiate a light of their own, and they've been crafted with intricate flourishes that cross and swirl. The extravagant beauty of the thing makes it no less of a prison. Inside, staring up at me from the swing is a faerie. Delicate and small as a fox, her ears protrude from her golden hair in soft points.

As a lion, I remain immobile except for my eyes, which travel the area to ascertain whether we're alone. Besides the birds, I can sense no one. And they are loitering in small groups, making hushed dove sounds to one another. When the woman moves her head to follow my gaze, my eyes are immediately drawn back to her.

Slowly but nimbly, she rises on the swing to reach for the part of Beam's necklace that dangles into her cage. No matter who she is—or what—or how captivating—that belongs to Beam. I snarl and gnash my teeth, leaving her motionless in mid-reach.

Finally, she speaks—or I should say that she makes sounds, soothing sounds like water in a brook. There are also rhythmical chirps and clicks. I don't know what she's saying, but she seems to be calming the birds who have grown agitated by my display. I'm about to drop the lion so that I can speak to her as a man when—*Caw!*

The stupid crow squawks from right behind my head and scares the crap out of me. I jump straight up from all four feet and round on it in annoyance. It doesn't back down. Instead, it attacks me—sideswiping me as it passes—and veers back for a second attempt. One swat of my paw sends it to the ground, where it lies dazed for a moment before it shakes its head. I've been *dying* to do that! It was very satisfying.

The small woman climbs down from the swing and bids the bird come to her with more watery noises, which it obeys. It even bows as she reaches through the bars to console it. Definitely some kind of faerie. I wonder if I'd be able to see her if Beam's blood hadn't gifted me with sight.

When the bird seems to cheer and the others calm down, the faerie extends her elegant fingers to me in what is at once a vulnerable invitation and an irresistible command. Who is she that this wild bird would take on a mountain lion for her? I pad forward on careful paws and press my nose to her palm. Now, she speaks to me in the language of cougars. Tells me how handsome I am. Tells me how noble. She smells of summer rain and blackberries. And bird nests. Or maybe that's just our company.

I shift into a man causing many a ruffled feather, and the faerie covers her mouth in surprise. "Leonid," she says.

Does she think that's my name? "I'm Chausie."

"But you are Leonid, aren't you? You come from the sky."

Umm. "Nope. I come from South Dakota."

She glances at Beam's catcher, now in my hand. "Are you here to free me?"

I sort of forgot she was trapped. I search for a lock or a latch, but I can't even find a door. Pocketing Beam's catcher—while the crow squawks at me—I try to pry off the roof, but it's like trying to bend iron. "How did you get in there?" I ask.

"I walked," she says ruefully and swats at a hanging ornament, causing it to swing back and forth. "The cage was twinkling in the moonlight, and this little charm—charmed me. I do love shiny things." She gazes at it. "I sat to swing—I didn't think of it as a cage at the time, but as a house—and while I was admiring it, a night dweller slammed the door."

I'm still trying to figure out where the door is. "A night dweller?" I repeat. "Like, a coyote?"

"A goblin," she whispers. "And not a nice one. He's going to sell me. He keeps muttering to himself about it. And now he's gone to fetch a cart."

"Does he have weapons? I mean, could I take him?"

"No," she says flatly. "He's cunning. He's skilled." She sizes me up. "He could *retire* off of what he could sell you for."

"Well, that's not going to happen. How do I get you out?"

While we've been talking, several of the birds have approached to deliver nuts and berries to my new acquaintance. She eats them gratefully, even offers some to me, which I decline because isn't food from faeries a big mistake? I'm walking around the cage, feeling for some kind of clue as to how to open this thing, when a fuzzy, young warbler drops an enormous, gooey-looking worm into the woman's hand. I abandon the puzzle of the cage for a moment. Will she eat it?

With what I assume is a message of thanks, the little woman speaks to the bird in the water language, but she has yet to pop its obese wriggler into her mouth. The bird waits. And now she falters a bit, but then she bestows upon the warbler the kind of smile men go to war over, and the little guy puffs up with pride and flits away. I lean in with anticipation. When I catch her eye, I give her a meaningful nod.

"What?" she asks.

"Eat it."

After a moment, she breaks into laughter—a sound like rain. I'm sort of in awe of her. I can't believe Beam's not here to meet her. She's still chuckling as she stoops to send the worm on its way without so much as a nibble.

"OK, stupid question," I say. "What are you? Are you a faerie?"

She considers it and says, "I suppose I am what you might call a faerie. We call ourselves"—here she makes a sound that I immediately can't remember, much less imitate. "At least, I am partly that. My name is Larkin."

She starts to say more, but I throw out a hand and shush her because something pricks my sensitive ears. "A wagon is rolling this way."

"It's him! The goblin!"

I do everything within my power to pull the cage apart. I lion up. I bite and claw and leverage my weight to use the strength of my hind legs. It's impossible.

"He's getting closer," Larkin whines. She's right. I can see him now, advancing underneath a dome of angry birds. He's just an old man, knobbly, with a hooked nose. He's sitting up in a wooden cart, holding the reins of a miserable pony. Birds dive-bomb him but then bounce off of some invisible force field and fall to the ground.

Clearly, the goblin possesses powers beyond my knowledge. What are the chances my brute strength can prevail?

"OK, listen," I tell Larkin. "I can't do anything about the cage right now." I scout for a place to hide myself. "I'll take him by surprise."

"If he knows about you," Larkin says, "you're as good as caught. Just follow us. Follow us and we'll think of something."

I nod my head to placate her, but the truth is, I don't have time for a long rescue mission here. "Hang on," I say and dig Beam's necklace from my pocket. Am I doing this? After a moment's hesitation, I shove it into the cage. "Wear this for now."

Larkin doesn't accept it. "To whom does it belong?" she asks.

"My heart," I say. "So use it well and give it back quickly."

She simply nods, but there is something doubtful in the gesture.

"It may protect you." I wave it impatiently. "May keep you from being seen."

"Yes. OK." She takes the round, woven frame in both hands and stares into it. "Will you hold the end?" she says. "I'm afraid."

"Just put it on, and—"

In the time I begin to protest, Larkin pulls the catcher to her face, but instead of wearing it, she *enters* it! I am at a total loss. I guess that's one way to pull her out of the cage. If she's not lost for eternity. No wonder she wanted me to hold the end.

I manage to fish it out of the cage and pocket it while I shift and claw my way to the first broad branch, where I silently position myself.

"It was worth a try," Larkin says. She's in the birdcage! I almost lose my balance.

"How are you back in there?"

"Frilk has me bound to it. Unless he frees me, I always end up right back." She sighs deeply. "I knew your heart lived outside of you."

"How's that?" I ask.

"My magic doesn't work on you."

The goblin drives his pony toward us while I crouch in wait. I'll just dive on top of him and subdue him right away. But when his cart clears my branch, what I see inside nearly causes me to lose my balance again! Lying in the back is a silky black panther, young like me but unconscious. Or dead? I concentrate on the ribcage and then the whiskers— what I can see of them through the rough rope that's been shoved onto her muzzle. There's a thin iron collar, too, chaining her to the cart. I can feel the sharp prickle down my neck, which means my hackles are standing.

Who is this guy? I'm well aware that there are black markets for exotic animals, and that's bad enough. But the faerie is human, or something like.

Anyway, now, I have two lives to protect, three counting my own, and none of them is the one I'm *supposed* to be protecting. All to say, I miss my chance for a clean aerial attack. The old-man goblin halts the pony in front of Larkin's cage and leaps onto the ground with the spry step of a man a quarter of his age. "Call off your birds," he gruffs.

Larkin is blocked from my view, but her voice is steady as she says, "They're not mine to command. They love me is all."

While they're talking, I sneak closer to the tree trunk so that I can see Larkin's face over the goblin's shoulder. I'm stealthy. Not a single leaf rustles. Even so, Larkin glances up, and her gesture begins to draw the goblin's gaze. I ready myself to pounce, but he stops, opting instead to shield his head with an arm already covered in pecks and scratches. "I swear if more birds come for me," he says, "I'll cut your ears off."

"Well, nobody's going to pay for a"—she makes the sound for her people again and, again, I can't remember it—"without pointy ears."

He considers that and finally says, "That's probably true. Come out." The front of the cage drops forward like a castle drawbridge, and Larkin exits as she's been told. "Get onto the seat."

When she steps in front of the pony, it shakes its reins, and she hugs its neck, murmuring into its ear. This causes the haggard animal to whinny like a foal. Even after Larkin leaves its side, its feet dance and it stands taller.

"Stop infatuatin' everythin'," the goblin grumps, but at this, Larkin cuts her eyes with an impish smile, and for a moment his face softens.

I don't understand why she doesn't just run for it. Will she just bounce back into the cage? I can't imagine she doesn't have a way to escape. But maybe her magic lies no further than her ability to make things predisposed to her.

"Damn ye, sprite," the goblin says. "Don't look at me."

Larkin sighs and climbs onto the seat when she catches sight of the panther in the back. "*Oh!*"

"Let it alone."

But Larkin is already over the seat at the panther's side. She removes the rope from its muzzle and strokes its black fur until its eyes drift open. Eyes as ice-blue as Beam's. And now I *have* to free it. Honestly. How did this situation get so convoluted?

"I said, let it alone!" the goblin repeats. "Get up in front, or you can forget about owning your clutch again!"

Ah. He has something of hers. That's why she's so docile.

Larkin sits back on her knees. "What have you done to this beautiful animal?"

"Don't worry about it. Cover it with that blanket and get up here."

Locating the blanket, Larkin spreads it over the panther, and while the goblin takes the reins, she lays a hand on its head. Then, with the briefest of glimpses at me, she takes the seat beside the goblin, and they begin a rickety trip across the meadow.

3

SCREAMING MAKES ME FEEL BETTER

BEAM

Chausie is purring with all the contented power of an idling motorcycle. I feel it inside my chest as if it emanates from me, and I smile against the soft yellow fur of his strong neck. I love waking up like this, but I did think we were through with beds made of earth and rock for a while. I hug him closer and say, "You're rumbling louder than all those noisy birds."

But I'm not awake yet. And now my dream turns strange. My bed is rolling. My four paws grab at the air like I'm running, but I'm lying down. See? That was so silly. I said *my four paws.* When I'm finally able to lift my eyelids, there is a big, bright moon lighting the night and an old man with his back to me directing a horse. A lovely, small woman is beside him, and she turns to stare at me.

Now, I am awake.

I try to sit up but I'm foiled by a heavy tug that constrains my movement.

In that instant, the reality of my situation becomes horrifyingly clear. I am chained down at the neck in the back of a wagon. I scream in denial—a scream so powerful and wild, that it shocks me. I do it again to test it. It makes me feel better.

It has the opposite effect on the old man. He yanks the reins, causing the horse to rear back, and the small woman to shush it with gentle words.

"Settle it down!" the man says. "Or else."

I think he means the horse, but the woman quickly crawls back to me, her hands outstretched, her eyes afraid. I try to scoot away, but I can't. She's not quite human. This wouldn't normally disqualify her from my circle of trust, but being as how I'm all chained up... I claw at her in warning and my lips curl like I'm going to chomp down on her— like I'm Chausie or something—like I'm a—mountain lion.

The woman is speaking to me. She sort of sounds like she's purring.

"What is happening to me?" I want to whine, but out of my throat come catty sounds.

"I'm Larkin," she says. "That goblin caught you. He caught me too."

"He's a goblin?" I ask. In cat language. She nods her head.

The goblin in question is down in the road berating the pony— which is not soothing it. The cart gets jerked around as it shirks from its master.

"Why aren't you in chains?" I ask.

She hesitates. "My chains are invisible." Now, she blinks slowly but I don't have time for her to do anything slowly.

"Get me out of here," I demand.

"I can't. But I can help you feel better if you'll just listen to my voice."

What is that supposed to mean? "I don't want to feel better! I want to get out of here!" My declaration is more of a wail, and it is answered by a freakishly loud scream—far higher and spookier than mine—from the woods to the right of the road. *Chausie.* I can't lift my head high enough to locate the sender, but I call for him.

"Stop it!" the woman says. "Frilk doesn't know he's out there."

I take it Frilk is the goblin. "Well, he does now," I yowl. He's halfway into the cart, searching in Chausie's direction, and breaks into a grin as he jumps into his seat. Compelling the horse onward, he scans the dark as we roll.

Pop! Who should appear, to my great relief, but my big-eyed, blue-skinned prowler buddy. I am so glad to see him, I could cry.

He leans in, looks me over, and says, "You're a lion."

"I am, aren't I?" I chirp. My voice is so weird as a cat.

"Oh, I don't speak lion," he says in English.

"You do so," I spit. "You spoke to Chausie that time Baalesh was inside the dead man." Our interaction has Larkin eyeing me in a new way. I'm not sure she can see Blue. Most people can't.

"Yeah, I *can* speak it," Blue is saying. "But I don't."

I exhale a little laugh and lay my head down to rest my neck muscles. I have to get out of this collar. I think about how Chausie rolls his shoulders when he drops his lion form, and I try it. I don't mind being a lion, surprisingly. It's pretty cool. But I don't want to be *stuck* as one. And I don't want to be anybody's prisoner in any form.

"Frilk will catch your friend too," Larkin says quietly. So, I guess she can see him. "You don't want *him* on display at Snatcher's Ridge."

"What is Snatcher's Ridge?" I ask. "Is that where the old man is taking us?"

Over her shoulder, Larkin checks on Frilk while Blue looks her over. The goblin is still concentrating on the darkness, and I get the sense he's hoping Chausie will follow us.

When Larkin notices Blue admiring her, he lets out a breathy, "Hiiiii."

She looks from him to me in question, but I just shrug.

Blue is undeterred. "Will you marry me?" he asks her. He's not much smaller than she is, and he is wholly smitten. I'm forming a hypothesis that Larkin has psychic powers over emotions.

"Stop doing your thing on him," I tell her.

"I'm not. I'm seriously not."

"What's your name?" Blue asks.

"Larkin," she says warily.

"Larkin," he sighs. "Will you marry me?"

She seems to weigh the offer. "Maybe. What's your name?"

"I am...whatever you want to call me."

"His name is Blue," I spout and throw him a warning glare before he can start giggling over the fact that he is blue.

"Could you be my hero, Blue?" Larkin asks.

I raise my objection, chains clanking along. "Don't get him caught. He's been a captive before. He doesn't deserve that."

"That's enough, sprite," the goblin gruffs. "Back up here now."

Blue dives behind me to hide, but I don't think Frilk can sense him at all. Anyway, once Larkin is up front, and Blue is sure he's not about to be found out, he starts rubbing my ears. "Oooo, you're soft. You're much softer than Chausie."

"Stop petting me," I grouse. "See if you can get me loose."

"No problem." He grips the collar with his four-fingered hands and nearly yanks my head off.

"*Ow!*" I swat at him. "Don't you think I've tried that already? Why hasn't Chausie rescued me?"

"There's some kind of ward in place that keeps him from getting close to the cart. I don't think he knows that the captured feline in here is you."

While Blue works on the chains, I try to eavesdrop on Larkin and her so-called captor with my cat-tastic hearing. Her chains may be invisible, but Frilk treats her more like an accomplice than a hostage.

Crack! Through some kind of prowler power, Blue frees the chains from the cart, and, with a blast of splintering wood, we tumble onto the dirt road. The cart lurches forward. The horse is spooked, and now the goblin is cursing and pulling on the reins with all his might.

"You did it, Blue!" I yell. It's not until I'm galloping into the dark—dragging these awful chains behind me—that I feel my little buddy riding on my back. He's clutching my collar like he's a Lakota warrior charging into the Battle of Little Bighorn—which the Lakota call Greasy Grass. It's where they killed Custer after the US government broke the Treaty of Fort Laramie. Yeah, I've been studying up. "Hoka hey!" Blue bellows.

A sudden *ck* sound to my left has me dumping my little blue mount and readying for a fight. But it's Chausie! He has his hackles raised. It doesn't matter to me. I'm so relieved to see him! I close the distance and rub my head under his chin, weaving back and forth and making happy little cat noises. It's kind of fun.

"Whoa. Hey. Personal space," he says. Only it's more like, "*Rrrah. Ck. Rah.*"

So, I slap his face with soft paws and laugh when he balks. His strange expression means he has no idea how to handle me. Possibly, he thinks I'm just a big flirt.

"It's me!" I tell him.

With a glance at Blue, Chausie assumes his human form. I think he expects me to do the same. When I don't, he says, "Are you a shifter or not?"

"Chausie!" I'm starting to feel perturbed, which is unfair. I should be glad he doesn't allow every she-cat to dab him up.

Chausie's all business. "Blue, get the collar off her." He looks toward the road where the cart has finally come to a halt. "We may be able to rescue Larkin, but he has something of hers, so I'm not sure if she'll come or not."

"*You* get the collar off," Blue sasses him.

The weight of Chausie's scowl falls like a brick. "What happened to obeying direct orders? Did you leave that obligation back in South Dakota?"

"That was before I found the love of my life. Larkin asked me to be her hero."

Chausie pinches the bridge of his nose. It's a gesture with which I am well familiar. "That's just her magic talking," he says. "Free this panther and then we'll go free Larkin. And then we'll go find Beam."

"I can't," Blue argues.

"Why not?!"

I've had it. I leap onto Chausie full-tackle and when he falls onto his back, I get in his face and snarl. "It's me!"

Finally, I have his undivided attention. I glare into his perplexed yellow eyes, remembering how they had convinced me that he was my lion when this situation was reversed.

"Beam?" It's so soft and so high-pitched, I can tell he hardly believes it.

"*Rawer,*" I reply helpfully.

"How— Are— What— *Huh.*" He takes my furry face in both hands. "You're a lion?"

I nod again.

"Did I make you a lion? The same way you made me an Elixir?"

I shrug.

"You're a *gorgeous* lion." He runs his hands down my sides.

"Isn't she soft?" Blue asks.

"How did that goblin get a hold of you?" And now Chausie's voice hardens. "Where is your uncle?"

I give Chausie room to sit up and stare at him dolefully as he works to free me from the collar. "It's like Larkin's birdcage," he muses. "I can't figure out how to open it. Is this the reason you can't shift?" He gives up trying and sits back on his heels to think.

How *did* that goblin trap me? I'm trying to remember when I notice Chausie biting back a grin, and then I realize I'm cleaning my paw—with my tongue. I set it on the ground and raise my chin indignantly.

"This is wild," he says.

"*Help me,*" I whine.

"Let's run back to my house. Mom's an ER nurse. She'll know what to do."

Blue pipes up. "What about my *wife?*" he asks. Chausie doesn't bother to ask who Blue's wife is, doesn't even respond. Just licks his lips and looks slightly pissed off.

"He means Larkin," I mew.

"I know who he means."

"Blue, I'm not sure I trust her," I say, causing Blue to gasp and his eyes to round in disbelief.

"How *dare* you?!" he hisses.

"You're an emotional basket case," Chausie says. He's searching in the direction of the goblin's cart. "We have to get out of here. We'll try to fix things for Larkin after that."

"Chaus!" I say in warning. A pale blue orb is rolling across the ground. It casts soft light as it draws near, and Chausie nudges me toward the tree line while gathering my chains to keep them from clanking. There's no way to be discreet, but still, we take cover behind some undergrowth. When the orb is close enough, we see that Larkin is strolling inside of it. I wonder if Chausie has the same doubts about her as I do. His nose quivers. I timidly take a whiff through mine—and smell something like rotting funeral flowers. Why does it make me want to go investigate?

Just when I think Larkin will pass us, the whole orb spins toward our hiding spot, and its blue light falls upon us. We stare into Larkin's eyes without speaking. "I'm sorry," she says.

"Larkin?" Chausie warns.

"Don't let him know you're Leonid," she says regretfully and seems to second-guess her next move, but then she calls out, "Over here!"

Chausie rumbles his displeasure and turns to me. "Can you find my house?"

I start to say no but realize that in cat form, I probably can. "Yeah, I think so."

"Then run hard. I'll keep him distracted. Get to my mom and—I guess have her call my dad to see what the lions can do. *Don't* go to your uncle."

It's so stupid of him to think I'd leave him in this situation, I don't dignify it with a response. Chausie becomes a lion.

The goblin steps into view by the light of Larkin's orb, and in that instant, Chausie pounces, biting into his neck and unsheathing long claws to tear his torso. The goblin is impossibly strong. He throws Chausie to the ground and—with almost the same movement—he flings a silvery net over me—a net that acts alive. "Chaus?!" It thoroughly wraps me up and anchors me to the ground.

The more I try to get free, the more it entangles me. It even ties up my feet.

Forcing myself to calm down and assess my situation, I regret my lack of thumbs.

That's when I notice three flashlight beams bouncing along the road. We all go still and quiet. I guess we're all wondering whose side these newcomers will be on. One and then all of the lights shine up at us. Chausie seizes the opportunity to leap upon the goblin again. The three lights rush up the hill.

"Oh, my lord, Ernie," says a woman. "It's a wild animal!"

Chausie is not the problem! I want to yell, but it's too late.

A zap of red trails through the air, followed by an acrid smell. Chausie shrieks in pain, a raw, animal sound that physically stuns me. I watch his back legs fail as he fights to remain upright, clawing with his front. *Damn these restraints!*

"Hang in there, Sir." I don't know who says it. *Ernie?* I guess? "That beast could have killed you!" I'm sure the goblin looks to these strangers like some sweet old man they've saved from being mauled.

"Oh, you're bleeding all over," the woman worries. "Mercy. Mercy. Mercy." She reaches for his side.

The goblin, who is hunched over dabbing his lacerations, shuns her ministrations. "No need," he grunts. "Much obliged." He casts a look Chausie's way.

Larkin's orb has gone dark. I don't think the strangers can see her. I don't think they can see me either, for that matter. My fur is blacker than the night.

Frilk tries not to show it, but Chausie put a hurtin' on him. I'm glad. I can see Chausie's lion eyes shining. He's panting in pain, lying on his side. "Chausie?" I yell, but of course, all anyone hears is a wild lion. I do sound pretty epic, but it doesn't bring Chausie any comfort. When his eyes land on me, the pain of my captivity seems to rack him even more. His muscles seize, and he curls in on himself.

"There's another one!" the woman says about me. Larkin, who has been inexplicably cheeping like a baby bird while Blue watches on, now grows silent.

A new kind of rage overtakes me. I always get bitterly angry when anyone hurts my lion, but there is an even wilder side to my psyche this time. My next roar is so loud, the three strangers cover their ears, and, even though I am bound, they fall back a few steps. The man who hurt Chausie aims his weapon at me, but the goblin steps between us with his hands bobbing up and down. "Now, don't get carried away. She's my pet. I've had her since she was a cub."

"Oh, *right,* you stupid, lying kidnapper!" I gnash my teeth at him. If his leg were a few inches closer, I'd snap it off. I wish I could get these people to understand what I'm saying. Yet, now that I notice the stilted way they're gathering, I begin to doubt their intentions.

"She doesn't act much like your pet," the one called Ernie says. Stun Gunner murmurs his agreement, and the woman removes something from her purse to palm it in her hand. I cannot further investigate because something is crawling over my body.

"*What the heck?*" I lion-whisper and slap at a bunch of field mice who have marched up my legs. "*Get away.*" I flick my paws free of them, but here they come back. What is happening right now? *Nibble. Nibble. Nibble. Nibble.* One takes a post on my left ear. I think he's the boss, directing the others by squeaking the same way Larkin did just now.

Upon further inspection, the mice are helping! They're chewing through the net! Didn't Aesop have a fable about this? And it happened to Aslan too, right? What is it with these brave little creatures and tied-up lions? I lie still and let them finish their work.

"Thank goodness we came along when we did." It's Ernie again. His voice is oilier now, and I no longer think he means to rescue an injured elder.

"Yeah, thank goodness," Stun Gunner says. "Makes our night a lot more lucrative." With another pulse of red light, Stun Gunner blasts the goblin!

Now—if any doubt remains—let it be known that Frilk is way more of a goblin than an old man. He reverses the charge of the stun gun with a flick of his hand, and it explodes back into the shooter, whose body violently convulses where it lands.

CHAUSIE

Topping the list of things I never wanted to feel? Electrocution. *Man,* that hurts. Are you *kidding* me with that? It hurts so bad I wonder if I'm going to die. But Beam's healing blood pumps through my heart, and it's going to take a heck of a lot more than that to keep me down. My body's nearly paralyzed for the moment, but my mind's working over time.

There is no way that three people just happened to be—no. There are no houses on this road. There's nowhere for them to go. Could they have been backcountry camping? No again. No way. They're not fitted out for that. And they're not fit. They were huffing and puffing just getting up the hill.

The man who tasered me got tased himself. I think the goblin used the current against him. He isn't faring as well as I am. He convulsed for several harrowing seconds. Now, he lies still. I think his heart stopped. The guy called Ernie thumps his chest a few times and gives up. If he were my friend, I'd work a hell of a lot harder than that. They'd have to drag me off him. I'd try to save *this* guy if I could move.

Ernie and the woman back away from the goblin as he towers over their dead companion. He doesn't look into their faces—just keeps glancing up from under his eyelids. So, they're at an impasse of sorts, each trying to figure out what the others will do.

Beam sneaks over to me, and even though her chains do make some noise, the others don't notice. She kisses my face with rough cat licks that make me smile despite the circumstances. "You gotta get out of here," I say. It comes out in English. I guess I slipped into human form without meaning to. "Here. Put this on." I want to get her catcher around her neck, but we're interrupted because my human voice draws attention.

"It's a man!" the woman says.

Ernie turns with a, "What the—"

But it's the goblin who most concerns me. There's a new glint in his eye, and Larkin exhales a worried sigh. I wish I hadn't revealed my shifter nature.

"Ernie, we attacked a man!" the woman wails.

"No, we didn't! You saw!"

The goblin sidles past them, dragging Larkin by the arm as if she's a child. Blue takes a swipe at him, but try as he might, he can't make contact. The goblin doesn't pay him one bit of attention. I don't think they operate on the same plane of existence. I don't understand how it works, but before Beam's blood bridged those planes for me, I couldn't see invisible creatures either.

Larkin looks forlorn. I almost feel sorry for her, but I don't have time for that, because Beam issues a low, threatening growl that swells in volume the closer they come.

"Back down," I command her. Not that she cares. The last time I wanted to keep her from the action, I had to convince a bunch of ghost warriors to restrain her. She never did hold me to task for that. Best not bring it up.

Blue tugs Larkin's free hand. "This way," he whispers, but she shakes her head no.

"I've seen paranormal creatures in my time," the goblin says—which is kind of funny since Blue is trying to tug his prisoner from his grasp while he remains unaware. "Sprites and talking bears," he continues. "Gnomes, cave trolls—I've even seen a satyr. But a real-life Leonid... Now, that is something." He seems to be lost in the notion.

Larkin keeps her mouth shut. I have yet to get to my feet. I'm not sure I trust my muscles and bones to do their job. But when the goblin turns his attention to Beam and says, "What about you, darlin'? Are you more than meets the eye?" Beam hisses an award-winning threat. She sounds like she's about to tear the guy to pieces. I owe her my life, and I trust her with it. But this goblin has tricks we know nothing about. His strength is uncanny.

"I guess we'll have to wait a few more hours until the drug wears off."

"What did you give to her?" I ask. Some drugs that keep us from shifting can have permanent consequences.

"Not to worry," the goblin says.

With his back to the others, the woman grows bold and risks an offer. "We could share the take."

"No, no," the goblin says through a dark chuckle. "Go, now." His eyes blaze red, and his features morph into such a savage and grotesque monster, that the woman falls to her knees. Ernie instinctively yanks her by the shoulders, and the two of them flee down the hill to the road.

While the goblin is distracted, I lion up, hoping that he won't expect me to be recovered enough to launch an attack. With my lips curled and my canines bared, a growl rips through my throat, and I spring on him from strong haunches.

But by the time I land, the goblin is gone. Larkin is gone. And so is Blue.

I spin around mid-jump, eyes landing on Beam whose wide-faced expression mirrors the surprise I feel.

Although Blue is a pedantic, quirky little being with large eyes and no nose, he has a combatant alter ego who can morph into virtually any force required. *Goliath.* And even though Goliath hardly ever makes an appearance, he did just now. Blue's small frame mutated and grew into a strong man and then a sail of a thing, blanketing Larkin and wresting her from the goblin's grip. At first, the goblin seemed to lose his prize, but then doubled his hold on her, and in the end, whatever happened, all three of them vanished.

Allowing myself to become man, I say, "Where did they—" when I am whipped from the ground by a long silvery strap that stings my legs as it seizes me.

BEAM.

"Chausie Louris," his mom scolds through the front door when I arrive and pat it paw after paw instead of knocking. "You told me things would be different from now on." She swings the door wide, her anger morphing to disappointment and maybe even to fear when she sees me there, a strange, wild animal on her front porch, and not her gorgeous, yellow son.

"Help," I say as a lion and sit back to appear less intimidating. I'm sure she's seen her share of big, furry felines—she was married to one. But she probably doesn't see a lot of them in Atlanta.

"What's wrong?" she asks. "Is it Chausie?"

I don't suppose she understands me this way, does she? "Yes," I start in. "Chausie's been kidnapped by a goblin called Frilk. I don't know where they went. I don't know what to do. I'm not usually a lion, but I can't stop being one right now. We have to call his dad. I think if you could get this thing off my neck..." I claw at the collar with both my front paws.

She has no idea what I'm saying, but she bends to get a better look. "You look like you've escaped from a roadside zoo. Are you a shifter?"

"I'm Beam," I tell her, but that doesn't help because she doesn't understand me. "Ms. Louris," I whine.

"I don't—" She looks beyond me. "Do you know where Chausie is?"

"I wish I did. Look, I need this thing off!" I try to say.

"You don't like that thing?" she asks. "Of course, you don't. Come in. We'll get you sorted out." That's how Chausie would've reacted— the measured tone, the dealing with the first problem first. It's very helpful.

His sweet mom shows me into the foyer and closes the door behind us. There's a full-length mirror where I look at myself as a lion for the first time.

"All those birds finally took flight," Ms. Louris muses. "It was the weirdest thing." She frowns and runs her fingers under my collar. "What kind of metal is this?"

"*Rawrruck,*" I say, which means I have no clue. I'm far less foggy-brained than I had been. The run did me good. The drug's wearing off.

"There's no latch. I don't understand how you got into it in the first place."

Neither do I.

"I'm going to get some shears I use for metalwork." As she walks away, she continues conversationally. "I took up a few new hobbies when—well when we moved here." I wonder if she could've finished that sentence with *when my husband took up a new wife.*

While she's away, I pad to the full-length mirror and study myself. This is bizarre. I have whiskers. I try to view my backside and flick my new tail. Then I bare my teeth. *Ooh. That's effective.*

When Ms. Louis returns, I stare at her dejectedly.

"It's not the worst predicament I've seen," she says. "You wouldn't believe the things that come into the ER."

At least I'm in good hands.

The shears are so large, that Ms. Louris has to use both hands to demonstrate what she intends to do. The steel makes a scraping sound as the blades meet. "I need you to be very still," she says. "Do you understand?"

I nod and brace myself while Chausie's mom maneuvers the lower blade between my neck and the collar. She clamps down slowly, but the collar just slides out of the chop. "I'm afraid I'm going to have to do this forcibly." She looks around for something, jogs away, and comes back with a few hand towels with which she pads my neck. I bet she's a great nurse. I bet the hospital can't run without her.

That's what I'm thinking as she slams the sheers together with an audible ring, like microphone feedback. It jerks me to the side, and I'd probably be cut by the blades, except she somehow holds on to both handles and keeps them from swinging. I am beyond thankful for the cushioning she has provided—and for my thick lion neck.

"What in the world is that thing made of? It doesn't look like it would be so difficult." She's speaking more to herself than to me. Her eyes light up. "I have a saw." Before she can say more about that, she's gone again.

There's a knock on the front door, and I chirp reflexively, hoping it's Chaus. His mom does too.

"Chausie?" she calls. She's hurrying back, holding a small circular saw. She must be committed to this whole metalworking thing. The way she opens the door leaves me out of view, and when I hear my uncle's voice sounding as thin and strained as it had earlier tonight, I'm glad to be hidden behind it.

"Sorry to bother you," he says. "I dropped off Chausie earlier. I'm Beam's uncle? Is she here?"

I try to glimpse him through the crack in the door. His long, black hair hangs freely. His kind, dark eyes look strained and swollen. Dark circles beneath.

"No, I'm afraid she's—not." Ms. Louris pauses, and I wonder if it's dawning on her that the black panther standing behind the door is me, Beam. I turn to check her expression, only to find myself face-to-face with Uncle Joel in that long mirror. I'm worried for him, but I can't trust him right now. I don't know how to convey that, so I simply slip around the corner as if I don't recognize him.

Chausie's mom sees all of this, and whether or not she suspects that I am me, she says to Uncle Joel, "Like I said, Beam isn't here. If I see her, I'll let her know you're looking for her."

I hear the door closing, but Uncle Joel says, "I see you have a black panther."

Ms. Louris' response cools considerably. "Chausie and I foster big cats who have been mistreated."

"What a good fit," Uncle says. "Are you trying to get the chains off of that one?"

"You should go. She's unpredictable around men—because of the abuse. Goodbye."

Go, Chausie's mom! Way to make stuff up. I hear the door close and lock. Then nothing. I bet she's making sure he leaves. I wonder if she sensed my apprehension or just felt that something was off about my uncle.

I relax, and now that I look around, I realize that the doorway I've ducked into is Chausie's. His room is neater than I would have imagined—though Chausie hasn't been here for the past few weeks. His mom probably cleaned it up while we were in South Dakota. A simple twin bed is covered with a dark brown comforter, and matching pillows are propped against the wall. Several trophies line a shelf to the side. *MVP* is carved into the base of three of them, and each one sports a golden basketball player in the middle of a jump shot. Next to those is a plaque that was awarded for the most three-pointers scored in a high school season—for the whole nation. Here is a family picture. His brother, unlike Chausie, takes after his mom more than his dad. His brother's away at college. And here's a picture of the whole basketball team the night they won the State Championship for us. Chaus was so happy. And so sweaty. And so very hot.

Chausie? I reach out to him with my mind, but I can't find him.

"There you are," his mom says. She studies me for a moment. "Are you Beam?"

I nod my head.

"I didn't know you were a shifter. What happened to you?" It's a rhetorical question. She knows I can't answer, and I assume she knows that I can't shift. I'm trying not to dwell on that part.

These chains I wear must raise concerns about her son's wellbeing. She glances at the saw in her hand. "You have to remain one hundred percent still for me to use this. You know that, right?"

I nod again.

"It will be uncomfortable, probably, with all the vibration. I'm going to stuff some cotton into your ears." She proceeds to do so and places goggles on my nose. That has to look hilarious. Goggles on a great big cat. She has goggles for herself, too. "OK, here we go."

I brace myself. The saw is cordless. Doesn't mean it's not powerful. It whizzes to life, and Chausie's mom proves as steady as a surgeon. She holds the collar away from me by standing on one of my chains, and with minuscule movements—and nerves of steel—this angel of a nurse works to saw through the awful collar. After several moments, she silences the saw. "I haven't made a dent."

I mew my impatience.

"We'll figure it out." She's thinking through the possibilities, maybe who to call. "Let me get the chains off, at least." This time, as she works, one of the chains clatters to the ground. "That's one," she says. The other comes away just as quickly, but in the process, it nicks the skin on my neck. "I'm sorry," Ms. Louris says. "It bit you a bit there, didn't it?"

She removes the cotton from my ears and uses a clean one to dab the scatch that must have brought blood. "At least it's a pretty collar, I guess," she remarks.

I am not seeing the silver lining.

Without a noise, the collar slips from my neck and onto the floor. Ms. Louris stares at it quizzically. The red cotton ball stained with my blood is still clutched in her fingers. She shakes her head. "I don't understand."

While I consider it, Ms. Louris turns the collar over in her hands, now a short rod instead of an unbroken circle, whose disconnected chains remain on the floor. "Are you able to shift yet?"

Maybe. I roll my shoulders and imagine myself human once again, but this time I feel something change. It's not unpleasant, but it's not all pleasant. I reverse the step. *What if I shift and I'm naked? Didn't Chausie say that part took practice?* I turn my back just in case and concentrate on what I was wearing. *Blue jeans. White T. Blue jeans. White T.* I begin to stretch and change. Things roll out of places and into other places. And I become me! I'm wearing clothes and everything. I kind of want to shift back just to get the hang of it, but I turn to address Chausie's mom.

What I want to say—*Thank you! That was the weirdest. I've never been a lion before*—dies on my lips because she has gone pale. "Ms. Louris, what is it?"

"What is this wicked thing?" She extends her arm to reveal the collar, now shackled onto her own wrist. I rush to pry it open. It has shrunk to fit her. The thing doesn't play by the normal laws of physics. You know how much I hate that?

It occurs to me why it came off my neck. I touch the place where I got nicked, but in this short time, it has healed. "I can open it," I tell her.

I run a finger along the saw's teeth hard enough to slice it, and I touch a drop of blood to the collar, which falls away from her arm and onto the floor. "Don't touch it," I say.

"Not going to." We both stare down at it with contempt. "Why did that work?" she asks.

"I'm not sure. I'd rather you not say anything about it if you don't mind."

Not a problem because she has more important things on her mind. "Where's Chausie? Is he in trouble? He ran out of here like his fur was on fire. He hopped right through that window there." She indicates the one she means.

"Do you know why?" I ask.

"No, but—he appeared to be chasing a crow. I think it may have taken something from these items." She waves at a bunch of feathers tied together on the floor. A thin, beaded pouch lies beside them, and a piece of paper that wants to roll.

"Chausie texted to ask if these were mine." The red and black beads on the flap of the pouch, when I open it, create a pattern of arrows that point down into the small bag, but it's empty now, so I pick up the paper, which turns out to be a note.

> Beam, I am not the man I appear to be. Until I can find my way back, please keep this on you at all times, and for goodness' sake, don't ever be alone with me. The visions are not complete. Parts were stolen. Uncle Joel

"Ms. Louris? Had you read this note when my uncle came to the door?"

She shakes her head and reads it now. "Well, that's bizarre," she says.

"You knew something was off about him, didn't you?" I maneuver Frilk's collar, or the short silver rod, into the purse.

"I knew you were avoiding him, and I've been a nurse, not to mention a woman, for long enough to follow your lead on that. Anyway, *some*body trapped you in that collar. Was it your uncle?"

I spill the whole story. Uncle Joel. Larkin. The goblin. Chausie's capture. The latter pulls her eyes tight with worry. "He told me to find you," I say. "And—" I don't know how she's going to react to this. "To tell his dad what's happening." *Your ex.*

She nods. "Yeah," she says dryly. "He'll know what to do." I can tell she does not love the idea, but she wants what's best for Chaus. Chausie's dad is a trained officer as well as a shifter—well, he stopped being able to shift, but still. He'll understand the implications of Chausie being taken.

Instead of heading for her phone, Ms. Louris simply sits on Chausie's bed and rests her head in her hands.

"I can call him if you want," I volunteer. "I just don't have his number. Or a phone. Uncle Joel took mine."

"No, it'll be faster this way, though last time he tried to contact me I forbade him to use it. Leo and I have a mated connection. It happens sometimes with the Igmuwatogla."

"Chausie and I have that!" I gush. "Where we can talk sometimes without being together."

"Can you really?" his mom asks.

"Oh, but we haven't—you know," I say like a doofus because hadn't she just said it was a *mated* connection? "I thought it was because he drank some of my blood."

She balks.

"I mean, because my blood calls to him. Because I love him. It's a long story. It's the reason he can walk again. We've been through a lot together in the past few weeks." Occasionally, my typically brilliant mind stalls out, and my mouth continues to spit words the way a car backfires.

Chausie's mom is eyeing me with curiosity, so I collect the shards of my dignity and end the verbal barrage with, "You should go ahead and reach out to Leo."

She doesn't ask for more of an explanation. She's probably thrilled that I've solved how to shut my mouth. Setting her face in her hands, she exhales deeply. I know what she's doing. The connection requires a type of surrender. You have to relax, but you have to focus too. You have to open yourself up. It's a very vulnerable act. I don't think I could do it for someone who betrayed me the way Chausie's dad did her.

I decide that I'm intruding, and when my eyes fall on the pretty little purse again, I pick it up along with the seven feathers and walk out into the hall. That last line from Uncle Joel's cryptic note comes to mind: *Until I can find my way back, please keep this on you at all times.* I suppose he was referring to the catcher, which must be what the bird flew away with. But just in case he meant the purse, I place it around my shoulder and neck, pulling an arm out of my sleeve to let it rest under my shirt. You can hardly tell it's there; it's so thin. I add the feathers to it. Isn't that interesting how it all but disappears?

Ms. Louris makes a breathy sound, and when I round the doorway again, she's pacing. She slaps her thighs in frustration. "I can't find him."

"I can't find Chausie sometimes either."

"But it's not just that Leo's asleep or distracted. It's like he's not even out there. Maybe our connection broke when he married someone else."

"I don't think he loved her," I say. "For what that's worth. She was very manipulative. Not that that gives him an excuse." Probably sounds lame. "Did you know he lost his ability to shift?"

"Leo?! No." I've alarmed her. She's gawking at me. Her lips move with the aborted starts of several questions. After a few moments, she simply sits down on Chausie's bed again. "He needs me." Now she looks up with a bewildered sadness. "Isn't that a crazy thing to say? But he must be suffering."

She still loves him. I guess you don't stop just because you have to protect yourself from your lover's recklessness. Why did he have to be so oblivious to the treasure he had in this woman and their sons?

"Could we call him on the phone?" I suggest. "Since you can't reach him?"

My question kicks her back into gear. She nods and jogs into the hall, presumably to find her phone. In the meantime, I eyeball the collar at the bottom of the purse. A few moments later, I can hear Ms. Louris returning and the phone ringing on speaker. Leo's answer is soft and hopeful, and I think the love his mom demonstrated must run both ways. "Sophie, is that you?"

"Leo." She sounds relieved to hear his voice. "It's Chausie. He's been kidnapped."

There's a slight pause. "I spoke with Chausie not three hours ago. He's a lion, for goodness' sake. Who could even pull it off?"

"Leo," she snaps. "I'm telling you that someone took him. Someone who knows what he is. Beam, tell him." She hands the phone to me and wrings her hands while I explain.

5

SNATCHER'S RIDGE

CHAUSIE

My hands are bound in front of me. A rough blindfold covers my eyes. I keep getting shoved from behind as we trek upward over rocky terrain. We've been moving for about an hour.

Frilk has been—well, let's start with how I know his name. When I was whipped off my feet—back when I was with Beam—I felt like I disintegrated, and I was sure that I had died. But then I reemerged into the world of sound and light, albeit the dark of night, on my backside.

We were tethered to some kind of anchor, and I get the idea that Frilk can only travel from one place to another using the same silvery whip he used to capture me. He got the jump on me, tied my hands with it, and hoisted me onto my feet. I have no idea where Blue went. Nor Larkin.

I, of course, began to shift so that I could fight my way out of the predicament, but Frilk snarled, "I'll kill her. I swear by the name of Frilk, the name given me as a goblin. If you shift—if you resist me in any way, I will appear before the panther, and I will slit her throat ear to ear."

The image of that threat subdued me, and I remained a man—more of a statue, really. I dared not even twitch. My blood flows through Beam as hers does through me. But if she were to lose it all at once... I don't suppose there would be any recovery from that. How does he know what she means to me? Was he only bluffing?

"Is that the kind of threat that keeps Larkin loyal to you?" I asked and got clocked for the question, then blindfolded, and then we began the ascent to where we are now.

This whole hike I've spent trying to reach Beam in my mind and thinking that if I can just buy enough time, my dad will figure out a way to find me. But he's not a lion anymore, is he? Maybe he'll mobilize the others.

Suddenly, I'm forced to my knees. The goblin falls on top of me and jerks my head to the side as he rips off the blindfold. "Take a look," he growls. "Snatcher's Ridge." His breath is hot and sticky on my neck. It must be around ten pm. There's a low cloud ceiling reflecting scant electric lights and puffs of mist nearer to the ground. "You're just property here, Leonid. Get used to it."

And there's that word again. I get that the Leo part has something to do with being a lion. My dad is named Leonhardt for that reason. They chose Chausie for me. Don't Google it. It's embarrassing.

Having crested the top of a ridge, I see that it plateaus into a shallow bowl of a field, but there are no trees and no grass—or at least what little grass there is has been trampled. Tens of people are milling about in clothes better suited to a game of D&D. Rigid cloaks. Long leather boots. Head coverings that make it difficult to ascertain individual features. But there are normal-looking people too—normal, like middle-aged Ernie and that woman whose companion the goblin killed. It occurs to me that this is exactly where they were headed.

No one pays us much attention—though it's clear I'm being held against my will. There are picnic tables in the middle of the space. Men and women are eating and drinking. No one lifts their eyes for long like there's some rule about minding your own business.

Booths dot the dusty ground. Some are like shacks made of wood that hide what's inside. Some are merely poles with burlap or blankets to divide one space from another. It's a market. Some booths sell food. Some sell clothes. There is one with a variety of colored glass bottles, and the smell coming from there is not good.

Frilk produces a phone. It must be satellite. He presses several numbers, pauses, presses several more.

"Keep moving," he demands. I dare not lion up in this place even without the threat to Beam. If he means to sell me, I don't want to give anyone reason to buy me. Frilk seems to know what I'm thinking. He says, "I can sell pretty boys like you for nearly as much as I can sell lions."

Well, that's great.

Into the phone, he says, "Tell Mauri I have two gorgeous animals for him. An honest-to-god Leonid and a *black* panther, a jaguar. Prettiest thing you ever saw."

I stiffen at the mention of Beam's feline form and begin to doubt the strength of his vow to kill her. He keeps a steady eye on me, but at some point, he'll get distracted, and in that moment, I'll lion up and make him incapable of doing anything with her at all. Until then, I'll memorize this place so that when I get free, I can come back with help to shut it down.

Frilk doesn't lead me through the center of the field. We skirt behind the booths, and now we come upon a more disturbing scene. There *are* boys for sale. They are standing bare-chested on raised islands of concrete, tied to columns that have been sunk into the ground for no other reason. The columns have iron circles cemented into them, and it is around those to which their bonds are secured. A single light burns at the top of each inhabited column.

A boy my age is scowling in my direction. His multiple locks of twisting long hair seem to create a mane. His dark brown skin looks angry—like he's been standing in the sun for days. He's thick and muscly and hostile.

I've played against guys like him. He'll slam the ball into the net before you even know it's out of your hands, and you'll only get to watch from where he laid you on your butt—when he can catch you, that is. I find myself almost smiling, which makes him look cornered all of a sudden. I wonder how he got here.

There are girls tied up, too, and now I search wildly for Beam, almost crying with relief not to spot her among them. I hate how they're being studied and even touched by men whom I assume to be buyers. How is this happening?!

We don't skirt the human market like we did the area with the booths. We walk right through the middle. Frilk must want to scare me into subservience. *Too bad, pal. I'm Igmuwatogla. I was born to handle monsters like you.* My defiant pep talk is short-lived when the muscly boy spits on me.

"What is your problem?" I spout and wipe my cheek with my shoulder. *Shouldn't we be on the same side?*

"Keep your mouth shut, *slave,*" one of the men says to me. As the truth of the word sinks in, I think about the pictures in our history book. Stolen men and women—and children—who had to endure conditions worse than this. That same man who called me *slave* says to Frilk, "I wouldn't mind seeing *these* two in a fight." I find the boy who spit on me now glaring at me. At the man who said it. At Frilk. At the whole world.

Another teenager catches my eye. I nod at her. Her skin is dark too. I pray it's a coincidence. That this isn't some twisted attempt to recreate the Old South. I'm from the Great Plains, so I don't understand sentiments like, "The South's gonna rise again." But I've lived here long enough to know there are still plenty of Confederate flags waving from pickup trucks.

I'm gonna get us out of here, I want to say to the girl, if only for my own benefit. *Don't give up.*

I don't think she will. I can see that she's brave. She stands tall. Her lips pucker slightly in a show of defiance. I bet she's fierce as well as brave. Now I see that a smaller girl is cowering behind her. She hides between the fierce girl and the column. Her cheeks are smudged with dirt and tears. She looks scared as a rabbit.

"Come out from there!" A hefty woman grabs the girl by the upper arm and drags her into the open while the fierce girl protests and jerks the rope that binds her hands to the column. "Stop blubbering," the woman demands. "Both of you."

I strain against my leash, but Frilk jerks me back. "Leave her alone!" I shout—and get punched in the gut for it. I'm doubled over, winded, for the moment while the woman leads the smaller girl away. She screams back, "Harriet! Harriet!"

The fierce girl, *Harriet*, calls after her, tells her not to be afraid, tells her Daddy will come for them.

I need my daddy too. I wonder if the muscly boy has anyone to hope for.

"I told you he's in the wrong place," Frilk gruffs at someone, and a hateful-acting man hops up to unlock the boy's chains—yes, chains, not just rope—and force him from the columned island.

The fierce girl's eyes trail from where her sister is being led away, to the boy, and then to me. She's perplexed and unhappy, but she's not broken. Not at all. We lock eyes in some sort of a pact. I can feel myself making the mean-looking face Beam says she fell in love with me for. The girl, Harriet, in her red hoody, looks just as determined.

I don't recover from the trauma of that place even after I'm shunted past it. Now, I enter the area where animals are for sale. I can tell by the smells. There are a pair of coyotes, a bear—even an orangutan! Where the heck did that come from? Cage upon cage, generally too small and too dirty, makes a border around a courtyard. The animals lie listlessly on concrete slabs as an occasional shopper passes by. None of them are shifters, that I can tell.

My bravado is fading. How are this many people OK with what is going on here? How do they even find out about it?

A gargantuan roar sends an audible earthquake around us. I've never heard anything like it. I whirl around to find a lion—I mean an *African* lion—tussling with his captors. Three of them try to wrangle him by his chains. His mane dances wildly. He gnashes his enormous teeth and clamps down on the arm of the man who called me *slave*. The man howls in pain and drops back to baby his blood-soaked arm. Another man shoots the lion with a taser. I guess that's the weapon of choice for these folks. It doesn't faze the lion at first. Another, longer current does, though. Just watching it reminds me of how much pain those things cause. The lion hits the ground inside the opening of a cage.

I don't realize that I'm being slammed into a cage of my own until I'm watching from behind bars. He's alive. Right? He's alive. His body is dumped out of the way so the gate can be slammed with a bang. He's panting, lying on his side. I know what that feels like. I'd tell him if I could.

"Don't forget what I vowed to you." Frilk is speaking to me through the bars. He flicks the whip that binds my hands, and it tears my flesh as it releases me. He curls it and hangs it from his belt like he's Indiana Jones.

"What's going to happen to me?" I ask. But he's ambling away.

So, now I'm in a cage. It's not the small kind that the other animals endure. It's big enough to walk several paces—as a man or a cat. The cage that the African lion inhabits is the same. They butt up to one another so that the side of mine is also the side of his. The lion has yet to move more than to breathe in small gulps.

"Blue?" I call out. *Where are you?* And then I reach for my Beam again, bowing my head to my hands like a prayer.

Chausie?! When her worried voice cries out in my mind, I smile with a sigh.

There you are, I say. Or maybe I just think it.

Are you OK? Are you hurt? Are you in a cage?! She howls the last with rising concern as she sees my dwelling from my point of view.

"Are you talking to Chausie?!" I hear through Beam's ears. It's my mom. That means Beam made it back.

Tell her I'm OK, I say.

I did. Don't worry.

Did you call my dad?

He's on his way. First plane out.

That gives me hope. *You should call your dad too,* I say.

Yes, of course I did. And your mom called a policeman who she says helped you when you had the wreck? She says it like a question.

Aiden. Yeah, that was smart. I know my tone is less than thrilled.

Not a fan? Beam asks.

I'm not not a fan. He's just always checking in like he wants to be my dad or something. And I have a dad. But it's cool. I'll take whatever help I can get at this point.

Do you know where you are?

Frilk called it Snatcher's Ridge. I don't tell her how awful it is, but I do say, *They have a few people for sale here. There was a young girl, like eight years old, and another boy and girl our age.*

How is that even possible? she asks. I don't want her to get mired in the evil of it. I kind of need her to stay unaware for my sake, if that makes any sense. It relieves me when she moves on. *Where is Blue?*

No idea. Or Larkin either. Maybe he was able to rescue her and they're off making weird, little, blue faerie babies.

Beam laughs, and it warms me like sunshine.

Was Mom able to get the collar off you? I ask.

Yeah, we got it off. Did you know she used to be able to talk to your father the way you're talking to me right now? She called it a MATED connection.

She did? Now it's my turn to laugh. *Well, I guess we have to mate, then.*

Chausie Louris!

Her indignation makes me laugh for real, and that draws the attention of the—snatchers? Is that what these men are called? Anyway, there are two of them talking on the other end of the yard. Maybe they're in charge of guarding us. One of them comes over, so I slump against the back wall of my prison and try to keep my reactions to myself. The next-door lion heaves a huge sigh.

There's an African lion in here, I tell Beam. *With the big mane and everything.* I watch him while we talk. *What do you think he'll sell for? And to whom? There are hunting ranges that specialize in exotics. Did you know?*

Oh, don't say that. Maybe he'll go to a nice zoo.

Maybe, I say, but I don't think anyone here deals with anyone *nice.* Beam hears what I'm not trying to communicate.

Chausie, keep your eyes open. And tell me everything you see so that I can help find you. We're all going to— Her field of vision whips to the back of my bedroom, and a rising fear clutches my heart. I can't tell if it's hers or mine, but its grip is like a vice. Staring in at Beam through my bedroom window is her uncle, and he looks crazed, peeping from the bushes like a deviant.

I jump to the front of my cage and shake the bars to get free, but it's not the market in front of me that I see, nor the bored hassling of the imprisoned animals, nor the business-like hardness on the faces of the snatchers. "Beam, get away from the window!" I yell out loud. A blunt baton strikes me through the bars, and I bow into it, clutching my ribs. "Settle down," the striker says.

"I am about *sick* of being pummeled," I growl back at him.

The African lion lifts his head off the ground and then lays it back, unimpressed.

My connection with Beam is lost. *Her dad is on his way to her,* I assure myself. *And Aiden. She'll be OK.* I've gotta get out of here.

I fall back to the wall furthest from any onlookers and sit down to consider my predicament. The guy who used the baton on me is now pacing the perimeter. Freeing Beam's catcher from my pocket, I fidget with it and look for other guards until I find one. Higher up, on a hill behind us, a man scans the grounds through binoculars. Further still, I can make out several birds circling the sky. Any chance Larkin is up there?

"Get in there, and feed it its dinner."

I pull Beam's necklace over my head and tuck it into my shirt before standing to find out what's going on. The hefty woman is forcing the small, tear-and-dirt-streaked girl to push a wheel barrel containing a raw animal carcass. It's too big for her. The whole thing nearly capsizes. The gate complains as it slides open, and the woman juts her finger in to signal where the girl should go. The lion doesn't rise to his feet. He must be used to living in captivity. *Gah, I hope I never am.*

The girl whimpers.

"Go on!" the woman says. "Or I'll give you something to whimper *about*. And then maybe you'll stop acting like a pathetic mouse."

The girl shakes her head back and forth, back and forth. She's terrified.

"Why do you have to torture her?" I call out. "Dump it there and let her go back to her sister."

The woman doesn't give me more than a sidelong glance. She yanks the girl from behind the wheel barrel and shoves her through the gate, strong-arming her until she can get the gate closed again with the girl inside. The girl fights valiantly, clawing at the woman's fleshy arm to get out, but that only irritates the woman. She curses and says, "Now you can stay in there all night! And we'll let the lion decide if you're a suitable substitute for the dinner you wouldn't feed him." With that, she shoves the girl down—the girl immediately bounces up—slams the padlock, and stalks away wheeling what would have been the lion's meal. The tip of his tail flips in annoyance.

"Whoever is hoping to get money for her won't like that," I shout. I'm grasping at straws here.

The girl presses herself to the gate and I would say that she doesn't move a muscle, but she's trembling.

"What's your name?" I ask through our common wall. Only her large eyes acknowledge me.

I try again. "I don't think the lion is interested in you. He seems very relaxed."

The lion heaves another miserable sigh.

I sit down and reach through the bars to pat the ground inside her cage. "Why don't you come over here and sit? I'll keep you company."

After a moment to ponder that, she slowly sidles over to me and stands in the corner with a rigid back. "My name is Rosa," she whispers. If I didn't have the sensitive ears of a cat, I wouldn't have heard her.

"I'm Chausie."

She nods, her eyes stuck on the threat within her bars. "I don't want to be his dinner."

"You're not gonna be his dinner. We're gonna get you out of there. In fact, we're gonna get out of this whole rotten place."

A tear slides down her cheek.

"Do you hear me?" I ask. "You're not gonna die."

"What if he is hungry?"

"He can have my dinner when it comes." *If* it comes.

Finally, she turns to look me in the face and seems to question the veracity of my statement with a tilt of her head. "Yeah," I assure her. "No big deal."

She sits down and folds her arms around her knees. After a moment, she says, "Are you super strong or something?"

I don't know what made her ask. "I mean, yeah. Look at me." I flex my bicep, and she grins. My strength is all lean and sinewy. I'm fit, but nobody's going to mistake me for a bodybuilder. "What?" I goad her.

"You must have noticed my obvious muscles, or you wouldn't have asked."

"You're in a cage instead of out there with the people."

Behind Rosa's back, the lion perks his ears. I register the movement without focusing on it, so as not to alert my young friend that he's tending to our conversation. "So are you," I remind her.

The gate to my cage creaks open and a fibrous, raw rib cage from some animal—a deer?—is dropped onto the ground along with an empty bowl. After the gate closes again, water is sloshed through the bars into the bowl.

Rosa's eyes grow wide. "Why are they feeding you that?"

I sum her up. "Rosa, you're pretty smart, aren't you?"

"I get the best grades in my class."

"What's your favorite subject?"

"Hey, I asked you a question," she says and makes me smile. She showing some spunk after all.

"If I tell you why they have me in a cage, can we still be friends?"

She considers me very seriously. "Are you some kind of a—" she begins.

I nod my head to encourage her. Maybe if she comes to her own conclusion, it won't be as shocking. "Some kind of a what?" I prompt.

"Feral person?"

"What is that?" I laugh. "No." I lower my voice. "It's just that I can take on a different form. And that form eats things like that." I point to the carcass with my thumb.

"Are you a monster?!" She scoots away from me. "Are you a vampire?!"

"No," I rush to say. "I'm just a big, furry cat."

"Oh." She glances at the rack of meat. "*How* big of a cat?"

Our conversation continues to draw the curiosity of the bulkier lion, and now he is silently padding our way in a direct register, each back foot silently falling into the print of its front counterpart. He's eyeballing me. Rosa doesn't notice. I don't think he's just a cat.

"I'm a lion," I answer her, but I'm putting our companion on notice too.

"I want to see!" Rosa says.

Is it because I'm in a different cage that she's not afraid of me? The African is smirking. I don't like his attitude. His expression is downright smug, causing the hair on the back of my neck to bristle. I check to make sure that no one else is watching, and I shift.

"Oh, how can that be?" the girl coos. She even reaches for me through the bars. "You're a *girl* lion!"

I jump back into human form. "No, I'm not! I'm a *mountain* lion. A very *male* mountain lion."

The African collapses and nearly chokes on croaks of amusement. Well, that's proof. He is clearly not an ordinary cat. He spends the next twenty seconds rolling on his back, writhing and yowling with laughter. It annoys the heck out of me, but it terrifies Rosa.

"He's not going to eat you," I mutter. "He's too busy feeling superior."

Her doubtful eyes ask me if I'm sure.

"I'll protect you."

At this, the lion scoffs, jumps to his feet, and shakes his glorious mane.

"You don't think I can put up a fight?" I ask him.

"From over there?" His language is interestingly accented, but I understand it. "Why don't you just haul that carcass over as you so sincerely promised?"

I roll my eyes and consider the carcass. "I'll bring it to you if you leave her alone."

He looks bored. "'K," he says flippantly and flicks his tail with the same attitude.

"No matter how long she's locked in there with you," I add.

He shakes his mane again and when he's finished, he's that punk-ass kid who spat on me earlier. "I guess that depends on how long you keep the food coming." His communications leave much to be desired, and hasn't he already made it clear that we're not on the same team?

I drag the meat to him in a show of good faith. I'm about to lion up so that I can shred it into pieces small enough to shove through the bars when Rosa identifies him. "Kofi!" He doesn't reply. "Kofi, it's me, Rosa." She takes a few steps to him. "Remember when you talked to me and my sister, Harriet?" Still nothing. "Why aren't you saying anything?" Kofi won't even look at her. She clucks her tongue in frustration.

"Just because we've met before doesn't make us friends," he says. He takes his lion form again and snarls at me to hurry up.

I might have snarled back if I wasn't distracted by a rusty bar. With some effort, I remove it, creating a larger hole through which Kofi's meal can be served. I wonder if Rosa is small enough to get through that hole. Maybe there are other vulnerable areas in these walls.

6

SEARGENT AIDEN GUNNOLF

BEAM

Uncle Joel is the only reason I'm alive right now. For years, he wanted to educate me about the power of my blood—ever since I was five and he knocked back a shot of it to prove it would heal his broken nose. My dad wanted to hide all that from me in the hopes of shielding me from danger, but Uncle Joel knew that was impossible. What he didn't know is that my blood can also annihilate people—or, well, it can annihilate hateful snakes. It works according to my mood.

Now, as Uncle gawks at me through Chausie's bedroom window, I don't know how I'm supposed to feel. Thankfully, Chausie's mother forcibly yanks the curtain shut. "The police are on the way," she says and pulls me into the hall.

Just then, a rapid pounding on the front door stops us in our tracks, and her eyes mirror my concern. More pounding. And then, a voice I trust more than any on Earth calls for me. "Sunbeam?!"

"It's my dad!" I break free from Ms. Louris's grasp and stumble over my feet to the door, but when I wrench it open, my dad is being attacked by my uncle!

"Get off of him!" I dive into the fray without thinking and end up dragging my uncle off the porch where we roll through the grass. When we come to a stop, Uncle clamors to his feet, one hand outstretched to ward me off. Now, here's where it gets weird. Er. Something else rolled with us, and now it skulks into the night, reminding me of a tall, skinny mime dressed in a black, whole-body suit that even covers its face.

"What is that?" I ask.

Uncle has a nasty set of scratches down his cheek. He looks bewildered. Nobody answers about the mime thing. It must be invisible. I turn my ire upon my uncle.

"What is wrong with you?" I yell and am tempted to gift him with a few more scratches, but I have to check on my dad. "Daddy?" He's gaping at me from up on the porch. His eyes are wide with...fear? When I trot toward him, he shrinks from me. My mom stands beside him but sort of cowers in the corner.

Chausie's mother acts as an interpreter. "They don't know who you are, Beam."

Everybody's staring. I look down at myself. Furry, black chest. Legs that end in large paws... I am not going to love a life of shifting without meaning to. Is that normal?

Chausie's mom kneels beside my father to take stock of his physical condition, and from behind me, my uncle says, "Someone is speaking inside of my head."

Crap. Blue jeans. White T. Blue jeans. White T. And here I am in my human form again, fully clothed. *Go, me! Two for two.* Once I've finished patting myself down to confirm my humanity, I say, "*Who* is speaking to you? That creepy mime?"

Uncle winces as if my words are too loud and uses his thumb to press the ocular bone above his eye. "I don't know." Blood drips from the lacerations on his cheek.

"Did something inhabit you back in the catacombs?"

"I don't think so, but it feels like I'm sleepwalking when the voice gets too loud."

"OK. *Um...* Ms. Louris?"

"Just call me Sophie." She's already coming down to us, passing me by with a towel to press against Uncle Joel's scratches.

"Did I do that to him?" I ask. "I didn't mean to."

"You're a predatory animal now," Sophie says. "You'll have to learn what that means and when to hold back." She leads Uncle to the porch steps, where she instructs him to sit and to apply pressure. Those scratches will be healed by the next time she checks them. The power of my blood remains in my uncle, so I'm not worried about him that way. I'm more puzzled by the fact that I caused them. I don't remember hurting him, though I do remember wanting to hurt him some more.

While Sophie examines my uncle's eyes, I think of the times Chausie has attacked people—only when they've meant to harm us. And only with a measured response. I'm guessing that takes a lot of control.

Up on the landing, my dad looms over my uncle while Chausie's mother tends to him. "Beam, what is going on?" he asks. "You can shift now?"

My poor dad. Until two weeks ago, our lives were very orderly. He established rules, and I obeyed them. His rules were things like, *Do not offer your blood to others. Do not talk to invisible creatures or journey into otherworldly dimensions.* I'm sure turning into a wild animal would have been banned if he had thought of it. "It happened for the first time today," I tell him. "I have as many questions as you do. Are you alright?"

"Fine." He waves away the concern about himself, and I know he means to speak again, so I wait for him to form his thoughts. He's not a verbal processor. "Is it permanent?" he finally asks. "Are there things we need to do to accommodate such a—thing?" I'm pretty sure he wants to use a word closer to *malady.*

"Don't worry," Chausie's mom says to him. "We'll guide her through all that."

"It's pretty *awesome,*" my mom chimes in. "Does it feel strange?" On the other hand, Mom digests reality with an insatiable appetite for details. "Having a child who is a shifter must present challenges." Sophie nods and I can see that Mom is about to ply her with questions, but I butt in.

"Mom, Dad, as you have surmised, this is Chausie's mother, Sophie Louris." When Sophie reaches out a hand, my dad moves forward with a wary eye on my uncle.

"Hawk Redfeather," he says. "This is Maggie. We've spent the last few days with your son. He's a fine young man."

Yeah, he is... I do a little finger dance behind Sophie's back making

Daddy drop his eyes to keep from grinning. He's a serious sort, but I've always been able to amuse him.

"Well, I hope that we can locate him very soon," Sophie says.

My uncle makes a sound that is a mixture of a groan and a sniff, which brings Sophie's attention back to him. "Beam says her uncle isn't acting like himself. His pupils are uneven."

"He probably gave himself a concussion when he jumped me for no reason," Dad says. Uncle Joel mutters a pitiful, "I'm sorry about that," which is muffled by the way he rests his head on his hands.

"He should be checked by a doctor."

"Won't the origin of those scratches be called into question?" Dad asks. "I'd hate for anyone to be on the lookout for a dangerous, wild animal because of it."

"The scratches are gone," I report.

Uncle raises his head to focus on me, and we see that it's true. "Why aren't you wearing your catcher?" he yells and jumps to his feet to lunge at me. This time, I do mean to shift. I bow up and hiss at him in warning. I sound fabulous. It stops Uncle Joel in his tracks.

"Hold it right there!"

I hadn't noticed the police cruiser pull up, but an imposing figure inserts himself into our standoff. His Army green uniform is at once rugged and official. He hasn't drawn his firearm, but his hand rests upon it, and he doesn't appear to be someone to be trifled with. Daddy immediately descends the steps, his hands held in surrender. "She isn't a threat," he says and places himself between me and the officer. But the officer isn't trained upon me. He's eyeing my uncle. "Sophie, do you know this man?" he asks.

"Aiden, don't hurt him. He's disturbed. He's not well."

Aiden's features are strong—prominent nose, sharp brow, keen eyes. He says to my uncle, "Sir, take your seat back and explain to me what's going on."

"It's just that she's not wearing her catcher," Uncle says. "She's not even wearing it." He sits back down on the step and moans into his hands. Officer Aiden observes each of us in turn. The badge on his left arm is gold, embossed with the words *City of Atlanta Police*. I'm not sure if I should, but I do become my human self.

My dad side-eyes me and then considers Aiden, but Aiden doesn't react to me being human now.

"I don't recognize the uniform," Dad says. "Specialized division?"

"APEX. Seargent Aiden Gunnolf."

"Aiden was the first to Chausie after his wreck," Sophie says. "He hardly let me get to him myself."

"Because he was a mess," Aiden says.

"And I'm an ER nurse."

"But he is your *son*."

They've clearly had this quibble before. "Wait," I say as it occurs to me. "You were already here when Chausie wrecked?" I knew it happened in this driveway and that his mom was home at the time.

"It's possible that me being here is what caused the wreck. My truck takes up half the drive."

"I'm not sure it was the truck that was the problem," Sophie says, and Aiden acquiesces with a knowing blink that leaves him gazing at her through his lashes. Just how close are these two?

"Seargent, what does APEX do?" my dad asks. "You were unfazed by my daughter's...condition."

"We handle the *big* Bads," Aiden answers without answering. "And we're used to...conditions."

"The shield on the side of your truck," my mom says. "There's a dog in the middle. Is it a K9 unit?" They're so nosey. Must be where I get it.

Aiden licks his lips in what looks like an attempt to hide a smile. "It's a wolf," he corrects. "And, yeah, it's probably accurate to say that it's a K9 unit."

I look at him anew. His ice-blue irises. His prominent nose. That faint scent of the outside my labrador used to track in. I lean forward and—forgive me, but I do it—sniff him. Loudly. "I'm so sorry," I blurt out when I catch myself. *That was appalling.* "But you're a shifter?"

He snorts out a laugh. "That took you a long time."

"Hey," I say defensively. "I've only just become one myself. I'm not used to—smelling people."

"Well, maybe don't be so obvious about it in the future," he says.

"Are you a *werewolf?*"

"Oh for the love of—no. Don't use that term. It's offensive."

"How was I supposed to know?"

"Why don't I start a pot of coffee," Sophie volunteers, though we're still hours from sunrise. "And maybe we can skip to the part where you find my son."

Aiden agrees with a flourish as he presents the door, inviting Sophie to lead the way. My mom follows and immediately voices more questions than Sophie can answer. She'll have their whole life story soon. Aiden directs Uncle Joel to go next. I guess he's not going to arrest him, but he doesn't want to walk in front of him, either. Honestly, I don't think any of us knows *what* to do with Uncle Joel. He's a bit green as he hunches over and walks holding his stomach.

"How did you get to know this family in the first place?" I ask. "Is there some kind of shifter registry?"

Aiden glances around to see if I'm serious, so I shrug. "No," he says. "That would be highly unAmerican."

"There's nothing *more* American," my dad mutters. "Ask McCarthy." He means back in the 1950s during the Red Scare when civil liberties were trampled due to the paranoia of communism. People lost their jobs and sometimes their very freedom with trumped-up accusations and hysteria. It's important to confirm the truth from reliable sources before reacting emotionally to hearsay—something my parents have drilled into my head since before I could walk.

"Or ask the so-called witches of Salem," my mom calls back.

"Well, that's not how we run things in Atlanta," Aiden says.

"KKK," my dad says through a fake cough. *So this is what it's like to be on the outside and not the victim of the mom-dad tag team. Huh.*

"Not on my watch," Aiden counters and Dad raises his hands good-naturedly.

You know what's cool? My parents are eyes wide open about the grievous sins perpetrated in the name of the United States—I mean, my dad is an Oglala Lakota Indian—but they still adore our country and, as lawyers, work hard to make it a safe home for everybody.

We crowd around Sophie's small kitchen—well, Uncle Joel slumps in a chair at the table—and as Sophie measures spoonfuls of ground coffee, I imagine the meals she and Chausie share here. Where does he sit? Does he help cook? "Sorry, what?" I say to Aiden.

"You asked how I knew them." He indicates Chausie's mom. "Not long after Sophie moved to town, I was finishing up a trail run and Chausie skidded into the lot like his hair was on fire. He jumped off his motorcycle and barely secured the kickstand before shifting right in front of me and running into the woods. Reminded me of a younger version of myself, so I ran his license plate and on my next day off, I knocked on the door to introduce myself."

From where she pushes the *brew* button, Sophie says, "I thought Chausie was in trouble for sure."

"Well, he may have been if his beautiful mother hadn't answered the door." When Sophie raises her head, Aiden winks at her. *Oh my gosh. Does Chausie know how they act around each other?* Aloud, I say, "I'm surprised Chausie would shift in front of you like that."

"He didn't know I was there."

I can feel the dubious smirk I'm making. "Not much gets past Chausie. You must be incredibly stealthy."

"I am," is all he says, and I believe him.

CHAUSIE

I wake up in the dark. This concrete floor is awfully hard, but that's not what woke me. Someone is sneaking through the ring of animal cages, scurrying shadow to shadow. I sniff the air and bristle. To my right, Rosa slouches against the bars that separate us. She's sound asleep. Kofi, as his lion self, rests on the farthest side of the cage—whether out of a desire to be left alone or to keep Rosa from being unduly afraid, I don't know. When his ears swivel toward the gate, I know that he has become aware of the skulking figure as well.

Strains of music float to us from that field I first traversed when Frilk and I topped the ridge. There are no guards around. The snatchers are probably throwing a big party to celebrate their catches. Tomorrow kicks off some kind of grand opening. I heard the guards say that all the buying will happen in the next two days. Other than the distant party sounds, the night is surprisingly quiet. There's a slight breeze.

The figure in question peers into the orangutan cage. I almost lose sight of him—or her, but I think him—because of how long he remains immobile. Finally, he makes his way to the cage of the sleeping bear. The next cages belong to us.

Emerging from the shadows, a sturdy-looking man, his hair tied back in box braids, glances over his shoulder and moves toward us. But now he has two lions to deal with because Kofi and I both leap to our feet, flanking the sleeping Rosa. He comes to a swift halt.

"Rosa?" He hardly breathes her name.

Kofi rumbles a warning. Is he *protecting* her now? I man up. "Who are you? What do you want?"

Though the man is visibly taken aback by my appearance, he answers, "I just want my daughter." His voice quavers. "Am I too late?"

"Rosa's your daughter?" I ask. And then I realize he thinks we've mauled her, so I rush to say, "No. No, she's just a good sleeper."

Kofi uses a soft paw to nudge her, something her father stifles a fearful noise over. He appraises the lion, who hovers over her, and kneels next to the cage. "Rosa, get up now. We have to go." With a glance around the cage, he asks, "How do I open it?"

"You don't," Kofi says flatly, having shifted into his human form. "They padlock the cages of animals who have thumbs."

Rosa blinks her eyes open and stares around sleepily.

"Rosa, do you know this man?" Kofi asks.

At the sight of him, Rosa's whole face opens up and she squeals, "Daddy!"

We all three *shush* her at once, but Rosa reaches through the bars for him and then erupts into tears. "They have Harriet. They have Harriet," she weeps.

"I know, Baby." He hugs her despite the bars that stand between them.

"How did you find us?" Chausie asks. "I need to get word to my dad too. He's in law enforcement."

"What's your name?"

"Chausie Louris."

"Nat Turner," he says, then looks at Kofi, who seems hesitant and offers his first name only.

Mr. Turner skips the formalities. "Harriet's a runner. She wears a small tracker on the laces of her shoes."

"Did you bring the police?"

He shakes his head. "They said she was probably at a friend's house, even though I insisted she would never do that without telling us. Especially not with her sister in tow. They said to get back to them after a full twenty-four hours. But I knew I didn't have that long."

"Do you have an address for this place?" I ask.

Mr. Turner shakes his head. "I just followed the map to the last place her tracker pinged. When the road ran out, I started hiking. Let me go now, Rosa," he says gently and pries himself from her arms. "Let's see if we can find a way to get you out."

"Can you come around back?" I ask. "There's a rusty bar I've been working on. I think if we could create some leverage, we could dislodge it. Rosa, can you squeeze through that hole?" I mean the one I pushed the meat through earlier.

Mr. Turner slinks around the side of the cage while Kofi glares at me.

"What?"

He doesn't answer, but I begin to understand him. Rosa may fit through that hole, but Kofi most definitely will not.

"Kofi, I'm not gonna leave you in here," I tell him.

He folds his arms with a look of disdain I'd like to smack off his face.

"Dude, what happened to make you this way?" I ask. I've been surly before. I've been hateful and pissed off. But I don't think I ever outright doubted the goodness of humanity the way this guy seems to.

Mr. Turner is behind the cage and asks, "Which one?"

I show him the bar I mean. "See how it twists? If we could pop it out at the bottom there..."

He nods his head and pulls with all his might. When it doesn't give, he says, "If we get it out, would you be able to fit through?"

"I'll make it work. But anyway, Rosa will be able to. I'll get her into this cage while you find some sort of a lever." Mr. Turner nods and sneaks off to search. "Kofi?" I ask. "Make sure there are no loose bars along your walls. I—"

He grabs my arm through the bars and jerks me into them. I'm about to put up a fight when he presses a finger to his lips.

I go still and listen while his nose twitches, even as a man. "Someone's coming," he says in low tones. The next thing I know, he's a lion padding the length of his cage.

"Rosa, come on," I whisper. The hole we've made is about four feet off the ground. She can't figure out how to climb up to it, so I make a basket with my hands for her, like a stirrup. But now that she is high enough, I need my hands free to pull her through.

What do you know? Kofi trots over without being asked and receives her weight with his head. It takes some tugging, but once we get her through, he begins pacing again. I think he's trying to make sure that any unwanted attention falls on him and not us.

Two drunken revelers, on their way back from the party, haphazardly shine their flashlights into cages as they pass. Lucky for us, they're in no shape to notice anything amiss. "Here, kitty, kitty," one of them says. He approaches Kofi, unsteady on his feet. "Here, kitty."

I ask Rosa to hide behind me. Maybe they'll want to look for her and open the door, giving Kofi a chance to escape.

The man's companion turns a dumb smile upon him as he reaches the cage. Kofi continues to pace. He gives a huff that has the revelers saying things like, "You're a big boy, aren't you? You want to eat my face off!" And then the first one swats Kofi on the hind end. He is so fortunate. Because Kofi turns on him in an instant, snarling and snapping his jaw around what would have been that man's hand if he hadn't already pulled it away.

"Hey, where's the girl?" the other one asks.

They shine lights around the cage and land on the pile of ribs left over from Kofi's meal. "*Oh.*" One of them points to the lion's belly. "I guess she's in there."

"Well, can you blame a fella for eating supper?" Both men guffaw, and the one whose hand Kofi nearly emancipated from his arm reaches through again! Kofi chomps again. And misses again. To uproarious, boozy-smelling chortles. Gross. Kofi sits back on his haunches, demonstrating the same look of disdain as a cat that he has as a human.

A huge yawn from one of the men suggests that he's about to pass out. He slurs something about the big day tomorrow and stumbles toward a small building that must work as a barracks. When the men move on, I say, "Kofi, how long have you been a prisoner here?"

He slips into his human form, still seated, and wraps his arms around his knees. "A few days."

"Where were you before that?" I have a growing hunch that he hasn't been free in a long, long time.

He shrugs off my question, but I keep trying. "Where are you from, I mean? Where's home?"

"What's it to you?" he snaps.

I stare at him blankly before I say, "You're not that fun to talk to."

"Then stop doing it."

Mr. Turner returns holding a steel pipe that glints in the scant light. "Here's something. It's not long, but it is strong."

"Let's try it."

He wedges the pipe between the base of the rusted bar and the next that he can use to crank it against. "If this works," he says, "it's bound to make a lot of noise, and we'll have company."

"I'll take care of it. You just get Rosa out of here. Listen, there's at least one guard up on that hill. I'll give you what cover I can."

"What about Harriet?" Rosa asks.

"Don't worry, Rosa," her father says. "Be very brave and do as I say."

Rosa silently agrees.

Her father reaches through the bars to grip my hand and makes us allies.

Out of the corner of my eye, Kofi pointedly turns his head away. He seriously thinks I'm going to escape and forget about him.

"I'm going to get you out," I tell him. But the only signs he hears me are the muscles clenching in his jaw and the upward trajectory of his eyes. I don't think he's had a single friend in his whole life.

"Come on, Rosa," I tell her. "Let's get over here in case the pipe flies out. I'd hate for you to miss your escape because you got knocked out."

Rosa giggles as she takes my hand. Her dad's presence has swallowed up all her fear. I daresay she could enjoy this adventure as long as he was with her.

"Here we go," he says. With the pipe in position, Mr. Turner hoists himself up Tarzan-style so that he can propel himself onto the pipe with both feet.

A ringing clang temporarily deafens us as the rusty bar comes free. At the same time, the pipe flies end over end, straight for Rosa's head. Thank God for cat-like reflexes. I pluck it out of the air and hurry Rosa toward the opening. "Here." I offer the pipe to Mr. Turner. "In case you need a weapon." With his daughter on the outside of the cage, he subtly lifts his shirt to reveal a pistol lodged in his waistband. "That'll work, too," I say, and, as a lion, I'm able to extricate myself.

Kofi watches us with the kind of expression that says it's a show he's seen before. Slightly interested but not that excited. I'm about to suggest we try to shoot off the padlock on his cage when several noises alert us that the snatchers are coming.

Figures emerge from the barracks. "What was that?" "Where did it come from?" "Who's there!" The two drunk men we'd encountered are among them. One is hopping on one foot, trying to pull on his pants. There's a confused swelling of voices but no focused action.

I catch a glimpse of movement, the swing of a branch in the distance. Mr. Turner must have picked up his daughter and run for it. Good for them. I quickly test each bar on the back of Kofi's cage and then hurry around the side.

"There!" someone yells, and all heads swivel. I haven't forgotten the brutal promise that Frilk made. If he sees that I've shifted, will he really track her down? With all these people coming for me, there's no way I'll get another chance to escape. I'll just have to avoid him and get to Beam before he can.

"I'm coming back for you, Kofi!" I say as a cat. And with that, I gallop through the middle of the courtyard. Maybe with all eyes on me, no one will look for the Turners. After all, Mr. Turner arrived under the radar, and Rosa was supposedly ingested.

The pathway narrows. Someone yells, "Get him!" Others are backing away in fear of me. I slash my claws through the fabric of a tent as I pass. It makes a satisfying *zip*. That, along with my throaty warnings, seems to clear the way for me.

With an anxious eye out for Frilk, I bound into the space where the humans were held. The islands are all empty now, and Harriet's scent is faint. It leads me back to the island where she was tied, but I already know I won't find her there. What I do find are two running shoes dangling by their laces. What kind of message is this? I seize the shoes and race away with them dangling from my teeth.

I lose her scent completely where tire tracks begin, and now I'm beginning to think Harriet is not only gone from the island but gone from Snatcher's Ridge. The bidding doesn't begin until tomorrow, though. I almost decide to make one more round. If I can find her now, I can get her back to her father. But my gaze snags on a figure who is stock-still in all the commotion. Frilk. When he catches my eye, his face remains stoic, and he drags a finger across his neck to remind me of his vow. And then he disappears.

Panic, in the form of pain, stabs my heart. He hadn't meant that he would track her down. He meant that he would actually appear before her. But he can't do that. How could he— I think back to the way the whip anchored us to that silvery object below the ridge. The collar.

Beam! The goblin is coming for you! Frilk is coming for you!

I don't know where to go except *out*. I sprint as fast as I can, and when I feel a safe distance away, I cry out for Beam again in my mind. *Get away from the collar! Throw it out!*

I follow my nose to Mr. Turner and Rosa. They've made good time. They're rounding the hill I told them to avoid, and I'm upon them before they notice me. Mr. Turner hastily draws his gun, but Rosa says, "It's Chausie!"

I drop the running shoes and man up. "I couldn't find Harriet," I pant. "But these were hanging up like they were begging to be found. I think they figured out about the tracker. I didn't want you to go into a trap. Listen, I have to get home. One of the snatchers is after my girlfriend. Can we get to your car? I'll come back with the police."

"I can't leave without Harriet."

"Mr. Turner, I am telling you she's not here."

It's a non-starter, and I don't have time to argue. He's not leaving the last known location of his daughter. He says, "I don't have cell service, but look here." He shows me the map on his phone. "Here we are on the ridge. And this dot is my car. Take Rosa with you."

I study the map until I have a good idea about the terrain and where we are in relation to the car. Anyway, I can scent the way. "Yeah, OK. Rosa, you'll have to ride on me."

"Daddy?"

"Go on, Rosa." He hands me the keys. "I'm going to find your sister."

"If I were you," I tell Mr. Turner. "I'd take out the guard on the hill and use his binoculars. Just keep tabs on who comes and goes. The bidding begins tomorrow—in a few hours. I'll be back with the police as soon as I can."

Mr. Turner almost smiles. "It's like you were trained for this."

"I was. Do you know what a mountain lion sounds like? The scream they make? That's how you'll know when I get back. Rosa will be safe with my mom."

I shift so that Mr. Turner can deposit Rosa onto my back. He tells her to hold on tight, and I gallop into the woods.

BEAM

"Do you know how to handle goblins?" I blurt out. Chausie is trying to communicate with me. He's worried about Frilk. I don't know if he's in immediate danger or if he thinks I am. We're standing around the dining table where Aiden is studying a topographical map on a video chat with an officer at his station. I've fed him all the information Chausie gave me—several times— but it's not enough to narrow down his whereabouts.

"No," he answers in a dismissive way I do not appreciate.

"Well, does anyone on your team know how to handle goblins?"

He turns his head with an impatient twist. "Goblins? Like, Rumpelstilzchen?"

"Yeah, maybe. Little old dudes with tons of scary magic." I shiver to recall the monstrous face Frilk made when the woman suggested they share the take. At the same time, I disregard the *tug* I feel coming from inside the purse that hangs under my shirt.

"That type of thing doesn't exist."

"*You* exist," I counter.

"Yeah, but shifters are natural. It's all about biology and the pull of the moon. You're talking about *magical* beings. I've been at this for a while now. They don't exist."

"Oh, Aiden," I say and allow my words to drip with condescension. If he only knew to whom he was speaking. "So, no ghosts? No invisible creatures?"

"Not that I've seen," he says sarcastically.

"Cute. And absolutely no help."

He tilts his head like he's listening for something. Chausie's mom turns toward us.

"The man who captured Chausie is a goblin," I continue. "He pulled Chausie off his feet with some kind of silvery rope—like a whip —and disappeared him. He put something like that on me." From the beaded purse, I pull the collar up to my throat, and as I suspected, it encircles my neck, becoming one solid piece. Aiden moves to inspect it.

"It seals itself onto the captive," I tell him.

"How do you get it off?"

"Well, the goblin—his name is—"

"Frilk." The bone-chilling voice comes from behind my left ear and leaves a wake of utter silence in the room until Daddy knocks a chair back in his hurry to protect me. From the pointy feel of it, the intruder holds a blade to my throat.

"Don't do it!" Aiden commands. He's nearly as close to me as Frilk is, though I'm between them, and the knife is closer still. It pricks my skin. I can see my dad advancing from the corner of my eye, and Aiden thrusting out a hand to stop him, though his eyes are locked on Frilk.

Frilk sniffs at me. "So, you *are* a shifter. Not a Leonid somehow, but I still could have made a fortune on you."

"I can see that you don't want to harm her," Aiden says with forced calm. "Put the knife down, and we can come to an arrangement."

"Can't," Frilk says. "I made a promise." Without another word, he slashes through my skin as he yanks the collar in the opposite direction. The collar simply lets go of me, and Aiden lunges for him. Meanwhile, I am spun forward, gripping my throat with both hands, blood spilling over my collarbones and onto my chest as warm as bathwater. I vaguely register that Aiden swings both arms right through Frilk, and then that Frilk is gone.

"Lay her down," Sophie commands. My knees give way as Aiden guides me to the ground. "Keep her throat higher than her heart."

Sophie is still instructing as she sprints down the hall. "Put pressure on it!" A cabinet bangs open, and she's already back, kneeling beside me.

"Let up, Aiden. You're choking her air off."

Things are going fuzzy. I try to tell them. Then I try to remember what I'm trying to tell them. Then I try to remember what I'm trying to remember. My mom is gaping down at me with the kind of horror I've only seen in movies. The kitchen light makes a sunset halo through her red hair. Daddy is fumbling for his phone.

I try to speak, but my voice won't work. I sputter and gasp for air. I'm drowning. I have to get loose. Aiden is fighting me. I slap at him, kick at him.

"She's convulsing. Hold her still." I barely register what's being said. I stop fighting—not on purpose.

"Get away from her!" My dad, who was issuing commands to Emergency on the phone, now shoves my uncle into the refrigerator.

"The blood, the blood," my uncle is saying.

"Is there an active intruder situation, Sir?" I hear Emergency ask my dad.

"No," he says and decks my uncle.

This would all be more interesting if I weren't chilling uncontrollably. I need blankets. I need to sleep. If I could get warm, I could go to sleep. When my eyes roll back into my head, it is a genuine relief.

"Sweetheart?" It's my mom sounding terrified and trying not to. My eyelids open halfway to see she's beside us on the floor. The knees of her pants are soaking up blood. She begins to sob. "Beam?!"

Daddy is kneeling beside us now. And there is Oonchi! *Oh, Oonchi! Have you come back to us?* Even as I think it, I realize that, *No. My grandmother has not come back to us. I am going to her.* There is a river that runs to meet the horizon, and I'm walking on it. At the horizon, it continues into the sky as a road made of stars. When I reach the place where water and stars meet, a woman waits for me, a woman with ears like Larkin's, made into points. In the language of lions, she says, "The purse holds the map." And the stars form arrows, much like the beads on the flap of the little pouch.

I don't know what she means, but I want to follow those beautiful stars.

"Only a cursed blade can reveal it."

"May I just...?" I indicate the star road.

"No, that is not yet your path. You're lion keens for you."

I hear Chausie's lion scream like in a dream.

The Larkin-like lady points to the stars. "His ancestors traveled the star road in reverse and made a home with the lions here on Earth."

"She has stopped bleeding," Aiden says hopefully when Sophie lifts a towel from my neck. I am at once lying on Aiden's knees on Chausie's kitchen floor and walking on the river road into the sky.

"I think it is only that she has no blood left," says Sophie, killing off the hope with the gentlest tone.

My body expels what breath is left in my lungs.

"Is she gone?" my mother rasps. My father is weeping.

"Not yet," Sophie says. The small pressure on my wrist is her checking for a pulse.

Somebody has mercifully turned on the heat. My body relaxes out of the painful chill and at last I can sleep.

The purse holds the map. They are the last words I hear before I awake. My mom has switched places with Aiden, and she is rocking me hard, holding me tight to her chest and wailing mournful, hoarse laments. I've never heard her sound so gutted!

"What on Earth is the matter?" I ask her.

The hushed voices and soft footfalls around me cease. My mom loosens her hold enough to peer down at me. Everyone is gaping.

I look down at myself. "Am I a lion again?" I ask. "Or...something else?"

Sophie nearly tackles me. "Get the sutures!" She measures the pulse at my wrist. "How? How-how-how?" She feels my forehead with the back of her hand and then stops everything to stare at my neck. Without looking away, she waves her hand for assistance. "A wet towel! Quickly!" Aiden rushes to deliver, and Sophie wipes my neck, softly at first but ends up scrubbing it. "There's not even a *mark*."

"You mean?" my mom begins.

"She's going to live?" my dad asks.

Uncle Joel cocks his head like a cartoon from where he slumps against the fridge. There are bottles of glue lying on the floor. I guess Sophie tried everything she could think of to fix me.

Now she appraises Uncle Joel, finally pointing to his cheek, the one I'd scratched earlier. "Is it some kind of Indigenous trait?" she asks. "Do you possess ultra-healing skin?"

"No," my dad answers and narrows his eyes at me. Chausie and I haven't told anybody that I made him an Elixir unawares or that his blood saved my life. I don't mind my dad knowing, but not now. Not here.

Aiden collapses into a chair, staring at me, covering his mouth with a blood-smeared hand. Now that I look him over, I see that he's bloody up to the shoulders.

"You're a mess," I tell him.

"Goblin," he manages.

"Yep."

My mom continues to rock me, this time out of sheer relief, not wanting to let me go. Silence falls upon the room until some time later when the front door opens and we hear shoes rush through the foyer. "Where is everybody?"

"Chausie?" his mom cries.

Chausie rounds the entryway with, "What in the–" His round eyes land on me, but I'm not bleeding anymore. I'm sitting up on my own. "Who's blood is that?" he asks. Yeah, it truly is a bath. Almost all of us are painted in it. It's still sticky underneath me when I raise my hand to claim it.

Uncle Joel, by the way, is slowly crawling toward me like no one can see him, but my dad hauls him onto a chair and demands that he stay.

Chausie seizes my shoulders and seems to be assessing whether or not I'm corporeal. "You're alive. Right?" he asks me.

"Yeah." I glance around. "*Uh*—I think so. They can all see me, so I must be." I'm a little befuddled.

"Is he gone?" When I don't answer, Chausie looks to Aiden. "Is he gone? Did you get him?"

Aiden shakes his head. "Gone."

Chaus sits back on his heels and runs both hands through his hair as he surveys the scene again. He blows out a breath that puffs his cheeks.

"Chaus, I'm OK," I tell him. "Don't go into shock."

"He told me he'd do it," he chokes out. "He swore it, and I didn't lion up because—but then I had to. I was going to miss my—"

"It's not your fault," I assure him. "And I'm OK." I reach for him. I'd stand up, but I'm woozy. "How did you get away?"

Instead of answering me, he crams the catcher necklace over my head—causing Uncle to sigh in relief. Chausie looks so sticken, I'm not sure what to say. I try, "Chausie, you warned me. I heard you. It's all Aiden's fault." On a whim, I twist and point blame at the wolf shifter, who lifts his hands to object.

But Chausie's mom cries a little, "*Oh*," and rushes to the entryway where a young girl peeks around the corner as pale as paper despite her dark skin.

Chausie cringes. "Oh, Rosa. I got her, Mom. You're a bloody mess."

True fact. I've bled on his mom and everybody else. Well, not Uncle Joel. Chausie hesitates, torn between this girl and me. "Go," I say. "I'll be here." Then he shoos the girl into the living room.

Daddy looks at me in the silent way of sage fathers and then traces my smooth neck where there should be a gaping wound. "The Elixir pumps through a lion's heart." He recites one of the lines from the Visions of Blood. It's a translation that differed from the one I learned.

The Visions of Blood were recorded in the 1800s. I haven't been able to study them because I only found out they existed in the past few weeks, but my oonchi used to sing them to me in a lullaby—in English since Daddy wouldn't teach me Lakota—and once, when I was dying— not today, but a different time—I remembered the song and realized that Chausie's blood would heal me. The power of it still lives in me as mine does in him—and in my Uncle Joel. But Uncle didn't become an Elixir over it, and Chausie did. "Let's get you home," Dad says, but I shake my head no.

"What if that evil creature returns?"

"I'm sure he believes her to be dead," Aiden says.

Mom asks, "How did he find her in the first place?" She's rummaging through the pantry and comes out with paper towels, a mop, and a bucket.

The collar. I grab my neck to find it, but I guess Frilk took it with him.

"We'll get you to a doctor right away," Mom says, but by *right away,* she must mean after she cleans up the congealing pool of blood because she waves me out of it and begins her attack. I think it's her way of dealing with the trauma.

"Has anyone seen the silver collar or did Frilk take it with him?" I ask.

"Is this it?" My mom pinches the ick-covered collar through a paper towel barrier, and we deposit it into the beaded pouch, which has managed to remain hanging over one shoulder under my shirt.

As Daddy helps Mom with the floor, I sneak into Chausie's room to borrow clean clothes and then into the bathroom for a quick wash-off. The beaded purse stares up at me in the mirror when I remove my shirt. I clean it off and study it, but there's no map inside. What is a stellar blade? Something made out of a meteorite? I touch the catcher for comfort and add it to the purse while I clean up. Then, I find Chausie kneeling before the couch to comfort the girl—who may need several years of therapy now. He holds his hand out to me when I enter and pulls me down to his side.

"Beam, this is Rosa. She's an incredibly brave girl who needs to hang out with us until her mom can get here."

Rosa has regained her color.

"What a horrible scene for you to walk into," I say. "It must have been very disturbing despite your courage."

"Did you catch the guy who did it?" she asks. *Good question.*

"No. But he won't come back."

Chausie silently indicates that he's not as sure about that.

9

THE ONE RIGHT IN FRONT OF YOU

CHAUSIE

I understand that the last thing on my mind should be the fact that Beam is wearing my basketball shorts and the jersey from our championship game. But for some reason, it's incredibly gratifying, and it makes me think in terms of the rest of our lives.

"I know how Frilk found me," she says and opens the beaded purse to reveal some kind of metal wand.

Even as she tells me not to, I reach for it.

"No, Chaus! It's—" Too late. It coils around my wrist with the strength of a python. "What the—"

"I can get it off you," Beam says. "Don't worry." Lifting the feathers from the purse, she uses the sharp end of one to puncture the skin on my thumb.

"*Ow.* What'd you do that for?" A red blood bubble swells on the fleshy part.

"I want to see if yours works same as mine." She touches it to the bracelet, and the bracelet comes free. With a flash of her brow, Beam scoops the thing back into the purse.

"He showed up where this was," she says. "It's small now to fit your arm, but it was around my neck before."

"The collar. What's it made out of?"

Beam shakes her head.

"Did he use the whip?" I ask. "That's how he took me to Snatcher's Ridge. There was an anchor set, and the whip pulled us to it."

"I'm not sure, but I felt a tug before he arrived."

Rosa must be bored with this conversation. She says, "Chausie let me ride on his back!"

"Really?" Beam laughs. "Was it fun?"

She nods emphatically.

"Well, it can't stay here," I say about the collar. "It must be invaluable. He could come back for it." I ask Beam to hand the whole purse to me—which takes a second, as she has to pull one arm out of a sleeve and thread the purse over her neck. But once I have it, I jog into the kitchen to consult my mom's doggy boyfriend. "Hey, Aiden, who would know about something like this?"

After a glance at the metal band, he turns back to his tablet. "Your mother?"

"No, I've never seen anything like it," Mom says. 'It's a wicked, snaky thing."

Now Aiden gives us his full attention.

"He doesn't believe in magic," Beam says from over my shoulder.

"You do know he's a werewolf, right?" The term irks Aiden. I use it whenever I can.

"Dammit, Chausie." *Score.* "For the record," Aiden continues, "I do believe in magic now. What is that thing?"

"This is the collar Beam was wearing. She thinks it's how the goblin showed up. What if there's a way to reverse-track him? We could trap him. Maybe we could free the others."

Aiden nods. "We have people who monitor that kind of thing. I just always thought it was a waste of time. I'll take it to them. I'm sure they'll have a nice laugh over my change of heart." Aiden reaches for the band, but all three of us speak out against it.

"You can't touch it," Mom says. "Or it will encircle some part of you and you'll be trapped."

"None of you are trapped," Aiden observes.

"But we *were,*" I tell him. I don't mention how we got out, that our blood is also magical. I think the fewer people who know, the better. Of course, he's going to ask the obvious.

"How did you unlock it?"

I try not to glance at Beam, but I do anyway. "We don't want to tell you."

"Well, then I don't want to take it to my other team members."

"Her blood!" Beam's uncle chimes in. "It was her blood, wasn't it?"

"Shut up, Joel," Beam's dad says. "You're delusional" He ushers his brother to a seat further off and instructs him to keep quiet. Then, with a small nod to me, which may be an affirmation of my attempt to keep the blood thing under wraps, he returns to his wife's side.

Meanwhile, even with his question left unanswered, Aiden says, "Wrap it up for me. I don't want it to stay here with your mom. Not if the goblin can appear with it."

Beam's the one who takes the purse and prepares the collar for transport.

"Chausie, take a look at this map," Aiden says. "Is this the ridge?"

I study it for a minute till I can find the road where Mr. Turner had parked. "Here." I point to it. "This is Snatcher's Ridge. This is where the cages are. And this is where the snatchers sleep." Aiden makes notes as I show him each area. "Harriet was held here, but where she was taken after that, I don't know. I told her father that when we get there, I'll lion up and yell so that—"

Aiden speaks over me. "Oh no, you're not going."

"What are you talking about? You wouldn't even know about it if not for me. This is what I do."

"It may be what you do in a national park, but it's not what you do with real crime here in the city of Atlanta."

I cross my arms and glare at him. "Aiden, you have no idea what you're dealing with. You need me."

Aiden's phone rings, so he holds up a finger and walks out the front door to answer it.

"Like I need your consent," I mutter. And then I remember Rosa on the couch. "Rosa, you hungry?" I ask. "I'm starving."

She hops up and joins me, saying, "That's because you gave your dinner to Kofi."

Kofi. Another reason I have to go back.

Beam's parents have taken care of the mess, using two full rolls of *super-absorbent paper towels*, now stacked in a bloody pile.

"They *are* super absorbent," I tell them. The red, gooey mess stands two feet tall. "We should pitch this idea to Marketing for a commercial."

Beam's mom rolls her eyes good-naturedly. Her dad does not.

"Around Halloween maybe," I continue because I'm an idiot. "No?"

No. The man does not want to joke about the copious amount of his daughter's blood that he has been soaking up. I worry this is how our relationship is going to go.

"Let me burn those," I suggest. "Last time we left something drenched in Beam's blood, a long-dead woman was reanimated."

"Good thinking," her dad says—so that's progress. "Maggie and I will do it, and then we'll get Joel home."

I point them to the firepit out back and proceed to pull out stuff to make peanut butter and honey sandwiches. "You want one?" I ask Beam.

"No. Are you really going back to Snatcher's Ridge?"

"Yeah, I've got to. You know the African lion I told you about? He's a shifter. I promised to get him out."

"Don't you think Frilk will be there?"

I suck peanut butter off my thumb and say, "I hope so."

"Chausie," she reprimands me.

So, I lean over to kiss her through a smile, but her blue eyes remain somber. "You know this is the kind of thing I'm devoting my life to, right?" I ask.

"I know. I just thought we could get through the last few weeks of high school first."

Rosa is watching us. "Are you guys boyfriend and girlfriend?"

"What gave it away?" I tease.

"You *kissed* her!"

I hold up the honey bear. "Honey, Honey?" Rosa nods. "Want some banana too?"

"*Ew*, no."

"It's good like that," Beam says.

"Really?"

"Here, try it." I add one slice. "If you like it, you can have more."

"I'm coming with you," Beam says.

"No, you're not. Sorry."

"Why?"

I drop the sandwich stuff to tick off the reasons on my fingers. "*Uh*, you're not trained. You nearly died today already. Your well-being will be a distract—" Using my fingers turns out to be a bad idea. Beam slaps my hand away.

"Since when does any of that matter?" she says. "I thought we were *partners*. I went to bat with Baalesh for you!" She has a point. That pompous, dragon thing would've broken my neck. I have the sense to shut my mouth before she remembers the time I— "And, by the way," —oops—"I still haven't forgiven you for the time you had those ghost warriors hold me captive." I scratch the back of my head and wait for her to finish. "I will *not* be sidelined by you, Chausie Louris, by you or by anyone else."

Setting Rosa's sandwich in front of her, we exchange a commiserating glance before I turn back to my angry girlfriend. "Understood," I say. "I just—I love you. I don't want you to get hurt again." I tug her to me by the hem of my shirt. "I like you in my clothes."

Her expression softens, and I take that as permission to comb her hair away from her face. "Anyway, it didn't take you very long to convince the ghost warriors to—"

"Chausie," she warns, but I shut her up with another kiss.

My mom rounds the kitchen door with clothes for everyone. When she sees us, she gets a funny look on her face.

"What?" I ask, but I'm pretty sure it's a reaction to me kissing a girl in the kitchen.

"It's just fun to see you happy. Are you really OK?"

"Totally fine."

"And you, Beam?"

"Totally fine," Beam echoes.

"I don't understand how, but I'm grateful." Mom presents her the clothes. "Do you think your parents would like to change?"

"I doubt it. They're ready to go home. But I'll ask. Thank you, Sophie. You've been amazing through all this." *Sophie.* I look between them.

"You were right about the bananas," Rosa chimes in. "May I have another sandwich?"

"I guess you didn't get to eat dinner either, huh?" I scarf down my sandwich and move to oblige her. I could use another one myself. That's when it occurs to me that Aiden hasn't returned from his phone call. Pulling back the curtain, I don't see his truck. "Mom, where is Aiden?"

"He left. Why?"

"I told him I wanted to go."

"Chausie, let the police handle it. You've done enough."

Anger shoots up my neck and burns my ears. "He *knew* I wanted to go. He left me here on purpose. What do you *see* in that guy?" I say it too sharply. Mom regards me with a stony expression.

I rein in my tone and try again. "People are depending on me, and he treats me like a child."

Mom seems to be choosing her words, and when she delivers them, they're softer than I expect. "You're one of the good guys, Chausie," she says. "You always have been. And you're going to help a lot of people. But you can't help *all* the people *all* the time. Sometimes, the ones who need you the most are standing right in front of you." She blinks in a way that means she's not trying to be harsh, and she wants to ward off any possible overreaction I might have. There is some history of me overreacting.

I open my mouth to speak, but I got nothing. Hadn't I promised myself to be better for her? I don't know why now, but it occurs to me that the wrinkles around her eyes are deeper than I recall. How many sleepless nights has she spent worrying or feeling lonely when my dad and I could have stopped to offer her—ourselves? "You're right," I concede. "What do you need from me?"

That brings a surprised smile to her face. "Stay here today. You gave the location to the police. Let them handle it. Anyway, we still have Rosa to care for." She says the last more cheerfully for Rosa's sake and takes a seat beside our guest. I can't help that my eyes trek back to where Aiden's cruiser should be. I could jump in Mr. Turner's car right now and maybe even beat him to the ridge. But I don't. I make Rosa's second sandwich and one for my mom.

In a minute, I yawn. Mom does too. Then Rosa. I don't realize I've dozed off—right here at the table—till I hear Beam quietly calling Rosa's name. "Your mom's here," she says sweetly. Rosa must have fallen asleep too. Beam bustles her out in a sisterly way, and I follow. My mom is speaking to Rosa's in the foyer. When we join them, Rosa's mother crushes her into a hug and looks her over, head to toe. She turns to me and squeezes both my hands. "Thank you for getting her back to me."

"She's pretty good company." I nudge Rosa off balance.

"Hey!" She shoves me back.

Her mom tries for a smile but she's still plenty worried. "You will call if you hear anything?"

"Of course. And we can drive Mr. Turner's car over—whatever you need."

"Chausie is a *mountain* lion, Mama," Rosa says. "At first I thought he was a *girl* lion."

Beam snorts a laugh that she tries to hide in a cough while I suck my teeth.

"Oh, OK, Baby," Rosa's mother says. It's fine with me that she dismisses the lion issue. The less anyone knows about us, the better.

When Beam and I follow Mrs. Turner out to the car, the smell of smoke from the paper towel roast still hangs in the air.

Mrs. Turner gets Rosa strapped in, shuts her door, and lowers her voice so that Rosa can't hear as she comes to stand before us. "Tell me the truth," she says to me. "How bad is it there?"

I don't mention Frilk or the creepy man who pawed at Harriet. "For the small amount of time I saw her," I say, "Harriet was in good shape. Head held high. Sure that her dad would come to the rescue." Kofi's surly face flashes through my mind. He didn't count on any kind of rescue.

"She was hopeful, then. That's good."

"Exactly."

"How was she held? Was she hurt?"

"Her wrists were tied together, but she had room to move them, so I don't think it was too uncomfortable. No bruises that I saw."

Of course, the only sign of her when I left was her running shoes. Again, I leave that part out.

"Mr. Turner refused to leave without her, so that's how I ended up with Rosa."

"Harriet and Rosa weren't together, then."

"Well, at some point, Rosa was brought to the animal side of the market and thrown into the cage next to mine." I rush past the question about why I was in a cage to say, "Your husband helped us escape."

"He hasn't called. His phone hasn't shown up since yesterday morning."

I'd like to give her some hope, but I can't bring myself to lie. I should be up there using my nose.

Mrs. Turner seems to read the gravity of the situation. "Let's pray," she says and proceeds to do so, so we all bow our heads. Beam takes my hand. "You're our father," Mrs. Turner tells God. "You always come for us, turning evil to good, saving us from our enemies and from our own sin. Bring my baby home, Lord. Bring my husband home. Put a bubble of protection around them and all those held captive. Let the evil fall upon the evildoers and not upon the innocent. Point the police in the right direction. Shield them. Deliver to them the victory that is yours to extend. We believe in your all-powerful arm, your all-seeing eye, your ever-loving heart. You are mighty to save. Do not rest until every lamb is returned home. In the name of Jesus..."

Mrs. Turner falls silent, and when I raise my head to see if she's finished, she's staring at me. "*Oh,*" she says reverently. "Thank you, Jesus. Thank you, Father."

"Did God just tell you something?" I ask.

"He showed me the light of the Holy within you. You're from the heavens. He'll use you to rescue *all* the captives." She addresses Beam. "And *you.* Judgment courses through your veins."

After a small pause, Beam says, "Well, that doesn't sound great."

"There's something else here too." Mrs. Turner searches the yard. "Something malevolent and accusatory lurks. It whispers." Without further comment, she bustles around the car to the driver's side and wastes no time pulling away.

"That was weird," Beam says.

"No weirder than anything else. What's up with your uncle?"

Beam searches around. "I'm not sure. I thought I saw something earlier, a kind of human figure all in black. It sort of rolled with us when I clobbered my uncle, and we hit the ground."

"You did what, now?" I ask with amusement.

"He was attacking my dad," she says.

I raise my hands. "No judgment." She punches me anyway, and I fold over, laughing as I cover my ribs.

"It's hard to be a lion!" she says.

I rope her in with an arm around her neck. "In what way?"

"It feels—prickly a lot. Makes me reckless."

Why does it feel good for her to get a taste of how hard it is to be me?

"I'm not sure I love it, Chaus," she says. "I mean, it's fun to run."

"I never thought I'd hear you say that," I tease.

"Right? But I scratched into my uncle's face. It was bad. I didn't freak out too much because I knew he'd heal up, but your mom said I'd have to figure out how to get a hold of that part. Said I was a predator." She lifts worried, blue eyes to me. "I don't want to be a predator."

Well, now I feel terrible. This is my fault.

"No, stop it," she says like she can read my mind. "This isn't your fault. It's wonderful. It's an amazing gift."

Doesn't sound like she believes her own words.

"It is," she assures me. "Maybe you can help me figure it out."

"Of course." I seize on the opportunity. "We'll have fun. We'll go on runs and hunts and—" I stop because the word *hunt* makes her flinch. "You just haven't had enough time to adjust," I offer. It's more of a hope. What if she hates being a shifter and I've saddled her with a life-long ailment? It's not something you can just decide not to do. It's always there itching to come through.

"You're doing it again," she says.

"Sorry. We'll figure it out. We always do, right?"

"Right," she says. "It makes me admire you, Chaus. The way you carry yourself. The way you know when to attack and when not to—how much force to exert—that kind of thing."

"I was taught all that. You'll learn it."

"I don't know. You're just so naturally lion. Even when you're human. I feel like an interloper."

I pull her to me and ask what I already know she'll find amusing. "What's an interloper?"

Gah, I love to make her laugh.

CHAUSIE

Once Beam leaves with her parents, Mom doesn't waste a second of our time alone. I field dozens of questions about Snatcher's Ridge, and when she exhausts that subject, she moves on to questions about the trip to South Dakota and even more about my feelings for Beam. I station my phone so that I can check the clock without being obvious. Aiden's been gone for hours. Can he not shoot me an update? When my phone finally buzzes, it's not him. It's my dad.

"Dad's about to turn in," I tell Mom, and I admit I'm relieved that another person will be joining our conversation, even if the two of them are estranged.

My dad pulls up in a bright red Dodge Challenger with black racing stripes. "Whoa! Sweet ride! They had a Hellcat for you to rent?" I walk all the way around it.

"You like that?" Dad says. "When I saw it, I couldn't resist." Dad looks me over the way Rosa's mom had done her. "Are you OK?" I nod that I am, and he thumps my head. "What about up here?"

"Yeah, Dad. Nothing really happened to me."

"Alright. Well, let's go catch the bad guys."

Mom waits for us at the front door. "Hello, Leo," she says. She's friendly, but ill at ease. Did she just now change into those tight jeans? *Huh.*

Dad stalls. Then nods. Then says, "You look great."

She doesn't acknowledge the compliment—just says, "Come on in. You still drink rye whiskey?"

I guess Dad forgets about the bad guys. He follows Mom into the house with a furtive glance that makes me laugh. What are the chances they could get back together someday? I want to text Beam about it.

Dad sits on the couch and Mom brings them both a drink. They even clink glasses, but the chair she sits in is the furthest away from him. I choose one that puts me equidistance from both.

"Have you ever dealt with a goblin?" I ask my dad.

It seems to take him effort to turn his gaze from Mom. "*Uh*...a goblin," he repeats. "Not sure we have goblins around the park. There are other extraordinary folk that I mainly leave to the Lakota. Their shamans have a lot more knowledge of that kind of thing than I do. Some of them can see the invisible—well, as you know, since Beam can, and now you."

"This guy's visible to everyone," I say, and my mom makes a *tch* sound, followed by, "*I'll* say."

Dad looks startled. "You've seen him?" he asks.

"He was in my kitchen. Nearly took Beam's head off. It was awful."

"*How?*" Dad demands and then scowls at me. "You let him follow you home?"

"No," I answer defensively. "He has outrageous powers. He showed up here—literally just appeared. We think he was able to track Beam because of a metal collar he had forced her to wear. Even Mom couldn't say what it was made of."

"Never seen it before," she confirms.

"Because you know so much about metals?" my dad teases.

"Actually, I do."

When Dad raises his eyebrows, she says, "Your drink is sitting on a table that I both designed and created. It's steel."

Dad regards the table. The metal part Mom sculpted to resemble a tree whose branches support the rectangular glass top. I think he's a bit shocked. *Go, Mom!* I catch her eye in time to see her look of satisfaction.

"That sconce is brass," she adds and points to the one she means. "And there are a few aluminum pieces on the back deck. The rest I sold."

She doesn't linger in her shining moment. "No, the thing that Beam wore was imbued with extraordinary characteristics. Makes me wonder if the study of alchemy found its way into the modern era."

"What is alchemy?"

"A quasi-scientific quest to change certain base metals, like lead, into precious metals—gold, for instance. *Huh.*"

"What?"

"No, it's just something Aiden said. When Beam asked if he knew about goblins, he said, 'Like Rumpelstilzchen?' And didn't Rumpelstilzchen turn things to gold?"

"If Frilk—the goblin," I add for my dad's benefit. "If he could show up where the collar was, then is there any way to *force* him to show up?"

"I have no idea, Chaus," Mom says and my dad indicates that he doesn't either.

"If we could, though," I muse, "what would we do with him? Kill him on sight?"

"Chausie," Dad reprimands, but Mom spits out a definitive, "Yes."

So, for like the third time in his short visit, my mom has left my dad speechless.

"I know the type," she continues, and her voice reminds me of that time Beam explained why the snake died—because she hated it. "Do you know how many women I've had to patch up? How many I couldn't save? *Wanton* disregard for innocent life. That—*thing*—that *goblin* didn't even stick around to watch Beam bleed out. Just slit her throat and left her on the floor to die in front of her parents. It was a *blood*bath. *You* weren't here." The last, she spits at my dad and I think she means it in the broader context of his desertion.

He's still as stone, eyes to the ground. He swallows.

Yeah, I don't think they're getting back together. I'm so glad I didn't have to witness Beam get mauled by that maniac goblin. I'm about to apologize to my mom for having to witness it, but Dad says, "I'm so sorry, Sophie," and lets it hang there. "I'm sorry for everything." He has yet to look up.

I stand and quietly point to my room. "I'm gonna..." Give them some space. But before I can move, we hear a truck pull up. Aiden. *Finally. Why didn't he just call?*

Mom hurries to the front door before he has a chance to knock. "Hey, Beautiful," he says, though his voice is flat. They must not have found the ridge. Or is it worse than that? He kisses my mom on the mouth and even clutches her behind as he pulls her into an embrace. *Heaven's sake.* I clear my throat, and as Aiden rounds the corner he says, "Chausie, there was nothing there, son. Just some—"

Aiden—in his awesome uniform—*dammit*—looking strong and fit and—young—let's just face it—he's younger than my mom, which makes him much younger than my dad—has just called me son in front of my dad, and he comes to an abrupt halt when he sees the other man in the room and questions my mom with his brow.

"Aiden, Chausie's father, Leo. Leo, Aiden."

"A werewolf," I add, but my dad reprimands me with, "That's not polite," and moves forward to shake his hand. "Chausie should have offered to go with you. His tracking skills are excellent."

Like I didn't try. Before I can defend myself—why am I having to? —Aiden says, "He offered. I wouldn't allow it. He hasn't been trained."

"He has been trained," my father argues. "In the most rigorous outdoor program available."

"I meant no disrespect. I'm not allowed to enlist civilians—that is anyone who hasn't earned a badge from Atlanta PD or received special clearance." Aiden says the last because Dad has begun to protest. Honestly, I haven't received a badge from Dad yet either. My motorcycle wreck interrupted training, but I'm not going to remind him of that right now.

"That's why I'm here, Chaus," says the Were. *Man, I should have been referring to him as a Were all along.* "I got the clearance."

That throws the switch on my attitude. "You did?" I ask. "That's awesome."

"You're eighteen, right?"

"Right," I say. Because I *will* be. In August.

"No, he is not," Mom says. "Not for a few months yet."

"Mom."

"Oh," Aiden says. "Sorry."

See? This is why I don't follow rules. They're stupid.

"But if, say, you and your dad wanted to trot off on your own..."

Dad can't shift anymore, so trotting isn't really an option.

"I'm sure they'll keep that in mind," Mom says with finality. "You ready for a drink?" Is she just blocking me from a dangerous situation, or does she know that my dad can't shift? Is she covering for him?

"Just water, Soph. Thank you."

I follow Mom as far as the kitchen entryway and lean in.

"Did Beam tell you that Dad can't..." I leave the sentence hanging because I don't want Aiden to hear that Dad's having problems. Mom nods.

"This whole visit is a little awkward," I say. She nods again.

"Do you think you and Dad could ever..."

"Out."

"Going."

Dad and Aiden are sitting in uncomfortable silence. When I reappear, they both try to speak to me at the same time.

"What?" I ask because I can't understand either one of them.

They both gesture for the other to go ahead, and I pinch the bridge of my nose in impatience. "Aiden, tell me what happened. You found the ridge, but no one was there?"

"One man was there with wrists and ankles bound. He had a large pump knot on his head. Booths were there. Cages. And those creepy mounds with poles sunk into them."

"That's where Harriet was tied," I tell him. "To one of those poles. Did you find Mr. Turner?"

"No, but I did find footprints up on the hill where the pump knot man was tied."

"Up behind the cages?"

"Yep."

"Good. I told Mr. Turner to take that guy out. He was a lookout."

Aiden makes a face that says it was a good idea.

"So, you have his scent?" I ask. "Mr. Turner's?"

"Yeah, but it went cold. Phone has yet to show up."

That makes me remember how Mr. Turner got there to begin with. "Did you find any running shoes?" I ask. "He tracked his daughter by something on her shoes. Somebody hung them up where she'd been standing—I guess they were sending a message. But I took them down and what if he has them?"

"Why didn't you tell me that before?" Aiden says and punches the screen of his phone.

"I probably would have, Aiden, if you hadn't left without me."

"Check the shoes that were found," Aiden says to whoever answered his call. "Is there any device attached, some kind of small tracker?" He listens and then says to me, "No tracker, but the laces of one shoe are missing."

"Mr. Turner's got it," I say.

"We don't know he's got it."

"Well, *somebody's* got it!" I run for my phone and text Mrs. Turner, who texts back within fifteen seconds. "She's sending a link to the tracker app and her password." I curse the phone for every extra second it takes to load. "Here." I show Aiden, and my dad leans over, too. "He's up in the Chattahoochee Forest."

"The *tracker* is up in the Chattahoochee Forest," Aiden cautions. "It could've been thrown into the back of a random truckbed."

"Sounds like it's the only lead you've got," my dad says.

Aiden acquiesces with a nod. "That and the man who was left behind. We'll send someone."

"Send me," I say.

"Hold your horses, son. Let's find out if it's a viable lead."

"It *is,*" I tell him. "Stop benching me." And stop calling me *son.*

"It's OK, Chaus," my dad says. "I've been dying for a chance to stretch the Hellcat's legs."

I glance out the window and a slow smile steals onto my face. The Challenger's extra wide grill looks as menacing as Frilk's monster face.

"It's fast," Dad says. "I bet it devours the mountain roads." My dad has his blind spots, but he rocks! *Road trip!*

Aiden sticks his fingers in his ears to show us he has no intention of owning what we're about to do and says, "That's good work, Chausie. We'll let you know what we find." And then he stands and calls out, "Sophie, I'm out, Babe. Gotta get back to it."

"You can't stay?" she calls from the kitchen. I think she loitered there to avoid the weirdness.

"No. I'm sorry. Walk me to the truck?" She takes his outstretched hand, and they leave together.

Dad looks after them and says, "How long has that been going on?"

"About a year, I guess."

He nods. "And I assume that the story about Beam didn't end in her dying, correct?"

"*Oh!* No, she's fine. Sorry. Yeah, no. She healed right up after Frilk got away."

"I wasn't sure when to ask about that part. It got a little heated. But I assumed by your countenance..."

I snort out a laugh. "She's fine."

It takes Mom a while to return, even after Aiden's truck pulls away. She doesn't seem that happy.

"Did Aiden upset you?" I ask hopefully.

"No, of course not. And you don't have to bristle every time he calls you *son*. Yes, you do." She adds when I try to deny it. "Did you find out what you wanted to know?"

"Yeah. Is it OK if Dad and I take a quick trip? We think we may be able to find Mr. Turner."

"Just up through the North Georgia mountains," Dad adds. "We could stay overnight and explore the place. You could come too if you'd like. My treat."

Ohhhh, wow. My mother has never looked more irritated.

"*Uh,* no, Leo, I would not like." She bites her tongue and strides a few steps away before she spins back around and uses her hands to punctuate the next lines. "I find it incredibly disrespectful of you to make an offer like that. We are not friends. *Your* fault. Even so, I have protected your reputation for the sake of your sons. And for what? So they could find out from someone else that you've been having an affair and are now *married* to that woman? Can you imagine how that must have felt, Leo, for Chausie? So, no. I would not like to go on an overnight trip with you. You are in my house because you are Chausie's father, and he was in trouble. As such, but only for as long as you can respect my boundaries, you are welcome to stay. Do not misconstrue this. Aiden and I are in a relationship. That may not mean much to you, but if you'll recall, faithfulness is essential to me."

After a ringing moment of silence, Dad manages to say, "I understand."

"Forgive my outburst, Chausie," Mom says.

I unroll my lips from where I've been biting them. "No, that's OK," I say. And because I want to lower the temperature, I add, "To be clear, you don't want to come?"

Mom snickers. "Correct. Thank you."

"No problem," I say.

But suddenly, Mom growls, "What did you say?" and she's mad all over again.

Dad just shakes his head and turns a mystified expression on me as Mom stalks off, pressing her temples like she has a headache.

So, no, I do not think they will be getting back together.

BEAM

Once I get home, I fall asleep on the couch in the den. We have a large, three-story house, and there is no way I'm going to rest way up there alone in my bedroom. Besides, Daddy is gone to take Uncle Joel to his apartment, and Mom tells me she's glad to have me close. She even offers to make shepherd's pie, my favorite, which she serves with ridiculous, old family stories of Ireland. Mom's great-great-grandparents were born there, and she still has cousins in County Clare. We visit at least once a year.

I'm reaching over the tall counter to steal a taste of the mashed potatoes when the mechanical hum of the garage door tells me Daddy's back from taking Uncle Joel home.

"Oh, that smells delicious," he says wearily as he trudges into the house, affectionate eyes resting on Mom and me in turn. "I can't tell you how happy I am to be back in the house with the two of you." He kisses Mom on the cheek. It's hard to believe that we were on a plane from South Dakota, hardly twenty-four hours ago.

"How was Joel when you left him?" Mom says. "I thought you'd stay overnight to take care of him."

"He seemed fine to me. Like whatever was plaguing him had run its course." Dad hands me my phone. "This was in his backseat."

"Maybe he only acts strange around me," I say.

"I wondered that. You do seem to bring out the weird in people." Dad raps my head playfully.

"Are you still covered in blood underneath that jacket?" Mom asks.

He nods.

"Go clean up, and we'll sit down to eat."

The pad of my father's leather-soled shoes disappears, and I rummage for a spoon. Mom is dipping the potatoes now. She has already spread a mixture of ground lamb and veggies that she'll cover entirely and then bake the whole thing, but she pauses to let me pilfer a bite.

As I savor it, Mom places the pie in the oven. "There are stories of goblins from Ireland, right?" I ask.

"Aye, that there are." She turns on the Irish accent. "What'd ye think of the ole leprechauns?"

"Short, little men greedy for gold? Nothing like old man Frilk."

"I'd say they're *just* like old man Frilk," Mom counters. "The stories we read ya were for wee lasses. Do you remember that coffee table book of Irish folklore?" Mom drops out of her accent and gestures to the bookshelf in the living room. I know the one she means. Daddy banned it after I told him I'd seen one of the creatures pictured in there—in real life in a park downtown. But he's not allowed to ban anything anymore. All of the secrets he kept nearly got us killed. Uncle Joel was right about that.

The thick pages of the book take effort to turn, and they depict lovely, large landscapes and features of Ireland. Flora, fauna, folklore— the kind of lore that most people regard as fiction. And maybe much of it is. But as I investigate, I find more than one fictitious creature I have both seen and interacted with. When I get to a chapter called *Púcas,* I see that the name is synonymous with goblins. There are several varieties. Some are mischievous, and some malevolent. None of them look too scary to me. But then I turn to the page labeled *Leprechauns* to find Frilk's vicious face staring up at me. With a sharp inhale, I resist the urge to slam the book shut.

"Did you find it?" Mom can see me from the kitchen. She's

collecting plates to set the table. The homey sound they make as they clang together settles my nerves.

"I did," I say. "You were right about leprechauns."

Leprechauns inhabit almost every county in Ireland and, indeed, as many boarded ships in their lust for riches, they reside worldwide. Leprechauns are vicious, cunning, ruthless creatures, who wield dangerous magic passed down from interstellar origins. While other púca are tricksy or talkative, leprechauns are secretive and ambitious. It is often said that they hide their gold at the rainbow's end, but that's just a tale. Leprechauns guard their take wherever they can stash it, and don't you dare think to search for it. Woe to the thief. Retribution will be swift and certain.

I swallow. How much would Frilk have made by selling Chausie? He was angry enough to murder me. If he thinks he succeeded, will that be the end of retribution?

My phone chimes with a text.

> You home, Sunbeam?

That's the first time Chausie's called me that.

> Yes. I've been studying goblins. Did you know in Ireland they define Frilk as a leprechaun?

The time it takes Chausie to answer makes me smile because I know I've surprised him.

> What else did you find out?

> That he's a vengeful, greedy, cunning word I'd rather not say.

> Son of a bitch?

No. Why should his mother be maligned?

Bastard?

Doesn't that place blame on the mother as well?

Or the father. Hey, I'm driving up to Dahlonega with my dad. Aiden found the ridge empty, but we may be able to track Mr. Turner.

Frilk's horrible face scowls up from the page.

Please be careful, Chaus.

I will. My dad's with me.

Yeah, but your dad can't shift anymore.

He can still shoot. 😊

I roll my eyes and get another text. It's a picture of a super fast-looking car. Then, another picture of Chausie behind the wheel. The man does love fast machines.

Have fun. Tell your dad I said hi.

Instead of begging him to be careful again, I send a little heart.
He sends one back.
Then I realize that he may be texting while driving!

OMG You'd better not be driving right now! That is against the law!!!

LMAO I'm not. But we are about to go. Love you.

It warms me how often and how naturally he tells me that.

Love you too.

"What are you smiling about?" Mom asks.

"Chausie texted."

"Oh, you two have it bad."

I smile broadly as I walk back over. I've been working on a way to tell my parents that I'm going to take a gap year after graduation and work on the Reservation. The job—that they don't know I've taken—is a fantastic opportunity and the perfect way to learn about my Lakota heritage, but I'm not sure how to convince them of that. We all agreed that college was the next step in the plan for my life.

The air crackles and a small, blue figure pops onto the counter between me and my mom.

I scold him with a hand to my heart to keep it from exploding. "You can't do that anymore! I was nearly killed today."

"Doesn't matter. You have to come," Blue's chirpy little voice says.

"Come where?"

My mom steps forward wielding a kitchen knife. "Who is it?"

"It's Blue, Mama. If you walked on the same plane, you'd be stabbing him right now."

"Oh, I'm sorry, Blue," Mom says. She can't see him, but she backs up and addresses him anyway. "Can you stay for dinner?"

"No, Mom, he can't stay for dinner. He can't eat that."

"Yes, I can," Blue says.

"You can?"

"You have to come!" he insists.

I wait for him to say more, but he just wriggles his four-fingered hand for me to follow.

"Blue, I am so tired. Can it not wait?"

"Larkin is trapped. She got sucked into a birdhouse."

Sometimes Blue stops his explanations well short of *explained*.

"Where did you learn to speak English?" I ask.

"I picked it up from you." He says this like I'm an idiot—like it's the most obvious thing in the world.

"That doesn't make any sense," I say. "You spoke it on the day we met."

"Larkin was sucked into a birdhouse and I can't get her out of it."

"I'm sorry for that. Believe me. But are you sure she doesn't want to be in the birdhouse?"

Blue eyes me in a way that makes me think he's about to throw a big, big tantrum. That is not something I can handle right now. "OK," I say to placate him. "You're telling me that when you dove on top of her —and Frilk—and knocked yourselves into some other place, Larkin was pulled somewhere you didn't mean for her to go?"

He nods enthusiastically. "Frilk fell away, but then I lost control of Larkin. Some other force sucked her—"

"Into a birdhouse. Got it. And where is this birdhouse?"

"I'll take you." He jumps into my arms, and the next thing I know, I'm in the middle of a glade that is bordered by trees. It felt like I turned into nothing. For the time it took, I couldn't feel anything at all. I couldn't breathe, and I didn't want to. I think, for a time, I ceased to exist, or my body did.

"Ah, Blue," I whine. "I was about to have Shepherd's Pie. Where have you brought me?" There are birds everywhere, and I feel that I've been here before, but it's fuzzy. "This is where all the birds went?" Blue is leaping ahead of me as I crane my neck to take it all in. The birds seem happy. They sit around in groups, twittering.

"Yes, they love my wife. They don't understand that she's caged."

"Blue, why are you referring to Larkin as your wife?"

"We got married. In our hearts."

"Both of you? Did both of you get married in your hearts? Or just you?"

Blue stops. "Why are you opposed to this relationship? Did I oppose your relationship with the lion?"

"No, you did not."

"No, I did not. Even though it was unconventional, I have been nothing but supportive."

"Wellll," I begin, but he follows that up with, "Apart from the morning when I couldn't believe you made him to see me, and I jumped on top of his side and screamed like a firetruck."

"You're right. I will be more supportive."

"Thank you."

This is how we cross the field and find ourselves before a large bird-cage. Inside, sitting on a little swing as if she had not a care in the world, is Larkin. "Looks pretty content to me," I mutter.

Larkin's lovely face remains open and receptive as we approach, and Blue falls over his own feet to be reunited. He hugs the outside of the cage as if he is embracing Larkin.

"Larkin, are you trapped in there or is this home?" I ask.

"Do I know you?" she says.

"Oh, *no,*" Blue moans. "She has amnesia."

"She does not have amnesia." I change into my lion self. I kind of just want to know if I still can. Larkin gets to her feet.

"It's you," she says. "You're not Leonid, though. How did you come to be feline?" She doesn't wait for answers. She has found a more important one. She touches her collarbone and says, "How did you escape the stellar material?"

"Stellar?" Second time I've come across the word in less than an hour. "Are you telling me that Frilk's collar is made of something from outer space?"

"Just like this cage," Larkin answers and I do see the similarities.

"Just like the gates of the In-Between," Blue says meaningfully. Now I get it. He wants me to unlock this cage with my blood.

"I thought the gates were made of frostwork minerals from the cave."

"It's an amalgam," he says.

"OK, see? You did not learn that word from me. There's no way you speak English by—"

Larkin interrupts us. I probably would too, in her position.

"If Frilk removed the collar from you," she says, "you'd be dead. Or stuck in something like this. So, how did you escape?"

Gone are the moments of Larkin's placid demeanor. She squeezes the bars so tightly, her knuckles lose color.

"*Tell* me," she pleads.

I'd like to. And yet—

"Tell me some things first," I say. "Why couldn't Blue take you away from here? What is this contraption?"

"It's my prison." She says it through gritted teeth. When I don't respond she says, "Any time I get away from Frilk, I appear back here."

"How does that work?"

Pushing her skirt to the side, she rests one small foot on the swing. A band of the same silver-grey metal rings her toe. A small green jewel is mounted there. "I don't know how it works," Larkin says, "but this ring is married to this cage." She bats at a hanging trinket making it spin and sparkle in the sunlight.

"Why did you give away our hiding spot?" I ask, and she drops her head.

"I have to do as he commands. He has my clutch."

The birds seem to be listening to us. They sway back and forth as they watch, and they've grown very quiet.

"A clutch?" I ask. "Like—a nest of eggs?"

Larkin nods her head but in the smallest of movements. Her eyes are full of tears, and I feel bad for her.

"You're going to have babies?" I ask.

"With me," Blue says.

"You're the father?!" That is slightly gross, but whatever. Maybe I *should* be more supportive of their relationship. I can't imagine Blue as a father. I can't imagine how he would go about becoming one. And now I bite back a grin thinking of how Chausie joked that they were off making little, blue, faerie babies.

"There is no father the way you're thinking of it," Larkin tells me. "I don't need a partner. I'm parthenogenic."

"Nooooo," I whisper. "Really? Like a Komodo dragon?" I read that amazing fact at our zoo's reptile house. "You can make your own babies?"

"Five of them." Larkin makes a sad smile that I take to mean she is at once proud and also positive she will never get to raise them. In that instant, I forgive her. If Chausie and I have babies—not that we're going to try that any time soon—I know he'll be fiercely protective of them. He'll be the best father in the world.

"Well, where does Frilk keep them?" I ask.

"She doesn't know," Blue says.

"Don't they need to stay warm? Won't they hatch and imprint upon Frilk if you're not around?"

"Now, do you understand why I have to do as he says?" Larkin asks.

"But won't you be disobeying him if you walk out of here?"

"If I get free of this place, I would be able to search for them. Any time he's through with me, Frilk flings me back here. If I don't have to stay put and he thinks I *am* here, then maybe..." Larkin leaves her thoughts unsaid.

"Now she has *us,*" Blue asserts. "And you can open this cage."

"Even if you're right, I'm not sure I can keep it open. She'd end up right back. What if we were to remove the ring?"

"You can do that?" Larkin asks. "What are you?"

"Never mind that." I throw a look at Blue to tell him to keep my blood secrets to himself. But how can I free her without her knowing about it? "Look, you haven't proven very trustworthy, not to me. If I help you, you can't ask me any questions, and you can't tell Frilk about me to get your clutch back. Nor Blue. You can't get Blue caught."

"She'd never..." Blue says.

"Promise me, Larkin."

"I promise."

"If you betray me, I'll put that ring right back on your toe."

"Aren't you going to open the cage as well?"

I think it through. The words in the book of Irish folklore are daunting. Vicious, cunning, greedy, vengeful.

"No," I answer her. "Frilk should think he still has control of you. He'll come to you here, won't he? Just act like nothing has happened? And I'll be far away by then."

"But what if he's mad at me? He doesn't know about Blue. He may think I tried to get away by myself when Blue tried to take me."

"Can you do that? Can you vanish from one place and reappear in another?"

"No," she admits.

"Can Frilk?"

"Not without using something stellar as an anchor."

All this talk about Frilk has me searching over my shoulder. "Let's get this over with before he comes back. Stick your foot out of the bar and look away."

Larkin thrusts her bare foot through the bars.

"Look away or it's not happening."

She complies but not without a sigh of malcontent.

"You're just going to have to trust me," I say and nod to my outstretched finger.

"*Oh,*" Blue whispers. Instead of finding a pointy twig or a stone, the shocking, little pixie exposes jagged rows of needle-sharp teeth, unrevealed to me until this moment. I've only just begun to protest when he chomps down.

"*Ow!*" I cradle my finger, now bleeding copiously, and glower at him.

"Is everything OK?" Larkin asks.

I gripe out a, "Yes. Almost done," and allow a drop of blood to fall on the toe ring. Then, using the bottom of Chausie's jersey—with the hand that is not bleeding—I pluck the ring from her darling little toe and deposit it into the beaded purse I have concealed.

"Can I look now?"

"Just a second." My finger is healing up quickly. I hold it away from us and use a leaf to wipe off Larkin's toe. Then I try to rid my finger of the red-streaked evidence as well.

"OK. All done."

Larkin investigates her foot and smiles up at me with the incredulous expression I'm beginning to think she reserves for me. "You freed me." She pumps herself back and forth in wide arcs on the swing, inside the cage.

"Kind of."

She doesn't ask where the ring has gone, and I don't bring it up, but she'd better keep her promise.

"I suppose I owe you," Larkin says. "I can tell you where the market is—though, your Chausie may be sold by now."

"My Chausie is just fine. He's on a road trip with his dad, driving a fast car, free as the wind."

Blue whips his head around.

"Oh, no, please do not go ballistic about not getting to drive the car," I say. "I don't have anything to do with that. You left us, so..."

I can tell he's about to shun me. "I haven't gotten to drive it either," I try, but he turns his back. "I have a picture."

Reluctantly, he gazes toward my phone and then gasps. I'm about to show him the one of Chausie behind the wheel, but the hobbling sound of wagon wheels puts me on alert.

"He's here," I hiss.

I imagine that if I were used to being a lion, I'd transform and bound silently away—or at least jump up into the huge tree. But I am not used to being a lion. It doesn't even occur to me. I scoot behind Larkin's birdcage and into the hollowed-out trunk of the tree. There is plenty of room for me to hide in here. It's huge. If I weren't afraid for my life, I would plan to throw a party in here. It would be fabulous. We'd bring in string lights and everything.

When the wagon has come close enough for me to hear its chains rattle and the horse nickering, Larkin says, "Have you finally come home? I thought I'd grow old in this space."

"By whose power did you go?" Frilk asks, and though I have been victimized by his brutal nature, have read about his savagery in my mom's book, he sounds almost vulnerable right now.

"It doesn't matter now. He took a shining to me is all. He is no match for you and he found that out."

"Come out, then." By the sound of it, part of the birdcage falls away.

"How was the market?" Larkin asks.

"Let's go inside, and I'll tell you about it."

Inside? Inside where?

Inside *here,* is the answer. Inside this very tree trunk where I am hiding. Larkin couldn't have given me a heads-up about that?

Larkin and Frilk, chatting like a long-married couple, grow louder as they come closer. I barely have time to move before they are standing in my spot. I keep feeling for the back of the tree, confident that I'm about to bang my head at any moment. But wait. I am not finding the back of the tree. I am walking a descending slope. Backward.

I consider taking feline form to utilize the spectacular night vision, but once I turn around and my eyes adjust, I can tell that there is glowing light at the end of the tunnel. So, there you go. I have successfully entered the underground lair of a leprechaun. Worse, I am being hemmed in by said leprechaun and his so-called prisoner/wife. Where the actual heck is Blue?

"I killed a woman today," Frilk says. "Showed up. Slit her throat."

"You almost sound as if you regret it," Larkin responds.

I have found a nook to crouch in, stationed behind an end table and two cozy-looking chairs. At the end of the room is a stone fireplace that Frilk goes to now, and after he procures a few pieces of chopped wood from a stack nearby, he proceeds to strike a match. It's all very quaint and honestly, if I didn't know who lived here, I'd be happy to visit.

As it is, I am full of dread.

"I do regret it," he says solemnly. "She was that black panther. I promised the Leonid I would do it, though, if he tried to escape, and so I had to."

"Yes, of course," Larkin says. "One must keep one's word."

"But she turned out to be a shifter too—not a Leonid, you see, but still... I would have liked to have sold her."

Well, that's noble. He has no qualms about slitting a woman's throat unless he could have earned a profit. I've gotta get out of here. *Blue!* I think. *You got me into this mess! Help me!*

I glance around as cautiously as possible. The great roots of the tree can be seen through the packed earthen walls. There is an open door to my right. Maybe if I were to crawl that way...

"Where are you going?" Frilk snarls and I nearly squeak.

"I thought I could splash some water on my face," Larkin says. "Maybe wash my hands. And then I could make you dinner."

Peering through the chairs from my hands and knees, I see Frilk offer a brusk nod. Larkin moves through the door I had been eyeing and flips on a light. Before she can close the door, she spots me, and there is a heartbeat in which I know I am betrayed. But she bows her head instead and ducks inside.

I hug myself to take up even less room and try to shrink into the ground behind the chair. When it creaks and dips back against my head, I realize that Frilk has taken a seat there. He groans like the old man he appears to be. Yeah, he's probably tired. He's been busy for the past few days.

A small hand squeezes my arm—gently, for once—and Blue holds a finger to his lips. I'm glad he didn't leave me. "Don't say anything out loud," he says—out loud.

Larkin throws the door open. Her damp face looks fresh and even prettier than usual, though full of alarm. Her hair is tied back so that her pointy ears are obvious. She's staring at Blue, where he sits beside me on the floor–directly behind the goblin. Then, she seems to come to terms with the fact that Frilk hasn't heard him, and she forces herself to look at Frilk and smile.

I can't see the goblin's face, but his question, "What's wrong with you?" lets me know Larkin's adrenaline spike has not gone undetected.

"Nothing. Nothing at all." Larkin must blast her words with whatever faerie dust she's got because even I want to kiss her. Blue exhales a long, contented *ooooo*. Thankfully, Frilk can't hear him.

Larkin softly touches Frilk's cheek as she passes by to the kitchen. She doesn't look back, but he watches her go. At last, he shakes his head like he's shaking her out of it. "Now, stop that," he says, but I don't think he means it.

After some inward deliberation, Frilk relaxes into the chair. My knees are getting stiff, and my ankles hurt. My feet are full of pins and needles. I hate that feeling worse than—well, it doesn't even rank anymore, come to think of it. I can probably just sit here a while longer.

Blue doesn't have this problem. He strolls around the room, checking it out. "Nice place," he says. Larkin, with her back to us, lights the gas stove and shows no indication that she hears him. "Sort of reminds me of my childhood," he says. I almost ask him to tell me about it, but then I remember that we are in a killer's underground cottage and that that killer can hear me just fine.

I am debating whether or not I will ever be able to use my feet again when Frilk begins to snore. He has dozed off there in the comfy chair by the fire. Why can't he just be content with this wonderful life? Why does he have to seek out riches he will never spend?

When the snoring evens out, and Frilk is truly asleep, Larkin, from the kitchen, while she continues to cook and hum a quiet lullaby—and now I realize that her song is at least part of the reason the goblin sleeps —motions with her head for me to get out of there. I unfold my legs, mouthing an *owwww* and rubbing the prickly pain from my feet. As I stand, my hip makes a popping sound, and Frilk repositions himself.

Larkin keeps humming. Blue is lying across the other chair. Asleep. I rouse him with a push, and he blinks his eyes open only to stare up in adoration at Larkin like he's on drugs. *Honestly.* Larkin gives me another nod to nudge me out the—tree. I leave Blue to his infatuation and slink around the chairs. I've made it as far as another interior door when Frilk rubs his eyes and yawns himself awake. I squat back down.

"Almost finished," Larkin says sweetly. "Will you want cornbread?"

Frilk stands and stretches in front of the fire. His eyes roam the air like he's trying to work something out. Then he sniffs.

"Smells delicious?" Larkin asks.

"Smells like that woman I killed." He sniffs his own hands and then his shirt.

"You're still sleepy. It's just dinner."

Frilk fixes on Larkin. She shrugs innocently.

Blue is finally on alert. He stands on his chair to monitor the situation.

Frilk sniffs once more. He's not going to give it up. There's no way I can get to the tunnel. As he turns my way in what feels like slow motion, I skulk into the unknown room.

"What is going on here?" I hear him say. His voice sinks into the sinister ugliness I expect from him.

Scanning the new space, I see that it is a workspace and that there is no obvious hiding place. Surely, my best bet is to remain close to the door and hope that Blue can give me a signal when the coast is clear. The goblin is taking his frustration out on Larkin, and while she does her best to calm him down, I creep around a table that takes up the middle of the room.

On the other side, there's a broad, built-in closet, and I may just fit inside. I open the double doors as slowly and soundlessly as I can. But instead of free space, the closet is full of shelves containing items that belong in a laboratory: balances, scales, microscopes, pipettes... The voices in the other room are growing angrier. Blue has joined the verbal fray, though Frilk can't hear him, so I'm not sure how that is going to help.

I should close the closet. What if things manage to go well, and then Frilk finds it open, ruining everything? I lay my hand on the middle shelf for stability so that I can use the leverage to close the right-hand door in silence. The blanket my hand lands on is warm. Warm, like a heating pad. I get that door shut, and as I'm closing the other, I see why all the warmth is needed. Cuddled in the blanket is a nest made of pine needles and twigs. It's small. It could easily fit in my hand. A golden chain is woven around the nest, and inside are five perfect, cream-colored eggs, speckled in dark brown.

What am I to do? What would you?

The argument has devolved. By the sound of it, things are being thrown. Larkin, in the peak of frustration, yells, "You're not helping, Blue!" And all goes quiet.

Then all erupts. Sounds of Larkin scurrying. Sounds of furniture overturned. "Where is he?" Frilk wants to know. "Who did you bring into my house?"

"It's no one!" Larkin says with some hysteria. "It's just a mouse!"

The nest, though small, is not fragile, and I scoop it up in both hands. The eggs are tiny like hummingbird eggs. I don't want to break them! I almost put them back. They'd grow up with Frilk as a dad, but at least they'd be alive. No, he could sell them, and who knows where they'd end up? That's probably his plan anyway. Maybe in all the chaos, I can bound up the tunnel unseen. I risk a peek out the door.

"No," Larkin is pleading. The plates have been overturned. Beans and cabbage stick to the wall and dribble onto the floor. Frilk is sending his whip out, lash after lash around the room. "When I find him, I'll kill him!" Frilk snarls.

Is that the kind of promise he made to Chausie about me?

Blue bounces ahead of the whip. I have a feeling that it can catch him no matter what plane of existence he inhabits. And then what?

I don't have to guess because the next crack sears his little blue butt, and he screeches in pain.

Act! Feline instinct commandeers my brain.

Striding out of the bedroom, I place the nest into Larkin's hands.

Her desperate cry of recognition hardly registers as I become a panther leaping over the kitchen counter and then from chair to chair, dodging the whip, crashing the table, springboarding against the wall. My claws tear the goblin's flesh, collar bone to belly. But that goblin is made of thick stuff. He forgets Blue, sending the whip around me instead. I don't want to be trapped as a panther. I remember the last time he ensnared me, I mourned the loss of thumbs. As the whip becomes like a serpent, snaking up my body, I shift. Sadly, my legs are soon tied together and my arms bound to my sides. Frilk shoves me to the ground and immediately turns his eyes upon Larkin.

Blue is gaping at me. I'm not brave or valiant or anything, but I do have strong—some might say rigid—opinions about what is right and wrong, and they dictate my behavior. It's wrong for those five little eggs to be smashed. Look at how protectively Larkin holds them to herself.

"Get her out of here!" I command Blue.

Frilk scans the area to find the interloper I'm addressing. He still can't see Blue, but he stalks to a bookshelf and I worry he has another whip.

"I am *commanding* you!" I yell at Blue who wants to grow into his Goliath self—I can tell—but I fear it will only get him killed. "For Chenoa!"

The reference to the woman who saved his life generations ago causes him to blink at me. In the next second, he flings himself onto Larkin, and they are gone.

And I am bound on the floor in the lair of a creature who has already sliced my throat once today.

12

CHAUSIE'S ROAD TRIP

CHAUSIE

Muscle cars. It's a great way to describe them. This one is a beast. She roars and snarls. She even purrs. "I'm not paying for a speeding ticket," Dad says. "And I'm not paying for a tow truck." He grips the dash when I take the curves too fast, but he's laughing harder than I've heard him do in years. This is the kind of thing I missed while we were all reeling from the divorce.

"Go back!" he says. "We missed the turn."

I skid to a stop and reverse for a few quick yards. These state highways wind through the mountains, and we haven't seen another car since we entered the forest. "There," Dad says.

"Is that even a road?"

"I think so."

Cell service is spotty. Dad shows me the app with the tracker's last whereabouts. I shrug and pull onto the dirt road. *Pathway* may more aptly describe it. "Does this car have all wheel drive?" I ask.

Dad scans the dash and points to an AWD icon. I push it like it's a button. It doesn't do anything more for the car than it's already doing. The potholes are substantial. "It doesn't appear to be a road," I say.

"Maybe I should have rented a Jeep."

Still, we continue and in the end, we come to a wider space that is a parking lot—whether or not it was made to be one. There are several jacked-up pickups, a Mercedes that may have been armed by a drug cartel, and a Hummer the size of an actual tank. No doubt it could climb right over the top of our Challenger—if it could catch us. Because this car is fast as—

"The tracker is close!" Dad's walking around the trucks, trying to make sense of where the tracker is in relation to where we are. I try not to think of what Aiden said. *The tracker could've been thrown into a random truckbed.* That would mean we've been wasting time chasing the wrong person going the wrong way.

"He has it," I say aloud to make it true. "He's here." I round the vehicles in a different direction than my dad. There's no one to be seen, but I feel eyes upon us. "Do you smell that?" I ask. Dad shakes his head. "That earthy, smoky smell?"

"Chausie, we're in the wild. I'm sure backcountry campers are trying to stay warm."

"No, not a campfire. Get a whiff."

The way my dad puts his nose in the air and sniffs is a half-hearted attempt to find the scent. I cock my head in question. This is not good. "Dad, did you lose your sense of smell?"

He averts his eyes, bites his lip. "Yeah. Sometimes I don't even know who I am anymore."

"Well, you're still an officer of the law," I tell him.

"Really? Because I don't work as one anymore. When your mom called and I found out you'd been kidnapped—I didn't even think. I grabbed a go bag and was walking out the door before I'd ended the call. It felt—alive. You know?"

I do know. "That day I met Beam… I'd been sidelined for so long, and she needed me. I felt like it was my one shot back into the game. I grabbed a few things, told Mom, and ran out the door."

"That's it," Dad agrees. "I was needed. I was back in the game. But about the time the plane took off, it occurred to me that I had no idea how to play anymore. I may be a liability here."

It hurts me to hear my dad talk that way. I don't say I'm sorry. I don't think he'd want me to. But I hate for him to feel diminished like this.

The explosive sound of a gunshot has us facing the trailhead. Dad steps to me, his hand on his firearm, and I don't lion up because he can't. It does occur to me how messed up that is.

Movement. A man lumbering toward us, clutching his side. He rasps something I don't understand and falls to his knees.

"Mr. Turner!" I rush to him through a clinging briar bush, and when I reach him, I pat him down to assess the damage. "Were you shot?" My dad catches up and stands over us, scanning every direction.

"They're after me," Mr. Turner says. He's out of breath. "I got Harriet unbound, but they split us up. She ran the other way."

I roll him over to get a look at his side, but he thwarts my efforts and clings to my shirt. "She's in there. Please! You have to get her. They just sold her off. They just sold my baby girl."

The man is barely keeping it together. He's bleeding from a small but open hole.

"Chaus, he's gotta get to a hospital," Dad says. "Let's move."

"No! Help her, Chausie." Mr. Turner chokes out the words in sobs.

"You take him," I say to Dad and toss him the keys. "Come on, Mr. Turner." I try to haul him up, but he resists. "I'm going to find her," I assure him. "But you have to go."

"Then how are *you* going to get away?" my dad says. "I'm not leaving you without an escape."

"There's nothing for it, Dad. Do the first thing you find to do first. Isn't that right?" This isn't the exact approach my mom takes. She's all *First, do no harm.*

Others are approaching. I hear their feet fall on the packed trail. Maybe my dad *can't* hear them. "Let's move!" Mr. Turner allows us to get him into the Challenger. Good thing the seats are black. I hate to say the next thought to my dad, but I have to. "Send Aiden for me."

The men in the woods are huffing loudly. "He can't be far," one of them says. "Here's more blood."

They'll be upon us very soon.

"Go." I smack the side of the Challenger and lion up. I don't wait to see it pull away. I hear it skid into action, and that's enough. Into the woods, I race and incapacitate the two snatchers before they even know

I'm upon them. From there, I use my nose to track their scent back to the encampment.

It's not as elaborate as Snatcher's Ridge. There's a small hunting cabin and a treestand lookout up high. That's probably the extent of what was here just this morning. Now there are a few tents as well. No cages that I can see. Just ropes tying some animals to trees. I don't see Kofi. I wish I did. I'd free him first of all. I wonder how many were sold and hauled off before the ridge was abandoned.

A thin, mustached man in a brown camouflage coat is yelling about the quality of business and demanding his money be refunded immediately. He must be the one who bought Harriet.

Only one guard, as far as I can tell—up there in the treestand on high alert, the scope of his rifle to his eye. I bet he's the one who shot Mr. Turner. He's the one I need to take out before I can do much else.

I slink into the forest and make my way along the outside of the boundary to the bottom of his tree. I won't be able to climb soundlessly, but I'm hopeful my speed will make up for it. Bounding from my haunches, I leap nearly as high into the air as he sits and then claw my way around, where I knock him to the floor of his stand. The rifle goes off with a deafening blast, but I'm not hit. All of this has greatly alarmed the orangutan.

Three men are pointing up at me and yelling as I pry the gun away and toss it over the railing. When the lookout faces off with me sans his rifle, he jumps over the railing himself! I wonder if anyone knows I'm anything more than a mountain lion.

Glancing around, I find a network of sturdy limbs and begin to canvas the forest, tree to tree, putting as much distance between myself and the range of a bullet as possible. I can always double back and sneak attack.

The orangutan makes my life easier when it tackles the three men who are following my progress, and now they have their hands too full to worry about me.

In my periphery, a flash of red darts from its hiding place. Harriet! She has covered a lot of ground, but three or four men are closing in on her. "Release the dogs!" one of them calls. Hounds are baying and straining against their leashes.

Don't release the dogs. I don't want to hurt the dogs.

I leap down a tree trunk, catching up to them to wage a war of intimidation. Harriet has armed herself with a tent peg, and she raises it at me, but I spin away from her to scream at the snatchers, who surround her. I brandish my front paws, claws on full display. I'm growling, hissing, snapping my teeth.

"Tazer it," one man yells.

No, I am not having the tazer again. I leap onto the man, and he crumples beneath my weight. I leap off again to make quick work of another and turn to check on Harriet, but she's off, running through the woods with no trail to guide her, as fast as she can—which is remarkably fast. She must set records for her high school team. Still, it's no match for me, of course, not on lion legs. When I've caught up, she swings the tent peg behind herself, but she keeps running. I man up to try to keep her from being afraid of me.

"Harriet, it's me. I was a captive too. No, keep running!" I overtake her when she turns to see me and plow on ahead. "Your father told me to come get you. Rosa is safe at home."

We don't talk again for fifteen or twenty minutes, and in that time, we cover a lot of ground. When we come to a road, we decide to keep going in case they're on our trail. I'd say they went back to camp to try again on their ATVs. "You're not hurt, then?" I say.

"I'm fine," she pants. In her red hoody, she reminds me of a feminist's dream of Little Red Riding Hood. She's built like a long-distance runner, tall and slender, with the stamina that comes from years of focused training. She makes a terrible victim. "Where are we going?"

"No idea." I pull my phone out to see if I have service. "Your feet must be killing you." She's barefoot. Well, we know where her shoes are, don't we? In the custody of the Atlanta PD.

"I can run," she assures me.

"I know. But let's stop and listen for a second." It's getting toward evening now. We step off the road and into the brush. I close my eyes but I can't hear anything besides the natural woodland sounds: trees rustling, squirrels scurrying through the leaves, birdcalls.

"We passed a sign that said there was a campground coming up," I say. "Let's go there and find a way to call for help."

"OK, but not on the road."

We remain in the cover of the woods but follow the direction of the road.

"How do you know my sister is safe?" she asks.

"I drove her from Snatcher's Ridge myself. Your dad helped us out of the cage we were in, but then he stayed behind to find you."

"He found me here." For the first time, Harriet's tone betrays her concern. "Someone shot a gun."

"He's OK. I saw him. My dad took him to the hospital, but he was conscious. He was just worried about you is all."

She side-eyes me. "I thought I saw you—I thought you were—something else. Something not human."

"I'm a mountain lion shifter," I tell her. Why not? If I deny it, she'll think she's crazy.

"You are, aren't you? How?"

"Uh, my dad was one." I never thought about it much more than that. He handed it down to me. "It's not unusual to have one born to a generation, though in mine there are three."

"Your siblings?" she asks.

"No, actually my brother isn't a shifter. He's studying to be an engineer." I haven't seen Zach in a while. He doesn't come home much. I'm sure he's had to deal with the divorce in his own way. And he has a job, has a girlfriend. "I met your mom when she came to pick up Rosa. She's worried about you. We'll have to find a way to let her know you're OK."

"I don't feel OK yet," she says. "We haven't escaped yet."

"Every step is further away."

"Then let's keep walking."

After several more minutes, Harriet points to another sign. "There's the campground," she says. "What happens if there are snatchers in there?"

I look down at her bare feet. She tries not to show it, but she's struggling. "We'll stick together," I tell her. "It's a State park. Let's find the ranger in charge." It doesn't occur to me that a ranger would be sympathetic to snatchers, but I guess money can buy loyalty. I check my phone again and try to call my dad. It goes through!

"Chausie?" I can only hear him in and out.

"Dad? We made it out. Harriet and I are walking—Dad?" The call goes dead. I text him instead and tell him where we are, what campground and road, and the nearest mile marker. Unfortunately, a small, red circle containing an exclamation point appears beside my text. It didn't send. I try one to Aiden too, just in case.

We turn onto the road marked *Campground* and find a small building like a guard shack with a crossing gate. A woman in uniform speaks through an open window when we arrive. "What can I do for you?" she asks. Since we're on foot and have no gear, she probably supposes we already have a campsite. "D'you go out hiking and lose your way?" Her eyes land on Harriet's feet and her demeanor changes. "You kids in some type of trouble?"

The radio on the ranger's shoulder could be our ticket out of here. I'm about to confess our whole plight, tell her how to contact Aiden and my dad, tell her where the encampment is with the animals that need freeing and the snatchers who need capturing—but Harriet says, "No, Ma'am, we're fine. I was wading in that beautiful river and the current stole my sandals."

Wow. She is untrusting. And a smooth liar too. What river?

"You camping with us?" the ranger asks. "I don't remember you."

"Yeah, my aunt's in there with the camper."

"What site?"

"Fourteen," Harriet says without hesitation. Looks the woman straight in the eye.

"Oh, go ahead, then," the ranger says and does something inside the guard house that lifts the gate. I don't know if she's aware of who's camping at *fourteen* or if she just assumes Harriet is telling the truth. Harriet walks in like she owns the place and I follow her.

"What was that?" I ask when we're out of earshot.

"Call me cautious," Harriet grumbles. "I've been kidnapped, tied up, and moved from location to location. I thought I lost my sister. My dad was shot. I didn't get a good vibe from that ranger, and I wish you hadn't brought us here."

I keep from halting in my tracks through a sheer act of will and only because I don't want the ranger to pay any more attention to us. "What choice did we have?" I say through my teeth. "You can barely walk. I know you're trying to tough it out, but..." I want to argue the point, show her why I'm right and she's wrong, but I do understand that she's been traumatized, so I exhale my frustration and say, "Just hang in there."

Harriet gives me a curt nod without looking at me and without slowing down. What she plans to do once we reach site fourteen, I have no idea. But here we are, trudging around a circle of campsites like we know where we're going, greeting over-friendly, middle-aged campers in lawn chairs, dodging kids on bikes, and trying not to appear paranoid.

"Why fourteen?" I ask.

"I saw that it was the furthest away from the guard shack. I figured it would give us time to scope the place out. Plus, it's the holy number seven—twice."

"You're a quick thinker."

She seems to appreciate the compliment.

"And a scary good liar," I add. That brings a smile.

"There's a bathhouse over there." She doesn't point, but I see what she means. "I need to go. Plus, we could get something to drink."

"Yeah, I could use that. I think we should stick together, though."

"I'm not going to the bathroom in front of you."

"That's not what I mean." It kind of is, though. I really don't feel comfortable letting her out of my sight. When she goes into the women's side, I hurry around to the men's, do my business, and hurry back. I'm gulping water at the fountain when she comes out.

"OK, it's possible that my feet are going to need amputation." She sits down on a bench to look them over.

"Yeah." I glance at them. "You've messed them up pretty good. I don't know how you've made it this far."

Over her shoulder, I spot an old woman watching us with a spatula in hand. She's cooking something on a grill that folds out from the side of a nice camper—the kind you drive like a big bus. Her eyes are kind. When she catches my eye, she waves the spatula, and I wave back. Then she beckons us over. "Come on," I tell Harriet. Maybe it's the tempting aroma of the meat she's cooking. "Let's go talk to that lady."

Harriet is hobbling by the time we get there. I direct her attention to the marker at the entrance to the site. *Fourteen.*

"I'm glad you saw me," the old woman says. "I could hear your stomach rumbling across the distance." She's a white woman with dreadlocks pulled into a pile on top of her head. She wears a stretchy, tie-dyed dress and sandals, giving me the idea that she's an old hippie who still travels from festival to festival after all these years. There's something about her that reminds me of Laurel Frost Flower. Maybe it's just her age. But no, it's more nuanced than that. It's the fact that her age doesn't diminish her liveliness—which is saying something since Laurel was dead.

Harriet's already sitting at the campsite's iron picnic table. Not sure if it's because, like me, she automatically trusts this lady or because she's beyond caring—with the pain in her feet. I wonder if she's had anything to eat since she was kidnapped.

The woman sets two big Gatorade bottles on the table. "You look parched," she says to us. "My name is Donoma."

"I'm Chausie." I take the bottle with a gesture of thanks. "And this is Harriet."

"You've been through an ordeal. You could use some help."

We both nod our heads. "How did you know?" Harriet says.

The bathhouse didn't have mirrors, but if Harriet could see herself, she wouldn't have asked. Sweaty, disheveled, hair gone wild, scratches on her face and arms from the briars and branches we ran through. I probably appear much the same, minus the scratches which have probably healed.

Although, now that I look at the woman, I notice that there is something strange about the way she studies us. I said her eyes were kind, and that's true. But they don't seem to land on us. That is, she looks around me without focusing on any one aspect, like my eyes—until she does.

"I see more than most," she says as if in answer to my observation. "You glow with the light of the heavens."

Harriet side-eyes me. "Does he?" she asks.

"And you, my dear," Donoma says to her, "belong to God. He means for me to take you home to your mother." She says the last with such peaceful assurance, I believe her. But then she lets out a yelp. "The burgers!" And slides them onto a plate. "Heaven's sake and no earthly good," she mumbles.

Harriet is laughing. It has a contagious effect. Soon, Harriet and I are scarfing down cheeseburgers and fried potato wedges. "Aren't you going to eat?" I ask. Donoma hasn't sat with us. Instead, she fills a huge stock pot with water and sets it on the stove.

"Oh yes. One moment." She disappears into the camper and reappears carrying a rubber tub which she places on the ground beside Harriet. Now she ladles salt into the pot and stirs. After a time, she wrestles the steaming mixture off of the stove, but it's too heavy for her. "Hang on," I say and rise to take it. "Where are you going with this?"

"Pour it in there with my thanks." She gestures toward the tub and says to Harriet, "Soak your feet in that, love. It will cleanse your wounds and set you on the path to healing."

I think Donoma sets more to healing than Harriet's feet. In the fifteen minutes or so that her feet remain in the tub, Harriet's whole countenance changes, and when she moves to empty the tub, Donoma and I both tell her not to. I dump the tub and clean up the plates. Harriet protests, but I press a donut to her mouth and say, "Stop fussing. You're going to undo what Donoma has done."

Harriet grins, accepts the donut, and relaxes into her predicament like a queen—if queens sat at picnic tables eating donuts. It occurs to me that simple acts of service are powerful medicine. Or maybe it's just a really good donut. I take one for myself.

"What did you mean he glows with the light of the heavens?" Harriet asks and studies me. Donoma does too, her chin resting on her hand. I'm sure I look uncomfortable while I bear their scrutiny.

"While the colors of one's energy blend and shift," Donoma says to Harriet, "there is generally one that remains dominant. Your dominant energy is red. You're a leader with a lot of confidence and a fiery temper —not always a negative thing," she says when Harriet objects. "But with Chausie, well, I'm not sure how to explain it. He has a terrestrial energy that is pink."

"*Pink?*" I protest and Donoma chuckles.

"Don't be chagrined. You're curious and loyal, non-judgmental, romantic. I bet you're able to assess situations and act on clues that most people would simply dismiss. And I see I'm correct. What are you grinning about?"

I didn't realize I was. "When I met my girlfriend, Beam—she's special—I mean not just because I'm into her, but because she's able to see things that are invisible to the rest of us—maybe like you can—but anyway, when she confided that fact to me, she was afraid I'd write her off as a lunatic."

"But you didn't," Harriet says.

I shake my head. "She was just happy to be believed. Pretty sure that's how I landed her."

Harriet rolls her eyes but returns my smile. "So what about the light of the heavens part?" she asks Donoma. "You told us about his *terrestrial* aura."

"It's like he was born from a star," Donoma says. "That's as well as I can put it. There's an illumination that I don't see inside of people."

Donoma packs up the cooking equipment and announces that it's time to go. I talk Harriet into allowing me to piggyback her up the camper's stairs—which is funny and awkward as she has to open and hold the door—and then I deposit her onto a couch. It's a deceptively large space. The side wall is extended to create more room, but now Donoma presses a button that causes it to slide inward. "We can't drive like that, you know."

My eyes refocus from the moving wall, through its window to the guard shack. The same tank-like Mercedes I'd seen at the encampment is pulled up at the gate, and behind it, the Hummer. "They found us!" I say. All three of us watch as the crossing rail begins to lift.

"Chausie, do you know how to unplug the water and electric?" Donoma asks.

"On it!" My mom and dad used to take me and my brother camping in one of these. While I race out the door, Donoma takes the driver's seat. The snatchers' vehicles creep around the campground's circle. It only takes a moment for me to unplug the two connections, though I don't know where to stash the cords, and anyway, I don't have time, so I just lug them back into the camper with me. I'm half inside, folding the stairs away when a great roar sounds from somewhere in the woods.

Kofi.

For the second it takes me to decide, I stall. I am this close to freedom with the captive I came to release. But not the one I promised to come back for. "Get her home safe, Donoma. Thanks for everything."

Harriet and I lock eyes, and I jump to the ground, slamming the door as Donoma pulls away. The snatchers are closing in. In a heartbeat, they'll have her blocked, but she guns it off the parking pad and skids past the Mercedes' bumper, gaining traction as she goes. The snatchers are after her until I shift into lion form, sprint forward, and leap over the hood. That's more than enough to draw their attention away from the old woman driver and onto me.

"Isn't that Frilk's cougar?" the driver of the Hummer calls through his open window.

"Not anymore," someone says.

They leap from their vehicles armed with rifles that they won't dare use on me. How could they sell me if they killed me? Unless for my skin. *Yikes.* I scamper into the woods, but not so fast that they give up on catching me. I have to give Donoma and Harriet time to get away.

I do too good of a job keeping within their sites. One guy fires at me. Another yells at him for it. I emit an earsplitting scream that has two of them covering their ears. The other two flinch, and one falls to his knees.

My scream calls up another thundering roar from Kofi, though from further away. If those guys think *I* sound scary... They're looking in the same direction. I think they're making a plan, but I'm not going to stick around to be part of it. I sprint in the direction of Kofi's scream, though I'm pretty sure he's being driven away in a vehicle.

13

REUNITED WITH THE COLLAR

BEAM

The undeniable truth is that I am at the mercy of a ruthless goblin, tied up on the floor, unable to move anything more than my fingers.

Frilk, with an undefeated scowl, stares at the spot where Larkin disappeared, and then he lowers his eyes to behold me. I sort of wish he would say something. It's torture not to know what he's thinking. Probably, that he wants to finish the job he started back in Chausie's kitchen.

To keep him from falling upon me, I say, "Don't you want to know where Larkin went?" The tremor in my voice betrays my fear.

He remains silent. But of course, he won't be bothered about Larkin's whereabouts. She's supposed to end up right back in the bird-cage at the top of this tunnel.

Sliding his dagger from a sheath on his hip, Frilk kneels to study my neck. He even lifts my chin to make sure—which makes my skin crawl.

What conclusions is he drawing about the fact that I'm whole and alive? That I'm an identical twin? That he botched the job? That he needs to sharpen his knife?

With the cold dagger, he pricks the skin on my left thigh. I jerk, but I can't do more than an inch-worm-type of gyration. Now, he sits back to observe. He's conducting an experiment! If he thinks *shifters* are valuable—try a shifter whose blood can heal people and open gates between worlds.

"Fascinating," Frilk says after he pinches my skin at the place he pricked. The small puncture must have healed instantly. He tries again, this time slicing deeper, and I grit my teeth to keep from crying out.

Frilk jogs to the kitchen for a towel to place under my leg—because God forbid my blood mess up his rug.

He waits.

It heals.

This time he looks into my eyes. Still, he doesn't speak to me. He crosses to a bookshelf and runs his finger along some interesting titles—*The Short Truth in Tall Tales*, *Stellar Bloodlines*, and *A Guide to Alchemy*—landing on a robust, leather-bound tome called *The Holy Grail: a Quest for the Elixir of Life*.

This is not good. He's too greedy to keep from sussing out all the things I'm capable of.

He flicks through the book and spends a few minutes reading pages in the middle. I wish I could read them! Don't worry. I have eyes on the prize—getting out of here. But if I could do that with some of those books...

Frilk leaves the room, and I hear him jostling things around. Glass test tubes? There is the *tch* of a flint lighter and the *shhh* of a blue flame. Yes, I know the color of a flame by its sound. I aced Chemistry.

He stomps back and slices my leg again! No warning. No explanation. I twist away, but he clamps down on me and collects my blood in a glass beaker. This time, he doesn't stick around to see if the wound will heal, so I seize the moment to try to smear the rope with my blood. It doesn't come loose. I don't think my blood affects it the same as it did the collar.

"What are you trying to test in there?" I call out.

Or maybe he's trying to *make* something. I glance at the bookshelf. *The Art of Alchemy*. It's one of those not-so-scientific sciences of the Middle Ages. They tried to change the composition of metals to make gold. And, yes, they sought after a way to heal diseases—think Bubonic Plague. It wasn't a very easy time to be alive. Literally.

Frilk is pretty smart. Diabolical as well, but smart. Where did he come up with the material he uses to capture everybody? Is it really from outer space? "You're not a Leonid," he had said. I scan my memory for the word and come up with the Leonid Meteor Shower. Every November, we see action from that, some years more than others. Mom and dad wake me up and we all go out to the backyard to watch. One year, we went camping.

Yes. I do have time to consider all this. Because Frilk is in his little lab doing little labby things.

This takes a long time. I am tied up on the floor. I almost fall asleep. Maybe Blue will come back for me. Maybe—

Frilk darkens the doorway and finally deigns to speak to me. "How did you get blood like this?"

"I was born with it."

"Why you?"

"I don't know."

Frilk considers my answers before he poses more questions and crosses his arms in front of himself.

"Are you able to heal others, or do you only heal yourself?"

The truth, Goblin, is that I never healed myself. Well, maybe indirectly. I healed Chausie and then he healed me. "Only myself," I say out loud.

I don't know if he believes me. He says, "Do you have any idea how much a self-healing predator would fetch at a fighting ring?"

That worries me on two counts. If he can't use me, he'll sell me to some ruthless fight pimp where I'll be untraceable. And if Chausie is found to be self-healing, he'll be even more of a target.

A surge of protective anger shoots between my shoulder blades. I blurt out, "I heal others."

"How do you do that?"

"Let me out of this rope and I'll tell you."

His lips pucker in thought, and then he lays hold of the whip which coils into his hand. "Wait here."

I will not. I eyeball the entrance.

With a crack of the whip that reverberates in my skull, Frilk snaps it so that the end snags on something invisible. That part disappears. Then

Frilk disappears. Now, what am I supposed to do? Get the heck out of there is what!

I dash to the bookshelf—don't judge—and gather up as many books as I can carry. Then I race for the tunnel up out of the tree. Again, I probably could have become a panther and made better time. Would the books have folded into my panther form as my clothes do?

The end of the whip snaps into view right in front of me, and, in reverse order, Frilk is back. In his right hand, he brandishes his knife, and it is dripping with blood. In his left, he holds the collar.

Some police officer is dead, I think. *Whoever was guarding the collar. It probably wrapped around their neck. I shouldn't have let Aiden take it. Oh god, what if it was Aiden?*

"Did you kill a police officer?" I whisper.

"Do you want to move about freely or not?"

He cleans the knife on his dark pants and holds the collar to my neck before he identifies the books in my hands—and actually laughs.

Once the collar wraps around my neck, it seals itself, and Frilk flicks the end of the whip, causing it to coil into a manageable belt ornament.

"How do you heal people?" Frilk asks.

"I don't know."

He backhands me across the cheekbone, causing me to drop his books.

I don't remember being hit before—not just like, right out hit. It makes me see stars for several long seconds. I grab my head and squint as hard as I can to make them go away. New fear rushes through me. He can torture me all day long. I'll just keep healing.

"You have to drink some of my blood," I confess through gritted teeth.

Again, he studies me with a look that says he needs to test my words. And off he goes to come back with a small, brown mouse. Does Larkin know he has test subjects? She would be so mad.

Frilk draws the horrible blade down the mouse's belly. Poor thing squeaks in pain and struggles. Next, Frilk cuts my arm—with the same gross blade, by the way—and then takes a drop of my blood to the mouse's lips. It laps it up. And then it heals.

A slow smile covers the goblin's face, and, there on the floor of his home, he lets the mouse go. It frolics and explores, eventually finding its way to the tunnel and presumably out into the beautiful world. I remember those first hours after being healed by the blood. Feels like you could accomplish anything. It's euphoric.

Frilk watches the mouse do its happy dance and escape. He says, "Your body churns out the Elixir of Life. It could be harvested daily and sold. It could be stored. It could be melded into the material. It could…" He simply raises his hands with the sheer joy of his dark imaginings.

"Hey! It is *my* blood."

A phone rings. *Really.* The goblin who lives in the basement of a tree has phone service.

He withdraws the phone and puts it to his ear without a verbal greeting.

"We found your cougar," I hear the caller say.

Frilk doesn't reply. He never seems compelled to hold up his end of a conversation.

"I can catch him, but I'll want more of the take. Hugo's men are after him. One of them shot at him like a damn fool, but he missed."

I draw in a sharp breath and hold it for a while.

"If you can catch him," Frilk says. "You can have twenty-five percent."

"Give me forty," the caller argues. "You're not having to do a thing."

"And just what are you going to do with a wild cougar and no connections? You won't get past the gate. I'll give you thirty."

"Thirty-five."

Frilk rolls his eyes showing how petty of a matter this is to him now that he's found the *Elixir of Life.* "Fine," he says. "Thirty-five. But you have to catch him before the sun sets or you can just keep him until the next market."

"I'll have him before that. Don't you worry. You just get up here and get your buyers in place."

Reaching for Chausie with my mind, I try to warn him as he had done before Frilk showed up with his bloodthirsty knife. *Someone's after you!* The concentration I'm exerting must show on my face. When I open my eyes, Frilk is watching me.

"What are you doing?"

"I feel sick," I tell him, which is not untrue. "I think you took too much blood."

I'm not sure if Frilk doesn't believe me in particular or in any human being at all. He stares at me blankly, as is his custom. "I'll have to take you," he says at length. "I can't leave you here. There are too many unknowns. You will stay by my side. You will not talk to anyone. You will not *look* at anyone. Do you understand?"

Hang on. He's going to take me to Chaus? "Yes," I assure him. "I understand."

"I suppose you *have* lost a lot of blood today," he says in a surprising twist. "It probably wouldn't hurt you to eat. I don't want you getting weak." He motions to the kitchen where Larkin made that lovely meal, and I spoon some things onto a plate. Biscuits and beans. Fried potatoes. Nuts and berries cooked into a jelly that makes me think of cranberry sauce. "Should I fix a plate for you?" I ask and clean up the mess of his original dinner. Why? Because Larkin's domestic kindnesses seemed to win him over.

He grunts in the affirmative, so I present him with his own plate and despite the odd company, the food is delicious. I hadn't realized how hungry I was.

About the time we're finished, the phone rings again. "Yes?" Frilk sits forward in his chair and abandons his food on the foot stool.

"I've got him," the caller says. "He's not that happy about it. Nearly took my arm off despite being drugged. But I've got him."

"On my way." Frilk ends the call and places another. "I have the Leonid. You still interested?"

I can't hear the response this time. Frilk says, "Pacific cougar. Mid to late adolescence. Handsome fella." The caller says more. Frilk responds, "An honest to god Leonid." Then he smiles and ends the call.

"How much will you sell him for?" I ask but get no answer. I try a different question. "Where are we going?"

"Don't worry about how much and don't worry about where. Just keep your head down."

Frilk nudges me toward the tunnel, so we traverse the incline and come out into the evening light where he stops to observe the empty birdcage. No Larkin.

"What is going on?" he mutters to himself. To me, he says gruffly, "Get up in that wagon."

I climb into the seat that Larkin possessed when I was a panther for the first time. I don't understand how this wagon will get us across the field, much less across the state—no offense to the pony. It's a good beast, but it's been sorely mistreated. I'd like to free it and find a lovely old farm with owners who would feed it juicy apples and allow it to roam.

"*Yah!*" Frilk slaps the reins against its neck, and off we go.

14

THE BUYER

BEAM

It isn't until we've cleared Frilk's field that I realize we're in an utterly different location. The sun is setting and the terrain is mountainous, with tree-covered boulders rising before us. We're on a paved country road but turn onto a narrower, dirt driveway. Around a bend, a man stands guard in front of an unexpected iron gate and waves us in while he opens it up. He must be familiar with Frilk already. He doesn't strike me as the type of man to tolerate strangers. Especially old goblin strangers driving rickety wagons. I keep my head down and only steal glances when I think no one is looking.

"He's at the camp house," the guard says and Frilk slaps the reins against the pony to urge it on. Signs posted point out the directions to *Registration, Guns and Ammo, Bows and Arrows,* and pictures of several exotic animals including antelopes, bison, grizzly bears, and African lions. *This is a hunting range.* My heart kicks in with a flight drive that is begging me to shift and get the heck out of there.

The camp house turns out to be a one-story shelter open to the elements. Smoke rises from the chimney. A few men—and women too, but mostly men—amble about, some stopping by the fireplace to converse, others moving about their business. Several of them hold long rifles or intimidating crossbows, not pointed and ready to shoot, but just in between killing things, I guess.

Frilk pulls the pony to a stop and doesn't bother to tether it to anything. It's a good, little pony.

"Is this the panther you told me about?"

I manage to keep my head down, but it takes a strenuous act of self-restraint. I said my head. I still do raise my eyes. The man speaking to Frilk is around Aiden's age. He's impressive in build, his biceps and shoulders strong beneath a long-sleeved t-shirt. The creases around his eyes make me think he smiles a lot. Surely this is not a man who buys humans.

Frilk redirects the man's attention from me to Chaus. "That's right, but she's no longer for sale. You'll have your hands full with the cougar. He's a real spitfire."

"Oh, no, I want the pair." The man sounds genuinely disappointed.

Frilk pretends to be sorry. Wags his head and says, "I've grown fond of her. Don't want to part with her now."

Pff. Translation: he can get rich off of me beyond his wildest dreams.

"I'm sorry. It's no deal if I can't have both. That's the agreement we made before you lost them."

Wow. To slide that subtle accusation in, this guy must not know the kind of monster he's dealing with. Maybe he's an even bigger monster. I sniff—not in the loud way I'd done Aiden—but quietly. I can't pick up anything animalistic or interesting. He smells good, is all, like expensive men's shampoo.

Frilk stares at the would-be buyer in a way I know too well, blank on the surface, cunning underneath.

The buyer tries again. "Fifty million."

And a small smile turns Frilk's mouth. Unlike the buyer's, it does not reach his eyes.

The image of the leprechaun in my mom's book comes to mind, as evil in memory as it had been on the page. Frilk loops a finger underneath my collar and gives it a yank. While I wear this, he can appear before me at any time, day or night. He's going to sell me and then double-cross this man by showing up to take me back—or to just take my blood. That way, he can remain true to the deal.

"Forty for this one," Frilk says silkily. "Ten for the other."

"Do you mean that in reverse?"

"I do not."

"You said the other was Leonid."

"That's right," Frilk agrees. "Do we have a deal or not?"

The buyer's confused expression softens as he figures it out. "You owe somebody a percentage for the Leonid, but not for this one."

Frilk shrugs.

"Well, then this is a good deal for you. Let's have a look."

How in the world could anyone afford to pay fifty million dollars for anything? How will he make it back? Dark fantasies come to mind. Things no human should be forced to do.

Frilk nudges me and I realize both men expect me to do something. "What?" I ask.

"Step down for the buyer to look you over," Frilk says.

Ew.

OK. So, every woman has to deal with being ogled because, let's face it, some men—not all certainly, but some—are pigs. They don't even pretend to respect us or treat us like equals. Instead, they take unwelcome liberties that can be menacing and even traumatizing. Makes me grateful to have found a trustworthy partner like Chaus.

Having said all that, the way this buyer looks at me is less like a pig and more like approval. His attention feels...safe. If that's possible. Don't misunderstand me. It's not safe. I know that. If he is looking me over to buy me, that is obviously dehumanizing, and nothing good can come of it.

Frilk orders me to climb down from the wagon. The buyer says, "I'm Mauri. What's your name?"

I shoot a sideways glance at Frilk who nods for me to answer. "Beam. Beam Redfeather."

"Redfeather," he repeats. "Is that Tribal?"

"My father is Hawk of the Mountain, a warrior of the Oglala Lakota." Dad's a lawyer, but—whatever. "We're the Tribe responsible for wiping out Custer and his men," I add.

"Excellent," Mauri says, less intimidated by my pedigree than impressed. "And your mother?"

"A civil rights attorney." Maybe that was the more threatening thing to say. Mauri nods curtly.

"Will you shift for me?" he asks politely.

"No," I spout. "I'm not a circus animal."

Mauri is pretty tolerant of my insubordinance. He even laughs good-naturedly. Why it should make him happy for me to deny his request, I cannot say.

"Shift for the man," Frilk says like his tongue is a dagger. "Or I will terminate the cougar, deal or no deal."

I *hate* Frilk. I hope he can feel it in his bones, the way I hate him, by the way I am glaring.

"I swear on my own name," he hisses down low at my ear. "On the goblin name of Frilk, I will do it."

It steals something from me. I abhor being forced to perform for these men. It is vile. But I understand the binding nature of Frilk's promises, and so I allow my anger to fold my body, extend my shoulders, raise my hackles, and snarl in the hideous face of the creature who has no regard for the free will of others.

Mauri emits a low whistle. "She's perfect," he says. "She'll be a star."

I become woman again and say, "I'm not going to be very exciting to hunt." Frilk checks me with an elbow to the ribs.

Mauri's hands go up. "There's no need for that," he tells Frilk. To me he says, "I haven't decided about you yet, but you won't be hunted here."

Will I be hunted somewhere else?

As Mauri calls his men over to prepare the payment, Frilk delivers another promise to me. "I have questions about how I managed to leave your collar behind when I slit your throat, so let me be clear. That collar is my permanent mark on you. If you find a way out of it, I will know, and the cougar will die."

CHAUSIE

The cage is short, so yeah, I'm in lion form, pacing back and forth and fantasizing about ripping that young, idiot snatcher's head off. He treed me with a bunch of coon hounds and shot me with something that made me woozy. I became human so that I could explain what a horrible mistake he'd made—which lasted for the few seconds it took to find out he already knew, and before I could fall out of the tree, he nabbed me with one of those long catch poles—the ones with the loop on top that tightens the more you struggle to get free.

He's been on the phone, but now that he's on his way to the cage, I give vent to my anger, hissing at him and flinging myself against the wall to swat at him through the bars.

"Keep it up, cougar," the young snatcher says. "The more ornery you are, the better price you'll bring."

We've been traveling for an hour or so. There's a tarp around the cage so that no one can see what's being transported, I suppose, but that means I can't see out. I tear a hole to remedy that. When we stop at an iron gate, there's a sign that reads

Posted
Private Property
No Trespassing
Live Ammunition

"Let's see what you've got," the gateman says. The snatcher comes round and both men stare into my yellow eyes as I glower at them through a hole in the tarp.

"He's a shifter," the snatcher says, not because he wants the guy to know, but because he's a self-satisfied jerk. He releases the tarp so that it falls away, and the guard strolls the length of the cage. "Get him to shift."

"Shift for the man," the snatcher commands.

I sit down and lick and lick a hind paw instead. It irritates the snatcher, and that makes me happy.

The gateman looks me over and shakes his head. "So, this is what we're doing now," he says. "Go on through."

I hear voices, and I smell Frilk. We pull up beside his wagon where the goblin and a man I can only assume to be the buyer are discussing their plans for me. The young snatcher throws the truck in park and steps out to greet them with the kind of triumphant smirk I'd like to punch off his face.

"You were right," the buyer says to Frilk. "He is a fine specimen." He raises his voice to me. No idea why. I could hear him across the field. "What's your name, son?"

Are you kidding me? You're going to call me son? Suddenly, Aiden's affectionate use of the term doesn't bother me.

I assume my human form and bump my head on the top of the cage. Gritting my teeth, I say, "Chausie Louris. My father is a law officer in South Dakota and he'll be here for me, so if you know what's good for you, you'll let me walk out of here right now."

"I like him," the buyer declares. "He'll fit in nicely." Then to me, raising his voice again, he says, "Don't worry, Chausie Louris, we won't be anywhere near here when your father arrives."

Don't know what I'm supposed to say to that. Every new place they take me to makes it harder to be found. "How many other hunting ranges do you have?" I ask.

"No, we're not going to allow you to be hunted."

"Just bought and sold."

One of the buyer's assistants wheels over a briefcase that Frilk immediately sets in the back of the wagon and opens to inspect.

"Ten for the cougar," the buyer says. "As we agreed."

Ten what? Hundred? Thousand? Hundred thousand?

"That's all you're taking?" the young snatcher demands and waves at the cage. "I spent that in manpower and gear! Not to mention the losses we've already absorbed."

"Not my problem," Frilk tells him and drops stack after stack of one hundred dollar bills onto the ground.

"This is a *Leonid!*" the snatcher continues to argue.

Frilk stops what he's doing to frown at the young man. "You want it or not?"

I'm still trying to do the math here. The total must have been in *millions.* Did this guy just pay ten *million* dollars for me?

Several rapid shots are fired from nearby. People can be heard congratulating each other. This place makes me sick. How hard is it to bag an animal that is fed by humans every day and trapped in a fence?

Junior drops to his knees with a huff and begins to consolidate the money. "You're just throwing it away," he says. "He should have gone for double that."

"We're done now," Frilk tells him.

"Yeah, we *are* done," he says and turns to the buyer. "Get your cat off my rig."

Mauri nods and, with a meaningful glance at Frilk—which I gather to mean they're in cahoots—he waves to a few young men standing by. I think the snatcher just got duped.

The men receive Mauri's wave as an order and approach the sliding door of my cage warily. They're smart. I have no intention of going quietly. I lion up with a series of low growls to let them in on my current mood.

Instead of opening the cage, one of them sticks a catch pole through. It's completely ridiculous. I evade it repeatedly with what must appear to be contempt even on my lion's face. Another one tries his skill with the pole. Then he calls for someone else.

"Bunch of amateurs," the disgruntled snatcher says. A noose comes from somewhere behind me and as I struggle to get free of it, the snatcher bounces around the cage and nabs me with another one. Now I am truly caught. I man up to use my hands, but they're upon me all at once, dragging me out of the cage and heaving me into another one. Soon, I'm being driven away, and the ambitious glimpse of the buyer I catch on the way out is disconcerting. It may not be a hunting range he has in mind for me, but it's not a zoo.

Good. That's just one more deplorable thing to shut down. I inhale deeply to isolate unique scent markers. I *will* be back. But as I mentally log the smells, one as valuable as my own skin registers. *Beam!* I keen for her automatically. I holler into the night. They've got her. Are they going to allow *her* to be hunted? I scratch the ground of the cage and throw myself against the bars.

"Settle down back there!" The driver beats on the back window.

Stop freaking out, I tell myself. *Reach for the woman. Find her light.* I close my eyes to concentrate. They're driving me away from her, and there's nothing I can do. When I'm exhausted from the effort and still can't reach her in my mind, I cry out for Blue and allow myself one last wail over the injustice of it all.

My ears prick as a howl goes up. A beautiful, flute-like wolf's howl in answer to my keening. Aiden? Is he on my trail? My dad could have gotten hold of him. *Would* have gotten hold of him. Do they know about Beam?

I call out again, but no answer comes. If it is Aiden, he won't want to give himself away. That gives me some hope, and I resign myself to transport, watching for road signs and trying to stay alert. No tarp this time. I don't want to miss anything that could give me a clue as to my whereabouts. It's dark though, and I haven't slept, except for when I was drugged, and I still feel drowsy from that. The lack of anything to see coupled with the rumble of the truck lulls me.

You know what's weird? Frilk was hardly interested in me anymore. He barely glanced my way other than a haughty acknowledgment of his victory over me. It's because he has Beam. He must. Which means he knows how special she is. I mean, she didn't die, did she? He'll be curious about that. How did he get to her without the collar?

I think about how I can spot her light and how Donoma could spot mine. Hers is like a door to the afterlife. Donoma—and Harriet's mom too—said I shone like stars in heaven.

And now I remember something that Laurel said that night we first got to her place, and Beam had already fallen asleep in a real bed for the first time in days. "Take care of her, Bloodkin. She may not know it, but her blood chooses you because she is a gate to the heavens, and you are made of stars."

Laurel was dead. I didn't know it at the time. And she had this unnerving way of answering my unsaid questions. I didn't trust her, but I was also strangely intrigued by her words because they felt weighty and right—even when I hated what they meant. But this one thing, I never had a chance to follow up on it. Now that I keep being identified as a Leonid, I wish I had.

The night wears on until we come to a guard house. This one's different from the one at the campground. Nothing pleasant or welcoming about it. The guard who checks the snatcher's ID looks like he could belong to a misguided militia. Shaved head. Tats. An AR-style rifle. *Shit.* What have I gotten myself into?

All he says, though, is, "Welcome to training camp," and waves us on.

Training camp. Training for what? A dozen thoughts flit through my mind. Summer basketball conditioning. Prizefighters. Cock fights. Dog fights.

We pull into a maze of fences, like at a prison. Once we come to a stop, the driver simply opens the gate of my cage and says, "No more of that. You're one of us in here."

Nothing about this guy screams *shifter* to me. I consider attacking him, but something about his demeanor tells me it would be of no use. I look around to find armed guards stationed up high in increments of about twenty-five yards. There's no getting out of here without keys and permissions.

The outside of the compound is lit with blaring prison lights, but the inside feels more like a neighborhood with softer lights on shorter posts spaced out.

I man up. "What did you mean, *one of us?*"

He's too enamored with the way I just shifted to answer at first. He says, "I'll never understand how that happens. I just mean we're all athletes. Fighters. You're among the best of the best here."

"Shifters?"

"No, that part's new. I'm not the one to ask about that. I'm hoping to become a coach—for the regular guys. Mixed martial arts fight clubs, endurance athletics. That sort of thing."

I keep expecting my guide to lead me into an area for animals like Snatcher's Ridge, but he shows me to a row of several tiny cabins. "This one's yours," he says, and we enter. It's comfortable, like a nice rental at a ski resort. There's a huge TV, muted but lit with a sports channel. On the opposite side of the room is a couch, and the wall behind it is also a counter for the kitchen. That's where he goes.

"Breakfast is from six to seven," the guy says as he opens and closes drawers. "Food's good here. Probably way better than you're used to from these kinds of places."

"What kind of places?" I ask.

"You know—places to train and hold preliminaries. Some guys fall in love with it. They get filthy rich. My advice? Put in your time, make a ton of cash, retire young, and go back to your life."

"Is that how it works?"

"Yeah. I mean—you have to be good. You have to be really good."

"And what if you're not?" I ask.

"Well...just make sure that you are." With that, he exits and the door closes behind him.

What are the chances I can just walk out?

Zero. It's locked.

With a sigh, I look around the place. It's equipped with healthy snacks and hot drinks. For humans. There's a half bath with soap and towels.

Most furniture doubles as storage, so the small space remains uncluttered despite being well stocked. I appreciate the spatial logistics. Stairs lead to a loft. I climb them now and find a double bed turned back and a desk with a chair. There's another bathroom up here, a full one with shampoo and conditioner, razors, a toothbrush... There are clothes in the closet with the tags on them.

A window looks out into the night where there is an enormous house—or a small temple—that butts up to a wild natural space with tons of trees.

Someone knocks on my door, not that I can open it. It swings wide and in steps the buyer I'd seen talking to Frilk. He probably made it here in record time with a Lamborghini or some other expensive machine. I watch him from the loft. When his eyes land on me, he smiles pleasantly.

"I realize it's late, Chausie, and I'm sure you're ready to get some sleep. We didn't get a proper introduction. I'm Mauri. Is there anything you need?"

I deadpan him. When he waits for a response, I say, "Are you serious right now? *Uh*, yes, there are things I need. Starting with a way out of here. This is criminal. I'm a human being."

"You're a marvelous human being," Mauri agrees. "Extraordinary. Do you know how many young men yearn to be where you are right now? I count myself among them. Only the privileged elite get to train here."

"You should give my place to them," I suggest. "And let me go."

"You're not a *prisoner*, Chausie. You're a valued member of the team."

"Then why can't I open the door?"

"Oh, that's only at night. They unlock at six am. Follow the sidewalk to breakfast."

"I want out." I enunciate all the words.

Mauri nods his head once and leaves it tucked. "Sleep on it. Meet the trainers and the other athletes. We just acquired a gorgeous black panther who I hope will—"

Before he finishes the sentence, I'm diving over the railing in lion form. He barely gets his hands up to block the blow and falls under my weight. "Where is she?!" I say, human again, my forearm on his throat.

He coughs and says, "She's practically next door, though I'm sure she's asleep." And now I suspect that he mentioned her just to keep me from trying to escape.

"What do you want from us? What is this place?"

I allow him to rise to his feet, and he says, "I just want your best. There will be games. Competitions."

"Combat," I correct him. "Cut the crap. You want us to fight."

"All athletic endeavors are battles, aren't they?"

"Not to the death. Is that what this boils down to? She's *female* for god's sake."

"How very liberated of you," he says sarcastically. *Not. In. The. Mood.* I swear I'm gonna rip this guy to pieces.

"She is not going to have a fair chance in a death match against bulkier lions who are stronger, faster, meaner."

"What about monkeys?" he asks. "Or apes?"

"What is wrong with you?"

"I'm a sports enthusiast, Chausie—and a showman. And I like to get rich. You can have your share of that. Don't you have plans for the future that a surge of cash could facilitate?"

I search my brain for a way to make this better somehow and land on, "Partner us up. If you let us fight together, we'll win. We've won every fight we've ever been in."

"So you do have experience."

"Real-life experience," I grumble. "Not some rich prick's degenerate pastime."

"How well do you know the young woman?"

I'm too emotional. I don't want to give him any more information than I have to. "Take me to her." I appeal to his ambition. "If you want victories from us, you'll partner us up."

His eyes slowly wander the ceiling and find their way back to me. He says, "I'll think about it. But you have to do what you're told and keep the conditions of our contract between us."

"Contract? You mean the fact that you paid money to buy me?"

"Isn't that what contracts are?" he says. "Tonight, get some rest. Tomorrow, we train."

"I want to see her. Now."

"Tomorrow," he says with finality. "Get some rest so that you can prove your worth. And then I might offer some leeway."

My eyes trail to the window beside the couch.

"They're riot-proof," Mauri says. "And they cost a lot. So...could you not?"

I try to act like I don't know what he's talking about.

Mauri leaves, and I allow him to. I hate situations like this where I have to sit on my haunches and wait. It's infuriating.

I unpocket my phone. No service. It's pretty spotty on the plains of South Dakota too, so I'm used to it. But still...you'd think this close to Atlanta we'd have more coverage. Probably why they built out here. Or maybe they're blocking the signal on purpose.

I have pictures of Beam stored on this phone. I scroll through a few of them now and trace her slender brown arm with my finger. Here's one of her laughing because she pressed her cold hands under my shirt right when the camera went off. I look ridiculous in open-mouthed shock. She looks radiant.

"Where are you tonight?" I ask the picture. "Are you as near to me as Mauri said?"

Beam? I call out to her but get no answer. So, I wander the small house and do things to get ready for bed—brush my teeth, wash my face —but really, I'm thinking through all the facts. Finally, I lie under the covers and stare at the stars through the skylight. I miss the way they shine in the Badlands. Millions upon millions. But I'm glad to see these all the same.

Beam? Stay strong. We'll get out of this. We always do.

I don't guess she can hear me. Maybe she's able to sleep. I shake my head to clear it. Maybe the drug is still affecting me.

"He was the best man I knew," Bear says.

Olowan watches her husband reminisce about his father as they stand over the grave. It's a good place to be buried. The towering butte overlooks the green prairie. *The buffalo are so plentiful,* she thinks. *Maybe the vision is wrong about their demise.*

"Your father was always kind to me," she says aloud. "Always checked on me after my own father died. He even saged my teepee once after I'd had a bad dream. Did you know it?"

"That same sage blankets his grave," Bear points out. "They must have dug up a mouse hole because once we replaced the dirt, the little varmints returned, dragging sage seeds all over the place, and they took root. It was a great comfort to me."

She smiles softly.

Bear cocks his chin to the side. "*You* told those mice to do that, didn't you?"

"I asked them too," she laughs.

"Wow. That took me a long time to figure out."

"I loved your father. And I loved you. It was difficult to watch you grieve."

Bear plucks some of the sage and rolls it between his hands to release the scent. Drawing near, he presses those warm hands to his wife's cheeks, and once she inhales the earthy scent, he presses them to her belly, now melon-round with their first child.

"We should go, my love," she says. "We'll fall behind."

Bear drops his hands to his sides. "I don't think we should." His words float like an autumn leaf in the breeze. Olowan takes that long to wait for an explanation.

"The messengers from Pilcher said that smallpox journeyed up the river with him. That's where the Tribe has decided to go. It spreads from person to person. We should heed his warning."

"You're not going to abandon your Tribe on the advice of a white man." It's not said with judgment so much as disbelief.

"You weren't there when it consumed the Cree," Bear says. "You didn't enter their camp and hear the suffering or smell the rotting corpses. The plaque has turned the great plain into one open grave. We'll rejoin the Tribe once it has passed." *If any of them are left,* he thinks. "Take me to the cavern where you received the vision, and we'll summer there. You can finish beading your purses, and we'll have the baby where it is safe."

Olowan nods in acceptance and takes Bear's hand as they walk. "I'd like to name her something ever green. Like Laurel. Something that survives the frost and flowers."

"You think it's a girl?"

She nods.

"What will the elders say about us choosing her name?" Bear asks.

"It was given to me in prayer, a sacred name for her quest. She will save us all from second death."

15

THE WILDS

CHAUSIE

It's five thirty am. I've been counting down the minutes till I can go search for Beam. May as well take a quick shower. Turns into a long one. The hot water feels so good, I stand under its soothing pressure long after I'm clean.

I dress in navy and white workout clothes—the expensive kind with stretchy fabric that moves with you. There are new packs of socks, high-end sneakers, and a jacket. Here's the thing: all of them fit me, and make me look the part. Dedicated athlete in his prime. This place was stocked specifically for me, with attention to every detail.

At six am, all at once, the doors and windows unlock themselves with clicks that echo through the cabin. As soon as I hear them I beat a path out the door.

Though the sun has yet to rise, the morning is clear, and a few jovial greetings are being exchanged between two guys who are dressed like me. I follow behind, watching them banter the way I do with my teammates, each assuring the other he will take him down today. Despite being held prisoner here, I'm warmed by the familiar interaction.

And I smell bacon. My stomach argues that Beam will likely be at breakfast. We can find her *and* eat bacon.

It all feels like the first day of basketball camp at a fancy prep school.

The buildings are red brick, bordered by manicured shrubs and ornamental trees. The sidewalks are paved. When I enter through the glass doors, the smell of breakfast hits me in earnest. I'm welcomed by a sweet smile from a woman who is bussing tables, and she nods toward three different lines with hot meals to choose from. Several men—and women, too, but not as many—are chatting as they select breakfast items and walk their trays to various tables. Everyone's clothes match, but I'm gathering that the subtle differences indicate who is an athlete and who is on staff.

It's nothing like a prison. It's cheerful and bright. Laughter bubbles from various areas and no one seems to be unhappy. Almost no one. As I stand in line and scan the room for Beam, my eyes fall upon a solemn figure eating breakfast by himself. He's wearing headphones, and even though his back is turned toward me, I'm pretty sure I recognize him. *Kofi.*

I mentally hurry the folks ahead of me. Maybe Kofi can shed some light on things. Maybe he's seen Beam.

I choose bacon and bacon—and a side of bacon. Also, toast, scrambled eggs with cheese, and fruit. *Damn.* I wish this *was* basketball camp. Then I wouldn't feel so weird about looking forward to this meal. Making a B line for Kofi's section, I find his seat empty. How can he be finished already? That's deflating. Should I go try to find him? Bacon says no. Bacon says he can't leave the compound, so what does it matter? He probably left because he saw me. Bacon makes some excellent points.

I sit where I can keep an eye on the doors. The only other person I recognize is Mauri, an impressive figure in his fitted t-shirt, looking like everyone's favorite coach. He's joking with some of the players—or fighters, I guess. When I catch his eye, he strolls over and takes a seat—casually, like we're friends.

"Too bad you don't like the food here," he teases. I wish I'd already bussed my table. I stack the empty plates to make them less obvious. "Don't be shy," he says. "Go back for more. You'll burn all those calories before noon."

"Where's Beam?"

Mauri checks his watch. "I'm sure she'll be along."

"Are you keeping her from me on purpose?"

Instead of answering, he stands and pats me on the back as he moves to another player—not player. Fighter. The guy seems to have genuine affection for him.

"Chausie Louris?" I look up at the sound of my name. When the woman who called for me sees me respond, she steps over to present a paper to me and then calls off someone else's name. It's today's schedule.

Chausie Louris, The Wilds, 17 yo male, feline shifter
6 - 7 a: Breakfast, Main Cafeteria
7:15 - 9 a: Conditioning, Gym 1 w/Berke
9:15 - 11 a: Skills & Techniques, DOJO w/ Quinn
11:15 - 12:15 p: Lunch, Main Cafeteria
12:30 - ?: Individual Trials, The Jungle w/ Rafe
5 - 7 p: Dinner, Main Cafeteria
8 p - 6 a: Cabins/lights out

"First day?" A freckly fellow with my height and build addresses me from over my shoulder, and I turn to assess him.

"Yeah. You?"

"Nah, I've been here a few weeks now. I'm Miles."

"Chausie." I glance around to see if anyone's eavesdropping. "How'd you end up here?"

"Same as you, I guess. I worked my tail off. I live and breathe martial arts."

"But, I mean, how did they trap you?"

"Trap me?" Miles laughs and shakes his head. "Took me three years to get accepted. That guy over there?" He points to a bulky-looking twenty-something. "Took him four! And he's already ranked."

Is this guy gaslighting me?

"Ranked in what?" I can't get any scent off of him other than human.

"He's UFC," he says. "I'm PFL, but I may be trading."

I know that UFC stands for Ultimate Fighting Championship. "What's PFL?"

Miles cocks his head to make sure I'm not messing with him. "Professional Fighters League? Dude, what are you even doing here?" He jerks my schedule from my grasp and peruses it with a drawn-out, "*Oooooo.* You're one of the Wilds. Feline? What kind? Lion?"

"Mountain lion."

"Oh." Is he disappointed now? "They got a *real* lion too."

"Would you like for me to prove to you how real of a lion I am?" I ask.

"Sorry. I meant a lion with the—" He draws an imaginary mane around his face.

"I know what you meant."

Miles concentrates on the schedule again. "You have Rafe this afternoon." I'm not sure how dramatic a fellow he is, but the way he says it sounds ominous. "Let me know how that goes. He is one scary weirdo."

Doesn't matter. Because as soon as I see Beam, I'm gonna find a way out of here.

Outside, I do not see Beam, but I do catch a whiff of her sage and prairie flower scent, just a hint. I let my nose lead me back to the cabins, where I peek into each one in turn. Strangely, none of them smell of her. Maybe I'm losing my mind. Each cabin has a long window where I lean in and cup my hands to cut down on the glare. I guess it's good everyone's out by six. Otherwise, I'd be labeled a peeping—

"*Yeow!*" I jump a few inches off the ground without meaning to— catty reflexes. I hadn't heard the wild-eyed monster of a man sidle up to me. How did he get that close?

The man sniffs me, and hardens his glare. Now, *this* is the type of man who joins a *fight club.* He's the MMA's ideal poster child, intimidating as hell as he towers over me without speaking.

I can't figure out what kind of shifter he is, but I smell it all over him. Honestly, he seems more animal than man. Maybe his natural state is the animal and being human is just the form he shifts into. He takes another whiff of me.

Our uneasy standoff grows uncomfortably long, two predators eyeing each other in motionless silence. *Are we gonna do this? I don't need any enemies here.* I choose the high road—or at least the one where I get to avoid immense pain—backing to the sidewalk slowly with a deepening sense of dread. He watches me all the way, cocking his head side to side like a paranoid bird.

I can still feel his eyes on me as I force myself to walk away. It's all I can do not to look back. Thankfully, I get swept up in a wave of guys who are going my way. "Are you in Berke's session?" one of them asks.

"*Uh*...yeah." I clumsily consult my schedule. "Gym One."

"Us too." He continues to talk, and by the time we arrive, I'm able to think of other things, like how the gargantuan room called Gym One is every athlete's dream. First of all, more than half of it is a playground. It's like parkour meets CrossFit meets trampoline party space. Bars and platforms, hazards, moving obstacles. For a second, I'm giddy. I want to jump in so bad! There are trapezes, huge thick mats, climbing walls—and traditional fitness tools too, like free weights and cardio machines.

What the heck is in Gym *Two?* Why would you even need another? "Who *funds* this place?" I ask without meaning to.

"We do," one of the guys says to me. "When we win." He flashes his eyebrows, and then our trainer claps three times. She's a woman in her thirties, I'd say, as fit as anyone here. Her thighs could snap me in two. Her biceps, shoulders—I'm dying to ask what she lifts. Besides her muscles, she has a strong demeanor. Confident, cool, yet friendly.

"Good morning, Fight Club."

"Good morning, Coach Berke," everyone says in unison.

"I hope you got your rest last night because today we go big."

A few of the guys cheer at the statement. One does not—Kofi—who stands apart from the rest of us, reminding me of the Grinch. I try to catch his eye. I wave, first with one hand, then both, but he's fixed on the trainer.

When the room goes silent, I look up to find everyone watching me waving like a lunatic. "First day?" the trainer asks. I nod, cheeks hot with embarrassment. "What's your name?"

"Chausie."

She flips through some papers while Kofi zeroes in on me. He almost seems interested—you know, in an *I'm interested in squashing you* sort of way.

"Chausie," the trainer repeats and comes up with a paper which I assume has information about me. She scans it from top to bottom. "Got it."

What she has *got,* I don't know, but she looks me over. "Thank you for your attention, Chausie. I'm Berke. I can send you home no questions asked."

Is that supposed to be a threat or an enticement? She must know that some of us are here against our will, right?

"Half of you come with me. The other half can attempt the course." Several of the guys run for the course with *whoops.* "Chausie?" Berke says. "This way."

While Berk explains which activities we're going to do, I watch Kofi destroy the course. He's not only strong. He's agile. He may be Spiderman.

"Chausie, do you have a crush on that guy?" Berke asks and the others laugh out loud. "It's OK if you do. It just can't interfere with my time. Do you want to be here or not?"

I study her dark brown eyes and say, "Do you know how he and I came to be here?" I point across the room at Kofi, who is starting the whole course again while most of the other athletes are falling into pits of spongy cubes.

"How's that?" she asks.

"We were bought."

"You must be good, then," she says. "Most are not lucky enough to sell their contract to Mauri."

"No contract," I say meaningfully. "I was bought. Kidnapped and then *purchased* from my captor. Kofi too."

When Berke realizes what I'm saying, she barks at the others, "What are you waiting for? Get to work," and pulls me aside. "That is quite an accusation."

I think she genuinely has no clue, but I jump on the chance to make her question it. "Did you know they lock us in our cabins at night? Why would they do that?"

"*Uh,* because you're a bunch of young, arrogant yahoos who are a danger to yourselves in packs."

She has a point. "OK, but look around. Why are armed guards stationed along the whole compound's perimeter?"

I think she has wondered this before, maybe has even questioned it. Her answer seems rote. "Whenever this much money is on the line, protections have to be in place. Our competitors would love to spy on our methods."

"Enough to break in?" I ask.

She's too entrenched. She believes what they tell her. I don't want to lose her as a potential ally by pushing too hard.

"Chausie, do you have any idea what most athletes would give to be where you are right now? You're new here, so let me save you some trouble. This is your shot at the big time. Now, get to work."

I don't think Berke is part of the trafficking. Not knowingly. I decide to do what I'm supposed to do so that I can stay in her good graces. I set up my weights, and very gently, I say, "I don't think you're complicit in what happens here, so I beg you not to turn a blind eye."

I guess I'm fortunate that Berke doesn't have a fragile ego. She hears me without reacting one way or another. But throughout the rest of the session, I catch her watching me, and a few times, she looks downright disturbed. Maybe she has her suspicions.

Despite all of this, I enjoy the workout very much, along with most of my fellow athletes. The parkour is the most fun I've ever had in training. It's probably not fair to all the normal guys that I retain some of my lion abilities while in human form. I'm going to be sore tomorrow—or, wait. I won't. My muscles will heal as fast as any other part of me.

At the end of our time, I help Berke collect the equipment just so I can keep talking to her. "How did you end up on staff here?" I ask.

"Mauri approached me when I retired from the circuit."

"You're a fighter?"

"She's a three-time UFC Featherweight champion. Undefeated." This from a guy who just benched three hundred plus.

"No kidding," I say to Berke. Even I know that makes her a badass.

"Got the belts to prove it," she says.

"When I get one of those enormous things, I'm gonna wear it all the time," the guy vows. "Will I ever get to fight you, Berke?"

"You better hope not, Copelan." She slaps him up the back of the head.

When he's out of earshot, she says to me, "You *can* leave here if you want to." It's almost a question. It's kind of a prayer.

"Can I?"

She's processing things, I can tell. I'm supposed to get to my next session in the dojo. But I take another chance. "I think Mauri bought my girlfriend too but he won't let me see her. I keep catching her scent, but I can't find her, and I'm an excellent tracker, Berke."

"Black panther?" she practically whispers.

"Have you seen her?" I'm working to keep my voice down and leaning forward with the urgency I feel.

She gestures somebody out the door when he appears to want to join us. "I heard we'd acquired one," she says. "This whole paranormal arena is new to me. New to all of us. I'll keep an eye out."

"Thanks."

As I turn to go, she says, "Hey, we should keep this between us. If something is going on—and I'm not saying that it is—these are rich, powerful people with connections. Got me?"

"I got you. But you have to know that even if they allow me to leave, I can't—not without Beam. I'll do whatever it takes to find her."

I'm relieved to have someone take me seriously. Someone who can walk out of here whenever she wants to. "Hey, can you use your phone here? Could you call the Atlanta PD? Sergeant Aiden Gunnolf is looking for me." She starts to protest, so I walk it back. "I'm not saying you believe me. But don't you want to err on the side of caution?"

With that, I drop it. I don't want her to block me. She has a lot to lose and no reason to trust me. I decide to follow the schedule. It allows me to check out the campus without raising suspicion.

Guess who is in my next session. Kofi. It takes place in the dojo, an uncluttered, minimalist hall with wooden walls around a white mat floor. *Skills and Techniques.* It occurs to me that fighting was never part of my training at The Outpost, not in any formal martial arts capacity. Now that I think about it, it seems to be an oversight. Why aren't we trained both ways? I mean, we learn to shoot. We learn some self-defense and how to take someone down to cuff them. But as I watch some of these lifelong fighters warming up with each other, I'm pretty sure I'm in over my head—unless I'm allowed to become a lion against them. But I'd end up clawing the mat to pieces.

"Kofi, I—" Before I get the words out, Kofi blasts me with a fist to the stomach. "What the *hell*, man?" I choke through gasps that force air back into my lungs.

He's no longer paying attention to me.

"I did not abandon you," I point out. I'd like to claw the obnoxious, surly attitude off his face—even if he did wipe the mat with me in return.

"Funny," he says. "I don't remember you being around when I was being bid on."

"I sent the police for you. They got there too late. I'm here now because I kept looking for you and got caught."

He puffs out a mirthless laugh.

"Look, let's stick together, and we'll get out of this," I say.

"What makes you think I want out of this? They paid twenty million dollars for me. This is my golden ticket."

I don't tell him that's double what they paid for me. Instead, I say, "Nobody wants to be a slave."

"Save it. Mauri offered me a contract—offered to train me, act as my agent, and then I get to make my own money. So, here's fair warning. I'm going to ruin everyone standing in my path to the top. It's nothing personal."

"No, of course not. Dude, I just want to get my girlfriend and get out of here."

"Your girlfriend's here?" Kofi looks around for her. "Which one is she?" I kind of wish I hadn't said anything.

"She's not in *here*," I say. "What's your long-term plan?"

"Put in enough effort to become champion a few times over and move to some sun-drenched island to retire."

"And how long will that take?"

"I don't know. Five years? And then I'll be free for good."

A new trainer calls us to order. His name is Quinn, but most of the guys call him *Sensei*, and we bow to him as we begin. When asked to partner up to practice the moves, Kofi quickly chooses me and proceeds to throttle me repeatedly. *Sensei* does nothing to help. Once, he even laughs outright. I suck at this. Give me a street fight—fists and grit—and I can hold my own. But all these fancy moves make me look like a fool. Quinn finds my information sheet as Berke had, and he gives me a surprised once over.

"Wilds?" he asks.

"That's what they tell me." I lick the corner of my busted lip to confirm that it's bleeding.

"Well, you won't need to know this kind of fighting, so don't take it too bad."

I limp out, swollen and bruised, but I enter the cafeteria completely well. Kofi does a double-take. When I come to sit with him, he abandons his lunch and stalks out. "You're sort of an asshole," I call after him and find some friendlier sorts to sit with.

While they chat, I try to gauge who is there of their own free will. All of them. All of them are super proud to have won a spot in this elite group of fighters. They tell me that ninety-nine percent of us won't last through the end of the month. I hope that means that the ninety-nine get to go home and not that their lives end.

Toward the end of lunch, I ask if anyone has the next session in the Jungle—and it's like I declared that I had successfully poisoned the food they just ate. Everyone at the table falls silent. Finally, one of them says, "You have to go to the Jungle?"

This gives me pause.

"Aw, man. I'm sorry," another says.

"What is it?" I ask. "You were all privy to the smackdown in the dojo. What's so much worse about the Jungle?"

"The *sounds* that come from there…"

"Yeah, we don't ever see those guys again. It's like they get fed to something."

Are they aware that we're shifters? Wild animals make wild noises. But their fear of the place puts me on edge. What if Beam has already been subjected to something awful?

"Just point me in the right direction," I say.

"Follow the path past the dojo,. You'll see Mauri's mansion, and it's the next road after that. None of us are allowed beyond. Not till we get to watch the inaugural event."

They're picking up their things and getting ready to leave. After we deposit the dishes onto the cleaning rack, Berke waves me over. "The black panther arrived yesterday several hours ahead of you. She was placed in cabin five."

I shake my head. "She's not there. I checked, and the scent's not strong enough."

After a quick frown of confusion, Berke makes an *Oh* sound.

"Yeah, my sense of smell... Anyway, I think Mauri moved her so that I wouldn't get to be with her. Do you see what I mean now? He's manipulating us."

"It's not the same thing as holding either one of you captive. I'm sure Mauri has his reasons. What's your next session?"

"Individual Trials in the Jungle."

"Already? With whom?" I wish she didn't sound alarmed.

"Rafe."

Berke's face remains impassive, but she swallows. "OK, well, I guess they want everything in order by Friday."

"What's going on then? What is the Wilds?" I ask.

"It's a new fight club devoted to athletes like you. Shifters aren't knowingly allowed in most fight clubs for obvious reasons. Unfair advantage. I mean, think of it." She waves around. "None of the guys in here could hold their own against that kind of thing. I mean, Kofi could, obviously."

"Obviously," I agree flatly. "What should I expect from Rafe?"

"From what I hear, the Jungle is just parkour in the wild, and you did great with that in human form. I wish I could come watch."

"Could you?" I latch on to that as if my life depended on it. Maybe it does.

She shakes her head. "I have a session."

"That's regrettable. You told me what to expect of the Jungle but not of Rafe."

She lowers her voice. "He's an unknown quantity. Just arrived. But he's supposed to size you up. Push you to your limit. Reveal your strengths—" She bites back the rest of the thought.

"And weaknesses?" I intuit. She gives a small nod.

"Do you know *what* he is, Berke? Some kind of shifter?"

"I'm not privy to that information. He's odd. Keeps to himself. But I'll tell you what I'd tell any of my guys. Keep your head on a swivel and all five senses sharp. And know this: You possess strengths that he does not."

"What, exactly?" I think she's trying to encourage me with a platitude about how everyone has their talents, but she lists specific traits. "Subtlety. Precision. A cool head under pressure."

She's not wrong. It's why Coach ran me at Point so often. I see the whole court at once, and I can knock down a shot from nearly anywhere. "You know this from one morning's session?" I ask.

"It's my job to know." She winks at me.

"If I'm forced to fight, will you be my coach?"

"Sure. If I'm allowed to. I admit that I've been studying animal tactics since I heard about the Wilds. You're a cougar, right?"

I nod.

"Cougars hold their own. And I heard from Quinn that you can take quite a beating." She says the last while trying to keep her face straight. "He's hard to impress."

I roll my eyes.

"Seriously, though, he thought it was admirable that you kept it together without shifting. I'll be your coach."

"Thanks, Berke." I start to walk, but she holds me back. "One last thing." Maybe she doesn't know if she should say what's on her mind. "I don't know if it was your girlfriend, but I saw a young woman riding with Mauri this morning. Black hair. Brown skin."

"Yeah, that's Beam. Was she OK?"

"She appeared to be."

"Where were they headed?"

Berke hesitates. "Toward the Jungle."

16
LEANDER'S PELT

BEAM

Thump! At first, the sound is in my dream. I'm trying to make sense of it subconsciously. The night has been dark and quiet and surprisingly comfortable. Yes, I am locked in this tiny, little cabin all by myself, but thankfully, the rest of the world is locked out, so I feel pretty safe.

The thump comes from above me, and since my bed is up in the loft, that only leaves a slanted roof above. Is it windy out? Was that a tree branch that fell?

I raise sleepy eyes to the skylight and come fully awake. What the *heck* is that thing staring down at me?! Kicking to a seated position, I pull the thick comforter to my neck. The creature leans forward to follow my movement. I have no clear categories for identifying it. Its penetrating eyes stare down from furry ocular orbits. It's vulture-like, but it's wolfy too.

Finally, its head rolls out of the frame and I hear it gallop across the roof—the sound is *thump, thump, thump,* gone. I race to the window to search the sky. Did it *soar* away? I scan the ground. It had better not be clinging to the wall outside this window where my face is pressed. I pull back into the room.

Well, I no longer want to fall back to sleep. I may never want to sleep again. Another horrifying jolt to my nerves occurs when all the locks in the house click simultaneously. I had been warned that these would trigger at six o'clock, but I was still unprepared. The clock on the bedside table reads six twenty-seven.

Before I can assimilate what's going on, there's a knock at the door, and I crouch down. No one is looking in through the glass, but I can see —from peeking around the dresser—that the visitor is fully human and not that unnatural bird/wolf thing. It's Mauri. After another knock, he lets himself in, and I rise to my feet.

"Good morning, Beam," he says when he spots me.

"Close the door," I hiss at him, and he does so with a curious lift of his brow.

"Lock it!"

"What's the matter with you?"

"There was a monster staring down at me through the skylight." I point up to where it had been and shuffle out of the line of sight it would have if it were still there.

Mauri appraises me with a look of concern.

"Why were the locks late in opening?" I ask.

"I staggered them so I could meet with you." Mauri's mouth quirks into a forced smile. "Dress quickly and come with me. I'll wait outside."

I almost ask him to stay while I dress. That's how shaken up I am from waking up to the vulture goon. I'm used to seeing strange creatures, and I don't usually feel the primal sense of terror that this one evoked, but it was far too interested in me.

Mauri must sense my hesitation. He says, "You'll be fine. Do as I say, and we'll talk on the way." He ducks out.

I have a bad feeling. I huff out a breath and quickly ready myself, making sure that my catcher hangs at my heart inside the little purse. Larkin's toe ring is in there too—an instant escape, should I need it.

As an afterthought, I feel for Frilk's collar. Yes, I am taking solace in the fact that a maniacal goblin can show up here to reclaim me. No doubt, he stayed up all night testing my blood in his tree basement lab. He'll need more before too long. He won't like it if these people allow something to end me.

I twist the front door's knob, but it's locked again. Mauri, who is standing on the porch, surveys the grounds before he lets me out. "There. You look very sporty now."

"I look like everyone else," I say. These are nice workout clothes, far superior to others I've worn. Dress for success, I guess.

Mauri escorts me up a few concrete stairs that lead from each cabin to the main path. The speed with which we move gives me the feeling that he doesn't want to be in the open any more than I do.

"Step in." He motions to a golf cart parked on the sidewalk and walks around to the driver's side to start it up.

"Aren't we going to breakfast?" I ask when we go in the opposite direction.

Last night, I ate in a cafeteria with a bunch of happy athletes who then meandered out to play pick-up games—soccer, basketball, volleyball... I was invited to participate, but I didn't want anyone to question my lack of athletic prowess. Anyway, I was keeping an eye out for Chausie.

"We'll brunch in my private residence, and I'd like for you to stay there with me from now on."

With an uncomfortable shiver, I consider bolting. I'm not ready to be someone's slave housekeeper—or worse—their slave in more degrading ways.

"Look," I tell him, "I don't know why you brought me here. Everyone else seems to be a gifted athlete. Since I'm not, I can only imagine that you want me to a) play an entertaining victim in the ring or b) become a pretty taxidermied mascot. Or c) I guess would be both. But I am not about to be some slave for your...private pleasure."

He looks taken aback. "That hadn't crossed my mind. What kind of person do you think I am?"

"The kind who *buys* people."

"No, I just want to keep you separate for a bit. I think it will help to motivate the others."

"How?"

"Don't frown so hard," he says. "It's nothing perverse."

"This whole thing is perverse."

We drive past buildings with doors open wide. They appear to be workout rooms. At the entrance to one of these, a woman waves hello, and Mauri waves back, calling good morning.

"One of our trainers," he says to me. "For the mixed martial arts fighters. Your class ushers in a brand new league—new players, new rules. We've developed a more appropriate place for your kind to train, though I'm sure you'll work with Berke some too."

I glance over my shoulder to find *Berke* watching us drive away.

"Who all is complicit in this kidnapping scheme?" I ask Mauri.

"What on Earth do you mean? Everyone here is living the dream. Don't you want to live out your purpose? Don't you want to find out what you're made of?"

"I already know what I'm made of. I want to go back home to my parents."

"Give it some time and see how you like it. There. That's my home." He doesn't need to specify. About a half-mile down a straight lane is an enormous white mansion whose portico is set with six huge pillars. The overarching triangular pediment reminds me of the Parthenon in Greece. I haven't been, but I have studied classical architecture. It's also like the White House. I wonder which one Mauri fancies himself: a Greek god or the ruler of the free world?

"Does it have a name?" I ask. Mauri shakes his head as I gape. "It should have a name," I decide.

The straight lane runs right down the middle of the front lawn—or should I call it a vast plain? It ends at the front door, and it's large enough for a truck. It's bordered by austere bushes and symmetrical gardens which spread on either side. They are truly lovely. The lush vegetation continues around the mansion. I can't tell what else is behind. It's not open space. It's more like a sudden jungle butting up to the back of the house. There's an iron fence back there as tall as the house itself—which is maybe four stories. Now that we're closer, I can see that the pediment is a frieze depicting men and women fighting valiantly, only this isn't the cavalry of ancient Greece. The figures are a modern celebration of hand-to-hand combat. In the middle of it, though, is the head of a triumphant lion with his wild, shaggy mane flowing around the rest of the fighters.

We park in front and climb the steps of—"Corinthia," I say aloud.

Mauri halts with a thoughtful frown on his face as he gazes at his bronze front doors—yes, bronze. A colossal light fixture hangs from the roof and highlights the shiny metal. "I like that name. You know your classical styles then. I can't wait to show you my pottery collection."

The tops of the columns are not carved with the typical leaves and flourishes, but with lion paws and faces snarling down.

"It's not—" I begin. Along with the course in architecture, there was a tandem course in Greco-Roman art. "It's not actual Corinthian pottery, right?"

"It most certainly is," Mauri says. "I only procure the authentic." Before we enter, Mauri gives me some time to absorb the details. I think he appreciates my interest. Once he swings open one of the bronze doors—tall enough for giants—I am again blown away, this time by the larger-than-life, 3D sculptures of what I assume to be Greek gods wrestling one another. They're three times the size of normal human beings, and there is still plenty of room for them. The ceiling is that high, and the foyer that round.

"Zeus and Kronos?" I guess.

"Come to the other side."

As we round the sculpture, one of the opponents is revealed to be a great, vicious lion. What a fantastic illusion! "Heracles," I say. "And the Lion of Nemea." After several minutes, in which I round the sculpture astonished, my eyes trail to an animal pelt hanging in the archway to the next room, golden and orange like blazing, furry fire. I've never seen the size of the lion that could have worn it. Its heavy paws hang from the arms, and its massive mane is tangled around saber-tooth fangs and scowling brown marble eyes.

"Where did you get such a thing?" I whisper.

"To the victor go the spoils," Mauri says.

"It's just a myth," I say, remembering how Heracles was awarded the lion's skin when he killed it.

We're staring up, side by side. "Mythical like shifters?" Mauri asks. "And yet, here you are in my parlor. And standing beneath your ancestor's invincible hide."

"Ancestor," I repeat, finally able to take my eyes off the extraordinary pelt.

"Leo," he says as if it's obvious. "The Nemean Lion. The great king of the August sky."

"You mean the constellation."

"I do."

"Not my ancestor," I say while trying to work out what all this means for Chausie. A real Leonid. Is he descended from the Lion of Nemea? Is that character even real?

Mauri moves further into the house where there is a library with wall-to-wall shelves so high, that ladders have been installed on tracks. I could move the length and the height of all the books on those things. If I were not a prisoner here... If I were free to come and go, I would add this place to the list of my must-visit-with-regularity sites.

"And here is the pottery," Mauri says. Truly authentic pieces—some from as far back as six hundred BC. All of them boast scenes of splendid lions preening, roaring, sitting in regal nonchalance, and eating helpless human beings in arenas.

"Generally," I say to Mauri as I return a priceless water pitcher to its showcase under a light, "I would consider this rude to ask, but since you purchased me like an animal—"

"You *are* an animal. Are you not?" Mauri asks it like it's a friendly joke.

I ignore this. "What do you do to have so much money? These artifacts are unattainable."

"I buy when the market is cold. I sell when the market is hot. I find ways to create wealth where others cannot. And I never lose my fights."

"To the victor go the spoils," I repeat.

"And to their children," Mauri admits. "There's something to be said for generational wealth."

I side-eye him.

"No," he assures me with a grin. "Heracles is not in my family line. Not as far as I know."

Mauri leads me up a curving staircase and gives me a choice of bedrooms. All three are fabulous, but one has a double window with a better view of what is growing in the back. It's not haphazard overgrowth that Mauri hasn't gotten to. Of course, it's not. Why spare the expense of landscaping in the back? There are wide, sprawling oak trees whose branches seem to me like balance beams, and I realize that it must be my new feline self, but I am itching to run along their broad expanses and leap from one to the other.

"It's something, isn't it?" Mauri asks. "It's the reason we chose this location. We call it the Jungle."

"It's like a playground."

"Oh, do I detect a hint of desire in your voice?" He looks at his watch. "Don't go out there without my permission, OK? It's not a playground. It's a battleground. We'll get you out there soon enough."

Hmm. Whether or not it's a battleground depends on who's out there, right? I study the area. There is one main open space like an arena, but dense vegetation around it. I can't see the other side. I imagine there are holes and levels in which to hide—or to lie in wait.

"I have to tend to something," Mauri says. "I'll be back for brunch. If you can't wait, feel free to raid the kitchen. Robyn, the cook, will be preparing things. She can help you."

After Mauri leaves, I look around the room and find myself drawn back to the view of the Jungle, where I get the bristly feeling that something is watching me from out there. Then, quick and heavy as a boulder, a dark brown figure dives for me and swings itself onto the wall of the house. Maybe it's clinging to the shutter. It's the monster I'd seen earlier, with its scary, deep-set, vulture eyes and its penetrating interest. Though there is a fence and a window between us, I feel extremely vulnerable. The creature leans closer to sniff me. Surely, it can't smell me through the window. I drop my eyes. Then I slide myself into the corner where it won't be able to see me. Still, it tries. It moves its awkward bird-like and yet lupine body and cocks its grotesque head. I watch its shadow on the floor.

Chausie? I ask. *Are you here? We have to go.*

Should I tell Mauri that the monster is not contained in his Jungle? Or is that what Mauri went to tend to?

I crawl below the window, and I snake out of the bedroom. I will not be sleeping there. That is not happening. I will also not be trying to let myself out the door. What would that thing do to me? What are we doing here?!

When I get to the bottom of the stairs, someone is coming through a side door and I yelp. The small woman locates me and says something in a language I don't understand. But it sounds kind. She's a pretty little thing, not to sound condescending. She is actually small, and now I notice her pointy ears.

"Did Larkin send you?" I ask with a hopeful hop from the stairs in her direction.

"I don't know Larkin," she says in English. "I'm Robyn. The cook."

"Robyn, are we safe here? There is something outside, something horrible."

"He is a poor wretch. He cannot help himself. But we are safe. We live under the cloak." Robyn points upward, and I know before I look. The Lion of Nemea.

"Well, it didn't help him much, now did it?" I mutter. "Wait. You live here?"

"Oh, yes, I feed Mr. Mauri and Ms. Sasha too when she is in town."

"Ms. Sasha?"

"His wife. Are you one of the fighters? You don't look much muscle-bound."

That makes me smile. "No, I'm not much. I'm to be part of the Wilds program, but I'm not much of a fighter. I just want to go home."

I don't think she hears the last part of what I've said. She has clapped her hands delightedly. "You are an animal? What kind? Show me—no, let me guess." And now Robyn, the small woman who must be the same thing as Larkin, circles me, humming *mmhmm, mmhmm* every few seconds. "Not a bird. Not a horse. Not a dog. You must be feline. No?"

I nod my head and she claps once more. "Will you show me? I've never known a Leonid before. And that really does put you under his protection."

"Mauri's?" I ask.

"Leander's." She indicates the lion pelt again.

"I thought his name was Leo."

"Oh, that's what the Romans call him, but not me."

With a bit of bashfulness, I think about how to shift, and I become my panther self. "Oh," Robyn erupts. "So beautiful. Simply exquisite." She holds my cheeks in a maternal burst of affection and gazes into my eyes. "Those big blues. Oh, girl, what a creature you are."

"Thank you, Robyn," I say and realize that I am speaking to her in cat language, and it is because that is how she is speaking to me.

"Not a Leonid, though? 'ts OK. He protects you anyway."

Something bizarre happens next. I lift my head to see the Nemean Lion's skin rustle against the wall, and I swear it winks one of its marble eyes at me.

"Oh, he likes you." Robyn wags her finger up at the pelt. "You naughty kitty cat! You big flirt!"

I swear to you, the thing chuckles when she pretends to reprimand it.

"I have a friend like you," I tell Robyn after I become human again. "She can speak to animals, and she's a good cook. She charms everyone around. How did you animate *him?*"

"Oh, he loves to chat, the big pussy cat. Your friend, Larkin...she is a —" Whatever word Robyn uses, I immediately forget as if I haven't even heard the sound of her speaking.

Robyn smiles softly and searches for a different way to describe what she is. "An animal enchanter. A *faerie* is probably as close of a word as you might know."

"Yes," I say. "She's like you, with the pretty ears and everything."

Robyn throws her hand forward to dismiss my compliment.

"She has a clutch of five eggs," I tell her. "They were stolen by a goblin—the same goblin who sold me to Mauri—but we got them back. Do you work here because you want to? Or are you forced to?"

Robyn shows more amazement with every phrase I utter. "I am free," she all but whispers. "But I stay because the Lion stays."

And now the Lion of Nimea is making a sound much like purring. This is beyond odd.

The front door opens and Mauri reenters.

"Good morning Mr. Mauri. Still brunching at ten-thirty? I'm about to set it out."

"Yes, please, Robyn. You've met Beam?"

"Yes. She was concerned about the monster you keep."

"The Lion of Nemea?" he asks.

"No," I say. "The one who was staring through my skylight this morning. He was at the bedroom window right after you left."

It's possible that this bit of news is not welcome to Mauri, but he says, "That's where I've been just now—to speak to Rafe. You won't see him again unless it's in the Jungle."

"Are you telling me that that creature is something I'm supposed to fight? Do you understand that I am not a fighter and it will kill me?"

"Come now, aren't all lions natural-born predators?"

"Maybe when they're naturally born," I mutter.

"What was that?"

"Nothing."

"Well, I think you're being dishonest. I heard that you've fought several times. I heard that you and your partner haven't lost a single match."

I know he means Chausie, and I get a sweet sense of relief that Chausie has been making it sound like we fight together—which we do, but not in the way that Mauri is thinking.

"Where is he? Can I see him?"

"So, you do have a partner."

"What are you playing at?" I ask him. "Yes. Chausie's my partner. Put us together."

"Easy," he says like he's talking to a spooked horse. "You'll see him soon enough."

I do not enjoy being treated like a horse. I am a smart, rational person whose passion is a helpful component of the whole. I'm not ruled by emotion. Nor am I hysterical. But I do feel my hackles rising, even in human form. "Have you been keeping us separated on purpose?" I ask. "Is that why the locks didn't open on time? Is that why you're holding me here at your home—because Chausie told you we were partners?"

Before he can answer, I spout, "You said before that you wanted to use me to motivate the others. I am *not* bait. I am not going to act the way you think I'm going to act. And neither is Chausie."

"I don't have any preconceived notions of how any of you are going to act. I don't know you, and I've never watched shifters fight. That's why we're going to test all of you separately over the next few days. Now, come. Let's brunch. Who else gets to enjoy my hospitality like you do?"

Robyn has been busy setting a long buffet with brunch foods. Thick bagels, guacamole, sushi-grade salmon, cream cheese, capers. I do like cream cheese and capers. Mauri pours coffee into a fragile-looking cup and tells me he'll set it in the conservatory for me—a bright, large sunroom with windows all around and even overhead. You guessed it. It overlooks the Jungle. It's like the rich people's glassed-in boxes over the sports arena.

After I dress two halves of a bagel, Mauri offers a selection of wicker chairs around a glass table, and we dine among a host of palm plants, orchids, blooming vines, and other plants that smell like lemonade. "Who's the plant lover?" I ask.

Mauri is happy to change the subject. "My wife and I both enjoy gardening," he says lightly. "But she has a degree in it. She's a beekeeper too. Works at the Atlanta Botanical Gardens."

"Is that where she is now?" I ask.

"Our main house is in Atlanta, and she lives there during the week, but she'll come tomorrow when we unveil the Wilds with a reception. We were lucky to have found you when we did! All of the coaches and athletes, as well as investors and honored guests, will come to meet our shifters and receive a demonstration of what you do."

"What I can do," I assure him around a bite of bagel, "as far as athletics will be underwhelming."

Maybe he thinks I'm being humble when I say I'm not a fighter, but he'll know the truth when I am attacked by some savage animal for sport, and I die in front of everyone—but I won't die, will I? *Oh, no.* I'll be recirculated into the fights to be tortured for a new kind of enjoyment. The freak who self-heals. I finger Larkin's ring from the outside of the purse.

"What is that?"

"Nothing," I say. "It's nothing." But he's not talking about the ring.

"The delicate, metal necklace you wear. May I?"

I don't want to discuss that either, but I sit still while Mauri runs a finger between the collar and my skin. "Will you take it off so that I can examine it?"

"I can't," I say. "Frilk put it on me."

After a pause, he says, "Is it a collar?"

I make a noncommittal shrug.

"What is it made of?"

If Mauri starts digging, he may figure it out. He has a whole lot of resources at his disposal.

"It's nothing special," I tell him.

"Then remove it, or—I'll saw it off."

"Won't work. I've tried."

"Well, I don't want you to wear it. Frilk doesn't own you anymore."

I raise my palms to let him know I can't solve the problem. "You know, no one should own a human being," I remind him.

"Well, you're not really a human being, are you?" He seems to have talked himself into this fact.

For the next several minutes, much as Chausie's mom had done, Mauri employs all kinds of things to break the collar off of my neck. None of them make my neck feel great, and none of them work.

I told you.

"This is infuriating. I'm going to demand Frilk remove it." Mauri slumps into his chair. "Except I don't want him inside the compound."

That's ironic since the collar is his personal portal here.

Mauri combs his hair with his fingers and composes himself. "Ah, well, it can wait. At least it's pretty."

Just then a large beast with a mass of grey and black fur is slammed against the window, and I jump to my feet as it hits the ground and races away. "What was that?!" I ask as it disappears back into the undergrowth.

Mauri is unperturbed. "Oh, just one of the jungle creatures," he says with a self-satisfied grin.

"You have jungle creatures?" I ask.

"Is that sarcasm?" When I fix him with a very confused and disgruntled look, he returns one that says, *Seriously?*

"You may not have been born in a jungle, but you belong to it all the same. You have the jungle...*weapons*." He motions to me as a whole as if I'm wearing teeth and claws right now.

I'm still clutching my chest where my heart is pounding. I need books. My real weapons are logic and knowledge. I don't even know what category a black panther belongs to.

"You act like you only became a big cat yesterday," Mauri remarks.

My expression must tell him the truth—I *did*.

This gives him pause, but then he dismisses it with a chuckle. "You're a jokester."

A shocking earthquake of sound goes up. I don't know what to call it. Some kind of screech that rattles this sturdy home and offends the delicate coffee cups—not to mention my constitution. I've only just recovered from the other scare, and now I grip the thick arms of my chair till my fingers hurt. "Was THAT one of your jungle creatures?!"

"No. No, that's Rafe." Mauri isn't nearly as self-assured. The sound set his teeth on edge too. I guess Rafe is what sent the first animal hurtling into the glass and then running for its life.

"What *is* Rafe?" I ask.

"I'm not entirely sure."

"And you trust him to be in your *yard?!*"

Mauri is watching out the windows now, and since it's *all* windows, he has a panoramic view—not to mention the wall of glass for a roof.

"This is thirty-one-millimeter laminate." He gestures toward the windows. "It can withstand a riot."

So, Mauri has created a jungle and acquired animal shifters to fight in it. "Is Chausie out there?!" I blurt out.

"Not yet. His trials are after lunch"

"Trials?" Now I'm starting to get mad. I slash my arm out to point. "Is that what *that* animal is doing? The one whose fur I can still see stuck to the window?"

"Yes, that is likely what is happening."

"Let us out of here! We're not giving credence to your psychotic imaginings. We won't be part of some delusional fight club zoo. We have to finish high school!" I know, but I do worry about the latter. Not finishing is right up there with death for me. Until a few weeks ago, I was on my way to being valedictorian. Now, that stupid Peter Mallory's going to get it. "When does Chausie's trial begin?" I spit. "I want to be with him."

Mauri's mouth bunches to the side. "*Hm...* I'll consider it."

A knock on the door has him frowning as he checks to see if the radio on his hip is working with a click and a *ckshhh* sound. When he rises to answer, I position myself to see who it is. A woman's voice says, "Sorry to disturb you, Mauri. I thought I should check in personally. I know the success of the Wilds is important to you."

I saw this woman on the drive over. She's one of the trainers. Her name started with a B.

"Not at all, Berke. Come in. Would you care for some coffee? Tea?" He gestures her inside. She says, "Well, I thought I might have a word with you about—" She spots me, and her sentence stalls. "I can come back when you're not busy."

"No, please. Join us." He guides her to the buffet and invites her to indulge.

"Some coffee would be great," she says and as he pours, she stares at me with what I define as a mixture of curiosity and concern.

"Here you are." Mauri brings the coffee and leads the visitor into the conservatory.

"I'm Berke," she says to me. "I haven't seen you around."

"I was kidnapped—" I begin, but Mauri cuts over me. "Beam arrived yesterday." He lays a heavy hand on my shoulder, and I shut my mouth. I don't want to get locked away in the room where the monster wants to stare at me. As soon as I see Chausie, I'm going to grab him and pray that the ring will whisk us both out of here.

"Oh, well, welcome," Berke says with some confusion. "What kind of fighting have you done that landed you in this fine facility?"

"None," I say flatly, and Mauri, whose hand is still on my shoulder, gives a squeeze. Then he takes a seat and says, "Beam is one of the Wilds."

"I see," Berke says. "How did you find out we were starting the new league?"

She's asking me, but Mauri says, "I recruited her. Beam is a black panther. Jaguar."

"Wait. Really?" I ask him.

He draws his eyebrows together and then breathes out a laugh like I've made a joke. But I'm a jaguar? Not a mountain lion? I did wonder why I looked more squared off than Chausie and his friends.

Berke appears impressed. "You all are coming out of the woodwork," she says. "That makes three in two days."

"What is it you wanted to talk to me about?" Mauri asks, directing her away from the fact that he found us all through a trafficker.

"It's about one of the Wilds, actually. The cougar shifter, Chausie." My sip of breath draws her attention.

"What about him?" Mauri says. "Did you have a chance to see him in action?"

"Yes—in human form. He can hold his own in the gym, but I'm sure he's far more capable as a cougar."

Mauri waits for her to say why she came. Berke's gaze travels from him to me and back again.

"I wonder if he's going to be too homesick to follow through here," she says tentatively.

"Well, he's committed now, isn't he?" Mauri says. "He'll have to hold out until it's time for him to go."

"What are the rules about that?" Berke asks. "I've never known any of the athletes to want to quit—not that he's made that decision."

"Because it's such an honor to be here," Mauri explains.

"Right," Berke agrees. "I certainly wish I'd had access to this place while I was on the circuit. But, I mean, we can't hold him here against his will." She laughs unconvincingly. "Can we?"

"He's under contract. I'll address it with him."

"Great. Thank you." Berke glances at me—quickly but meaningfully—making me hope she understands who I am and that she's on our side. "Probably, if he didn't feel so alone, he'd be able to focus on fighting better."

"Is that your opinion as a coach?"

"Yes, Sir. He tried to befriend one of the other fighters today and received a beat down for it. Handled it well, but I think we'll get more out of him if he has one or two trusted teammates around."

Mauri ponders her words while I raise my hand to volunteer for the job.

"Anyway," Berke continues, "I gotta set things up for this afternoon's session. Thanks for everything." She motions with her delicate cup before setting it on the table. "Good coffee," she says, and shows herself to the door, leaving me to wonder if I imagined her goodwill.

17

RAFE

CHAUSIE

"Hello?"

I suppose it would be too much to ask that Rafe, who has been described to me as a *scary weirdo,* would just show up at the set time and guide me through whatever these *trials* entail.

I stroll through the Jungle's entryway of vines and leaves that flap like elephant ears, into an open space bordered by a curved row of sturdy bleachers. It's sort of like an arena but with no real fighting ring or cage. Well, fighting for the Wilds won't be contained the same way. What would be the fun in that?

Honestly, I don't hate the thought of competition in here. From the arena, several pathways run, some over mounds, some up along the trees. It's wild. Which is appropriate.

"Hello?" I call again. "I'm Chausie?"

A dull thud hits the ground behind me and I turn to find the creepy, wild-eyed man who freaked me out early this morning. The lowest branch of the nearest tree is still very high. But he must have dropped from it.

"You're Rafe," I say as it comes to me.

"You sound more sure of who I am than of who you are," he says.

His voice sounds like shatterproof glass when it's being tested—not an explosive tone, but a fracturing, crunching concussion.

"What?" I ask. "No—I was just trying to figure out where to go."

Rafe cocks his head like a bird—like he can focus better from the side—or like English isn't his first language.

"What are you?" I ask. I can't help myself. This guy is so weird. "Are you—human?" *Shouldn't have asked. Shouldn't have asked.* His pupils dilate, his eyes round while his nose shrugs into a vicious snarl. At the same time, he roars—a sound so foreign and threatening that I automatically shift and, you know what? That branch isn't as high as I thought. I'm up there in half a second—running away from that horrible *thing*. But he is—impossibly—in front of me now, perched on the end of the branch—not as a man—nope—he is not human, no way—he is some horrific bird of prey—and maybe a quarter wolf or—hell, I don't know what. I leap up into a different tree and before I know it, I'm a quarter mile away.

Rafe flaps great, skeletal wings and, with a dismount that causes the whole branch to crack, he comes for me. How can he track me with such precision? I remain motionless—completely hidden in overgrowth —until it's obvious that Rafe's evil talons are going to pluck my eyeballs out. I've never fled from a bird before. I've caught plenty of them.

If I dive to the ground, I'll just end up under him. Instead, I leap upwards at the last moment, so that he flies underneath me, and when he twists to find where I've gone, I come down on him, sticking claws through the feathers and skin of his chest. We fall to the ground, though he flaps and scratches to get rid of me.

Now, Rafe is not a small bird—and, honestly, he is not a bird at all —he's some kind of wolf/bird hybrid thing. He's huge—the size of a large man. So, we fall hard, me on top, and I jump off of him without tearing through more of his flesh. I don't want him as an enemy.

He jumps to his feet. He's bleeding. And now he shifts into something new. He is humanoid—that is, he stands on two feet—but still wolf-like in his elongated muzzle and ears. The eyes retain their rounded bird-of-prey look. He is furry and barrel-chested, and he springs upon me, but my reflexes are sharp. I bound away, springboarding off a tree trunk to switch directions on the fly.

He doesn't follow me in this form. He's not agile enough. He morphs into a wild boar. What the heck *is* this guy?! But wild boars can't climb trees, so that is where I go, traipsing along the wide branches of these spreading oaks. "What is the point here?" I ask as a lion.

Now he is a tiger—bounding up the tree where we face off, him nearest to the trunk, me getting perilously close to the branch's thinning end. Can he shift into anything he wants? Is there a way to force him into one true form? I think of what mountain lions can do that huge, bulky tigers cannot, and very few things come to mind. I can purr, but I really don't think that is going to be helpful.

I can climb. I'm more agile. My tail is better equipped for the tree tops.

So, up I go—into the tallest trees, looking for places that will barely support me, and so will definitely not support him. Of course, won't he just turn into a bird then, and let himself down with wings?

Gotta try. Up I go. One step ahead. Berke was right. I'm quick with solutions, and I can do this all day. He's spending so much energy on shifting, I bet I can outlast him.

At the top of the tree, as I suspected, he plummets. But he grows wings—as a tiger. That is, he doesn't shift into a bird. He's a tiger with wings. It's bizarre. He flies at me and climbs into the treetop, but his wings are too big, too awkward. He lets himself down to the ground and turns into the man—well, a man that only mimics a real human being. From there, he stares in my general direction.

"Come down," he calls up. "I concede that you can flee from me all day long, and I grant that it is helpful in a fight, but it won't land you any points."

I work my way to the ground but keep a wary distance. "I'm just trying to stay alive here," I tell him. "I don't know what you want from me."

"You will fight the African tomorrow."

"Kofi? I think he's African-American."

Rafe does the cock-head thing where he tilts his chin and looks like a bird.

"Kidding," I mutter. "It's a—joke—'cause he's—never mind." I don't think Rafe *can* joke. Just one of several human sensibilities he seems to be missing. To be fair, I tend to joke more in extenuating circumstances. I joke more and I joke inappropriately.

"You will fight tomorrow," Rafe says with his crunchy voice. "If you win, you will fight again the next day. But you have to do more than run away. You have to land punches, claws, teeth..."

I can't help but to stare pointedly at his bleeding chest. My claws did that. He looks down and says, "You should have done more. You should have finished me."

"No, I'm not going to *finish* people. It's not a death match." He doesn't reply. He just stares. "Is it?" I demand. "Just what are the rules? There's a point system? Is there a ref?"

"The rules are that you win. No matter what the cost. You win here, whatever it takes, and then *maybe* you make the team."

"There are teams?"

"Eventually, you will go out in threes against other fight clubs. So far, we've kept a bear, a few wolves, a lion, and now you."

"And a jaguar. Right? There's a black panther here."

Rafe shrugs.

"You don't know? Aren't you in charge of the Wilds? Haven't you been testing all the shifters?"

I think of the guys at lunch who balked when they heard I'd be tested by Rafe in the Jungle.

"So, where are the rest of them?"

"I found them lacking."

"And what happens to the ones you find *lacking?*" I say with more heat. "You send them home?"

Rafe pauses. "Home. Is that one of those words people use to mean something else? Those never make sense to me."

I scowl at him. "The word *home?* Where are they now, Rafe, if not their literal home? The others told me that they're never seen again." He didn't kill them. He wouldn't *kill* them. Mauri paid a fortune for us.

A series of weird head tics makes me want to un-ask the question.

"Have you tested the panther yet?" I stomp up to him, get right in his birdbrained face. "Have you tested the panther?!"

A slow, snaggle-toothed smile spreads across his mouth, and his canines seem to elongate.

"Answer me!"

"I sent her...*home*," he says.

I shove him down without thinking about the ramifications. "I swear to god, if you harmed her, I will end you. Where is she?"

"This is very interesting," Rafe says from the ground. "We spent over an hour with you running from me like a rabbit. All the while, only once did you unsheath your most effective weapon. And only then, under direct assault. *Now* you go on the offensive?"

I bend down with my face inches from his, my hand wrapped around his throat, my claws extended through my human skin. "Where is she?" I growl.

Even though I doubt Rafe is at all intimidated by me, he gives me an answer. "The last time I saw her, she was on the other side of that window." He points to Mauri's mansion, what we can see of it through the branches. "She is fascinating, isn't she? Not really a shifter at all. But she is *something...*"

"She's my partner. And she doesn't belong here. She's not a fighter —not unless she has to be."

"Maybe her job is to make *you* a fighter."

The truth of that statement punches me in the gut. Beam isn't here to fight. She's here to lure me to fight. Even into a death match? I'd take on anything for her sake. I think I just proved it.

"We want out," I tell him. "We didn't sign up to be here. We don't want any part of it."

"You want to go...*home?*" he asks. He's enjoying the euphemism too much. It's probably the first time he's ever been able to employ one. To back it up, he raises the skeletal wings as he shifts into the bird of prey/canine combo and screeches.

It's all I can do not to flinch, but I don't. "Are we done here?" I ask.

"Done," he says in a wild, crackly, bird tone.

I get as far as the lane to Mauri's stupid mansion. *Screw it. I'm gonna find her.* I lion up and dash through the gardens toward the house, squatting low to make myself invisible. I crawl around the ground where stairs ascend to the front door. She was here. Her scent is unmistakable. I keep crawling around the house, peeking into windows, and listening for conversation. I have in mind to climb up to the window Rafe had pointed out because, in my imagination, Beam is being held prisoner there, tied up, gagged, all of it. But I halt at the next ground window when I see her in a room surrounded by books. She's at a table, reading studiously, writing notes even. She doesn't look like someone being held against her will. I laugh to myself. She probably takes great solace in a room surrounded by books.

I man up and peck on the window. She's concentrating too deeply to hear me, so I knock. When she raises her head and sees me, she practically trips over the chair to get to me and falls to her knees at the window, which still puts her at a higher level than me. I signal for her to lift the window, but she shakes her head. *It's locked,* she mouths and glances over her shoulder to check that no one is there.

I scan the area for something to break the thing with, though I don't know where we're going to go after that. Beam holds out a hand to stop me. She doesn't want me to try to break it. I trust her. *Then what do we do?* I raise my palms to ask. Displaying one finger, she rushes to the desk and shows me the covers of two different books. One is *The Leonid Meteor Storm of 1833,* and the other is *Leo's Lost Claw.* Behind the title is a muscly man wearing a lion—a lion that puts even Kofi to shame. Its dark mane wraps around its back and torso. It's larger than the very large man who is wearing it like a coat.

Is this the most important thing for Beam to communicate right now?

"Can you get out of there?" I ask.

She looks over her shoulder again. Moving back to the table, she scribbles on the notepad and walks it over to show me.

It's locked. Glass is riot-proof. I saw what I think was a wolf thrown against it earlier!

She writes something else. *Frilk knows I heal.*

I figured. "Why are you wearing that collar?" I say at the lowest volume and touch my neck. "Can't he get to you?"

What? she mouths.

This is stupid. I close my eyes and reach out to her in my mind. *Can you hear me?* I open them to find her nodding.

Why haven't I been able to reach you like this? she asks.

I was drugged—like you were when Frilk caught you.

Are you OK?

I'm fine, I smile. Her concern always has that effect on me. *It's good to see you.*

She presses her palm to the glass, and I meet it with mine. *Chausie, I think we should stay and play along.*

I'm not sure we have a choice.

We do! Beam lifts her shirt to reveal the small beaded pouch. *I have Larkin's toe ring in here.*

The bewilderment must show on my face, because Beam laughs at me. I have no idea what she is talking about.

It's a long story, but it will whisk us to Larkin's birdcage, and we can let ourselves out.

"That's amazing!" I say aloud.

Yeah, but I think we should stay because I think something nefarious is going to happen.

The whole thing is nefarious.

Even more so. I think Mauri is scheming something even worse.

Kofi's here too, I say, but I don't mention how he beat the heck out of me earlier. *Have you done any training?*

No. I'm not sure what's going on. Mauri treats me like a guest—who can't leave. We have a view of the Jungle, and that's where the wolf got slammed.

Beam's eyes suddenly go wide, and she jumps to her feet. "Chausie, look out!"

I spin to figure out what's freaking her out. Scaling the corner of the third floor of the house is Rafe in his creepiest of forms, the vulture wolf combo on two legs. My sudden movement startles him, and with a guttural sound, he launches himself off the building and soars down to me on wings.

"Chausie, run!" Beam cries.

Rafe lands, chattering with croaking sounds too close to my face. If I had to guess, I'd say that this is his natural form. Curiosity gets the better of me. "Rafe, what exactly are you?"

He stops chattering.

I'm not comfortable with him, but Beam is horrified. She's pressing herself against the glass in solidarity. *It's OK, Sweetheart,* I think and touch the window to ease her fear.

Now Rafe, with his jerky movements and uncanny eyeballs, zeros in on Beam, which shoots me with a spike with adrenaline. "Step back," I command him. He steps forward instead, wholly absorbed with her. "Rafe, step *back*." I shove him, not hard, but hard enough to make a point. He remains fixed on Beam, studying her as if he's never seen anything like her in his life. He's obsessed.

Another form appears in the room behind Beam. Mauri. He places a hand on her shoulder and looks down at us blankly before gesturing us toward the front of the house and nudging Beam out of sight. I make sure Rafe is moving with me before I get too far away.

Mauri meets us at the doors—ridiculously shiny doors that are too tall for human beings—though, now that I think about it, who knows what kind of beings he expects to entertain?

Beam is standing off to the side, as Mauri welcomes me in. I don't think he feels as hospitable as he sounds. I want to rush to Beam, but I don't want to give him any more leverage. If he's using her to get to me, it's better that he not know the depth of my affection. Anyway, I'm sort of stunned by this place. What the *actual*? It's giving Natural History Museum meets Antebellum plantation—if they were stuffed into the White House. You can't even walk through the room because two huge statues are wrestling in the middle of the floor.

"Beam, will you show Chausie to the conservatory?" Mauri asks. "I'll join you momentarily."

She's pleased to do it if the lightness of her step is any indication. She takes me by the hand while Mauri asks Rafe to remain outside and says something about how he thought they had *come to an agreement.*

As soon as the door is closed, I sweep Beam into a swinging hug and then scan her head to toe.

"I'm fine," she says. "I'm good. What *is* that thing? It scares me to death. It keeps spying on me through windows."

"That's Rafe—one of the trainers. He can shift into animals that don't even exist, like whatever he thinks up, those are the traits he takes on. I don't think he's one bit human."

"I don't like him."

"Me either. He has no moral compass. Wants us to fight to the death. I don't think there are any rules at all. I'm supposed to fight Kofi tomorrow." When Beam tenses, I add, "Not to the death. It's a training thing." I just hope Kofi knows that.

As Beam leads me around the statues, I get the prickly sensation that I'm being watched, and I look up to find the head and mane—and whole great coat—of an enormous lion hanging above the entryway into the next room. "That's the Lion of Nemea," Beam says. "He's sort of alive."

The lion emits a low throaty growl, and Beam flashes her eyebrows. "Check out his right paw. It's missing one of the claws. That's supposed to be how Heracles ended up killing him. His skin was impervious to attack except for his own teeth and claws."

I turn to observe the wrestling statues. "I take it that's the two of them in action?"

"Yep," Beam says, popping the P.

"Life is never boring with you," I tell her.

"The cook is a faerie like Larkin. Her name is Robyn. She's here to stay close to the lion." Beam points up at the pelt. "Did you know that Heracles wore that pelt into battle?"

"Because it's impenetrable?"

Beam nods and leads me into a sunroom, where I spend a few moments looking into the Jungle. "I was in there running for my life a while ago. I didn't know if Rafe would kill me or not. I'm not sure he hasn't killed other trainees."

"This can't be allowed to continue," Beam says. "I think that's why we're here."

I rub her arms because she looks cold to me, and she buries her face into my chest. "We can leave any time, right?" I whisper. She nods without looking up.

"But only if we're together. Only if we're holding on to each other."

"Well, that takes some of the pressure off, doesn't it?" I kiss her head, and move to kiss more than that.

"I think you are more than partners," Mauri says. I guess I was too distracted to hear him return. I don't let go of Beam because what's the point? He already saw us.

"Berke tells me that you're too homesick to stay here," he says. "She thinks you'd be a more focused fighter if you were more settled."

"She's right. Let me stay with Beam, and I'll focus."

Mauri mulls it over. "Then you'll do as I say and put all your effort into it?"

"Yes. But not if Beam has to fight."

"Would you rather we treat her like the bikini-clad women who strut around the ring carrying posters?"

"Excuse me?" Beam says.

Mauri ignores her. "She has to be tested," he says. "I paid fifty million dollars for the pair of you."

"I thought you paid ten for me," I say—like it matters, but for some reason it does.

Mauri waves it off. "That was just a ruse that Frilk came up with to keep more of the money for himself. You're a Leonid, Chausie. You have star stuff in your DNA. Beam will be tested as you were."

"No. Rafe's insane. And he's unusually interested in her."

The shadow that passes over Mauri says that he agrees. "We'll have someone else test her," he suggests. "You do it."

"What do you mean?" I ask.

"I want to see what the two of you can come up with in the wild. I haven't had the pleasure of watching cats yet in my Jungle."

"I'm not going to fight my girlfriend."

"We could go *play*," Beam says, surprising the heck out of me.

"There," Mauri says. "She wants to."

"Where will Rafe be?" I ask.

"With me. Observing."

"When?"

"Now?"

I've been working out all day at this point. Even super-healers need a break. But I can tell that Beam wants to do this the way I wanted to do the parkour, which must be the panther in her, and the more I think about it, the more excited I am to share that with her.

18

IN THE JUNGLE

BEAM

I know. It's not like me. It's so silly. But I haven't been able to shake the desire to get out there. I'm a little giddy with anticipation. I kind of skip-run once we're out the door with Chausie laughing as he jogs behind. Mauri seems pleased. He waves us off and tells us to have at it. Chausie shifts and pretends to nip at me, his teeth snapping before they bite my behind! So, of course I shift as well, and we run together for the first time as big cats.

It's pretty fun. I feel single-minded as a cat. Not as driven by the thousands of angles and options I generally analyze about everything. I guess this is what it means to act instinctually.

We plow past the iron fence that separates the house from the Jungle, and I leap onto one of the low-hanging branches, romp across it, and skip to the next. My muscles are strong. My spine is flexible. My brain processes potential next moves like a computer. Jump, climb, run, balance—I'm a cat. I stop to scratch my front claws down the trunk of one of the oaks.

Chausie can't stop laughing at me—even in lion form. He chases me, bounds ahead, tackles me. I'm so pleased to experience this with him.

The Jungle has layers and levels. I hide from Chausie in a cave-like formation and pounce on him when he trots by. In the last few weeks, we have traveled many miles, but I always slowed him down. Not this time!

I sprint into yet a new area we have to explore and nearly barrel into the biggest canine I have ever seen. I have to skid to a stop to keep from colliding with him. Or her. I don't think I should try to look underneath to find out. That's probably rude.

The beast is baring its teeth, its lips pulled back to reveal a blue gum line and sharp, white fangs. Chausie rounds the corner and almost collides like I did, but he manages to leap to my side where he goes stock-still.

I've never seen a wolf in the wild. There were a few red ones at a conservatory I visited, but they were quite small by comparison. And friendly. We tossed rat popsicles into their pin, and they leaped upon them with joyous yips. This huge grey one is not yipping. I don't think it is joyous at all.

Two other wolves flank the first, and though I still don't know if it is male or female, I am positive that it is in charge.

Intellectually, I know what it means to work as a pack, but seeing it in action is awesome. And awful. The two fan out to triangulate, and one nips at my heel. I whirl around.

Nobody told me that it's not a good idea to turn your back on the alpha. If you're ever in this situation, don't do that. But if someone nips your heel, you'll find out that it's not that easy to ignore.

"We're not here to fight," Chausie says but they don't speak cat, do they? He shifts into human form. "Mauri sent us here to play around. We don't want to fight you."

"Oh, yeah?" the alpha says, also after shifting. She's female, by the way. "Well, Mauri sent us to settle the age-old conflict. Cats vs dogs. Get ready to be in pain." With that disappointing quip, she shifts back into a wolf and lunges for me. She hurts my bottom. It's embarrassing. But Chausie makes her pay for it. Not enough to keep her from trying again.

Meanwhile, the one who nipped my heels takes another bite, this time from my ear! I don't have time to think. I swipe both claws at the same time to stave off the attack. Chausie is tussling with the alpha, and the other two are separating me from him. As I said, the pack sense is strong with them. They attack me at the same time, but I'm able to spring over them so that they tangle with one another. Then Chausie is all of a sudden fighting both of them. One emits a sharp whine but is still very much in the fight.

Now, the alpha, while Chausie is dealing with the other two on my behalf, has decided to see to me. So, to be clear, I have an alpha wolf bent on a physical altercation, and I have never so much as slapped anybody in my life. There was the incident with Baalesh, but that was really more of an accident.

"Beam, climb!" Chausie growls and skips fights again to exchange kicks and bites with the alpha.

Right. I use my strong hind legs to leap high through the air—with such propulsion, I could have cleared the whole staircase in Mauri's mansion—and I land above the two wolves, both of which begins to ascend the mound on which I've perched. I think Chausie could've dealt with that alpha more quickly if he hadn't been worried about me. That's what he meant back at his house about being distracted by my well-being.

"Come on, Chaus," I say, and without giving him more reason to worry, I scramble up a tree. I get clawed and my skin gets ripped, but I make it out of their grasp, and I'm feeling pretty good about it—until I realize that all I've done is make the wolves lose interest in me. And so they all three turn on Chausie.

He's good. He fights valiantly and takes one of them down. But he's outnumbered, and he's getting hurt. Snarling as I bound back down the trunk of the tree, I land in the skirmish, and yet *another* wolf appears. He's a he. I just know. He now claims the biggest canine ever spotted by me position.

He doesn't take time to assess the situation, but bounds into the fray. We're going to get hurt. But I'm already committed. I charge into the wolf in front of me, knocking it off Chaus, leaving him to deal with the two others and the one on the way. I can't decipher what else is happening because I have a bone-crunching alpha wolf—whom I so want to call the B word because it would be appropriate on two different levels, and I think that's funny, but I don't say that word because I respect women—chomping on me.

Chausie cries out and, as usual, something primal takes over when I know he needs help. I go for this thing's throat, ripping flesh and fur. I don't have time to entertain her. She's in my way, and she has to go. The wolf howls in rage. I taste its blood in my mouth, which—I may regret telling you—fills me with a wild, triumphant thirst for more. I turn to chase it down as it runs from me.

"Beam!" Chausie's human voice snaps me back. I whirl around, teeth bared, furious, and ready to brawl.

It takes me more than a few seconds to come to terms with what I see. I still want to fight. I still want to rage. But the wolves skulk out of the area—all but the latest addition. And he is standing with Chausie as a human, both of them grinning ear to ear. He fought *with* us.

The strangest part is the disappointment I feel. Glancing down the path where the wolves retreated, I'm tempted... Chausie gives me a sympathetic smile and draws a deep inhale, pursing his lips as it flows out again. He means for me to do the same, and as I mimic him, the blind fury subsides. I find myself seated on the ground as a woman. I keep breathing.

"Well, I take it back," Chaus says. "I think she has a big future here."

The man with him laughs, and my mind clears. I want to thank him for helping us, but I just need to sit. They're busy assessing their wounds. Chausie faired much better than I expected. Or else he has already healed.

"Aiden?" I'm finally able to say. "How are you here? Are we free to go now?"

The police officer/wolf shifter staunches a gash in his thigh. I bet it hurts. "Sadly, no," he says. "Chausie's dad called to tell me Mr. Turner had been shot and that Chausie had gone to find his daughter. I was always a step behind. Followed you to the campsite. Followed you to the place where they were buying and selling. Followed you here—and applied to be a fighter. They don't know who I am, other than that I'm a shifter. And they were more than happy to let me in."

"There may be cameras in here," Chausie interjects. "Microphones too."

Aiden nods that he understands. "I'm just happy to have been accepted into the program," he lifts his voice to say. "This has been a dream of mine for ages."

Undercover work may not be his strong suit. Chausie and I trade a look.

"Well, well..." Mauri and a man I assume to be Rafe—I've only seen him in his vulture form—join us at the entrance to the Jungle. "I think we've found a strong combination for our lead team." He singles me out. "Well done, Beam."

"Thanks," I say and feel flustered by how proud I feel. I probably really hurt that person. "Where are the wolves we fought?" I ask. "Are they OK?"

Mauri waves it away. "Sure. We have excellent medical staff." He motions to Aiden's leg. "Looks like you could use a stitch or two yourself."

"I think the better question," Chausie cuts in, "is why were the wolves there in the first place? We agreed to *play* in there. You ambushed us."

"Didn't you enjoy the rush?" Mauri asks. "The thrill of power and victory?"

Kind of. I'm conflicted. It's one thing to compete. It's another to rip into someone's sinews.

"That's not the point," Chausie says. "If we're going to fight for you, we have to be able to trust you."

"Oh, I think that ship has sailed," I mutter.

I keep trying to ignore Rafe, who was apparently never taught that it is rude to ogle young women. He is frowning at me and tilting his head at odd angles. "You should have finished them," he says in what sounds like a very old parrot's voice. He even whistles at the end. I try not to keep eye contact, hoping he'll just stop staring. Chausie steps forward between us somewhat.

"We've been through this," Mauri says to Rafe. "Those athletes were a huge investment. We do not kill them."

"Some of them were bad investments," Rafe comments. He's still concentrating on me. He's starting to creep me out. "You have to put them down," he tells me. "Or they will get up. And you will go down. You smell like birds. Are you a friend of birds?"

I guess Aiden is uncomfortable too because he changes the subject by saying to me, "Your name is Beam," like he's never met me before. "And what's yours?" he asks Chausie.

Chausie squeezes his eyes shut, probably to keep from rolling them. "Chausie," my love answers flatly.

"Yeah, Chausie. We make a good team, don't we? For never having met before." Aiden is overdoing it.

"Your shirt is ripped," Rafe says to me and puts a finger through the hole to touch my skin. His finger, by the way, is rough the way a toad is rough—dry and bumpy. When Chausie protests the move, Rafe knocks him to the ground. Then, ignoring Chausie as if the physical assault was nothing more than a reflex, he adds, "Your skin isn't."

"My skin isn't what?" I ask while Chausie hauls himself up.

"Ripped." Rafe continues to scan me, even walks around me. "There is blood." Now, he gets low to point to my leg where one of the wolves about clawed it off. But there's no wound to go along with the dried path that trails around my calf. I think Chausie is preparing to make an ugly end to this meeting. I squeeze his arm.

"Must belong to the wolf I beat," I say with bravado I don't feel— because the last thing we need is for our ability to heal to be revealed.

"You are both remarkably unscathed," Mauri agrees with Rafe.

I shrug. "Too quick to catch."

That seems to mollify him. "Indeed. Rafe, let's scratch tomorrow's fight between the lions in favor of keeping them healthy enough for the inaugural competition. These three will take on the lion, the bear, and the wildcard."

"Fine," Rafe says. I know it's one small word, but I don't like how he says it.

Since it's well past dinner time, Mauri invites us humans to eat in the mansion. Rafe is not invited to come in. While he cranes his neck to see what's inside, Mauri closes the door in his face. Now that he's gone, I find myself more relaxed. I even imagine what it would be like to buy into Mauri's delusion of how fortunate we are to be here. The place is comfortable. The food is delicious. And as we recount the fight, we feel united.

"Level with me, Mauri," Chausie says. He has finished everything on his plate, and now he sits back in his chair and crosses his arms. "Where did you find Rafe? What is he?"

Aiden usurps the answer. "You don't know?"

"If I did," Chausie says with a scowl. "I wouldn't have asked."

"He's a werewolf."

"What?" we both ask.

"No wonder it bugs you to be called a werew—" Chausie begins, but then remembers he's not supposed to know anything about Aiden and makes what could have been an innocuous statement as awkward as can be. Flushing pink and stammering as he tries to cover it up, he says, "I mean, not you personally, but you, as in all of you wolves—"

Aiden plays it off. He says, "It's OK, Chausie. Lots of wolf shifters get the slur thrown at them, and you're right. We don't like it."

If Mauri is suspicious of this clumsy interaction, he doesn't show it. He addresses my question. "I had been looking into the league, asking around about trainers and athletes. Rafe was very knowledgeable about shifters, and he understands that I hate to lose." Mauri watches his coffee as he swirls it in the cup. "Between us, his kind is stranger than I realized." Aiden stifles a snort. "It may not work in the long term. We'll see."

"Has he been killing off the trainees?" Chausie asks.

Mauri's head pops up. "Why would you say that?"

"Seems pretty bent on fighting to the death, and you're a little lean on fighters as far as I can tell."

"Well, we have to work out the rules with the other clubs. Nobody wants to lose their investment so...terminally." He rises to his feet. "Aiden, would you like for me to drive you back? Chausie and Beam will be staying here up on Heracles Hall tonight."

My head whips up. *He's not making Chausie leave?* Chaus squeezes my knee under the table.

Aiden frowns at us. "You're not staying in the same room, are you?"

"What business is that of yours?" Chausie asks.

"Your moth"—here, Aiden understands that he's about to reveal the connection he has with Chausie's mother, so he extends the word and even makes it plural—"motherrrrs would want you—both—to be wise, I'm sure." *Smooth.* "But what do I care?" he continues. "I'm going back to my cabin." He mutters something about *plausible deniability.*

Heaven's sake.

"I'll drive you back then," Mauri says, and we all rise to our feet.

Chausie grips Aiden's arm and the plaintive change in his voice draws us all in. "Aiden? Thanks for showing up."

He winks at Chaus and says, "All in a day's work. Y'all get to sleep. Big day tomorrow."

Chausie looks after them as they leave and admits, "Aiden's a pretty good guy." Then grins at me and says, "Don't tell him I said so. Oh, hello!" He says the last because Robyn walks in front of us with arms full of plates and utensils.

"I can help clear those," I tell her.

"No, no. Won't take a minute."

Chausie says, "You remind me of someone."

"I was about to say the same about you." Robyn's large, Larkinesque eyes have turned a bit devious. "I wonder what he'll do with you staying in the house all night. He sleepwalks."

"Who?" Chausie asks. But Robyn continues on her course to the kitchen.

"Is everyone here committed to exploding my brain with cryptic nonsense?"

He looks so perplexed I have to laugh. "Come on, Chaus. Do you want to pick a bedroom?" I tug him toward the long, curving staircase, and we explore each room in turn. Each has its own full bathroom and king-sized bed. They're all ostentatious, just—over the top. I mean, who needs a chandelier in every bedroom?

When we get to the end of the hall, I say. "This is the room I picked until Were-Rafe climbed the fence and stared in at me."

Chausie gazes out the window into the dark and then rakes the curtains closed. "No more talk of him tonight." He falls onto the bed, resting against the headboard with a heavy sigh.

"What all have you done today?" I ask because he looks exhausted and I don't feel weary at all.

"Oh my gosh. What haven't I done?" He yawns and rubs his eyes.

"Weight session. Mixed martial arts. Kofi used me as his personal punching bag for a while."

"Kofi is here? Is that the lion they were talking about?"

He nods.

"Was he happy to see you?"

"Not really, no. He thinks I abandoned him. I may be just one in a whole string of folks who have let him down. I don't know. I get the feeling he was *born* in captivity."

"Nooo. That is awful. So, is he completely maladjusted?"

Chausie yawns as he thinks about that, and I sit beside him. "He has his moments. He guarded Rosa, though he would probably deny that he did. He did things to make her feel less scared of being locked in a cage with him. But he doesn't *people* very well." Another yawn. "I'm gonna get him out of here." Chaus rests his hand on my leg. "What about you? I thought I caught your scent by one of the cabins, but it was so faint."

"Mauri came to fetch me around six-thirty and we had brunch here. Then I studied in the library, as you know. There are so many books! Most of them have to do with ancient Greece—architecture, pottery, myths, culture—and then I found one about the Leonid Meteor Storm of 1833. It had pictures—drawn, not photographed—of different people who had seen the meteors fall all around the world. There was one of a Cheyenne family cuddled together under the brightly lit night sky outside their tipi. It got me thinking. What if The Vigilance had a record of that meteor storm from the Oglala Lakota point of view? Remember how my people kept Winter Counts?" I turn my head to accept what is coming: Chausie biting back a smile because I called them *my people*. And I admit, it does feel good to own that part of myself. I didn't realize how much of me was missing before I went to South Dakota.

But Chausie is not teasing me. His eyes are closed, and his head rests against the headboard. "Here," I whisper and stand to pull the covers back. "Scoot down and go to sleep."

He makes a sound of protest. His eyes come open. "I'm listening."

"No, you're not," I laugh. "But that's OK. Lie down before you get a crick in your neck. I insist." Chaus allows me to guide him into place, remove his shoes, and cover him up.

"Don't go away," he mumbles. "We get into trouble when we're apart."

"We get into trouble when we're together too," I say. His face, in its unusually relaxed state, draws my loving scrutiny. He's all angles except for his full lips—which I kiss, and then they wake up to meet mine.

"Stay asleep, Chaus," I whisper and rest my forehead on his. I know he likes when I do that. He's told me before that it's a cat thing, and sure enough, it makes him smile.

"You kicked that wolf's ass," he says. "You're my queen."

"That's *right!*" I vault over him to land on the bed with a *cush.* "Don't forget it."

"Well, now I'm awake," Chausie laughs. He rolls on top of me, making me squeal, and his yellow eyes seem lit from within, the way they gleam when he's a lion. He traces the side of my face with his thumb. "*Gah,* you're beautiful." He has said that before, but I don't get used to it.

"Do you love me, Chaus?" I ask up at him.

"Yes." He lowers himself to kiss me—and says again, "Yes." And kisses me again. "I love you." Now, he maneuvers us so that I'm on top of him and steals my line.

"Do you love me, Beam?"

"Yes. I love you."

"Will you kiss me, Beam?"

"Yes. I will kiss you."

"For as long as I want?"

Whatever playful eagerness is on my face makes him rumble and flip us over again.

There are a hundred things we should be worrying about, but I push them away, opting instead to burrow against Chausie's warm body and lose myself in his affections.

19

A MIDNIGHT VISIT

CHAUSIE

At some point—and don't ask me how—we fall asleep. There is nothing in the world better than being snuggled up in bed with this woman. When she yells, "What is that?!" I am so deeply entrenched in a dream that it takes effort to fight my way out.

I have an arm around her head. I'm stroking her hair. *Is* this her hair? It isn't as soft.

"Chaus?"

Her voice doesn't come from the head I am stroking. "*Yahheee!*" I do not care what un-masculine sound just escaped me. I am scrambling up and away from it, to where Beam is standing. It's dark in here, but my night vision confirms that there is a stranger in our bed.

"What the— Was its arm around me?!"

Seconds go by. It doesn't move. It doesn't appear to be breathing.

Someone is climbing the stairs down the hall. "Naughty *boy!*" we hear. "How long have you been gone? I can't close my eyes for a minute!"

The bedroom door is open like a gaping hole into the rest of the house. I closed it before we fell asleep. I'm sure.

"Naughty. Naughty." Robyn's small figure appears holding a flashlight. "What has he been up to?" she asks.

"He?" I point.

I vaguely register Beam leaning toward the bedside table and clicking on the light. That dead-ass, shaggy-maned lion skin that hangs downstairs is now lying on our bed.

"You are very naughty," Robyn says at it, her voice softening as a mother's would. "But you wanted to cuddle your cub."

I have horror movie visions of that thing clinging and crawling unnaturally down the wall, then traversing the stairs like a giant slug. *How did it get up here?* I start to ask.

Beam wants to know something else. "How are he and Chausie related?"

As is often the case, Beam has asked a question I don't react to because I don't want to appear dense, but what is she even talking about?

"He was banished to the sky, right?" she says. "By Herac—"

"We do not utter that name here," Robyn interrupts with malice.

"I'm sorry," Beam says.

"He's a liar and a thief. Leander was a sweet soul. Yes, he was a lion, and he had to eat. But that liar tricked him, killed him, and wore his skin around like a suit of armor."

"Disgusting," Beam says, taking on the inquisitorial persona she learned from her lawyer parents. "When that horrible thing happened," she says, "Leander's life light was broken into pieces, right? That's why we see the constellation? And why so many cultures all over the world refer to it as a lion?"

Robyn nods and rounds the bed to collect the limp skin. She picks it up like a massive, empty baby, cradling its oversized head to her shoulder. It dwarfs her, but she makes it work.

Beam continues. "What I don't understand is what that has to do with shifters here on Earth. Something about the marvelous meteor storm back in 1833?"

"The meteors, as you call them, were sentient beings created when the Lion's light broke apart. The supposed hero, whom I refuse to name, hunted them down to further humiliate Leander. Those who escaped to Earth naturally found their way to big cats and were able to live as both cats and humans. Shifters were born."

Robyn combs her fingers through the Lion's mane, and the thing blinks its eyes.

"Was he a shifter in life?" Beam asks. "None of the stories say so."

"He was born a lion but raised by me."

Beam appears dumbstruck.

"How *old* are you?" I ask.

"Chausie," Beam reprimands, but Robyn chuckles.

"I had already hatched my clutch when Leander was born." She pats Leander's back. "He was a darling thing." Leander makes a noise that I imagine to be his version of cooing.

"You imbued him with your magic," Beam guesses.

"He was near death when I found him. A hunter had killed his mother. I simply asked him to thrive."

"And then he became impervious."

"To all but himself."

Beam lifts the paw that is missing one of its claws. I can't tell what she's thinking, but she's got the face that means she's sorting through the information.

Robyn falters under the weight of her gargantuan child. "Here, let me do it," I say. "Where are we going?"

"Oh, he would love that," Robyn says, and I come around to figure out how to hold the thing while it dawns on me that Robyn is speaking in cat language.

I try to imitate how she was holding Leander, and he nuzzles my neck. When I side-eye Beam to communicate how bizarre this is, she just smiles.

"Carry him downstairs before Mr. Mauri finds out," Robyn says. "He won't understand. He'll be irate."

Off we go. I'm negotiating the stairs without being able to see around the lifeless—and yet not—marble eyes and bushy hair.

"What is this?" an angry voice sounds from below. "What are you doing with that? Is it not enough that I've opened my whole home to you?"

I've never heard Mauri speak sharply before, so I'm not sure how to respond.

"We're replacing it for you," I say.

"How did it get MISplaced?!"

Apparently, Mauri is not privy to Leander's sleepwalking habit.

"Give it to me," he barks. I glance down at Robyn, who nods for me to do what he says. The Lion sighs.

"I can help you hang him back up," I offer. We've come to the bottom step.

"No, I will not be leaving it in the open for the time being." Mauri heaves the pelt out of my arms and checks it over, especially its paws. Then he stomps away in pajama pants, the Lion's head and arms dangling unsanctimoniously. As an afterthought, he halts and says, "Did Rafe put you up to this?"

"No," I tell him. "No one was up to anything. The Lion came on his own. There was no harm done."

Mauri puffs out a derisive breath. "You are here to become an elite and indomitable team. You are not here to—" Seemingly incapable of words strong enough to describe our dereliction, he huffs again. I find myself crossing the floor, not to get up in his face but to ensure that Robyn and Beam don't take the brunt of his temper.

"No one has crossed you," I tell him. "No one has stolen or harmed anything you own."

He throttles the Lion in a tantrum. "You took this!"

"No. I was bringing him back to his place."

Mauri throws up his hand in a stop sign. "If you don't prove yourself in the Jungle this evening, you can forget this place. I'll sell you before the guests are gone and ship you to the highest bidder—far away from here. Where they will treat you like the possession you are."

My jaw locks down, and I can feel the muscles straining. Even so, I try to calm him down, try to make him see reason. The last thing we need is for Mauri to go off the rails. I've seen how quickly he makes deals. He can force us into different, unknown locations before we have a chance to vanish with the ring.

"I'm done talking." He wheels around with the Lion in tow and is soon out of sight.

"Be good," Robyn calls to Leander. A door slams on the other side of the house. Robyn sinks to sit on the stairs, and Beam takes a place beside her. I'm still looking after Mauri, wondering how long his anger will last and how punitive he'll be.

"Have you followed Leander from owner to owner all this time?" Beam asks.

"Yes, I can't bear for him to be alone, not when he is aware. He gets frightened and confused."

Beam heaves a sigh. "This is awful," she says, and I agree.

Robyn observes us, me leaning against the stair rail, and Beam slumped with her elbows on her knees and her head resting in her hands. "It's still a few hours before sunrise," she notes. "Mr. Mauri may cool off. Go get some more rest, and take these." She indicates two stacks of folded clothes lying on a console table beside the staircase. "They're for tomorrow. You will receive other clothes for the reception. I'll have breakfast ready at six-thirty."

I gather the clothes and drop them on Beam's lap before I hoist her into my arms and up the stairs while she giggles, which is what I was hoping for.

When we lie down, she rests her head in the crook of my arm. We're both pretty bummed. We talk it through repeatedly, and, eventually, Beam dozes off, but I can't let it go. Should we disappear right now? Hope the goblin won't see us if we show up in the birdcage? I don't like the idea of Leander's skin remaining here as a trophy—especially when he's the reason I have shifter abilities. Does Rafe want the pelt? Is that why he keeps spying through windows and doors? Or is it because he senses something special about Beam? I'm still mulling these things over after the sun comes up. Beam is spooned against me. I kiss her head and tiptoe into the bathroom to clean up.

You know who could prove helpful here? Blue. But I'm not going to reach out to him while I'm in the shower. It would be just like him to finally show up while I'm undressed.

After the shower, I walk out with a towel tied around my waist. Beam is standing in front of the window hugging herself.

"What do you see out there?" I ask and scoop up my set of clothes. When she doesn't answer, I say, "Beam?"

Her shoulders convulse, and she folds in on herself.

"What's the matter?" When I go to put my arms around her, she turns to sob against my chest, squeezing my arms so hard that I fear my hands may lose feeling.

"What is it, Sweetheart?"

She stills as she observes our situation and then laughs through the words, "Are you naked?" as she rubs tears from one of her eyes.

Looking down at myself, I say, "Partially. Why are you crying?"

"I don't want to be a lion," she whispers like it's shameful. "I don't want to, Chaus. I don't like the way it feels to want to tear someone apart. I'm sorry."

"What are you sorry for?" I ask. "I don't mind if you're a lion or not. You remember when you asked about it in Laurel's cave? You thought I'd want a *little lion lady,* as you put it." That earns me a smile. "You remember what I said?"

"You said you just wanted me to be Beam."

"That's right. I want you however you come. Feline or not." I wipe tears from her cheeks. "Happy or sad."

"But I'm stuck with it." The words sound like she has to cough them out, and I'm suddenly aware that she feels trapped and that it's my fault.

"Beam, I'm so sorry. I didn't mean to give it to you. I didn't—"

"No, stop it. Don't feel bad. I feel terrible that you saw me crying about it."

"No-no-no. I want you to tell me. OK, look, I won't feel guilty about giving it to you if you won't feel guilty about not wanting it. You can be as upset as you need to be, OK?"

This brings on a bout of ugly crying, which is still pretty cute.

"Did I say something wrong?" I ask.

"No, you said everything right." She looks up at me, her beautiful blues magnified by tears. "You have to teach me how to handle the impulses."

I put my forehead to hers and nod. "I will. But maybe we can figure out how to put you back to normal."

"Would you mind, Chaus? If we could?"

"I just want you to be happy," I tell her.

"I enjoyed it today—before the wolves showed up. I loved running with you and playing with you as equals."

"Yeah, that was *great.*"

I shouldn't have emphasized the *great.* She's crying again.

"But, I mean, I can run like a lion with Grant. That's not what I need from you. The things I need from you, I can't get from Grant." I smile down at her in a way to let her know what I mean.

"You're OK with that?" she asks doubtfully.

"Beam, I'm human before anything else," I say. "And I love you. If there's a way to get rid of it for you, I'll do it."

"But this evening, we have to fight people. And they haven't done anything to us."

"OK, first lesson. It's not a fight. It's a competition. Aren't you the kid who stacked the Candy Land cards in your favor?" I get a smile for that one too. "Find the joy in this with me, and we'll be fine." I sound more confident than I feel, but if I believe in anything, it's that Beam can rise to any occasion. "If we need to disappear with the ring, then we will."

"No, I know. It's just—" She stalls out.

"Go on."

"What if I kill somebody?"

"*That's* what you're worried about?" I laugh.

"It's not funny! What if I do?"

"You're not going to kill anybody. I won't let you. And honestly, it's not that easy to accomplish."

"*Uhck,*" she says by way of protest.

"We're going to stand up to them. We're going to give chase. And they're going to retreat. Just like yesterday." *Except for Kofi,* I don't say, *who has made it clear he will fight or die.* "Let me have Kofi," I add.

"Yesterday, I nearly ran after that alpha wolf to finish her."

"But you didn't. Listen, I know you haven't been a shifter long, but how many bizarre, life-threatening situations have we made it through together?" When she doesn't answer, I lift her chin.

"Quite a few," she admits.

"You're the same person with or without claws, and I trust that person implicitly."

I can see I've gotten through to her because she stretches up on tiptoe to hug my neck. "Thanks, Chaus."

Every time I hold her close to me, all is right with the world. From the day I met her in that coffeehouse, I knew that she was part of my purpose, my *reason*. Like God used her to track me down and put me back on course. And I'm going to live up to it—even if, at some point, the unthinkable happens.

BEAM

"Larkin is a good cook," I tell Chaus. "Did I tell you? It must run in the faerie family."

Chausie and I descend the stairs at six-thirty, famished. I think shifting gives me a big appetite. But there are no delicious smells coming from below—nor any sounds, for that matter, from anywhere in the house.

"Are we early or late?" Chausie asks.

"Maybe Robyn overslept? It was a big night, what with Leander's pilgrimage."

"Look here." Chaus picks up a notecard from the console at the bottom of the stairs and reads aloud.

Good morning Chausie and Beam,

The front door will remain unlocked today for your convenience, and a golf cart is available out front. You may breakfast and lunch in the cafeteria. Berke has volunteered to act as your coach, so take time to strategize if you wish.

Your clothes for the reception will be hanging in your room after two this afternoon. Reception begins at four. After that, we will all journey to the Jungle.

Fight bell rings at five-thirty.

Regards,
Mauri

I make a beeline for the kitchen.

"Where are you going?" Chaus calls.

"I want to see Robyn. She said she'd have breakfast for us."

"Breakfast food in the cafeteria is good."

"I'm not worried about the food, Chausie." I swing the kitchen door wide. It's all clean and clear of activity of any kind. Step stools at every station are a bittersweet reminder of the small, pointy-eared woman I seek. I march through a door on the other side, and, as I suspected, there are living quarters fitted with faerie-sized furniture.

"He kicked her *out*," I huff. "Or worse." I open the closets and drawers to confirm they're empty.

"*Ohhh*," Chausie cottons on. "You think Mauri took his anger out on Robyn and sent her away."

"Yeah, I do. She'll be grief-stricken. She's cared for Leander since he was a cub."

Peck. Peck.

Peck. Peck.

Chausie and I stare at one another, and then he motions for me to follow him back into the kitchen.

Peck. Peck.

"There!" I point to a window, where a red-breasted robin flutters behind the glass and whistles to us in short, sharp bursts. Chausie rushes to run his fingers along the window frame.

"Is there no latch?" he asks.

"None of the windows have proper latches."

That way, the robin seems to say and points with its beak. Chausie moves to the counter by the wall, causing the bird to twitter with excitement. He continues to regard the bird as he moves further out, taking cues from it like in a game of *You're Getting Warmer.*

"No, that's not it," I say, when he lays hands on the toaster. He touches the coffee canister next with a questioning brow. The bird turns its whole body back and forth in the air. *Nope.*

"Is it these keys?" I ask and present a lanyard hanging from a hook. "Maybe Robyn wants us to free Leander." I leave them alone when the bird gives no indication that that's what it wants us to find.

Chausie studies the robin, who is doing a wonderful job of hovering in the air where we can see her. "What are you trying to say?" he asks and then surges to the window as horrible Rafe, in his vulturiest form, streaks through the air, jaws agape, and swallows the robin whole.

Chausie pounds the glass with his fists. "*Why?!*" Rafe doesn't stick around to answer.

With a sudden jolt, Chausie spins and says, "You don't think that robin was *Robyn,* do you?"

I shake my head. "I don't think so. I don't think shifting is one of her...skills. But I do think the robin was trying to deliver a message for her."

And I do think Rafe is capable of it.

I keep searching for something else the little beast could've meant for us to find. It must have been important for Robyn to have given it the assignment.

"Poor thing," Chausie says. He's still staring out the window.

"Chausie, are you mourning for that bird?" I ask him.

"It was trying to help us." Now, he turns to me, his gorgeous yellow eyes filled with the injustice of it. "I hate that its life is over. Werewolves suck."

I can't keep from smiling. "Yeah, they do. But you're great."

He doesn't know why that's what I think to say, but it's because—despite his being a predator—he's sorry for the little bird.

CHAUSIE

We do another sweep of the cabinets and drawers, but if there's something for us to find, we don't. Anyway, we need to get to the cafeteria. Connecting with our team is top priority. We trade Robyn's quest for a ride in the golf cart and catch Aiden in the middle of bacon and eggs, gabbing with younger athletes who seem to hang on his every word.

I'd probably enjoy the guy too, if we'd met under different circumstances.

"Sleep well?" he asks in the loaded way of a mom's snoopy boyfriend.

"We slept great," I inform him and keep it curt enough to let him know I have no intention of entertaining his thoughts on our bedroom arrangements. "Were you able to find out who the other two fighters are?"

A small flick of Aiden's finger from around his biscuit has us sizing up a big ole boy who is surrounded by several heaping plates of food and a few stacks of empties.

"Brown bear shifter," Aiden says. "Big freaking kid, isn't he? The other teammate's still a wildcard. They're not telling us."

"OK, well, bears aren't fast enough to catch us. They're just hard to bring down. Beam, maybe you can get him chasing you in circles and wear him out."

"I can do that," she says. "Who do you think the wildcard will be?"

Aiden raises his brow to say, *Your guess is as good as mine.* "I asked around, but the only other shifters I heard about were the wolves."

"Let me have Kofi," I say, "the African lion."

"Racist."

I roll my eyes and say again, "Let me have him. Whatever the wildcard is, you can make short work of it and then come help me with him. He'll be the one to beat. He's committed to this program now, and I'm pretty sure he'll pay whatever it costs to be their champion."

Berke saunters over in a friendly way, hands stuffed in her jacket pockets.

"Mornin', Coach," Aiden says.

"Mornin', Team."

"Thanks for volunteering," I tell her.

"My pleasure. I heard you impressed Rafe yesterday."

"All I did was evade him. I didn't know how or even if I was supposed to engage."

"He had some mighty claw marks on his chest. That's what I heard."

"Dude's weird," I say because accepting the compliment feels like a bad omen before a fight—and maybe I want to downplay how good it feels to hear her say it.

"Yeah," she agrees. "He's a real wildcard."

I wouldn't have thought twice about the word choice, except that Berke backs it up with a meaningful pause, and I blurt out, "You think *he's* the wildcard? Is he allowed to put himself on the team?"

"I don't know. But we should be prepared in any case."

"How are we supposed to prepare? He can change into anything in the world." Beam stiffens beside me, and it occurs to me that she and Berke haven't been introduced. "Beam, this is—"

"Berke," she says and holds out a hand. "We met yesterday. I think she was playing detective at the time."

"Guilty," Berke agrees. "Especially when a wolf showed up with the same first name as the officer Chausie told me to call."

"*Aw,*" Aiden cuts in. "Did you need me, Chaus?"

I ignore this. "So, are you our inside woman now?" I ask Berke.

"Looks like. No, Sergeant Aiden was available to take my call at the APD. And then this wolf shifter shows up. Last night, he gave me instructions for a range of worst-case scenarios."

I question Aiden, who flashes his eyebrows. He must have been working on making a partner out of Berke while Beam and I were snuggled up. "Good job, Aiden," I tell him.

"Don't act so shocked," he says. "And be sure to tell your mom how great I am."

"I'll be sure to tell her how you spent the evening with a baddie named Berke."

"Fine. Then I'll be sure to tell her how you and Beam shared a bedroom."

Our laughter is a welcome thing as we zone in to discuss strategy.

A while later, Aiden notices someone over my shoulder and raises his voice to say, "Hey, good fight yesterday."

I smell them before I turn to see the three wolves from the Jungle in human form. The alpha, with a huge bandage around her neck, plods over. My instinct is to step in before she can stir things up with Beam, but she pats me on the arm and reaches across to fistbump Aiden. To Beam, she says, "Great moves out there. Give 'em hell today."

"*Oh,*" Beam says. "Thanks." And they move on.

"She was so nice," Beam says under her breath. "I was not expecting that."

"Yeah, good thing you didn't kill her," Aiden remarks.

I immediately try to squelch that with a *cut* motion across my neck. But Beam doesn't reveal to him how fragile she feels about her new tendencies. She says, "Shut up, Aiden, or you're next." Which makes me snort out a laugh. Also, I like that she doesn't share that vulnerable subject with him. Makes me feel like I can provide something for her that no one else can.

"Hello, Wilds," Mauri looms over our table. He doesn't sit down or clap me on the back like he did yesterday. His whole demeanor is far cooler this morning.

I glance at Beam, but I can't tell what she's thinking.

"Morning, Mauri," Aiden says. "I don't suppose you want to give us a hint about who the wildcard is."

"Well, then it wouldn't be much of a wildcard, would it? Suffice to say it will be the start of something spectacular. Better bring your A-game." Here, Mauri eyeballs me and says, "After last night's little stunt, I expect nothing short of *everything* you've got. The consequences I outlined last night, stand."

"What stunt are you referring to?" Aiden asks.

Mauri rights himself from where he had bent to keep the last part confidential. "I'm sure your teammates will fill you in." He resumes his morning greetings to the other athletes, leaving Aiden to silently question me.

"He's delusional," I mutter. "He thinks I tried to steal from him." I want to say more, but I don't want to be overheard. "Let's drive around. He gave us a golf cart."

"Can't," Berke says. "But I'll be at the reception, and we'll talk more then."

The morning is warm for early spring—maybe not for a Georgia spring. South Dakota may have snow on the ground. We pile into the golf cart and, at Aiden's suggestion, I drive along the perimeter of the compound. Beam is beside me in the front, Aiden in the back. He says, "See how each section is guarded up top?"

Sure enough, the same number of armed guards I'd seen the night I arrived are stationed at regular intervals.

"I think Mauri fancies himself a king or a lord," Beam says, "and this is his fiefdom."

"Berke thinks the guards are here to protect the athletes," I inform them. "Said it was for all the fight money on the line."

"Those guys are more than security guards," Aiden says. "That's serious hardware. Like they're expecting a siege from a small government."

"Yeah, well, when you buy people for sport, you need to protect your investment," I say, and Beam says, "The art in Maurie's mansion is worth a fortune on its own."

We know one item that is. The Lion of Nemea. "Aiden, do you think there are any other fighters here against their will?"

"It's hard to say without asking every one of them—which is what the police will eventually have to do. But everyone is so grateful to have the chance to train here..." He leans in and taps my shoulder. "Slow the cart."

We've just passed the end of the gymnasium complex, and Aiden points to an out-of-the-way covey where the sidewalk ends. "Mauri and Kofi are having a little chat."

"Where no one else can hear," Beam adds.

I pinch her ear lobe. "We can." The three of us strain our sensitive hearing to find out what's being said.

Mauri is talking. "You have a real shot at a future here. Isn't that what you want?"

"I want to win fights," Kofi says. "Fights that lead to more and better fights and make me money."

"Then join me. Lions have to stick together. You can't advance if you can't do what it takes."

"I will do what it takes." Kofi's voice turns hard. "I already told you. If I have to—"

Beam smacks my thigh. "Go!" she whispers. "They see us." Sure enough, Mauri and Kofi are both staring in our direction.

As casually as possible, I punch the gas pedal, but you know how golf carts are. There's no way to take off smoothly. It lurches—the best I can do. "*No, we're not eavesdropping on you,*" I mutter so that only Beam and Aiden can—"Where is Aiden?" He's no longer in the cart. I try not to glance around so as not to draw attention to him or to the fact that we were spying. "When did he take off?"

"I'm not sure," Beam says. Now that we're out of the direct line of sight, she's looking back. "I'm pretty sure they saw us."

"They saw us," I confirm. "But who cares? We're just driving around." Even so, I check the rearview to make sure we're not being followed. "Mauri's the reason Kofi's latching onto the idea of fighting for a living. He's grooming him. Tried the same thing on me—or started to."

"What does he want him to do?"

"Who knows? Kill us all?"

"What was that thing about lions sticking together?" Beam asks. "Join him in what?"

"No idea."

"I need to go back to the house."

I scan the area for Aiden again. "OK. Why?"

"His words about lions reminded me of something that was underlined in one of his books."

The cart tilts as a big wolf jumps into the back seat.

"Oh, Aiden, you're beautiful that way." Beam reaches back to pet him, and his whole back leg twitches like she's tickling him.

"Dogs are weird," I say. "Where'd you go?"

"Making myself scarce is all." He's a man again, and Beam draws back her hand in disappointment. "Drive down there." He directs me down a lane behind the gym.

It's a basketball court. I must be staring at it with longing because Beam laughs at me. "Is it calling your name? Let's stop."

"Yeah?" I ask. Shooting is meditation for me. I have to be present with the mechanics of my body, the physics of the arc, the distance to the net, the rebound, the bounce. Just thinking through it helps to ground me. "What about the things you want to check out at the house?"

"We're not far from there. Drop me off and come back."

When I hesitate, she says, "I'll be in a library." As if that makes her invulnerable. She probably feels like it does. "Chausie, you want to do this. Maybe you need to. Spend some time here, and then come back to me."

I appreciate the suggestion. I drive us down the stupid straight lane of the driveway to the ridiculous, oversized house, where Aiden and I walk in to make sure all is secure. Instead of Robyn, caterers are bustling in the staircase room and the kitchen. I leave my brilliant girlfriend in the library with a kiss. "See you soon."

Back in the cart, Aiden says, "You really like that girl, don't you?"

After I decide it's a sincere question, I abort the smartass comment I'm about to make and say, "Yeah, I do."

"Is she your boo?" he asks.

"Shut up, Aiden. And don't call her a girl. She'll fight you."

When I start hitting shots, the tension melts from my shoulder, my neck—my very brain—until I'm in the zone. One ball after another falls into the bucket, and Aiden stands underneath to feed them back to me.

"Damn, Chaus. You sure you don't want to go play for a college team now that your leg is healed?"

I dribble in and out of the three-point line and fake out a non-existent opponent to shoot a lovely arcing—*swish*. "I thought about it. But working at The Outpost is all I've ever wanted to do. So, what's the point?"

"It's all you've ever known to do, right? But now you see that there's a whole world for shifters."

"Did Mom put you up to this?" I ask him.

"APEX could use a guy like you. We had one retire recently."

I stop dribbling. "Are you offering me a job?"

"Do you want a job?"

I'm not sure how to answer that. I kind of shrug my shoulders. "Nah, Man. My path was laid as soon as I began to shift. My dad was ecstatic." Not to mention that Beam is going to be working at The Vigilance there and living in a magic cave-house with a hot spring.

"Well, just keep in mind that there are other possibilities. Things closer to your mom."

It's true. Mom is far, far away from South Dakota now. "Man, I'm just trying to shoot for a few minutes."

"Don't let me bring you down." Aiden slaps the ball and tries to steal it, but I check him, dribble around, and lay it up.

"My go," he says.

This is way more fun than talking about my mom being sad. For half an hour, I don't have to think about anything at all as we play, and then a large shadow appears and asks if he can cut in.

"Oh, you wanna have a go in *my* dojo?" I say to Kofi—complete with the cocky palming of the ball in his face. And so he strips me of the ball, charges to the basket, dunks it, and hangs off the rim just to rub my nose in it.

Honestly, this is the best thing he could offer me. I beat him handily. Point after point. Even converting his surges into my points.

But the higher I drive the score, the rougher Kofi becomes. Aiden finally intervenes. He says, "Dude, save it for the fight."

I'm cut. I'm bruised. But it is so worth it to be better at this than he is. I'm probably smirking. And it's probably not a nice look. Probably pompous. Definitely self-satisfied. And maybe even the reason that Kofi chucks the basketball at my nose.

It breaks. I hear the sickening crack as the blood drains from my face. I can even see its new orientation. You know that feeling you get when something happens, and you're hyper-aware that it's bad? I don't have time to dwell on it, though, because Kofi follows up his rocket-propelled basketball with his rocket-propelled fists. He topples me and pummels my ribs mercilessly, saying, "I can't lose this! I won't!" And other similar phrases over and over as he beats me.

Aiden's on top of him now. He tries a choke hold, but Kofi flings him off. Dude is strong! And he's still going on about how he can't lose when I realize he's sobbing the words now and weeping. The punches slow. He curls onto himself and covers his face, wailing and groaning and having some kind of emotional breakdown.

Aiden leans over me, his eyes full of concern. Everything hurts, but I wave him away. "Give me a minute," I manage. The fetal position seems like the best idea. I close my eyes and just try to breathe through my mouth.

When Aiden understands what's happening to me, that I'm healing, he checks on Kofi—even puts an arm around him. Kofi reacts with surprise. "Get off, me," he says, but Aiden sits down instead, right beside him there on the court.

"What's the matter, Kofi?" he asks. "What are you so afraid of?"

Kofi sniffs and wipes his eyes like they have to be punished for crying. He looks miserable. And angry. And caged. All at the same time. He catches me watching, and I think that, if he knew how to, he'd apologize.

"It doesn't have to be this way," I tell him. I'm still lying on my side, bracing my ribs.

"It does," he says. "There's no way out for me except for doing what he wants. I'm never going to be free."

"Yes, you will be, Kofi."

He shakes his head and stands to go. Aiden rises, too, and while he's pretending to be casual, I know he's angling to keep Kofi from doing any more damage. Kofi positions himself so that his sneakers are about an inch from my face, and he talks down at me. "Don't show up to fight. Or I *will* kill you. I won't have a choice."

"And what are you going to do to Beam?" I ask. "You think I'm going to stay away so you can kill her?"

The sneakers walk away.

"Nobody's going to kill anybody," Aiden calls after him and bends down to me. "How're you doing?"

"Getting better," I grunt. With assistance, I sit upright, and Aiden studies my face.

"You didn't use to heal like that," he notes. "What gives?"

I'm beginning to trust Aiden, and if it were my secret alone, I might tell him. But the more people who know about Beam, the more danger she could be in. Of course, no one can put her in more danger than Frilk can. What was I thinking, leaving her when she wears his collar? As I get to my feet, I think up a lie for Aiden. "There's a hot spring in South Dakota. Its healing properties are legendary—lasts for a long, long while."

I don't think he believes me. It's just as well.

"I'm gonna check on Beam," I tell him. "Want a ride to your cabin?"

"No. I'll see you at the reception."

"Alright."

Before I drive away, he says, "Beam's gonna be fine, Son. And so are you. I'll see to it."

For once, I don't cringe or roll my eyes or hate on him for calling me *son*. The stakes are high, and I'm glad he has my back. So, I just nod.

This time, as I drive down the stupid lane to the stupid house, there's a guy waiting in front of the portico. He wears a maroon suit jacket and stands at attention. When I stop the cart, he hurries around to me. "May I park that for you, Sir?" he asks. I think I've seen him in the cafeteria.

"Mauri hired a valet?"

"For the big fight and the reception. Loads of special guests will be arriving. Even people in government."

"*Huh.*" I leave the key in the ignition and climb the steps. I wonder if any of those guests are already here. By the time I think to ask, the valet has pulled away.

The door is unlocked, and other guests *have* arrived—or at least one. Mauri's wife, maybe? Would she be here this early? Maybe it's not as early as I think. The woman is standing with her back to me, dressed in a silky sapphire-blue dress that falls over her hips just right. She's studying the marble wrestlers, and she bends from the waist to inspect the lion's paw. When I find myself staring, I avert my eyes—not because her shape isn't something to see, believe me. She's not mine to love, you know?

"Chausie, what in the world happened to you?"

The gorgeous woman is facing me now, and my mouth comes open, but no words come out. It's Beam. She rushes to me, worry fueling her movement. The dress has enticed her eyes to a deeper blue. Her lashes are thick and curled upward. Her lips shine, and her hair—gah, her hair

—is pulled into a haphazard knot on top, with loose tendrils kissing her face.

"Say something," she says anxiously and scans my shirt, which I now realize is gunked up with blood from when Kofi broke my nose.

Speak, Chausie. You're freaking her out.

"You are stunning." It's all I can come up with, but it pleases her. Her cheeks flush, and she turns her head with a shy smile.

I can't embrace her. I'm a sweaty, gross mess. I'm scared even to lean in for a kiss, but I allow my eyes to feast on her the way I wouldn't before. I take my time, walk all the way around her.

"It's just me," she laughs.

"Just you exploding my mind. You found a way to stash the little purse, didn't you?" This is really just a ploy to touch her neck, but again, I'm filthy, so I draw back.

"I want to keep the ring on me at all times," she says, "and the pouch is a very stashable size—for fashion that has no pockets."

"Why were you studying the sculpture?"

"I'm glad you asked. Come look." There's the tone I know. She's been doing research, and she's uncovered something. When we get close enough, she points to the statue of Leander's front paw.

Seconds pass without her speaking. "Is this the part where I'm supposed to say something intelligent?" I ask. "Something about the lion's foot?"

"How many claws?"

"Oh, he's missing one. Just like the pelt."

Next, she points to an item in Heracles's hand.

"And there it is," I say.

"The claw," she agrees. "This scene is the moment before Leander dies."

I glance up at where Leander's pelt should be hanging.

"Mauri hasn't returned him yet," Beam says. "Why would he purchase such a sculpture and place it front and center in the foyer of Corinthia?"

Corinthia? I only mouth the question.

"My name for this mansion. Keep tracking. Why is this important to him?"

"Beecauuuuse...he likes to show off big, expensive, one-of-a-kind art?"

"But why *this* art?" Beam pushes.

"Were all of the adjectives I just threw out not enough?"

She laughs, "What I mean is, why *these* moments?"

"I think you're giving him too much credit."

"No, he likes for his things to mean something. He's very precise and very dramatic. The ancient pottery he collected is primarily covered in lion images. Not just any lion. This lion. The top of the columns outside? They have lion heads snarling down. And do you remember what was carved front and center into the triangular pediment?"

I do not. She tugs me out the door so that we can gaze up at it. There's a magnificent lion in the middle, larger than the fighters that surround him. His mane weaves around them.

Back inside, I consider the sculpture again. "If Leander was invincible to all but himself, how did Heracles get the claw off?"

"That's a great question, Chaus!"

At first—mistakenly—I feel proud of myself for coming up with a question Beam had not, but that didn't last long. She had already thought of it. She says, "Turns out, there are several different versions of the story. Some don't include the claw at all. But the one that rings truest to me says that Heracles forced the claw into Leander's heart while it was still attached—apparently, the sculptor didn't know that version—and then he removed it and used it to skin poor Leander."

"I hope Robyn wasn't around to see that."

"So do I." Her mournful countenance gives way to hurry. "You have to change. You're going to make us late." She shoos me to the stairs, and I obey, taking them as quickly as she does.

"Late for what?" I ask.

"The reception. It's going to be held right here."

"Have I got clothes too?"

"A tux! I think you'll need another shower."

"Well, yeah."

Beam motions to where the tux is hanging. I've only worn one once —for a cousin's wedding. This one looks nicer by far.

"There's a razor too," Beam adds. And I stop at the bathroom door.

"Do you like for me to be clean-shaven?" I ask.

The question makes her bashful again. "I like you all the ways, but it's a dressy occasion, so—yeah."

"You got it." I look her up and down. "You know that I adore you, right?"

She moves to get close to me but stops and frowns. "*Why* are you bloody?"

"Because Kofi sucks at basketball, and he's a sore loser."

"I've about had it with this Kofi, and I don't even know him."

When I don't do anything but look sorry for him, she says, "Oh, my gosh, you are such a softie."

"I just feel bad for the guy. Whatever deal Mauri made with him must make him feel that his head is clamped in a vice. And it's not like he has an Aiden to lean on. Though Aiden tried."

Beam bites her bottom lip to keep from smiling.

"Yeah, I heard it," I say. "Well, it *is* nice to know Aiden's here. He didn't have to check himself into the place without backup, did he? He's here for us. And tonight, he's our very capable teammate."

"Yes, he is."

"Is that what you're going to wear to fight in?" The dress isn't skin-tight, but it's not exactly loose enough to run in, and her shoes have thin, peg-like heels. Really pretty. Not really practical.

"I suppose it's all part of Mauri's theatrical debut. Who knows what other surprises he has in store? Did you know he has a first edition of Shakespeare's *First Folio!*"

When I make it clear that doesn't mean anything to me, she says, "A printed version of Shakespeare's plays from 1623! That's why I don't think Mauri would have randomly selected any of his art. And this dress... My mom splurges to get me nice dresses from time to time, but this one—" She mouths the word *Wow.*

"You should wear it to prom," I say. I reach out—and stop myself before I contaminate her. "Ima hurry so I can..." I don't finish the sentence, just make an *mm* sound that pleases her, and then duck into the bathroom where I catch my blood-splattered reflection in the mirror.

We've got the ring. Right? So, we just can't wait too long to use it. I think of Kofi, though, and Aiden. And Berke. And who knows how many others need to escape.

It's remarkable how steaming up a bathroom to soothe quick-healing muscles and bones under the water, and knowing your gorgeous girlfriend is waiting to see you in a tux can wash away thoughts of danger.

BEAM

I've never seen Chausie in anything other than joggers and jeans. And he looks great in them! But him standing before me all cleaned up, curls combed out of his eyes, chin smooth, in a tux?

"*Oh*," I say—intelligently. Chaus grins that lopsided grin he saves for when we're alone.

"*Oh*," he says back, closing the distance at a pace so slow it feels like the best kind of torture. He makes me nervous. When I swallow, his eyes dart to my throat, and he rubs the pulse point with his thumb. "I can hear that."

"My heartbeat?"

"Yep. Racing."

I listen. Dig into my feline senses. And inhale as I realize I can hear his as well.

"It's not all bad, right?" he asks. "Being a cat?" He's so close now, I can feel his breath. I shake my head and swallow again. It's a reflex.

He wets his lips and meets mine so softly, I don't even kiss him back. Until I do.

"I love you," he tells me. Even though he's not finished kissing.

When he pulls away, I open my eyes and tell him to come back, which makes him smile. "You wanna skip the reception?" he teases.

"Yes, I do." I know we can't, but I do think we'd have a lovely time in here by ourselves. I push him toward the mirror where I take pictures of us with my cell-less phone.

"The suit fits like it was tailored for you." It's streamlined to emphasize all the right things. His height, his shoulders, his waist. Even the sleeves hit his wrists at just the right spot. How? "We make a nice-looking couple," I say.

"Truth," he agrees.

When I set the timer for one more picture, Chausie knocks me off balance to kiss me harder than before. He doesn't stand me up again till well after the *click.* So, that one's a keeper. Love how that one turned out.

I show it to him. I could have already told you the face he'd make. That cocky raise of his eyebrows to tell me he thinks it's a job well done.

Chausie presents his arm to escort me, and I have to remind myself where we're going. It's not our party. Not our prom. It could very well turn out to be something tragic. But we have the ring.

The crowd is gathering. We can hear them from here, and they only grow louder as we traverse the hall. At the top of the stairs, we stop to marvel at all the lovely outfits, the gold watches, the flashy jewels. Jazz music streams through built-in speakers.

The console table now boasts a variety of hors d'oeuvres. "Want some?" Chausie asks, but I'm feeling too distracted to eat, and this is why: I'm missing a piece of Mauri's plan. He says that this reception is supposed to mark the inauguration of his new fight club, and maybe that's all it is. But I can't imagine he won't do something outrageous.

What does a man like Mauri want most? He's not a shifter, not a goblin, nor a faerie. And yet he manages business with all of them. He's just a normal guy—granted, a guy with vast wealth. Is it enough for him to be seen and to have his acquisitions praised? Is it enough to be in charge of paranormals? "What does he want?" I think out loud.

"Who?" Chaus asks and takes a bite of a smoked trout croquette. It says so on the little sign in front of the serving dish.

"*Oo,* that does look good," I tell him, so, he holds his small plate out for me.

"Mauri," I answer and loft a croquette in thanks. "He got so angry at us last night. I said plenty of bold things yesterday that could have angered him, but he stayed calm and pleasant. He did everything he could to win me over. Did you know he was keeping us separated on purpose—before he decided it would better suit his needs to allow us to be together?"

Chausie indicates that he does know. "You sort of forget how diabolical he is, don't you?"

"Exactly," I agree. "So, what was it about last night?"

"Leander," is all Chausie says.

"Leander," I agree. "That pelt is beyond priceless. Though some of the other things are as well. Mauri practically begged me to handle the pottery. Didn't act territorial about it at all. Just charmingly proud."

"As much as he likes to show off, you'd think he'd have returned Leander for his guests to admire."

"You're right, Chaus." I look at Leander's place to confirm he's not hanging there. "Do you really think he means to sell us off and separate us?"

"He bought us, didn't he? You heard him. We're investments. His real gift is the ability to lull us into a false sense of freedom. He gave us the run of the house, a bedroom together... We rode around in a golf cart, and now we're eating these delicious smoked trout thingies, but we're not free. Not at all." Chausie's eyes wander as if he's had a new thought. "I bet this is the closest thing to freedom Kofi has ever known. No wonder he's willing to fight for it."

These are the issues Chausie and I are weighing when many of the partygoers begin to gasp and *ohhhh*. Like everyone else, we crane our necks to find out what is drawing such admiration. An enormous, shaggy lion head enters the room on the shoulders of a man. "What the actual—" Chausie begins. "Is he *wearing* Leander?"

"Just. Like. Heracles," I say in disgust. Honestly, I'm not surprised. He's obsessed with the story.

Mauri's guests gather to see what I now believe to be the guest of honor. I can't even find the words. Leander's arms come down over Mauri's like sleeves. "Welcome!" Mauri says from within the teeth. He's all smiles. "I'm so glad you've all made it!"

"Now we know why he didn't hang it back up," Chaus says.

The feeling of someone too close to be a stranger, along with his *tch* of disgust, has us turning to welcome Aiden, who is scowling at the lion-wear.

"I know—can you imagine?" I guess Chausie is envisioning his own head and shoulders being worn as a suit coat, but at the moment, I'm too distracted by these men in their tuxes to care. I demand Aiden move closer to Chaus for a picture. "If we ever get out of here," I tell them, "Sophie will love this." I have to take repeated photos until the grumpy men/animals produce real smiles, but I finally snap a few that won't make the cover of *Hitmen Hotties* and immediately know what I'm getting Chausie's mom for Christmas. I wonder what kind of frame she'd like.

"Is that our senator?" Aiden asks.

Mauri, intent on working the room, is now addressing a woman who fists Leander's mane in both hands as she greets him.

"I think it is," I say. "How far up does this thing go?"

"I intend to find out. Let's play it cool. Like we're undercover."

Chausie and I exchange a look.

"What?" Aiden asks.

"Aiden, I hate to break it to you," Chaus says, "but you are not that great of an actor."

"Sure I am. Drinks?"

"Tea, if they have it," I say. "Thanks." Chausie goes with him to see what's there, and I people-watch. Over by the sculpture, I spot the bear shifter looking ill at ease in his formal attire. His friends, just a bunch of normal guys as far as I can tell, look better suited for a frat party than a reception, and they're trying to talk him into something—I don't know what, but I know it's stupid.

The wolf women appear out of nowhere and surround me. I have to keep from laughing. They even act as a pack at a party. "You look amazing!" the alpha says, and the two others agree. The nippy one pinches the fabric at my waist the same way she'd bitten my leg yesterday. But she comments kindly on the fabric, so I'm going to assume she's only interested in the texture of the dress and not my internal organs.

"Don't touch her," the alpha snaps.

"Sorry," Nippy says to both me and her alpha.

"You three look nice, too," I offer. "It's interesting to see everyone all dressed up." I don't mean for my gaze to snag on the gauze wrap that covers the alpha's neck—the lacerations made by my teeth. I bit that woman and tore her flesh. At the neck.

I must appear pained. She says, "Don't worry about it. It's part of the game."

"I never fought before," I admit. "I don't like the game."

After an incredulous bark that is a laugh, she says, "Wait. Are you serious? What are you doing here?"

I guess that answers whether or not she's here of her own free will. I check the expressions of the other two, but the nippy one gives me a quick, mirthless smile.

"Come on, ladies," the alpha says. "Let's hit the food table. *We* don't have to watch our fighting weight tonight."

I grip Nippy's arm to detain her. "Are you here against your will?"

Her eyes round in fear, and she shakes her head too fast.

"I am," I confide in her. "And I know a way out. Do you need one?" She checks on the others, and before she rejoins them, she says the softest, "Yes."

OK. So that's at least one more. My eyes trail over the room.

And there is Kofi. His very presence commands attention. He certainly looks the part of a warrior as he stands off alone. When I unwittingly catch his eye, he holds contact. It's not flirty or electric. It's also not hateful or intimidating. It's just curious. He's sizing me up, and I guess that's what I'm doing to him. He's as much of a wildcard as whomever the wildcard is. It occurs to me that Chausie's caring for him may be detrimental to us in the upcoming fight.

When Chausie returns and offers me a drink, I break eye contact with Kofi to accept. Into my ear, Chaus says, "You are absolutely gorgeous," and withdraws with a kiss. Kofi drops his head, and in that passing moment, I get why Chausie wants to save him. Despite the mountain stack of the man's chest and shoulders, his thick twists of hair pulled neatly into a mound, his hands clasped in front, revealing arms like tree limbs in his fitted tux, there is a vulnerability, a lostness, maybe even a sense of shame.

Chaus follows my gaze and gives Kofi an upward nod, and now Kofi leans forward in amazement. He almost loses his balance, and the longer he stares at Chausie, the more puzzled I become. "Why is he looking at you that way?" I ask.

Aiden, having procured his drink, says, "I'll tell you why. Kofi pummeled our boy to a pulp this afternoon. Broke his nose and probably a few ribs. Now, here he is, not three hours later, like he stepped out of *GQ* without a scratch on him. That hot spring must be incredible."

Aiden leaves room for me to respond, but "What?" is all I think to say. And then he nods, his lips pursed, and eyeballs Chausie, who chuckles and claps him on the shoulder. "Well done, Detective," Chausie says.

"You want to tell me the real reason you two heal so fast?"

We both shake our heads, and I wave at Berke who greets us with, "Well, if it isn't this evening's champions…"

"*Woooo,*" Aiden sort of howls, "aren't you something?" She is. She's wearing a strapless gown that showcases her strength and powerful femininity.

"And here they are now," Mauri croons loudly for the sake of his guests. He strolls over to wrap one arm around me and the other around Berke, at the same time waving his glass to include Chausie and Aiden. "Kofi?" he calls. "Wolves and bears as well." When the crowd murmurs with excitement, Mauri says, "That's right! It's Jungle night at the mansion!"

Kofi, the wolf women, and the bear take their places with us. "These are a few of the athletes and one of the coaches you'll have a chance to marvel over tonight. The Wilds will be on full display with a grand surprise even the athletes can't anticipate."

What is that supposed to mean? Chausie and I exchange an uncomfortable glance.

"When you're ready, please make your way to the Jungle. We have carts out front, and of course, you're free to enjoy the gardens if you'd rather walk. Just follow the signs to the central arena."

A woman steps out front to take our picture. I've seen her working the room. She has a real camera, and I think it's her job to record the event. Mauri smiles his widest. I don't think any of the rest of us do. Maybe the bear. Is it weird to want a copy, though?

Without another word, Mauri all but dances into the crowd as they disperse.

"Well, that is quite a suit," Berke mutters, her eyes on Mauri's back. "He's sure feeling festive."

"I'd say he's feeling jealous," Chausie corrects. "He wants to be a shifter so bad, it's pathetic."

Aiden says, "What's the surprise he mentioned? The wildcard?"

"That's what I took it to mean."

Berke searches the room. "Where is Rafe?"

"Mauri doesn't allow him in the house," I say, and Chausie says, "He's more of an outdoor werewolf."

CHAUSIE

Dressed in Leander, Mauri stands on a floating platform above the crowd. The snazzy party guests bob their heads from their reserved box seats. Trays of food and drink are being served, and they raise their glasses while Mauri basks in their attention. How many of these people are here because it's a *who's who* event, and how many are complicit in human trafficking? I look from face to face while Aiden advises Beam how to deal with bears.

The athletes from the other side of camp are showing up, excited to experience the Jungle at last. They file into the bleachers, calling out their support, mostly to Bear Man—the only name by which people seem to know him—but I hear my name too, and Aiden's, and Kofi's. Nobody calls *Beam,* but everybody is talking about her. What kind of shifter is she? Why has she been kept separate from everyone else? Is she single?

"She is not single," I inform the guy who asked the last. "She is very coupled." Yes, I had to swiftly and soundlessly approach the spectators to school him. His wide-eyed shock is my reward. He had no idea I could hear him from that far away. With a quick, humorless smile, I'm gone again.

Berke rejoins our team after tending to some pre-fight business.

"They'd like for all the shifters to weigh in as you're introduced. Not just the teams, but all the Wilds." She motions to the platform where Mauri now holds a microphone. "Maybe the 'wildcard'"—she makes air quotes—"is simply that other players will be allowed to enter the competition at various points."

"I don't think so," Beam asserts. "If so, it's news to the wolves. Back at the reception, the alpha mentioned eating whatever they wanted because they didn't have to fight."

"She could've been trying to throw you off."

"That's true," Beam admits. "But I don't think so."

We ascend a column of stairs that appears to have been flown in from an ancient Greek temple. Mauri, inside of Leander's teeth, rotates to wave at his adoring crowd.

As we crest the top, he speaks into the microphone. "Welcome, esteemed guests, coaches, and athletes. We're delighted to have you join us for this inaugural match of the Wilds Fight Club." With a sweep of his arm, he presents us and allows the uproarious applause to continue for several long moments before he calms it down to say, "As you may have heard and may have seen by now, this club is quite nuanced. It's a niche league of superb fighters with paranormal skills. Just think of it. To possess the skills of a wolf pack or the strength of a bear. Is there any price you wouldn't pay to command the prowess of a mighty lion? Here in the Jungle, the king of the beasts reigns!" More applause.

"Why don't you just go ahead and hand Kofi the trophy?" I say under my breath.

"The rules of the Wilds are much the same as in UFC matchups," Mauri broadcasts.

"I didn't know there *were* any rules," Beam says out loud. "It would probably be nice to have a list." It almost makes me laugh. The woman loves some rules. Mauri either doesn't hear her or doesn't address it. He says, "Even so, there are sure to be dramatic moments with cataclysmic clashes and—let's face it—more blood than you're used to."

The crowd cheers. Someone yells, "Not more blood than Berke can draw!" Berke accepts the joke with a bow and a flourish.

"When do we find out about the wildcard?" another voice shouts. Mauri chuckles. It's the most annoying thing I've ever heard. He says,

"Some of you have heard tell of a *wild* surprise. Indeed, the wildest you can imagine..."

Beam repositions herself, crosses her arms in front, and scrutinizes Mauri as if she'd like to read his mind—no doubt trying to decipher what he's up to.

"He means Rafe," I guess. "He's keeping him hidden so that he can release him as a spectacle."

Beam nods in agreement. "That does sound like something he'd do."

Starting with the wolves, including Aiden, the athletes are weighed as both humans and animals, and the information is announced. I gotta give it to Aiden. He bounces around like a prizefighter—like Rocky! Maybe his acting skills are gaining ground. Or maybe he's just pumped.

Next up is the bear. The crowd goes wild. What a goofy kid. I don't know how old he is, but his chubby, red cheeks scream *boy*. I'm glad we gave him to Beam. He won't land a blow. What's he even doing here?

Mauri announces my name. A contingent of fighters I'd met yesterday stands to yell for me—including a pretty woman whom I helped run the parkour. Beam side-eyes me, but I just smile and shake my head.

Then Mauri calls Beam to the scale. There are hoots and hollers from all around. I clap along with them. She's an unusual beauty—as a cat and as a woman. Her panther self is all sleek muscles rippling under shiny black fur.

When she's finished, she crosses the platform to rub her feline ears and neck against me, essentially claiming me in front of the crowd. I kinda dig it.

Kofi is last. Yeah, he's something, too. He shakes his glorious mane and fixes his sullen glare on the world at large.

Now is the first time Mauri seems to stumble. He scans the platform and then the Jungle. Finally, he announces Berke's name with a gesture in her direction. "Coach Berke, would you step forward?" As he shares a few facts about her career, he seems distracted. "Do you have a team name picked out?"

She turns to see if we have one, but when we don't, she says into the mic, "Berke's Battlers."

"Berke's Battlers!" Mauri repeats. Off the mic and falling out of his emcee persona, Mauri says to Berke, "Have you seen Rafe?"

Is this all part of the show?

When Berke questions him with a dubious smirk and shakes her head to say she doesn't know where Rafe is, Mauri says, "He's supposed to serve as coach."

"Do you really not know?" she asks. Then Mauri leans over the platform's wall to say, again, off the mic, "Quinn? Will you serve as coach?"

"Sure." Quinn leaps the boundary wall and jogs up the stairs so that Mauri can introduce him the way he had Berke. Mauri comes up with his own name for them. "Heart of Heracles!" he says. *Applause. Applause.*

"Fighters!" Mauri call out. "Meet us on the ground in fifteen minutes, and weeeeeeee'll FIGHT!" The *weeeeeeee'll* rises in pitch, and as he yells the last word, the crowd takes it up as a chant.

"Fight! Fight! Fight! Fight!"

Beam becomes woman to say, "I think I'm gonna throw up."

"That's good." This from Berke. "You want to be a little nervous."

"Why didn't I spend time on tutorials this afternoon?"

"You know what you need to know," I tell her.

"And you can tap out at any time," Berke adds. When she sees Beam's shocked expression, she adds, "Not that you'll need to."

"What does that even mean?" Beam asks.

Berke taps her fingers on Beam's arm. "Tap on your opponent or on the ground if you get into too much trouble. You'll forfeit, but they'll stop ripping into you."

"Wait. The whole team would forfeit?"

She shakes her head. "Just you."

"Still no wildcard," Aiden says, looking around.

"It has to be Rafe," I say. "Who else is there? Certainly no one worse."

Beam doesn't react, except maybe to grow greener. Aiden mutters a curse, which quickly morphs into a strategy session. "OK, well, you're the only one who's dealt with him, Chaus. Let me take the lion. I'll join you when I can."

Berke keeps her mouth shut, but I think she disagrees. "Speak your mind, Coach," I say.

"You think I should take the Were?" Aiden asks.

"No," she says. "Chausie should take Rafe, like you said."

"You think I should take the *bear?*"

"I think you should take the bear *down.* Emphasis on down. And quickly. You know about bears. You're both more...terrestrial. Felines will have a better chance against felines."

"You've been watching too many *Who Would Win?* animal videos," Aiden says.

"I really have," she replies in all sincerity. "Ever since I found out about this. Listen, if Rafe is the wildcard, give Kofi to Beam."

"You're kidding," I erupt. "He's nearly as violent and unhinged as Rafe."

Berke frowns. "Quinn said he didn't dish out any more than you could handle."

"Well, I *was* fighting back."

"So will she," Berke says. "Look at her. She's tough."

"No doubt. You should've seen her tear into the wolves. I'm just saying Kofi's a big guy—and a bigger lion."

"I don't think he's murderous, though," Berke counters. "I mean, I don't think he wants to *lose,* but..."

I let her non-comment settle and say, "Is that supposed to be reassuring?"

"You want me to take on the *lion* lion?" Beam asks, and when I raise my hands to ask, *Really?,* she says, "I'm sorry, Chausie, but—I mean, he's huge, and he's not friendly. And his life is on the line. You said so yourself."

I hear the anxiety in her voice and want to hide her away, call the whole thing off, but before I can flake, Berke gets on her level and says, "Yeah. You're gonna do it. You're lithe. You're quick. You can climb. Aiden'll get killed by that thing."

"No, I won't," Aiden objects.

"Yes, you will. And—forgive me, but I've been doing this a long time—Kofi's the kind of guy who will have a harder time committing to

Beam as an opponent. She's a lady, after all. She certainly looks the part tonight."

"That's what you're banking on?" I ask.

"I think it will factor," Berke says.

"Seven minutes." The announcement echoes through the clearing.

My girlfriend exhales a big breath that puffs her cheeks and then nods.

I've seen her accept improbable challenges before—the way she sets her face into a flinty mask that erases any signs of fear. And that's what she does now. The sight of it makes me feel better. She's scanning the Jungle like she turned off the misgivings and on the calculations.

When Berke is satisfied by Beam's resolve, she says, "Draw him into the trees. He can't climb like you. He *can* jump. He can jump far out and high up. And he is *so* very strong. But mainly, he's bulk and jaws." As an afterthought, as if she hasn't been clear enough, she adds, "Stay away from the jaws."

"Got it," Beam says. "Just another day on Isla Nublar."

Aiden doesn't get the reference. "*Jurassic World,*" I tell him. "Dinosaurs. The Indominus Rex."

"What were those tiny, little, quick ones that ate people up like piranhas?" Berke uses her hand to mimic a small dinosaur nipping my arm.

"Compsognathus," I say and laugh when Beam gives a fake shiver and says, "Just give me the lion."

"Alright." Aiden puts a stop to our banter. "I cripple the Bear Man and join Beam to take on Kofi. Chausie, why don't you just keep Rafe on the run until we can subdue the lion? And then we'll triple up on him."

"Yeah," I nod. "And I'll lend support in the meantime as I can."

"Nope," Berke reprimands me. "You know better than that. Let your teammates do their jobs. You're the one dealing with the unknown. Don't take your eyes off of him."

We fall into a tangible silence.

"Three-minute warning," Mauri calls.

"Man, it looks like that dead lion suit is snarling," Berke says about Leander.

"Probably is," Beam says. "He's not as dead as you'd think."

Kofi and Bear Man are swinging their arms while Quinn speaks to them.

I'm still watching Leander's face. It does look more animated than usual. "What if the wildcard is Mauri?" I'm kind of just saying it out loud to try it on for size, but Beam demands that I, "Say more," as if she's been waiting for me to explain this for hours. And that makes it seem less unlikely.

"All that *we lions* we heard him say to Kofi, for starters."

She's nodding for me to continue.

"The way he worships Heracles. I mean, he named the team *Heart of Heracles.* Does that sound like a team he could resist fighting on? He practically told us that the *king of beasts* was going to win. He's already wearing Heracles' trophy."

"Let's bring it in," Berke says. We form a circle, arms around each other's shoulders. "We're going to assume the wildcard's Rafe. If it's Mauri, then all the better."

"But nothing can get through the pelt," I say.

"So punch him in the face. Hamstring him. Bite his feet." She's just getting warmed up. I cut her off to say, "I got it. Whatever's not covered."

"We got this," Aiden says.

"We got this," I agree.

We look at Beam. "Y'all just stay out of my way," she says.

At least she's feisty.

As a unified line of interlocking arms, we hike to the center of the arena, and Berke makes her way to the coach's block. Kofi and Bear Man wear matching gear, but they don't look anything like a team. Bear Man looks forlorn. I think he'd like to join our side. The wildcard is still conjecture at this point, and Mauri's such a drama king, I think he's getting MMA confused with WWF.

With his microphone, Mauri now stands among us and reintroduces each player without asking for our input or dispensing any biographical information. I mean, what would he say? *At least three of these six people were forcibly abducted and sold to yours truly. Give it up for my money and human trafficking!*

"Who's their third fighter, Mauri?" Berke yells.

"Oh, you'll see!" he answers like it's fun for us all that the secret of the wildcard is allowed to mess with our heads.

He instructs us to shake hands, which we all do without incident. There may be some posturing, some scowling—the normal stuff—but there's no trash talk. Except for Aiden. He tells Bear Man, "You seem like a nice kid. I hate what's about to happen to you." And he wolfs out with the menacing glare of his kind, pinning the poor guy in place like a deer in headlights.

"If things go South," I murmur to Beam, "do not hesitate to use the ring and get out of here."

"K," she says in the blankest way possible to let me know I'm an idiot to think she'd leave me behind.

"It's time!" Mauri says to the crowd. "FIGHT!" No sooner is the word out of his mouth than Aiden attacks. Bear Man hasn't completed the shift before he lets loose a boyish howl of pain that is instantly replaced with a big bear growl.

Kofi and I glower at one another. I'm certainly not going to leave Beam to him before a third player enters the arena. She has yet to lion up, but I don't think too much about it. I'm standing here as a human, too, but my lion senses are on full alert.

Mauri hasn't left the arena, and the conniving smile he wears is unsettling.

"Heracles never used Leander as anything more than a suit of armor, right?" I ask.

Beam whips her head my way, dawning comprehension lighting up her steely expression. "I know what Robyn meant for us to have."

And then the wildcard arrives, so whatever we think we've unearthed gets reburied. An airborne creature in his natural form, Rafe casts a shadow over us as he mounts the floating platform in front of the audience. A collective gasp ascends, and he squawks out a terrible warning.

Mauri looks surprised. Way more surprised than we do. He probably had a big build-up planned, and Rafe just ruined it. "And here is Rafe," he announces. "The head trainer for the Wilds."

"What is he?" is the question that gets hissed throughout the stands.

And then shrieks go up as Rafe dives toward them from the platform. He circles over them as he comes into the arena hot.

I lion up, and I'm off—abandoning my girlfriend to the lion that is Kofi—to track Rafe. Wildcard or not, he's in here, so he's fair game. Up into the trees, Rafe roosts on a wide limb where he has eyes on Mauri. Is he awaiting instruction? *Eyes wide, Chaus,* I tell myself. *He's unpredictable.*

Kofi roars that bone-throttling roar that is every bit a weapon as his bulk and jaws. He towers over Beam, who has still not shifted. What is she waiting for? She stands before him without flinching, my beautiful girlfriend in her stunning dress, small before the massive beast.

I pay for my distraction when Rafe surges from the sky and sends me somersaulting. Clutching wildly, I catch on to a branch in time to swing out of his waiting talons and haul myself across the Jungle, thinking that he'll give chase. What predator could resist after a near miss like that?

One who has other prey in mind.

Just like that, Rafe has separated me from my partner. He knows I'm able to keep away from him. He played me.

I can't see Beam from here, but I am pounding the earth back to her.

When I enter the clearing, she's still in her human form! Kofi is mad at her, flailing his human arms and hollering at Mauri to make her play by the rules. "No one is required to shift," Mauri laughs.

All in all, I'd say it's a brilliant strategy. She remains unscathed. She didn't have to go up against the larger lion or even flee. She simply had to remain Beam.

In the commotion, Rafe, the winged creature, dive bombs the scene, skeletal talons extended. To my disbelief, he goes for Mauri, but it is Leander who roars. Or is it? Mauri takes a swing when Rafe buzzes him and pulls back claws dripping with Rafe's blood.

Rafe circles the scene. I'm really not sure what I'm supposed to be doing. Kofi is shouting threats at Beam. Telling her he's going to attack her whether she shifts or not. Over the crowd, Berke yells, "Focus on Rafe, Chausie."

As an osprey ensnares a fish, Rafe changes tack and grabs my Beam.

He simply explodes through the space and is gone again, having dragged her off her feet.

Aiden races in on all fours, and Kofi lions up again in time to receive his full-on attack. Aiden's a big wolf. It shouldn't surprise me, the vicious slashes he scores in Kofi's skin, but that mane is coarse.

"Go!" Aiden grunts at me, but I never planned to stick around for him anyway, not with Beam in the grip of the Were.

I don't spare a thought for Bear Man. I'm sure that, even with his girth, he was no match for Aiden. Probably tapped out right away.

Mauri narrates what's happening, and the crowd is unintelligibly loud. He should climb up to his platform. It's too wild for him in here, even inside the Lion. But that's all background noise to me. I'm scenting. I'm stalking. Laser-focused on movement of any kind, eyes sharp, ears on a swivel. Rafe can't perch exactly, certainly not high in the thinning treetops, so I scour the lower parts of the Jungle. He's had a lot more time to study the terrain than I have. He probably had a hand—or a wing—in developing it. I don't want to consider what he was plotting to do with Beam after he decided to draw himself as the wildcard, not when he has taken every chance to spy on her through the windows. I shouldn't have allowed Mauri's showmanship to distract me.

"Beam?!"

The only answering sound is Kofi, and I think he may be tearing Aiden to shreds.

"He's tapping out!" Berke's voice rises above the crowd. "For god's sake, Mauri!" She flings a towel and then herself into the ring. "Kofi, you have to stop! If you can't control yourself, then you can't fight!" She has some nerve taking on Kofi in that state—gotta hand it to her.

Kofi stops mauling Aiden. I try to decipher how badly he is hurt by a glimpse at Berke's face. He needs me. But so does Beam. I don't understand why her smell disappeared, but then it comes to me. It's one of Rafe's abilities. It was the same that day I couldn't get a hold of her scent at the cabin. Rafe himself was within inches of me before I knew it. Same thing when I showed up in the Jungle and had to call for him.

He must cloak his own effects and maybe the effects of his—prey. I'm sure Kofi is coming for me, but I close my eyes and plead with Beam to speak up, to shine out, to let me know where Rafe has hidden her.

"Beam?!"

BEAM

Rafe flies through the levels of the jungle with clinical precision. I'm folded upside down by the hips, mind, and he clears seemingly impossible obstacles within a hair's breadth. If I hadn't jerked myself into a ball, I'm pretty sure my head would've been knocked off. Maybe that's what he's going for—the way a sea otter knocks its clams on the rocks before it eats them.

Through a small opening, we fly, and I am dumped onto dusty, red clay in a space where several rocks lean together to make a shelter. There is nowhere to hide and no other way out, so I press myself as far back as I can.

At the opening, Rafe fans his great wings like he's airing out the place. It reminds me of the way President Tumbling Rock spread the sage smoke through The Vigilance, but there is no appealing smell—there's suddenly no smell at all—and there is no crow-man dropping out of the ceiling. I raise my eyes just in case. Nope.

Once Rafe is satisfied with his wafting, he shrinks in size to become an ordinary grey rat snake. You might think that I'd pounce on him, right? Shift into a panther and eat him up? But I'm so curious as to why he picked a small, seemingly harmless animal, that I just watch. He lifts his head and chest—he *stands* with a significant portion of his body—and dances.

Swaying in graceful rhythms, Rafe-the-snake may be trying to hypnotize me. Isn't that what the snake in *The Jungle Book* did? What was that one's name?

"Kaa," Rafe-the-snake says. Did he just answer my question? I avert my eyes. I don't want to be hypnotized.

When he loses my attention, Rafe drops to the ground. His scales give way to jelly, and soon, he becomes a huge slug—a small animal but a large mollusk. He climbs the wall. This takes less time than you'd think. About halfway up, he drops himself by a rope of slime and grows a large, blue pustule.

What is happening here?

Rafe-the-slug swings on a gooey web at the whim of a non-existent breeze. I'm not being hurt. I think it's possible I'm being courted. My eyes feel heavy, and I find myself yawning. The slug's head takes the shape of a lion's, like Kofi's, but it's still a slimy slug.

The lion says, "I don't want to kill you."

"That's good. Then don't."

"I didn't want to kill the robin."

He transforms into a robin and hops in front of me on two small feet. Tears fall from his tiny, round eyes. Rafe-the-robin speaks—or, he makes robin sounds—but he's trying to get a message across.

"I don't understand bird language, Rafe," I say.

A human head manifests where the bird head has been. It has pointy ears and chin-length hair, but Rafe isn't able to hold onto that form. He cries, "He's coming to life! He must be stopped!" and contorts into the slug again.

"Rafe, are you not the wildcard?" I ask, and I swear he scorns my mental capacity with his slug face. "Well, I'm sure what you have to say is very important," I say petulantly, "but this also seems pressing. If you're not trying to fight me, then who is?"

The slug grows a great lion paw, its mighty claws straining against an opponent until they are turned onto itself.

Then he makes the claw into the shape of Robyn and Rafe-the-slug eats her.

"Did you eat Robyn?" I ask.

Beam! I hear it in my head and jerk to attention. I feel that Chausie is racked with concern, and here I am, lulled into a dreamy conversation with a werewolf who isn't making any sense.

Rafe's slime string breaks, and he falls to the ground in his usual form, the bird of prey/wolf combo, but he's weary. He can barely open his eyes.

Before he can stop me, I dive out of the opening—which I should have thought through a little better because there is no ground on the other side. I'm freefalling as a human being, so I twist into panther form on the way down to the ground! It's awesome! Just like Chausie can do! I claw onto vines and sprint along the branches. I scent him, and as I lay eyes on him, I see Kofi bearing down, nearly on top of him.

Chausie isn't even paying attention! He has his eyes closed in concentration.

"Get away from him, Kofi!" I roar. Turns out, I have a big girl roar. I have a lioness roar! Kofi flinches. I mean, not that much. In truth, it may have been more of a muscle twitch. But anyway, he does look up.

Unfortunately.

He hurtles over Chausie, and—remember what Berke said about his ability to jump? All. True. So high and so far—and so coming down to end me. There is blood all over his whiskers, mane, paws, and chest. I'm not sticking around to add mine to it.

I dash down the tree branch—oh my gosh, I'm fast—and meet up with a relieved, though terse, Chausie. Kofi skids as he spins to face us.

"Is that *your* blood he's wearing?" I pant.

"Aiden's."

Chausie's tone is flat, even by cat standards, and I worry that Aiden may not have survived.

"Where's Rafe?" he asks. He's compartmentalizing. That's probably good.

Kofi is seething, his lion breath sprays flecks of spit.

"No idea," I answer. "Last time I saw him, he was a slug."

Chaus merely nods—because that's a normal thing to hear.

"I think it's time for the ring," he says, eyes on Kofi, head down, ready to clash.

"What about Aiden?"

"I can't think about that right now. Berke's with him. Kofi doesn't want to go with us. Mauri is a lunatic. I can't see how this ends well."

"Let's do it." I proceed to woman up so that I can fetch the ring when Kofi rockets at me from his haunches, but Chausie's ready. He meets him in the air and knocks him off course. Chausie is on *fire*, not literally, but with the knowledge that he has to fight twice as hard and fast to bring Kofi down. He slashes, and, quick as lightning, he bounds away, readying himself for another round. I'm standing on two feet as a woman. Kofi tries to keep an eye on each of us.

"I *told* you," Kofi says as a lion with a deep accent. "No more mercy in human form." That's what he'd said earlier. After all, he can't advance into Mauri's fight club if he can't do what it takes.

He really is majestic. He looks every bit the king, complete with a heavy brow to hold the weight of what he feels burdened to do—namely, to destroy me.

"Kofi, listen up," Chausie says, assuming human form. "I know you think that there is, but there is no future for you here."

Kofi resumes his human form as well, just to argue. "There's no future for me anywhere else. I may have *killed* that guy. You think they'll let me live in the human world after that?" His voice cracks. If Aiden did die, I know in my heart that Kofi will never get over it.

"No, he's—no, he's not dead." Chausie inadvertently turns like he can simply find Aiden sitting on the bleachers, and then he looks at me, his face ashen, and I know exactly what he's thinking. *I should have saved him.* The thing about being an Elixir is that it gives you a messiah complex. You feel obligated to save everyone.

"You can't think about that right now," I remind him out loud, and then I get mad. "Kofi, there is no reason for you to continue this stupid fight. You come with us right now. Chausie is the best friend you've got. He got Harriet free. He got Rosa free and even Mr. Turner. Yeah, he had to leave you behind before. And he hasn't stopped obsessing about it ever since. Why do you think he's here? Heck, why do you think *Aiden* is here? To get you out. Now, stop being such a sullen brat and come with us so that we can get out of here."

I think my tirade stuns him. I'm just so sick of all of this, and Mauri, on his stupid microphone, is getting on my last nerve. "Shuuut uuuuuu-uup!" I roar at him. And yes, I have slipped back into panther mode. The crowd cheers. I roll my panther eyes at them. And then I give Kofi a little hiss for good measure. He backs it up a step. *That's right; you back it up,* I think, and make sure to become human again before I do something I'll regret.

"You really have a way?" Kofi asks. He barely moves his mouth, and he throws a look at Mauri, who is issuing a verbal invitation for all other shifters to join the fight.

"Yes. I have something that, as soon as I touch it, will put me into another place." He's gonna do it.

"Give it to me," he says. He's not gonna do it.

"You wanna go by yourself?" I ask. I don't know if he means to leave us behind or if he's putting us through some test. "It doesn't work that way. You need me to open the door on the other—"

"You think I don't know what that is?!" He stumbles toward me and would've yanked on my collar if he hadn't received a mighty check from Chausie. Over Chausie's shoulder, Kofi rants, "You think I haven't worn one of those before? You work for that goblin! You're no more than a slave yourself!"

If his words were solid, the force of them would've bowled me over.

"I am not his slave. Look." I glance at Chausie. This is the same predicament he was in when it was my neck on the line. Do something to test the veracity of Frilk's vow. "I can take this off, but I fear it will summon the goblin, and he has sworn to kill Chausie if I do."

"What a bunch of bull," Kofi spits.

The wolves are entering the arena, and there appear to be others of which I was unaware. Maybe they're the ones who never returned from their encounters with Rafe.

"We have to leave him, Chaus," I say. "There's no convincing him."

"Hang on." Chausie comes to me like he's in slow motion, each step heavy and seeming to cost him something. He lifts his hands to my neck as gently as if he means to kiss me. The intent behind his eyes is no less full of love for all of its regret. It fills me with inexplicable sadness.

"Chaus?"

"I'll find a way," he says. "Don't leave him behind." He comes away with the collar.

23

FRILK'S RETURN

CHAUSIE

The next moments are a blur. The collar chooses me as its next attachment. I assume my lion form and sprint further into the undergrowth of the Jungle.

"Oh, no, you don't!" Beam shouts. "Chausie Louris! You stop right now!" And she's on my tail in a heartbeat.

Kofi is following both of us. I'm not sure what he hopes to get out of this. Maybe it's just his prey drive kicking in.

When it's clear I'm not going to get far enough to keep Frilk from being a danger to them, I whip around. I do admit that I'm pissy. "What are you following me for?" I snap.

"Throw it away," Beam chides. "At the very least. Don't *wear* it! What is wrong with you?" She's busy trying to find fresh blood on one of us when Frilk appears.

All three of us cats back up on twelve legs. Of all the monsters I've faced, Frilk is the cruelest and—unfortunately—the smartest.

He raises a dagger, the tip of which is wedged between his fingers, positioned to hurl. I can see the inevitable rotation of it in my mind, but he stops himself before he flings it. He's eyeing the collar on my neck, and then he searches Beam, who has no collar. He's thinking through the possibilities, eyes narrowed, brows furrowed.

Finally, he pulls out a vial and tosses it to Beam. "Your blood. Now."

She obliges, shifting into a woman and searching for something sharp to make a wound. Frilk closes the distance and slices her forearm. Kofi stiffens.

When Frilk's small vial is full, he tells Beam to stay put, and you can tell she's scared to death. She starts pleading with him, her voice all trembly. "Take me. Just take me with you now and leave Chausie. He hasn't done anything. He hasn't—just take me!" I remember what a bloodbath was left in the kitchen the last time Frilk kept a promise. I don't want Beam to relive the horror with me in her role.

But there is no dissuading Frilk. He's intent upon me, and ultimately, I'd rather that. Beam has the ring. So, let him come.

"Kofi, get her out of here," I say as a cat. "Let her take you to the meadow and set you free." And then I shift into my more vulnerable human form.

"No!" Beam yells. She rushes forward, but Kofi blocks her path. As she fights to get around him, Frilk spills a drop of her blood onto the collar, and the collar comes loose, falling to the ground.

"How about that?" he mutters and then stabs me through the throat without warning. How is he so quick?

Beam shrieks and Frilk turns on her. I'm spurting blood through the hole in my neck, but I swear I don't feel it. *Get out of here!* I try to *will* her to use the ring. I stagger to my knees, trying to tell her I'll be OK. Frilk doesn't know that I heal the same way she does.

Lion Kofi is staring down at me, aghast. For all of his surly declarations, I think he's seen enough blood. There's nothing more I can do to entreat him to force Beam to escape with the ring. Frilk's going to disappear with her and use her as his blood well for the rest of her long, long life. I try to speak out again, but it's all gurgling sounds.

My panther doesn't know how to quit. She gets by Kofi and is now fighting Frilk so hard that even his whip is having trouble tying her up. I don't think she cares about being captured. She's just trying to get to me.

I'm lying on my side, struggling for air. It's like breathing through a straw with a tear in it. Does that mean he stabbed through my trachea?

Something switches in Kofi. He looks away from me to watch Frilk struggle with Beam—who is so angry, she is gnashing her human teeth.

"Let her go to him!" Kofi growls.

I don't know if Frilk understands cat language, but he appears to understand being pounced on. Kofi lands on top of him with a snarl that knocks Beam free of his grip, and he utters a string of curses as he falls under the weight.

Beam doesn't wait to see what comes of it, but clamors over the grass to me. "Chausie? Please keep breathing." Tears stream down her face.

You know how on TV shows, the guy who's bleeding out says he's cold? I don't feel that. I feel like I'm on fire. I point—inasmuch as I can lift my finger—to where Frilk and Kofi's tussle has come to a quick end. They're both lying in the grass. I don't understand how the goblin can take on a lion hundreds of pounds heavier, but Kofi is whimpering. He makes a motion to stand but slides down onto his furry belly. Looks like he's been stabbed multiple times. Meanwhile, Frilk grimaces and appears to have sustained as many gashes as he has dealt—I'm happy to report.

"Go see," I tell Beam, though there's no voice in the sound—just whatever noise the consonants make in my mouth. "Kofi."

My neck must be healing because she agrees to leave me. "Kof?" She bends to pick up his huge lion head by the mane. "Kofi?"

He's gonna die. That's what her mournful eyes say when she raises them to me.

Help him, I beg her. *Please.*

She nods and produces a claw of her own without shifting—cool trick—to scratch a deep gash in her arm. Kofi's huge mouth lies open as he languishes, and his eyes, which are half rolled back in his head, come round when Beam fits her arm against his tongue.

"Drink," she says. "Go ahead."

It doesn't matter if Kofi wants to or not. The blood is pouring into his mouth. Frilk watches with an addled listlessness.

Before long, Kofi grows stronger and lifts his head to assess what's happening to him. When he suspects he's healing, he becomes very still;

only his eyes roam. After a moment, he heaves an enormous inhale and inspects his chest for proof.

Now, he believes it. He stares at Beam, bows his head, and licks the length of her bleeding forearm in gentle lion kisses that I try not to begrudge. Finally, he shifts into his human form—without the scowl for once—and leans back on his hands where he sits staring at Beam like he wants to worship her. I know the feeling.

Sadly, I have stopped paying attention to Frilk, who, though he is hurt, has regained plenty enough strength to yank my head back by the hair and hold his dagger to my throat. Since I'm late to the play, I slump as if I have no strength and little life left in me. "Woman," Frilk calls out. "I require your resources. Don't make this man suffer any more than he has to."

She doesn't turn her head at first, but I can see the hard expression forming, the one that means she is OVER this, and it will end NOW. When she rises, I don't know what she has in mind, only that it's gonna be fabulous. She stands tall and stares down her nose at the goblin. So, I don't remind him he already has a vial of her blood on him.

"Come to me, or his whole head comes off." Frilk is hurting. He grunts the last words. But his grip on me is fierce, and I'm too weak to mount a counterattack.

I don't tell her not to do it. Honestly, I'm so enraptured at this point, I just want to watch.

"Open your wound and drip it into my mouth," Frilk orders. "Do it!"

Beam's sapphire eyes are sharper than the goblin's dagger. My god, she's gorgeous.

"I will *do* it!" Frilk growls and draws blood from below my ear. I wish I didn't flinch, but I do.

Without taking her eyes off of Frilk, she does the cool trick with her cat claw in human form and walks—I should say stalks—to us. Her hair has come down from where she had it tied up, and it's all messy now, giving her the air of a war goddess. Her square jaw is set like stone.

When she arrives, Frilk grabs her arm in one hand and jerks her to the side, pushing me to the ground. I think I can get up now, but for some reason, I relax. Kofi seems to be under the same spell. He can't take his eyes off of her.

Before he drinks, Frilk says, "I'm going to enslave the African for the rest of his life. And I'm going to find others to kill in front of you just for spite. And that one?" He gestures toward me. "I'm still going to hack off his head."

That may be what does him in. Beam doesn't say a word as that abomination drinks from her. She stares him down the whole while.

Kofi shakes himself from his stupor, but I block him from going to her aid.

And then, the goblin stumbles back, drops his dagger, and clutches his heart. It's like a giant vacuum sucks his insides out. Like the snake that bit me back in South Dakota! He sort of implodes and falls—as a rubbery piece of jerky.

After half a minute goes by and Beam still hasn't done more than glare at Frilk's corpse with contempt, I quietly call her name.

She turns that look upon me until it softens. "You're better now?" she says.

"Yes."

She visually checks on Kofi, who is almost *smiling*. He's a mixture of awe and joy, and I don't know what else because I don't care. He's not the one I want to watch.

"OK, stop staring," Beam says to both of us. "We have work to do."

I tilt my head to receive my assignment.

"Let's go get Leander."

Kofi looks ready to march into a freaking war zone for her.

"Feels pretty amazing, doesn't it?" I ask him. I remember the day I drank from the woman. She healed everything that was ever wrong with me.

Kofi rolls his head my way and says, "I could take on anybody. I could take on everybody."

I chuckle at how amazed he sounds, but I nod my head. "I know what you mean." And to Beam, I say, "What's the plan, my queen?"

"The plan is to get our so-called liege to actually show up and obey an order." She lifts her head and yells, "BLUE! You better get your butt right here, right now!"

Pop. And there he is. "You called?"

Beam starts right in. "I am very upset with you."

"What for? *Ew!*" Blue uses Beam to swing away from the thing that used to be Frilk. "What is *that?* Is that Frilk?!"

"Where have you been?" Beam demands.

"At home with the kids."

"Oh, the babies hatched?!" she squeals, so I guess all is forgiven. Blue nods enthusiastically. "All five?"

"They just needed their dear dad around," he says.

"Do you love them?"

"They're incredible."

"And Larkin's OK?"

"She's great. I mean, she's never home. She goes to talk with the animals."

"What *is* he?" Kofi asks me.

"You can see him?"

"Grant could see the invisible for a while," Beam says. "Probably won't last."

Blue side-eyes Kofi, but says to me, "You'll have to come visit. We fixed up the house."

"What house?"

"Laurel's."

"Blue, that is *Beam's* house now," I say while Beam asserts something to the same effect.

He shrugs. "We like to skinny dip in the hot spring."

I don't even... Beam laughs outright at my dismay. Blue says, "Who's the lion?"

"That's Kofi," she answers. "Listen, Blue, I need you to go get Larkin."

He splutters, "Then who will care for the babies?"

"Can't you just bring them with you? I want to meet them!"

"I guess so. Now that ole Beef Jerky is dead."

"And will you please come when we call you from now on?" Beam asks. "We've been very anxious."

"*Uhf!* What do you think I have been?!" He pauses with a look of expectancy. Is it not rhetorical? Pause over. "You and Chausie don't understand because you don't have kids, but there is no time—not one millisecond—to do anything but take care of them. How could I possibly get to your psychic nine-one-one calls? I am exhausted all the time. Look at my eyes." Four fingers on each hand spread the skin around his gigantic eyes. They are rather bloodshot.

"*Oh,*" Beam says dejectedly. "Well...I didn't know. I'm sorry."

"No, Iiiiii'm sorry!" Blue wails, causing Kofi to look concerned. "Iii-iii'm sorry. You are my bosom friends! I'm—I'm just so exhausted!"

This degenerates into agonized sobbing. It may be too late to intervene.

"Alright, little buddy." I pat his heaving shoulders. "Keep it together. Listen, do what Beam says, and guess what."

He sniffs, his tiny chin trembling, his giant eyes brimming, but I do have his attention.

"My dad rented a bright red Dodge Challenger Hellcat—the one with the wide body. And we're gonna drive it."

"Can I come?" Kofi pipes up.

Trying not to laugh in astonishment, I say, "Absolutely." *As long as Blue doesn't throw a fit.* But Blue likes the idea. He says, "Just us guys?"

I latch onto it. "Yeah, just us guys. You, me, and Kofi."

"And Beam will babysit?"

"*Uhhh.*" I glance her way.

"Of course I will. Just go get Larkin, OK? And bring her back. We'll be in the arena."

"I don't know where the arena is."

Beam stretches her arm to point in that direction. "It's—"

"I don't need to know." And *poof.* He's gone.

The super-sweet tone gives way to grumbling as she says, "Then why did you mention it?"

She surveys the flattened goblin and collects his things—the whip, the dagger, and the vial of her blood—which is good because what is left hasn't congealed. Goblin must have added some kind of anticoagulant. The collar, she picks up through the material of her dress.

Beam looks down at herself for a place to stash those items. "No pockets?" I ask and offer to take them.

"No pockets," she says and hands them over, except for the collar. "Which pocket are you least likely to reach into as a matter of habit?"

I unbutton my jacket and offer her one on the inside.

"You should take the sheath for that dagger," Kofi says. He swipes it from Frilk's belt and hands it to me.

"Why don't *you* take it?" I offer.

"Really?"

"Yeah, you should," Beam tells him. "The metal is from outer space, and you're a Leonid. If Chausie keeps the whip, you'll both have something made of it, and I have a feeling it will serve the two of you better than it will anyone else."

Kofi accepts the gift and even steals Frilk's belt to wear the dagger with his tux. He's a mix between James Bond and a pirate.

Now that all that's done, Beam observes him. "You still feeling good Kof?"

He offers her a genuine smile. "I feel great."

"Good. I have some work for you."

CHAUSIE

"*That* was the judgment," Beam says without context. She's marching us back to the arena to rescue Leander. How we're going to pull that off, we don't yet know.

"*What* was the judgment?" I ask. "What your blood did to Frilk?"

"Yeah, remember what Mrs. Turner said? How judgment courses through my veins?"

"Turner?" Kofi asks. "Like Harriet?" He adds, "And Rosa and their dad?"

Hmm.

Beam throws him a look, and he freaking smiles like he's been caught. I'm not used to this side of him. "Kofi?" she asks. "Are you crushing on Harriet?"

After a slight hesitation, he positions his thumb and index finger close together to indicate *just a little bit.*

"Oh my gosh!" I erupt. "Is it Beam's blood that's making you so... soft?"

"I am not soft."

I mimic the way he'd used his fingers to measure his affection for Harriet and turn it on him. "Just a little soft," I whisper.

"Shut up," he laughs. "She was just so composed. Like she didn't belong in that place as a matter of being."

"None of us belong there as a matter of being," I say.

"Yeah, but she wore it like a crown. She is nobody's slave." He mutters something that may have been, "Unlike me."

"Yeah," I nod. "She was fierce."

"Good for her," Beam says. "And good for you. Chausie has her mom's number, so you can get in touch with her and ask her out."

"Oh, I don't think that..."

"Yes, when we get out of here, that's what you're going to do."

It's funny how bossy she gets. I have to laugh when Kofi acquiesces with a small salute.

"Do you think *my* blood holds judgment?" I ask.

"Well, you turned me into a freaking cat shifter," Beam says, "so why not? Of course, Mrs. Turner saw *the light of heaven* in you." She makes the words thick to tease me for being praised in such a way, though we both know it's her soul that lights up like the sun.

A lot of noise spills our way from the arena, not cheers so much as shock and—objections?

"What do you think's going on?" Beam asks.

"I'll scout it out," I suggest.

"Let's stay together."

As we skirt the main arena, we see that the audience is on their feet, and an eery silence replaces the noise we heard. Our senator and her people are leaving, their heads hung or turned away from the action.

"They're sneaking out," I note. "Whatever went on while we were gone was over the line. They don't want to be associated with it."

A majestic golden lion paces back and forth. Yes, a lion with a mane. Yes, he is glorious. He puts Kofi to shame—which is saying something because as much as I hate to admit it, Kofi's pretty glorious himself— especially right now with Beam's blood giving the ultimate glow-up.

This lion has someone's blood too. It's all around his mouth, and a wolf is lying on the ground in his path. She looks broken. Her condition must be the reason for the silence. One of her pack members is guarding her body from the beast. Every time he gets close, that guardian wolf bares her teeth and issues a throaty threat. She's no match for the lion but valiant all the same. The last pack member has become human and is weeping over the first, stroking her fur and trying to make her open her eyes.

Several other fighters have come into the arena. Maybe they're trying to get in on the action or maybe they're trying to stop the atrocity. Right now, they're all just standing still.

"Is she dead, Chaus?" Beam whispers.

"I think so, Babe."

"It's Chesnea," Kofi says dolefully.

"Chesnea's the alpha?" Beam asks.

He nods and says, "That woman crying over her is Journey."

"Journey—she's the nippy one. She was forced to be here like we were."

Kofi questions her with his eyes and then turns them upon the crowd. I know what he's thinking. *How many others?*

"Who is the lion?" I ask, but no one has the answer. Or else no one wants to share it.

"He looks like he's been AI-generated," Beam says. "He's not quite believable. Too brilliant. Too perfect. His mane lifts in a breeze that doesn't even exist."

Now that she mentions it, he does look that way. "He's real enough to kill," I remark.

The incredible lion sniffs the air, zeroes in on us, and recognizes us with a slow, stately bow of the head. So, I guess our cover's blown. He sits on his haunches like he's sitting on a throne and waits for us to make a move.

"Rafe is the only one who can manifest surreal characteristics like that," I offer. Not because I think it's Rafe but because I don't want it to be a creature of epic myth.

Kofi sniffs the air. "That's not Rafe," he says. "It's Mauri."

And finally, I say what we all know to be true. "That's the Lion of Nemea. He has come alive in Mauri somehow."

"We have to get to the mansion!" Beam blurts out. She shifts and leaps into action, racing for the Jungle's exit.

"What happened to sticking together?!" I yell and bound after her.

She nearly makes it to her goal, but the Lion is faster than any animal I've ever seen. My heart sinks as he overtakes her, and her whiskers tremble when he snarls in her face.

Before, when Beam faced off with Kofi, I said that he dwarfed her. No. This thing makes her look like a doll.

Kofi and I dash to her defense, but another monster gets there before we can. Rafe. The werewolf beats to the ground in a bizarre mish-mash of animal traits and is covered with eyeballs, which is gross to me. He has a set of human ears and another set of pointy ears like Larkin's or Robyn's. The real trouble is his saber-tooth fangs, which he exposes viciously as he propels his head in search of victims—or that's what I think.

When we skid to a halt—on the Rafe side of Beam—Rafe doesn't even turn one of his many creepy eyeballs upon us. And they're not on Beam either. They're all focused on Mauri.

This standoff lasts only long enough for the Mauri Lion to express his displeasure. I don't know who moves first. There is a tense pause, and then everybody jumps. Kofi and I hurl ourselves toward Beam, and the three of us roll outside the impending skirmish.

Beam is up on her feet again, tearing for the opening as Mauri flings Rafe through the air with his mighty jaws. But Rafe shifts into a long-beaked, massive-winged pterodactyl and soars right back into action.

"Kofi!" I yell because he's watching the opponents clash. When he hears me, he gives his head a shake, and soon, he has caught up to me.

The noises that trail us make my skin crawl. Snapping and ripping, crunching, howls of pain. By the time we hit the steps of the mansion's portico, there is a roar so great that it seems to fill the whole Earth.

"Get inside!" Beam commands, and after we pile in, I lock the brass doors.

You know, as I scan the doors' length, I finally understand why they are so tall. "He's coming," I warn them. "He'll have full access."

Beam has already disappeared behind the marble wrestlers. Kofi and I catch up to her in the kitchen, where she's emptying the knife block. "Sweetheart, claws are better suited for fighting than those knives."

"That's what I'm looking for!"

Kofi and I exchange a puzzled glance while Beam overturns the drawers so that utensils clatter onto the floor. "She had to have had it. She had to. What else would she want us to find?!" Her voice grows shrill as she beseeches us to come up with the answer, and her eyes fall past me.

"A key," she says and then repeats it as a question. "A key? Not those by the door. Something that could—because she wouldn't have kept it in here. She would have locked it away. Or no—what if *he* locked it away? But still, she may have had a key." All the while Beam is ranting, she's jogging around the kitchen overturning things. She stops and shakes me by the lapel. "Help me, Chausie!"

"Is this it?" Kofi asks. An old-fashioned cast iron key rests in his upturned palm. The key is tied to several coal-black feathers—our feathers, if I'm not mistaken. Beam immediately tugs the beaded pouch from where it hangs inside her dress. She searches inside, then refers back to the feathers quizzically. The way Leander's pelt loved Robyn, maybe the feathers did too. Maybe *they* sleepwalked.

We both gape at Kofi and the key in his hand.

"It was in the cookie jar," he explains. "That's where my grandma used to hide things."

I don't know what is more shocking. The fact that Kofi found a key attached to sleepwalking feathers or the fact that he has a grandmother.

Beam comes to her senses and drags Kofi down to kiss his cheek—which startles him more than anything else has, if you can believe that. "Good job," she says and strokes the feathers. Is it the movement of her hand, or do the feathers flap on their own? Either way, she's back in business. "Now, to find the lock. Did Robyn have possession of it? Or Mauri? It may be on Mauri's side of the house."

"Would Robyn have had access to Mauri's personal rooms?" I ask.

"I don't know. Let's split up."

Kofi raises his hand and says, "What do we think is locked away?"

Beam smiles. She's feeling hopeful again. "There is only one way to pierce Leander's invincible hide."

"His own claws," I say. "And one of them is missing."

"You think it's here?"

"It makes sense. Robyn could've been present when Heracles figured out what made Leander vulnerable." My mind leaps ahead. "What about upstairs? Mauri called it Heracles Hall. That's a good name for a place to keep his weapon."

"Yeah," Beam nods. "I mean, we had free rein, but that may have been a joke to him."

Another roar goes up and shakes the windows—the riot-proof windows—reminding us that we need to work fast.

"OK-OK," Beam says quickly. "If Mauri has it, it's probably in some astonishing thing. A priceless sarcophagus—jewelry box-style. Something with lions carved into it. Something old. Chausie, search Heracles Hall and then the sunroom. Kofi, take the library and the room filled with pottery. If I can't find it here in Robyn's space, I'll go to Mauri's private wing. Let's meet there."

"Be quick," I tell her. "He's coming for us. He'll barge in as soon as he's free of Rafe."

Whatever else I want to tag onto the warning, I don't take the time. I sprint away, wondering why Rafe is going up against Mauri at all. I skip most of the stairs and enter the first door. All the rooms up here, as showy as they are, remain uncluttered. Nothing in the drawers or closets but essentials—like in a hotel. It doesn't take me long to clear them.

I search the sunroom, or the conservatory as Mauri calls it, but unless it's hiding under one of the planters, it's not in here either.

A suppressed yowl comes from deep within the house, sounding like Kofi's tail was caught in a door. One thing I've got on that overgrown feline is a fantastic, long, bushy tail. His looks like a snake wearing a poof on its head.

I head toward the yowl, checking the foyer as I pass. This takes a moment because there are several shelves of artifacts—but nothing that looks like a box with a keyhole. As I round the sculpture, I eye the Heracles' marble hand, holding Leander's claw aloft. I check it. I do. It would be just like Mauri to hide something so precious in plain sight. But this one is made of marble.

"Chausie," Beam calls from the direction of the kitchen, "the feathers showed us where it was! We would never have found it, but Kofi noticed what they were doing." At the same time, the front doors push open, and Mauri enters the cavernous threshold as a man—a man inside of a lion coat.

Two sets of footsteps slap the floor behind me. "Go back," I yell to them.

But they round the sculpture—and Beam's face falls. She found the claw. But Mauri found her. Beam obscures the discovery behind her back in not as subtle of a move as one would hope, but what choice does she have? She has no freaking pockets. I am really starting to internalize why women gripe about that.

OK, well, there are three of us. As long as Mauri doesn't use Leander-power to become a legendary monster of mythic fame, we should be able to take him. And if he does, well, we've got the claw. And if it goes sideways, we'll use the ring to disappear and regroup somewhere safe to form another plan.

Kofi makes a sudden move—and this is how much misplaced trust I have in him—I don't react. I let him wrest the claw from Beam's grip and then hold the very dagger she gave to him to her throat! He challenges me with ferocious, curled lips, though he is in human form, and I can't advance because my Beam is at the end of his blade. In the smuggest tone possible, he says to Mauri, "You were right. She led me right to it."

"Kofi, no!" Beam pleads.

I can't believe what I'm hearing. He betrayed us. After all we did for him. After saving his life! The clearer I see it, the hotter I become. But I mean, why not? He declared to me plainly enough what his intentions were.

OK, new plan. No more chances for Kofi. He can endure the fate he has chosen.

I don't interfere as he drags Beam across the foyer to present Mauri with the cursed claw of the Lion of Nemea. He has the strength of Beam's blood in him, and right now, I just want to keep her safe. I try to speak through our mated connection. *Time for you to go. Use the ring.*

"Well *done,* Kofi," Mauri says and turns his prize over admiringly. "I knew you were a champion. I knew you'd come through. And just in time for our big finale."

Whatever that entails.

Kofi holds his head high, looking very much like he did that time he spat in my face. It's all I can do not to pounce on him, strength of blood or not.

"What did you plan to do with this, Beam?" Mauri asks. "Certainly not turn it on me. Not after I gave you access to my home and opportunities you never would have had the privilege to enjoy."

I almost can't wait to hear her retort. Her ability to fight with words is unparalleled. Phrases so sharp that her adversaries don't bleed for several silent seconds of reckoning.

But all she does is cast a hurt glance at Kofi. She can't believe it either. That makes me angrier than before. She saved his life. I guess her blood's not a perfect judge of character after all. And now I feel guilty. I'm the reason she gave Kofi second chances. She had him pegged.

The power to shift overtakes Mauri—and it's not natural—not the easy slide into form that real shifters make. Leander's pelt engulfs him, and he sort of gets stuffed down into it—like when you have to change your pillowcase, but your pillow is too bulky. The lion then fills up the foyer, and next to the sculpture, he looks like Leander's AI-generated twin. He huffs out a breath of catty satisfaction that makes me want to punch him in the nose.

"What have you done to Rafe?" Beam asks.

Pause. Blink. Is Rafe not the least of our worries?

"Or was he acting too?" she adds. "Do you have *everyone* trained to do your bidding? Are you not happy until *every* knee bows to the magnificent Mauri?"

Ahh, there she is. Is now the time for the caustic wit, though?

"And did you *have* to kill the wolf?!" she continues. "Do you think that makes you a big, strong champion?"

Mauri's whiskers twitch, and since he could devour us both at the same time, I think we should go.

"Sweetheart?" I ask, though Kofi still has an arm around her collarbones and a knife to her throat. "The ring?"

Mauri—in Leander's lion body—slowly pads around the sculpture in the opposite direction of us. Of course, if he continues that route, he'll soon show up behind us, and we'll be in an even more vulnerable position—if that's possible. There is no getting past Kofi without a fight. He'll be nearly invincible for days. He's glaring at me. Maybe I was glaring first. But now, he points with his eyes down at the hand that imprisons my girlfriend, and he does her trick, where only his arm becomes lion.

OK. So?

Beam looks down.

I look harder. One of the claws is much shorter and smaller than the rest. I hadn't noticed that before. When I was ten, one of mine was ripped out. Took forever to— But it wouldn't take Kofi's forever. Not today.

The Lion of Nemea has come around the back side of the sculpture now and is breathing down my neck. I don't shift because I don't know how much control Mauri has over the thing—which gives me an idea. How much of Leander is still in there? And now it occurs to me why Beam wants Larkin here. Perhaps Larkin can reach Leander as Robyn had done. Her ability to speak and persuade in any language is unparalleled.

"The fight's not over," Kofi proclaims. "Right, Mauri?" He shoves Beam into my arms and sheaths the knife. "Guests, your investors—hell, the whole training camp is waiting to watch us triumph over any who want to come onto the field and try."

Instead of a reply—I'm beginning to think Mauri doesn't know any cat language other than the roar—he tosses his mane.

"Hello again." Blue appears between Mauri and me. Over and around his shoulders, a baby sling is tied, and in that sling rests a nest, padded and secured in its own compartment. And in that nest are five teacup-sized babies, each with pointy ears, wide eyes, and a large smile. Blue shrieks when he sees Mauri and jumps into my arms. "Why do you have so many lions?!" he demands. "Can *that* one see me?"

"No," I say as subtly as I can. I cradle Blue and back away from Mauri because while Blue remains invisible, the babies do not. Mauri licks his lion lips and sniffs loudly. *What have we here?* he seems to say.

Beam steps out front of me to obscure his view. This is all going from bad to worse. "Blue, get them out of here," I say through my teeth.

The lion bats Beam out of the way and lunges for me. As I spin out of reach, Blue flies from my arms like a fumbled football. The children, by the way, thoroughly delight in this. Their fits of laughter echo through the foyer and would be wholly entertaining if said children were not about to meet a swift and tragic end.

Kofi catches Blue, and all Blue has to say is, "Don't you wish we were already riding in that cherry red Challenger?"

"I never said it was *cherry* red. It's TorRed." Not that that's important right now.

Mauri roars in annoyance—not the earsplitting kind, but loud enough to refocus us, the babies in particular. They begin to mimic him with their baby voices. "Rahhhhhr! Rahhhhhhr! Rahhhhhr!" All five of them—at different times—repeatedly and exuberantly. They say other things, too. "Good kitty!" And "Do it again!" In baby voices, yes, but in lion language. "Big, strong kitty cat!"

Mauri tilts his head to listen. Only, I'm not sure it *is* Mauri who is listening.

"Get back to the arena," Kofi barks at us. "The finale will begin after the allotted break time."

"Let's go," Beam says. She becomes a panther and jogs past Kofi. I remain a man so that I can nab Blue and his nest of children. Kofi is only too happy to hand them over. Everything in me wants to beat him down with my fists, but somehow, I control myself, with only a scathing look as a parting shot.

Once we're out of earshot, I tell Blue, "You have to disappear with those kids."

"I thought you wanted to meet them," he objects.

"Well, yeah, when we're not being cornered and betrayed by deranged predators!"

He starts in with the sing-song voice, and I rub a hand down my face. *Please, not the sing-song voice.*

"Blue, come here. Blue, not now. Answer our calls. Bring the babies. Take them away."

"He's going to throw a tantrum," I tell Beam because she's the only one who can make short work of those.

"Blue, we do not have time for that right now," she scolds him—as a cat. She keeps circling me to keep tabs on the mansion since I'm on human feet. The lions aren't giving chase. They're more moseying and talking to one another as they follow us to the Jungle. Probably discussing how long they want to play with us before they kill us. Or perhaps, if they should eat the children first as appetizers.

"Is this the direction we want to go?" I ask.

"Yes, we have to try to rescue Rafe."

Of all the perplexing things my love has said... "Why?" I ask.

"Why? Why?" the babies chorus. And one of them yells, "Becauu-use!" And they all burst into giggles.

Beam womans up to get a proper look at them. "Oh, Blue, they're adorable." Then, narrowing her eyes, she says, "Blue? Why is one of them blue?"

"Babe, focus in," I say. "*Why* are we going to rescue Rafe instead of using the ring to get out of here?"

"Oh—because werewolves aren't natural creatures. He's something else. He's as trapped in his weird body as we are in this place."

"And you know this how? Mauri had a book on it?"

"No, it was something Rafe said when he flew away with me. He didn't want to kill anyone. He was compelled to."

I make a scoffing sound. "I bet that's what all the serial killers say."

"He didn't want to kill Robyn's little bird messenger. And don't forget, he protected us from Mauri just now when we had to get back to the house."

"A lot of good it did us."

Beam blocks my path and grips my arms. "Chaus, you're going to get everyone out. That's what Mrs. Turner told you. She was right about the judgment in my veins. She's right about you."

"*Was* she right about the judgment?" I ask.

"Take my hand."

I don't know why I'm holding Blue like an infant, but I adjust him to clasp Beam's hand. "Don't look," she says when I begin to check what sharp, curved object she has placed between our palms.

"Is that the claw?" I ask.

"Is that the claw?! Is that the claw?!" the babies chant, and I shush them, so now they are *sh—sh*—shushing me back.

"You got it back from Kofi?"

"He never took it."

"He did. I saw him."

"The one he took was his own. He was acting."

I cringe. "He tore out one of his claws for you?!"

"Hey, I saved his freaking life."

That's a valid point.

25

RAFE'S TRUE FORM

BEAM

Chausie's not ready to forgive Kofi for taking me hostage at knifepoint —even if it was pretend. "Kofi's a good actor," I say to lighten the mood. "Maybe he could give Aiden some lessons." As you can imagine, this doesn't help because it just reminds Chausie that Aiden is, at best, gravely injured. And that Kofi was the one who did it.

Inside the Jungle, birds are gathering. I have a sick feeling that they are carrion birds coming for Chesnea, but upon closer inspection, I find that Larkin is their focal point, and they are creating a shield between Larkin and Rafe.

Rafe is in the vulture/wolf form we've grown to fear, but he has been subdued with a deep row of bite marks across his torso. Even so, he chomps at the birds if they get too close. But he whines when he does it. "I don't want to! I don't want to!" The words are clipped because he says them through his beak.

Larkin, who is kneeling as close to him as she dares, smiles sadly as we approach. "Thank you for summoning me, Beam, but he is beyond my magic."

"Well, he's not the one I was hoping you could enchant." I get down beside her to assess Rafe's condition.

"There are more of my people here?" Larkin says.

Huh? I'm befuddled. "Is this werewolf one of your people?"

"We were attacked—ages ago—and many of us were turned. They used our own magic against us. This poor, strong soul is one of my kin. See how he still fights?"

"You and Rafe are related?"

"Is that his name?" Larkin's olive complexion goes grey, and she bows into a full Child's Pose, her nose to the ground, saying, "Your Majesty."

Rafe is in bad shape. Tears leak from his eyes.

"This is your king?!" I ask.

"He was the first to fall—protecting us. We have to help him."

Chausie is only half-tending to our conversation. He stands with his back to us, fidgeting with the claw and waiting for Mauri to show up. He's also still holding Blue like a baby, and that means he's still holding Blue's babies.

At the far end of the arena, Mauri stomps a paw the size of a serving platter to announce his arrival.

"Beam?" Chausie cautions.

"*That's* the one I want you to talk to," I tell Larkin.

She spares a glance, but she's far more concerned about Rafe and the suffering he endures. "I don't think I'm the one you need. He's a false animal."

"Look closer," I say. "The lion essence in him is what created the Leonids."

"Are you saying that this is the lion of the constellation?" Larkin asks.

"Kind of. His semi-living head and pelt made a very bad man able to become that."

"My magic," Rafe whines. "Didn't want to."

Instead of advancing, Mauri sits down the way he had done earlier, like the world is his personal throne room, and when he sits, he reveals that he isn't alone. Kofi, in lion form, stands behind him, a smaller but more realistic version of the king of beasts. For all of his toughness, he looks uncertain and a little scared.

All of this time—if you've been wondering why Blue hasn't been blurting out inappropriate, half-baked ideas—it's because our exhausted little papa has fallen sound asleep in Chausie's arms. Chausie bends to show us. "What am I supposed to do with this?" he asks.

But as he says it, the babies begin to tumble out of the carrier one by one like fledgling birds. Chausie catches each of them before they can hit the ground, but he's holding Blue in one hand and now two—no, three—faerie babies in the other, with two more about to dive. "Blue, you gotta help me," he says.

Blue opens first one eye and then the other. "Oh, name them!" Blue shouts as he comes awake and hops to the ground. "We have to name them! Let them fly."

Chausie raises his doubtful eyes to me, but Larkin nods, so he relaxes his hand.

Apparently, as it is with chickadees, this is quite a milestone for faerie babies. Anyway, Blue shouts a name at each of them as they hit the ground. "Oriole! Rufous! Quetzal! Uhhhh.....Barbet! Phoebe!"

You'd think the mischievous babies would want to run to their mother, but no. They scurry toward Rafe! "Children!" Larkin cries. I scramble to my feet, but before any of us can stop them, the babies hop along one of Rafe's long wings and climb up his back.

Some of them stand on his shoulders, and some on the back of his neck. One stands on top of his beak! They clasp each other's hands and sing a game of *Ring Around the Rafie* while Rafe goes crosseyed, trying to focus on them. He snaps his beak, which reveals canines and other savage teeth.

Larkin sinks to the ground with a grief-filled wail. She's reaching for her children but doesn't dare advance and risk making things worse. Blue stands aghast. The children, however, are having a marvelous time. One of them sings, "I see a werewolf, werewolf, werewolf. I see a werewolf. Come—and—play!"

They rotate turns so that the next faerie child can perch on the beak and take up the song. "I see a birdie, birdie, birdie. I see a birdie. Come—and—play!" They rotate again. "I see a tiger, a ti"—you get the idea. They go through all kinds of animals. A caribou. A marmoset. They sing about animals I've never heard of. Maybe they're making them up, but I get the idea they see into Rafe's mind all of the wild things he has become.

After about seven rounds of this, Rafe begins to wretch—like he's coughing up a hairball. And one by one, animals escape from his mouth. First of all, a robin, like the one we saw fluttering outside the window—the one who pointed us toward the key. I think the faerie babies are freeing the ghosts of Rafe's victims!

"Beam, the feathers!" Chausie says. He points at my chest, and I look to find the feathers have escaped my hidden purse and are flapping to get out of the top of my dress.

"Give them to me," he says, and I oblige him.

"What are you gonna do?"

"I'm not sure yet. The ghosts remind me of the seven spirit crows that flew out of the fire back at The Vigilance."

The feathers want to be part of this. They're directing Chausie to Rafe like a dowsing rod.

Birds continue to gather. They don't care about walls and armed guards. They fill the arena and light on all the surfaces. Rafe is still chomping and writhing. He must be fighting himself to keep from eating the babies. When Chausie takes another step closer, he flails his wings. "No, Chausie," Larkin pleads as I say, "Careful, Chaus!"

He halts on the spot but slowly reaches for Frilk's whip, which he has managed to hang from his pocket. I'm not sure Chausie has ever used a whip before—let alone a whip made out of extraterrestrial material, but he winds it over his head like he's in complete command and says, "Blue, stand him up."

When our small, blue friend manages the task, Chausie sidesteps Rafe's furious wings and hurls the end of the whip around him. I pray it's enough to bind the creature without harming the babies. I shouldn't have worried. It's like the whip knows what Chausie wants and obeys him enthusiastically. It snakes behind and binds him chest to foot, wings included.

"Larkin, do you know what I should do with the feathers?" Chausie asks.

"Yummy! Yummy!" one of the children cries. "Yummy! Yummy!" the rest of them repeat.

"Feed him the feathers?" he asks the kids.

"Yummy! Yummy!" Now, they're rubbing their tummies with

ridiculous looks of euphoria. I do see the influence Blue is having on them.

"Rafe? Open up." Chausie says. I guess he's trusting the two-day-old faeries to know what to do.

Rafe does not oblige. "Rrrrafe?" he growls.

"Rrrrrrafe," the kids say. "Rrrrrrafe."

He wraps his fingers around Rafe's razor beak and pries it open, exposing the hybrid vulture/wolf maw. "A little help here?" he grunts, but I'm on it. I grab the feathers and stuff them down Rafe's throat.

Rafe coughs and sputters. So do the kids. They topple to the ground and wander about pretend hacking. *Cuh. Cuh. Cuh.* Blue scoops them up. Larkin looks like a week's vacation is in order. I think I'm ready for one myself.

With Chausie. Let me just say that he never looks so good as when he is intensely focused on solving a problem. When he realizes I'm standing beside him, he gently pinches my thigh. "Thanks, partner," he says without looking away from Rafe.

There's a flash of green light, and instead of what we thought was Rafe's true form, there is now a small, comely man with a golden circlet on his head. Pointy ears rise to either side of it.

"Your Majesty!" Larkin says. "Are you well? Chausie?" She calls to Chausie because the whip won't come loose for her, but when he touches it, it coils neatly into his hand. Pretty cool.

"So, *this* is Rafe's true form," I say.

Larkin falls upon him with tears of joy but quickly rights herself as she realizes she is molesting her king. "He's hurt. Will someone—" Before Larkin can finish asking for help, Mauri thunders in from the periphery, a false charge that scatters the wall of birds protecting them and ends in Mauri pacing side to side instead of running us over. He chuckles and grins through wicked teeth. I've never seen anyone so high on their own power. Power that isn't even his!

Chausie tests the weight of the whip in his hand. Would it bind the Lion of Nemea as it bound Rafe? Or is the only way to end this to drive the claw through his heart? Chausie says, "I feel responsible for him. Like he's a little thing to protect instead of an ancient monster whose only capable enemy is a mythic god—and now a jealous billionaire."

"I know what you mean."

"Leander?" Chausie calls out. "Can you hear me? Don't listen to him. Don't let him take your power like Heracles did." The Lion snorts. His lips lift in a snarl, and he stamps his front paw. Larkin joins us, blocking Chausie with an arm that hardly reaches over his knees but, he allows her to proceed. She stands to height and looks the Lion in the eye. She did manage to survive Frilk, so who knows?

"You gorgeous beast," she says. "You formidable creature. Champion. King."

Who is she talking to? Leander or Mauri?

The Lion changes his tune. Makes a snort of appreciation.

The look on Larkin's face is pure adoration, and she hums as if she would like to sing his praises.

"What a player," I mutter. I know she's doing this for the greater good, but she had better be sincere in her affections for Blue, or she's gonna have to fight more than that Lion.

Beam. Chausie uses our connection to reprimand me. *Same thing you did to Baalesh. Give her a chance.*

True.

"What's his name," I hear Larkin whisper to Chaus.

"Mauri."

"Help me to my feet," King Rafe says.

Larkin looks back. She'd drop everything to obey him, but I wave her off and brace the king under his shoulders so that he can stand.

"Robyn cared for this beast," King Rafe says and steps directly in front of all of us, nose to nose with the Lion—and to do that, the Lion has to bow its head. Rafe, though a king, is a small, delicate man, and next to the Lion, he may as well be a mushroom. But his voice sounds wise and is laced with the sympathy of a benevolent elder. "Where is she?" he asks the Lion. "Where is Robyn?"

Mauri—or Leander—avoids his eyes, and the great Lion turns his head away.

"Leander," the king asks, "are you confused? Do you want to come away from the man so that I may speak with you?"

The Lion whines—such a mournful sound, I feel sadness in my bones. I can tell that Chausie does too.

"Leander?" the king asks, and at the same time Robyn says, "Mauri?" So, they're trying to divide and conquer.

I think it's going to take. I think my hopes for this encounter are about to be realized. Leander and Mauri seem to come apart from one another. But just as quickly, they come back together. The Lion roars, and despite the king's ability to communicate with the animal, I fear Mauri will devour him.

Chausie attacks. He lions up—instead of driving the claw into him as a man—and he is sorely punished for it. So I lion up. And I am sorely punished for it.

Both of us will heal. But Larkin won't. Rafe won't. None of the faeries...

As if he hears my thoughts, Mauri turns on Rafe, and Chausie shifts into a man. I know why he's doing it, to use the claw, but his human flesh is now laid bare.

That's not what he's concerned about. "I hate what I have to do," he murmurs and then lifts his voice to Kofi. "I need you."

It's like Kofi was waiting to be asked. He instantly attacks the Lion with a vicious utterance that comes from deep inside. He takes Mauri by the scruff, but Mauri turns on him with a jarring hiss. They clash. Claws and teeth scrape and snap. Muscles and weight bump and collide. The savagery of the Lion of Nemea is staggering. But Kofi is running on my blood, and he's a far better match for Mauri than we were.

Chausie fists the claw. He's ready on his toes the way he must be on the basketball court, waiting for the time to act. Who knows if he'll get a second chance?

Kofi is so full of strength and stamina, that I finally get why people enjoy fighting as a sport. He flips the Lion of Nemea onto his back— and Chausie pounces, driving poor Leander's claw down into his rib cage.

But the Lion twists at the same time, and the blow misses his heart. He roars in pain and anger. His enormous jaws clamp down on the back of Kofi's leg and then he jerks, tearing through Kofi's thigh, hamstringing him. I cover my mouth in shock. It's gross—all the stringy parts that wave in the open. Even so, Kofi doesn't stop snapping and growling.

Chausie tries again. He is in a terribly vulnerable position as a man between these two lions, but he fights smart and takes the opportunity to drive the claw upward into the soft part of the Lion's jaw beneath his teeth.

What was it that Berke said? Stay away from the jaws!

Everybody's in motion, and nothing goes as planned. Mauri chomps down on Chausie's arm, and he screams in pain, which stings me as well. Kofi knocks Mauri onto his side. That may be why Chausie still has his hand, but as he pulls it into himself, it's wounded to the point that I doubt the power of healing.

The claw is in the lion's stomach. Our only chance of victory over the Lion of Nemea was just swallowed whole.

Chausie has turned pale and he just stands there blankly, his mauled arm hanging limply at his side.

"Leander?" the king calls over the din. "Where is Robyn?"

"Robyn?" asks one of the babies. "Robyn?" ask the rest. Their heads pop out of Blue's carrier, where he has only just managed to settle them, and they carry the call like they're now playing Marco Polo. "Robyn? Robyn?"

The Lion is distracted from his brutality and turns curious eyes upon the children who bounce up at him, hands raised high. "Eat us! Eat us!" they say and giggle.

"No!" Larkin yells. She scoops up two of them, but the Lion beats her to the other three and snacks on them all at once.

Larkin wails the way my mother did when I was dying.

"They're not dead," I tell her.

"They were swallowed whole!" she says.

"Yeah, but..." I got nothing. "They're going to be OK," I finish lamely.

The king slides to his knees in slow motion. Whether he's succumbing to his wounds or to the horror is anybody's guess. "Blue?" Chaus says. "Get them out of here."

"I can't! My babies!" Blue looks horrified.

"Beam?" he says. "The ring. Take as many as you can save!"

He's right. "Larkin, your king!" I yell.

She is so torn. "Take the two you have!" I tell her.

She clings to her two remaining children and wraps an arm through her king's, but her face is frozen in shock and disbelief. Because she has no free hands, I pour the ring onto her arm where it encircles her near the elbow, and all four disappear.

Chausie's furious that I didn't leave with them. If looks could kill…

"You should know by now," is all I say.

He shifts and prepares to continue this doomed fight when we hear gunshots. The fighting doesn't end. If anything, the shots add to our frenzy. But then there's an awful ripping sound like canvas being torn, and we all go still to identify what it is and where it is coming from.

The Lion jumps back onto his hind legs and complains as something punches through his belly from the inside out. We watch, unsure of what we're seeing. The puncture tears, severing the skin and creating a gaping hole. Out of that hole and onto the ground plops a very cranky—and very gooey—Robyn. Along with three faerie babies who blink around and then begin to chat her up.

Blue rushes to corral them and stuffs them into the carrier as they struggle to get free.

Leander and Mauri separate, the latter falling to his knees as a man and the prior covering the ground as a magnificent, if not quite dead, pelt. Interestingly, Mauri is not split wide open the way he had been as a lion, but he's too stunned to move. He only holds his middle as if he can still feel the ripping. Chausie, with his one good arm, though the other looks much better already, shoves him over and binds him with the whip. Then he thinks about it and opens his jacket. With some finagling so as not to touch Frilk's collar, he gets it to wrap around Mauri's wrists like cuffs.

I check on Robyn as Chaus goes to Kofi. "I just need to rest," Robyn says. "I was able to convince Leander's innards not to harm me."

Blue hugs her and the babies spill out onto her lap where she pats them with one hand and hoists the claw into the air with the other. "Thanks for this!"

"That was all Chausie."

He observes his slowly healing arm and says, "I can't say it was my pleasure. But you're welcome."

Kofi is panting and *aurrrring* in pain as he becomes human. Chausie rolls him to assess his wounds. "Is it bad?" Kofi asks.

"Yep. Looks like you got shredded. Your leg's barely attached."

"Could you at least pretend to care and get me some help?"

"I care," Chausie says. "But Beam's got us both covered. Check it out."

It's difficult for Kofi to see that part of his leg, but his tendons and flesh are knitting back together, more slowly than the way he'd healed earlier, but steadily. Chaus drops to the ground beside him with a huge exhale, and I take a seat too, once I'm confident that Robyn's OK.

"What have you done with the rest of my family?" Blue asks me.

"I sent them back to the birdcage to get them out of harm's way. You can pop on over there if you want."

"I need you to come with me to get them out."

"No, let me rest for a minute."

"Here, Blue." Chausie offers what's left of my blood in the vial that Frilk collected. "Use that to get them out of the cage and put a drop on Rafe's tongue if he's badly injured."

"You have to stop saving everybody," I say to him.

"Why?"

"Because of what President Tumbling Rock said. It's sacred. It's supposed to stay secret."

Chausie shrugs.

I'm not sure why the man doesn't believe that rules apply to him. It half exasperates me and half makes me want to kiss him.

BEAM

Shouting. Men and women. Wolves and gunfire. And then, a whole section of the wall that surrounds the border of Mauri's compound comes down. Debris flies. Kofi becomes a lion again, but it pains him to stand.

Leading the charge through the gap are tens of officers in uniforms that match Aiden's. And they mean business. They rush in with long, black guns and immediately round up the athletes and audience members who have remained. "Form two lines," a commander shouts. "One on either side of the bleachers." Nippy stands among them. They had to drag her away from Chesney's body, which someone has covered.

Chausie's dad marches in wearing a long-sleeved APD t-shirt and a holster around his waist. I can't help but feel sad to see him with a firearm in hand. I know he carries one as a matter of course, but he generally relies on his shifter abilities, and those are gone. He scans the arena and waits for the other officers to move as a unit—until he sees us sitting on the ground in the open arena, and then he stealthily but quickly jogs over.

The others sweep past us, some of them continue through the Jungle, shifting into other forms as they go.

I wonder what they think of us sitting around in the dirt wearing clothes designed for a formal occasion. Leander's bloody pelt rests among us, and beside it, there's a woman as small and as icky as if she has just been born—which she kind of has.

I slap Chausie to make sure he's aware that his dad's on the way, and he scrambles to his feet.

"Chaus, you good?" His dad crashes him into a hug.

"All good."

"Beam?" he asks over Chausie's shoulder.

"All good," I repeat. "And very glad to see you."

"How about the lion?" Dad nods to Kofi. "Is he a shifter?"

"Who is that?" Kofi asks in cat language, and when Leo answers him because he understands him, Kofi relaxes some and takes his human form.

"I'm Chausie's dad. Leo Louris. Do you need medical attention?"

Kofi side-eyes us and almost grins. "No, I'm fine," he says.

"Good. We're gonna get you home."

Leo's assurance doesn't seem to comfort Kofi. Kof just flashes his eyebrows with an upward nod and a smile that disappears as soon as Leo looks the other way.

"Do you have one?" Chausie asks.

"No," he answers after hesitating. "Not for—I don't know—since I was eight."

"Is that when you were kidnapped?"

"By my uncle." Kofi stares ahead. "After he found out I could shift, he sold me, and since then, I've been sold or stolen three more times. I've been in zoos, and I've been forced to fight."

"Would you like to find your parents?" I ask.

"I lived with my grandma. I was told that she died, but yeah, I'd like to know for sure."

"Is that why you protected Rosa back at Snatcher's Ridge?" Chaus says. "Because you were around that age when it happened to you?"

"Maybe. Probably."

"*Uh*, no," I break in. "He did it to win points with Harriet."

Kofi smiles and lies back with his hands behind his head to allow the healing to complete its work. "Man, it feels good not to hurt."

"Doesn't it?" Chausie agrees and watches his dad interact with

Robyn. I don't know if he's ever seen a faerie before. "Ma'am?" he asks Robyn. She is a sight. Her wet hair clings to her face and her pointy ears stand out indignantly as she strokes Leander's pelt.

"That man ate me!" she says, pointing at Mauri. "I served his family for a hundred fifty years, and he ate me!" She turns back to Chausie's dad, and after a brief inspection of him, she gentles her tone. "*Oh.* You've lost your animal essence. I'm so sorry."

Leo doesn't confirm it—just makes a quick non-smile and directs another officer to handcuff Mauri, which allows Chaus to retrieve the collar and the whip. This he does with style, using the whip to pop the collar—turns out, the whip releases it just as our blood does—and then uses the whip to deposit the collar into his pocket, allowing it to coil back at his side. He flashes his eyebrows at me. He's really digging the whip.

"I demand to speak to my lawyer," Mauri says. "I demand my rights."

"Why don't you start with the one to remain silent?" Leo quips.

Robyn continues to pet Leander. "If only Leander's essence could reside in *him,*" she says about Leo. "But there's not enough now to transfer."

Pop!

Blue inserts himself into our midst along with Larkin, Rafe-the-king, and all five babies. He's bouncing on his toes to keep them happy, and he hands Chausie the vial along with a small wrapped package, which I assume to be Larkin's toe ring. "Did your dad-the-lion drive the Hellcat here?" he asks. "Oh, wait. I guess he's dad-NOT-the-lion now."

"Don't call him that," Chausie says. "And I don't know, Blue. I've been a little busy."

Rafe is glowing. Literally. I guess he got a sip of my blood. He bows to me and makes a motion that zips his lips. Did Blue tell him to keep it a secret? How discreet of him!

The babies tumble out of their carrier to bounce on Robyn's knee, and the faeries discuss faerie things in a language I don't understand. I wonder if Blue does.

Chausie's narrowing his eyes at me in thought, full of possibility—another one of his best looks.

"What do you have in mind, Chausie Louris?" I ask.

"Beam," he says with the kind of seriousness that brokers my full attention. "Would you really be happier without the shifter side of you?"

The way he asks forces me to give it real thought. "I know it's a gift, Chaus. And I know you said you don't care either way, bu—"

"Stop. Without my opinion factored in. Would you remove it if you could?"

"Yes. I'm sorry."

He waves away the apology, then says carefully, "If it could be transferred—safely, of course—to my dad, would you want that?"

"Oh my gosh, yes! Is that possible?"

"I don't know. Something Robyn said makes me think that maybe."

"What happened to him that he can't shift?" Kofi asks.

"It's a long story," Chaus says. "We'll tell you another time. Because you're going to stop beating me up, and we're going to be friends."

"I'm not going to stop beating you up."

"Oh, but we can be friends, though?"

"I guess so. I'm friends with Beam, so I probably have to tolerate you."

With a snort of a laugh, Chausie stands and stretches and walks toward the circle of faeries.

The police officers are allowing most of the crowd to disperse with directions I can't hear. A few have been rounded up, and Nippy is one of them. I bet the others with her were also kidnapped or coerced to be here by some other means.

Leo directs an officer to speak on his radio. "Inform the Redfeathers that we have their daughter, and she is unharmed. And will you reach out to Ms. Louris? Her son Chausie is also in good shape. Tell Sergeant Aiden Gunnolf, too. He'll want to know."

"He's alive?" Kofi sounds at once hopeful and ashamed as he asks Leo for more information.

Leo nods. "We're going to stop by the hospital to get everyone cleared, and you can see him then if you'd like." Leo must not know who tore Aiden up so bad. When Kofi looks appalled, Leo adds, "Don't worry. He's in bad shape, but he'll survive. Is there anyone I can have the officer call for you?"

Kofi clears his throat and says, "I haven't seen my grandma in ten years. But if she's still alive, I'd like for her to know that I am too."

While Leo instructs Kofi to divulge more of his information to the officer, Chausie jogs up and practically drags me and his dad over to the faeries. "Tell them what you told me."

"Rafe should have the mansion," Larkin proposes.

"What about Robyn?" I say. "She lived there for ages and worked all the time. Rafe ate her bird."

Robyn gasps, and Rafe makes an apologetic face.

"Not that part," Chausie says. "The part about Leander."

"Oh, yes," Robyn says. "Let me ask him first." In lion language, Robyn says, "Leander, would you like to heal one of your cubs? It would mean that you would no longer wander about in this pelt. Your magic would be dispersed to him."

"I thought he didn't have enough essence," I say.

"But you do," Chausie tells me. "I asked her if she could use Leander's magic to transfer your essence to Dad."

His dad's eyes go wide. "No, I could never take that away from someone," Leo says and backs up a step.

"She wants to, Dad. It doesn't feel natural to her like it does to us."

Leo questions me without words.

"It's true," I tell him. "I'd love to give it to you. It's who you are."

Chausie gets more excited. "They think that they can make it happen since there are so many faeries here and since Beam is so extraordinary."

We all turn to question Robyn. "Leander says yes," she says. I didn't hear him say anything.

"How do we do it?" Chausie asks.

"Are you sure?" Leo asks me. He looks just like Chausie when has says it.

"I'm sure." And I am. But I do also feel a small pang of loss. Chausie must know. He whips his head around and says, "We can wait. Give you more time to consider it."

"No, I've had enough. Let's do it."

Robyn instructs me and Leo to stand back to back. The three adult faeries surround us with the babies perched on their shoulders. Robyn covers us with the pelt of the Lion of Nemea, and they hold hands, fencing us in. They chant words in unison, in their language, and just like the name of their people, I cannot describe or even remember what it sounds like, except to say that it sounds like wind and water.

The pelt heats up. Or I do. I am compelled into my panther form. The Lion becomes heavy upon me, weighing me down. At the same time, I feel what may be part of my soul being sucked out of my back. For a brief moment, the Lion becomes himself, fully embodied—on top of us! He roars mightily, but that sound diminishes even as he is making it. I lose my panther form. I guess I lose my panther *self*. And then the Lion is only a pelt. And Leo and I are both lying on the ground.

Chausie appears slightly worried from outside the ring of faeries. I look around trying to assess myself. "I'm OK," I say. "Leo?"

The faeries drop hands, and Robyn collects her Leander with tears in her eyes. "Thank you, dear boy," she says. The pelt doesn't blink. It doesn't purr. I don't think there will be any more sleepwalking.

Chausie's dad is a lion again! He stands on his hind legs to hug me and licks my face. I almost lose my balance, but I'm laughing and hugging him. Then he bounds into the Jungle, Chausie on his heels. He looks larger and shinier. I think he's had a glow-up.

I watch them romp around and tackle each other, and I do feel a twinge of regret. That part was fun. But I'm so happy for Leo. I know Chausie is, too.

"Thank you, Faeries," I say. "Robyn, I see that it cost you."

"It was the right thing," she says. "It was time. And it looks like I may be needed elsewhere." She means the babies who are now swinging from her hair.

"Yes, please!" Blue says as an impassioned plea. "Visit us often. I'm exhausted."

27

WHAT BECAME OF THE WOLF

CHAUSIE

From the training camp, we drive to the hospital. There is a busload of athletes behind us who need medical clearance as well as counseling, and that is where they'll be reunited with their families. Beam, Kofi, and I ride in the Hellcat with my dad. Blue is with us, too, standing on my dad's lap with his hands on the wheel. We told Dad he was there, but he can't sense him in any way. Even so, Dad said he was happy for Blue to tag along.

"Blue," Beam says. "I thought of a fantastic surprise you could give to Larkin."

"What's that?" Blue doesn't take his take his eyes off the road or his hands off the wheel, though he is having zero effect on the world around him. I still don't understand what makes him able to act upon certain things and not others.

I glance back at Beam to see what she's up to. She's definitely up to something.

"A place where Larkin's faerie heart would truly feel at home," she says, laying it on thick. "A place where every child's dream comes true because there is a precious pony in need of loving care."

Blue forgets to drive and bounces onto the middle console.

"A place that is married to the earth in a way that would also allow you to feel at home. And the best part? Robyn will be close enough to pop over and babysit, giving you time to rest and enjoy this part of life. It is cozy and vacant and move-in ready."

"You're a realtor now?" I ask.

"*Sh.*"

"Where is this place?" Blue asks. "How can we nab it before someone else snatches it up?"

"Well, you would have to move fast. You know what? Don't even worry about going back to Laurel's. Chausie and I will take care of it."

It's hard not to hide my burgeoning grin.

"You would do that for me?"

"Of course, we would. You're part of our family now."

"Really?"

"Really. This place is built in a huge meadow so that the pony can entertain your kids out the front door. You've been there before. It's dug out beneath a beautiful tree, and the roots frame the ceiling."

"Do you mean Frilk's place? That's brilliant."

"Yeah, he's not going to use it."

"Move-in ready," Blue says.

"Move-in ready."

And just like that, he pops away.

I clap my hands for Beam's performance. "*Nicely* done. That was very smooth."

"I thought so," Beam says.

"Don't even worry about going back to Laurel's," I repeat, laughing, but less so when I glance at Kofi. He's been in a funk since he found out we were going to see Aiden at the hospital.

"Yeah, stay out of my house," Beam laughs.

"Stay out of your hot spring!"

"Are you all talking about the dead woman's house?" Dad asks.

"Yeah, she left it to Beam."

"Legally?"

"I'm not sure about legally," I answer. "I don't know who owns the property. It belongs to the Tribe, I guess. But since the entrance is magical, I don't think anyone's going to question it."

Beam checks her phone for the fiftieth time. She's dying to touch base with her parents. "We *will* have cell service when we get there, right?" she asks.

"Any minute now," Dad assures her. "Keep checking."

Kofi grows moodier the closer we get. When we park, I think I may have to wrestle him out of the car. Just as I'm about to yank his door, he expels an explosive breath and propels himself out.

"Mom?" Beam finally reaches her parents and chats with them into the building and up the elevator. It's probably the best thing to distract from Kofi's somber silence.

When we reach Aiden's room, it's open, but Dad knocks anyway and Aiden answers with a weak but cheerful, "Come on in."

My mom's in there, too. She crosses the room to hug me and says, "You're wearing a tux."

I know she's trying to be cheerful, but her voice is strained.

"Thank you, Leo," she says to my dad.

"I really didn't do anything. They had it taken care of." Dad raises his voice to Aiden. "You hanging in there, Sarge?"

Aiden doesn't look so good. He's breathing on his own, but it's labored. I bet his lungs were punctured. He has white bandages taped to him in several places. But he answers in the affirmative. Kofi hangs back by the door.

Beam, who has been about to burst, now blurts out, "Aiden, Rafe is a faerie king! He's back to normal now, not a Were anymore. And Mauri *swallowed* Robyn, not to mention three faerie babies. But Chausie and Kofi fought Mauri, who had turned into a big lion, and they got her out of his belly—well, really, she got herself out of his belly. But they helped! You missed out so much!"

"I'll let you all catch him up," Dad tells me. "Come find me in the lobby when you're done so that we can get you cleared through medical." Kofi has to move to let my dad out, but he doesn't venture further into the room.

Aiden listens as we gush, but his eyes drift shut from time to time. Even so, after a while, he says, "Kofi? Come on in here, Son."

Kofi looks like he'd rather be beaten to a pulp than for Aiden to speak softly to him.

I'm not gonna lie. It makes me a tiny bit jealous to hear Aiden call him *son*. Isn't that weird? But more than that, I am genuinely glad that Aiden isn't harboring any hard feelings toward him.

Kofi moves slowly, but when he gets to the bedside, and Aiden reaches up a hand, he bends forward, and Aiden cups the back of his neck.

"Sit down," Aiden says and pats the bed.

Kofi sits, but he doesn't say a word.

"What's going on inside?"

Under the pressure of that simple question, the dam inside Kofi fails. "I thought I killed you," he says and chokes back a sob. "I thought I'd crossed the line. I lost myself. I was a total asshole. I'm sorry. I'm sorry." Aiden lets him cry. I think it brings tears to all of our eyes.

"You were under incredible pressure, and you did what you were told to do. Look at me." Kofi raises his head. "You didn't kill me. OK? You didn't kill me."

"I was going to. And not just to you. And then I 'bout got killed, but Beam heal—"

"That's enough," I interrupt before he can divulge that Beam manufactures healing properties in the form of red and white blood cells.

She steers the conversation away with, "Kofi was spectacular. And he's a way better actor than you."

Aiden makes a face full of pretend shock and betrayal.

"He made it possible for Beam to destroy Frilk," I say. "The goblin."

"He's dead?!" Aiden asks with sudden hardness. His eyes flash with a dark satisfaction. "That goblin butchered one of my men."

"I'm so sorry," Beam says. "I knew that's what must've happened. He showed up with the collar, and he was speckled with—" She doesn't finish the sentence. Instead, she says, "I'm so sick of talking about blood."

"*You* tell me the story, Kof," Aiden says. "Starting from when you let me go instead of finishing me off. Thank goodness it wasn't up to Beam, right? She would've ended me, no questions asked." Aiden laughs at his joke and then groans in pain, clutching a pillow to his side.

Kofi finally relaxes some. He begins to tell things from his perspective, leaving out the part about Beam healing him but making us all sound like superheroes.

When he's finished, Aiden furrows his brows and studies each of us in turn. "*How* did Beam kill the goblin again?"

"Wwwell..." Kofi glances at Beam, but she seems more interested in her fingernails.

Aiden says, "And why did neither of you help her?"

"It's not that we didn't help her," I say.

He waits for me to explain, but I don't.

"You say you fought this epic lion." Aiden sounds like he doubts it very much. "Yet none of you have any visible battle wounds."

We're all averting our eyes. Aiden allows the silence to deafen us.

"Oh, here," I say at last and slap the vial of Beam's blood onto the pillow over his wounded torso. "Drink that."

I feel Beam staring at me and add, "But keep it secret."

She rolls her eyes, and I lift my hands to ask, *What were we supposed to do?*

"Seriously?" Aiden asks. He rolls the vial between his fingers. "Who's is it?"

Beam raises a finger.

"Your blood has the power to heal people?"

"And faeries," Kofi says.

"How did it get to be that way?"

"I was born with it. Same as you were born a shifter, I guess."

"Is this why your uncle acted so strange?"

"He's not usually that strange. He's actually quite level-headed. My parents and I would likely be dead right now without him, and Chausie would still be limping."

"Why are we talking about that?" Mom asks. "Aren't people allowed to act strangely once in a while?" She stomps out of the room leaving Aiden with the same look of surprise I feel on my face. That is not how my mom acts.

Beam watches her go with a curious frown. "Sorry," she says to me. "Did I say something?"

I shake my head. "You didn't do anything." What the heck is going on with Mom? Is it because Dad's here?

"Well, anyway," Aiden says, "getting that intel out of you was way too easy." He hands the vial to Beam.

"You're not going to drink it?" Kofi asks.

"Nah. Listen, if you're gonna work for me, you're gonna have to learn the rules of interrogation."

At first, I think he's talking to me, but I already gave him my answer on that. He's talking to Kofi. "What do you mean?" Kofi asks.

"I mean, you have to learn how to question someone and how not to be manipulated. *You* have to control the conversation."

"Not about interrogation," Kofi says. "What do you mean about working for you?"

"I'm offering you a job with APEX. We're gonna go shut every last one of those snatcher's down. Pay is not outstanding, but there are decent benefits. World's best boss ever." He smiles. "And free rent till you get on your feet. You think about it."

"Are you for real?" Kofi asks. "After what I did to you?"

"Hell yeah, I want you on my side."

Kofi's broad smile spreads across his whole face. "Yeah. OK. You got it."

Aiden offers his hand, and they shake on it. I'm struck, once again, with what a good guy he is.

"You should call Harriet," Beam says, "and we'll celebrate."

I scoff at that because Kofi's going to dismiss it out of hand, but he says, "Maybe I will."

Two knocks reveal Berke. "Hey there, gang. How's the wolf holding up?"

"Ah, my savior," Aiden says. "I'm good. I have to stay a few days. But Sophie and I are taking the kids to the lake next week, so I'll have a nice place to recuperate."

"Glad to hear it. Everybody else OK?" As her gaze slides from face to face, she must wonder if we fought at all.

"We're good," Beam says.

"Did you hear about Chesney?" I ask her. "The alpha wolf?"

"Yeah. I'm so sorry. I had no idea Mauri was capable of that kind of brutality or of course, I never would have been a part of it."

"But she's going to be OK?" Kofi asks.

Beam and I exchange a look. Does he not know? He was with us. He had to have seen her body.

"No, Kofi," Berke says gently. "She died."

"But I saw her downstairs waiting on somebody in the lobby. She was...fine."

Berke continues to shake her head. "Must have been someone with a similar look."

"What about the other wolf?" Beam asks. "The nippy one. What was her name, Kof?"

"Journey," Kofi says, but I can tell he's not ready to move on from the Chesney issue.

"She's fine," Berke says. "I mean, she's going to need some ongoing help. You know... But her parents are here to take her home."

"Maybe you could give her my number," Beam says. "In case she wants to reach out."

After we find my dad and get checked out by the doctor, Beam's parents are waiting to take her home. It's hard to let go of her. If we were married, we could just drive home together and never say goodbye. "Text me when you get there," I say into her ear.

"I will."

"I love you."

"I love you too."

I watch her walk away and wave when she looks back.

"I think he's smitten," my dad says to Kofi.

"Oh yeah, he's lost it," Kofi replies.

We take seats in the waiting room, where the police have made a staging area, and wait for my mom. This isn't the hospital she works at, but she's helping out anyway. No one else seems too badly hurt.

"I think I broke your mom," Dad says to me. "She's not nice anymore."

"Yes, she is. She's just stressed out." But he's right. She's been through stress before. This isn't how she handles it.

When she's ready to go, we all walk out together. "Why don't you drive with your mom? I'll get a hotel room tonight and Kofi can stay with me."

"No, Leo," Mom says. "There's no need. We have a guest room. You too, Kofi. You stay with us until Aiden is well enough to go home."

I think he's relieved to know where he'll be sleeping and that he'll be with other lions.

TV news vans are set up along the curb outside the ambulance bay. They want to ask us questions, but we don't stop. Even so, they point microphones at us. "Were you with the fighters at the training camp? Can you tell us what happened? We heard a young woman died."

"No comment," Dad says and shields my mom from them. He's used to handling these sorts of situations.

It's already well into the night. When we get home, I take a quick shower, quicker than I want to because I know Kof needs one, too. And while he's in there, I bring a blow-up mattress into my room. Dad takes the guest room, which is my brother's when he's home. And, oh man, it feels good to lie down. Beam and I text for a bit. Kofi gets done and forces me off the blow-up mattress and into the real bed. He says he won't even use a bed if I don't give him the one on the floor. So we switch, and I turn off the lights.

I'm falling asleep when Kofi says, "You really have Harriet's number?"

"No. I have her *mom's* number. Wait. Do you even have a phone?"

"Nah. But that's the first thing I'm gonna get. 'Cause I have a job now."

Makes me laugh. "I'm glad for you. Maybe Harriet can come to the lake with us next week."

"Am *I* going?"

"Yeah, we're practically brothers now. My mom and Aiden are serious."

"What's the creepy dark shadow thing that follows her around?"

Click. I sit up and turn on the light in the same movement. "What are you talking about?"

"That dark—it's like a shadow. I don't know how else to say it. It sticks to your mom li—"

"Mom?!"

I'm in her room before she can invite me. She's been crying, her face in her hands, sitting in an armchair in the corner of her room. For one instant, I see the thing Kofi means. Looks like it's whispering in her ear. It jerks its head up when I barge in and slides behind her chair.

"What was it saying to you?" I demand.

"What?" Mom stands and pats her cheeks. She turns back the covers on her bed.

"Mom, what was that thing saying to you?" I search behind the chair, then around the room, then under the pillow. Where did it go?

"Chausie, is there something that you need? It's been a long few days."

Am I going crazy? Was it a trick of the light? Or did I just imagine what Kofi described? I scan the room one more time. "Sorry. I guess I— I don't know. What's wrong with you?"

"I'm just exhausted. Get some sleep, baby," she says. "We could all use some."

28

THE WAY TO THE GRAVE

BEAM

It is the best time to be alive. The sun beats down on our skin, and the breeze cools us. Kofi, Chausie, Aiden, and I lounge on the second story of a floating dock at Aiden's lake house. He has been regaling us with tales of his summers spent here. Now, he and his siblings rent it out most of the year, but they reserve certain weeks to play. So...yay!

"I feel like one of the Disney princesses," Kofi says. "Rags to riches." He sips thirstily through a steel straw to emphasize the point.

"You look like one," Chausie says to him.

"Time to cool off, kids." This is from Aiden, who proceeds to cannonball into the lake below. The splash is so great that drops of water land up here.

Chausie frowns. "Is he supposed to be doing that?"

I shrug.

"No," Kofi says. "When is Harriet getting here again?"

"Soon," I laugh at him. "In time for lunch."

After Aiden swims to shore, he shouts, "I'm gonna go check on your mother." Chausie's mom has a migraine or something. She hasn't come out of her room this morning.

Chausie watches him go. "I can't even see any wounds," he says.

I shrug.

Kofi is stuck on Harriet's impending arrival. "Her whole family is coming."

"Is that a question or what?" I ask.

"Should I wear clothes?" Kof looks down at his bare chest. He's built like an elite athlete—all bulk and no fat.

"I mean, maybe to meet them initially, but I don't think you should feel weird about wearing a swimsuit when we're all enjoying spring break at the lake."

"Don't you guys think it's odd?" Chausie asks. "The doctor said he should take it easy."

I shrug. For the third time. And now he narrows his eyes at me. "Sunbeam Redfeather. You laced his drink. He gave you back that vial of blood, and you tricked him into drinking it anyway. You are such a hypocrite."

"I don't know what you're talking about."

Kofi's booming laughter suffuses the air around us, and when I can't keep from joining in, Chausie flies at me, scoops me up, and dumps me over the railing.

I shriek all the way down, and the impact at the bottom forces water up my nose. Chausie splashes in after me. I'm at once laughing and choking. Thankfully, he swims me to the ladder where I can recover, but as soon as I do, he's kissing me.

Slippery legs. Muscled arms fastening us to the ladder. Chill bumps on skin. All the sensations. Like I said, it is the best time to be alive.

Pop!

"What are the two you doing?" Blue asks.

Chausie, who is slightly breathless and looks like he might cry, lays his head on my shoulder and says, "Please go away."

"We have things to tell you."

"We?" Chaus squints his eyes, even though we're in the shade, and scans the lower dock to find every faerie we know gathered around us. "Hi," he says to everyone. "Blue, we need to set some rules."

"I thought you didn't believe in rules."

It's all I can do not to crack up.

The babies are busy making wet smooching sounds. Well, one of them is fabricating the roar of an engine as he sits on top of a jet ski's handlebars, pretending to drive. "They are just like you, Blue," I say.

"Aw, thanks, Beam."

"Not a compliment," Chausie mutters.

When we climb back to the top dock, Kofi greets our visitors like old friends. The babies flock to him, vaulting into his arms to sit on his biceps. "Flex!" they demand and show off their own tiny muscles.

"Kofi, can you still see Blue?" I ask.

He lays eyes on him as he hoists the kids into the air. "Am I not supposed to?"

"Maybe it *was* Chesney he saw at the hospital," I tell Chaus.

Chausie's demeanor takes a dive, and it's not because of Chesney. He says, "I think my mom's being harrassed by something. She's not acting like herself. She's downright volatile."

"We've all been through a lot," I offer.

"Yeah, but Kofi said he saw a dark figure shadowing her."

"Chausie, that's what I saw glued to my uncle! You think it transferred to your mom?"

CHAUSIE

I wait impatiently while Beam consults her uncle about his experience, and King Rafe asks about my dad. Exact opposite of how my mom is doing. He's ecstatic. He insists that he's faster and stronger as a lion than ever before. He's even considering coming out of retirement. I convey these sentiments to Rafe as Beam finishes her call.

"Uncle Joel doesn't know why it detached," she reports. "He used words like *oppressive* and said it kept making him think dark thoughts. Shameful. Violent, even. He thinks it may have come from Kimi's drill shaft, as we supposed. Do you remember how Mrs. Turner said that something accusatory was lurking around your house? She said that it whispered."

"It was whispering to my mom. The way she reacted when I saw it made me doubt. But now I think she just couldn't see it like I could. Excuse us," I say to the faeries. "We need to make sure my mom's OK. Kofi, will you come?"

It takes a few seconds to rid him of the faerie children, but soon, we're racing to the house.

I bang open the back door and run up the stairs. "Mom?!"

Aiden, in contrast to me, is closing her bedroom door as quietly as possible. "Not now, Chaus. She doesn't feel well."

"I know what's wrong with her. I think we can help."

I take a calming breath before I knock softly and let myself in. I don't want to bother her, but more than that, I don't want to freak out the whisperer. When I came in hot the other night, it immediately hid from me. "Mom?" I say. "It's me."

The shades are drawn, and the room is dim. Mom's lying under the covers. That sneaky form is crouched at the top of the mattress like a gargoyle. It doesn't think I can see it.

"Please, Chausie, just leave me alone for now." I've never heard her sound so weak or anxious. It makes my heart hurt for her, and if I'm honest, it makes me afraid.

"There's an explanation for the way you're feeling," I tell her. "It was the same thing that plagued Uncle Joel—Beam's Uncle Joel. But you're not going crazy, and you're not going to die. "

Mom's voice tightens with emotion. "Are you sure? I keep thinking horrible things. I don't want you to know them. I don't want anyone to know."

"I'm so sorry. We're gonna fix it."

Kofi is standing at the door with his eyes locked on the whisperer. It hasn't moved a muscle. "Can't we just lion up and devour it?" he says in his lowest tone.

"I'm not sure if we can interact with it physically or not, but I don't think this room is going to support you going full lion."

"Here!" Beam jogs through the threshold with her catcher in hand. "Sophie, I'm going to put this necklace over your head."

As Beam approaches, the whisperer slides behind the bed and out of sight, but once Mom allows Beam to place the catcher around her neck, she breathes more easily. "That may have helped," she says and assesses herself. "It's like the bad thoughts can't speak up anymore. Like I have only my normal thoughts now."

"That's so good," Beam says. "I don't think you're going to have to worry about that thing anymore."

Beam catches my eye, and I know what she's thinking. It could attach to any of the rest of us instead.

I'm looking under the bed and around every nook and cranny. Kofi scans the ceiling.

"I feel like I just woke up," Mom says. She already sounds stronger. "Is this what your uncle was suffering?"

"Yes, but we didn't know it at the time. You should come outside and enjoy the sunshine. I'll get you some coffee." Beam opens the blinds for more light, but that's where the whisperer is hiding! "Grab it!" I yell as it darts past Kofi. He was so close!

We pursue the black figure through the house in a series of jumps, slides, one spectacular couch dive by yours truly, and some stellar team-work—Leonid pun not intended, but absolutely fantastic. We finally corner it in the living room, in front of the fireplace.

"Outside, men!" Aiden admonishes us. "Your mom feels terrible." He can't see the whisperer, and I dare not take my eyes off of it. I don't have time to explain.

"If I were a lion, I could nab it," Kofi complains.

"Maybe we could herd it into the game room," I suggest. "We wouldn't have as much to break."

Aiden says, "Go play outside."

"Not playing," I reply. Kofi and I keep the whisperer from escaping in a very predatory dance. He's right. It would be easier to catch if we were lions.

Beam studies the situation from across the room. "Do you think it is body or soul?" *Blood for body. Light for soul.* It's something one of her Lakota ancestors taught her. She can become a gate of light to move souls on. And we all know the effects her blood has on bodies.

"I don't know *what* it is. Maybe a combo."

"Do you think it's something like a prowler?" she asks. She hollers for Blue.

"What is it?" he appears and asks. "Also, could we get some drinks out there? This place is fabulous."

"Focus," Beam tells him and snaps in his face. "Do you know what that thing is or how to subdue it?" She points to the whisperer, who is suddenly trembling in fear.

"Are there *multiple* beings in here that I can't see?" Aiden asks.

"Yep." I zig-zag to keep the whisperer from dashing past me.

"Oh, I love those!" Blue coos. "May I?" He reappears right in front of the whisperer, utterly disfigured. Having elongated his head to ten times its normal size, his jaw drops wide open, and he chomps the whisperer into his mouth. Not whole, mind you. It takes quite a lot of juicy-sounding mastications that make me want to gag. When he finally swallows—we're all watching with rapt, if disgusted, attention—he says, "That one was licorice."

We can't stop gaping. He smacks his lips and says, "Sorry. Should I have saved you some?"

Beam gives her head a tiny shake.

"Can we get those drinks now?"

BEAM

"That was fascinating," I say to no one in particular, though Kofi and I are making lemonade for the faeries, so I direct my next thought to him. "Good job dealing with the whisperer. You didn't freak out a bit."

"I like being able to see extra things. Do you still think I'll lose that ability?"

"I don't know. It's something I was born with, but my blood gave it to Chausie. The only other people who have drunk my blood can't see anything more than usual."

"Well, one of them can't because he's dead. What are you?"

"I'm still figuring that out."

"Whatever you are, you're scary."

"You think so?" I look up to gauge his sincerity.

He nods with his face all squished up to underscore the point. "I don't know why you didn't want to stay a lion."

"I was afraid I wouldn't be able to turn it off. When I went into that zone with Frilk, I didn't feel vicious or out of control. I wasn't even doing anything except allowing him to take what he deserved. But when

I was a lion, I felt driven to inflict harm. I can honestly say that I'm relieved to be rid of it."

Chausie slides between us to place the catcher around my neck, pulling my hair free and finishing with a kiss on the top of my head. "Mom doesn't need it anymore. Why don't you keep it on you?" It's more of a firm suggestion than a question.

"Because I don't want to lose it in the lake and have it swim away in the gullet of a catfish." I rummage through the cabinets and come out with a serving tray. "Aiden?" I call out. "Do you have any faerie-sized glasses?"

"Aiden took Mom on a walk," Chausie says.

"Well, these will have to do." I place the smallest glasses I can find. "Will you guys take this to the faeries? I need to check my email real quick."

Kofi takes the tray. "What are you expecting?" Chausie asks.

"When I sent my excuse for absence, I asked all my teachers for the catch-up work I have to do. Have any of yours written back?"

Chausie's blank expression tells me all I need to know. "You haven't reached out to them, have you? I'll copy my email for you to use."

"That's OK."

"Don't look at me like that, Chausie Cat. I have a shot at vale-dictorian."

"Do you? Of course, you do. You know, you've never asked what kind of grades I get."

"Oh, I had one of my hacker friends look them up."

"You did what?"

I roll my eyes. "I'm sure you do just fine."

"I haven't done great for the past few years," he confesses.

When I don't respond—because I'm thinking about something else —he says, "Does that bother you?"

"What? No. You're perfect. You know, one of the guys on my debate team really is good with computers. Maybe he could tweak some of the grades I missed." *Did I just say that out loud?* I look up to find Chausie visibly perplexed.

"I'm beginning to think you don't care anything about rules at all," he says. "You just want to have control over outcomes. This is very interesting."

"Hey. I *deserve* to be valedictorian."

With a chuckle and a shake of his head, he says, "Come on, Kof. Thirsty faeries are dangerous."

Kofi isn't engaging. I bet he hasn't been to school since he was kidnapped, around third grade. I wonder how well he can read. While he trails Chausie out the door, I open my laptop. We're not going to be able to help him with that stuff once we move to South Dakota. Seems cruel to have bonded with him only to leave him behind. He's set, though. Good job. Good people to live with. That's what I'm thinking as I check my email.

None of my teachers have replied. It's like they're not even checking their email. Like spring break is a real holiday. It's not. I probably only have one or two more weeks to get everything turned in. They won't be accepting grades through the end of the year. Heck, we graduate before the official end date.

My phone vibrates with an incoming text from Chausie. An official announcement of valedictorian from the school's website. And it's me! The salutatorian is pictured as well. *Haha! That's right, Peter Mallory!* Oh, that's not nice. He's a good guy. But wait, can they take it back? Was this published with the belief that I would continue to turn everything in and get As?

I send back a kissing emoji because I know Chausie is glad he got to ease my mind. But I'll have to follow up to be sure it's correct.

When I rejoin them, Kofi and Chaus are sitting with the faeries in a circle. It seems to be a faerie thing to do. I take my place across from them.

"We came to express our gratitude," Rafe says. "It is no small thing for _____________ to be beholden to other creatures." He uses the word for their people, but you know how that goes. No idea what the word is. I did sort of hear the sounds this time. Or maybe it was a fish jumping.

Rafe says, "We bestowed upon your lions the gifts of Leander. To Chausie, his father's shifter abilities. To Kofi, Leander's pelt." Sure enough, Kofi lifts Leander onto his head. Not like Mauri did. At least, it doesn't have the same effect. It's fitting for Kofi to wear him. I think Leander would be proud.

Chausie's staring at it enviously.

"Trade you for the whip," Kofi says under his breath.

"I'll think about it."

"What would you ask of us, Beam?" Rafe says.

Oh. That's a broad question. They've helped so much already. Of course, King Rafe was stuck as a werewolf. As I look around the circle at those of us who escaped the ties of Snatcher's Ridge, I remember one who did not. "Is it within your power to summon or locate the soul of the wolf shifter who died?"

"Chesney?" Kofi asks.

Yes, I nod. "I may be able to become a bridge for her to the afterlife."

"You think I saw a ghost?" Kofi asks. I hold up a finger to let him know I'll answer that later.

"Still think it's cool?" Chausie mutters.

"It is beyond our ability to summon anyone," Rafe says. "And beyond our ability to speak with the dead. But we can send out the message that you are looking. We have many messengers." Even now, a few birds collect and seem ready to deliver. One, in particular, soars elegantly and lands in the middle of our circle closest to Robyn. A dignified brown owl with white bars across her wings. Through a yellow beak, she hoots to share the latest forest gossip. I can feel Larkin's nerves from here. She sits straighter, licks her lips, and fidgets.

"Beam?" Robyn asks. "Where did you get the beaded purse you wear?" My catcher resides inside the purse now, and I wish I'd left them both inside. I don't know why.

"From Chausie," I answer.

"A crow brought it to us," Chausie reminds me. "Along with the seven feathers we made Rafe eat."

"You must have done something very special to have been so gifted. Did you find anything other than the feathers?"

I tug out the catcher. "This necklace was mine already, but I had lost it, and it came back to me in the purse."

Robyn shoots a look at Larkin and hoots to the owl, who clarifies her position. The corners of Larkin's mouth twitch in a non-smile. I'm missing something. Maybe I shouldn't skip the start of faerie gatherings to check email.

"Frilk had my clutch," Larkin says defensively. Her eyes brim with tears. "We were all scattered. We had no king."

"Don't give me that *we had no king*," Robyn says. "If you cared about the old ways, you wouldn't have been a slave to begin with. And you wouldn't have enlisted a crow to steal a magical object that was gifted to someone else. Your convictions are twisted and gnarled. We will speak more of it at Counsel."

"I offered the necklace to her," Chausie volunteers. "If that's what this is about. I mean, not at first, and only on the condition that she would surrender it back to me."

"He did." Larkin grasps Chausie's words like a lifeline. "He offered it to me of his own free will."

"Which made it of no use to you," Robyn says. "He is true of heart. Where would we be now if he were not?"

Rafe curls in on himself and rocks back and forth. I guess we'd be someplace bad.

"What did you mean to happen to me?" Chausie asks.

"She meant to trade your freedom for hers," Robyn says. "You could have been lost to the catcher forever."

I feel sick. Would I have worn Chausie around my neck for the rest of my life, not knowing he was in there? Oh gosh. Blue is married to this woman. They have kids together. Kind of. The kids are all watching with solemn expressions. "I've repented," Larkin says.

"We'll see," says Rafe.

"Did the crow deliver anything else with the purse?" Robyn asks.

It's Chausie who answers. "It brought a knife, the blade from which no wound can heal." The memory of the blade causes me to shiver.

Robyn is nodding her head like this all makes perfect sense, and the owl is hooting. "A cursed blade," she says. *Those words are familiar. Why are those words familiar?* From the folds of her skirt, Robyn withdraws the claw of Leander. "I think this will reveal what you need it to. Take it with our blessing, and now I think our debt is paid."

The slam of a car door on the driveway by the house makes us look up. Aiden's cheerful voice greets the Turners. "Glad you could come! Good to finally meet you."

He and Chausie's mom are shaking hands with Mr. and Mrs. Turner. Rosa's waving at us from the driveway, and beside her, Harriet gazes our way. Chausie positions his hands on both sides of his mouth to say, "Come on up!" I'm waving, too. Kofi, from inside Leander's teeth, looks ready to puke.

"We must go," the faerie king says. "Until we meet again..."

Blue disappears them just like that. I bet they don't reveal themselves to just anyone. Otherwise, we'd all have faerie tales.

CHAUSIE

When we reach the lower dock to greet them, Rosa throws herself into my arms and reaches to hug Beam at the same time. "Hi Kofi," she says.

He gifts her with one standoffish nod. He's still wearing Leander. Black shorts. No shirt. And this over-the-top lion's pelt. I guess he's done pretending to be a Disney princess.

"Good to see you free and in the wild," Harriet says with a friendly yank on Leander's mane. Her smile falters when it's met with a scowl—not the rizzy kind that is my go-to, either. Harriet turns to me. "How're you, Chaus?"

"Great. How are the feet healing?"

"Much better now. Is this your girlfriend?"

"And our school's official valedictorian."

Beam, who is giving Kofi the stinkeye, quickly rearranges her features. "Just Beam. It's nice to meet you, Harriet."

"Your man is very proud of you," Harriet says with a handshake.

"He's spoken well of you too."

"Can we climb up?" Rosa asks.

"Sure!" Beam shows the ladies up the ladder and then I round on Kofi.

"What is wrong with you?" I whisper-yell.

"What is wrong with *you?*" he says back to me.

"That's brilliant. Look, I get it. You're nervous. But can you at least stop acting *mean?*"

Kofi begins to launch a counterargument but gives up and says, "I'm not sure."

"Well, try. And take off that stupid lion head." A spasm of guilt has me waving a hand in front of Leander's vacant eyes to make sure he's not in there.

"Harriet grabbed onto the mane," Kofi says. "Did you see that?"

"Yeah, you doofus, she was trying to flirt with you."

"Do you think she'll try again?"

"No. Not if you don't give her a reason to."

"How do I give her reason?"

"I don't know. Stop grunting at her. And would it kill you to smile?"

He nods and begins to climb the ladder.

"And take off Leander," I hiss at him.

"Nah, man. She likes it."

BEAM

"Kofi wore that ridiculous pelt all day long," I laugh. Now that the Turners have gone and everyone else is in bed, Chausie and I steal a few minutes alone in my room to decompress.

"Yeah, but Harriet seemed to dig it. Gotta hand it to him."

"Do you think she understands that he can shift?"

"No idea. But I don't think it'll be a problem. She's pretty cool."

"She's lovely," I agree. "Oh my gah, when she asked if he wanted her number, I thought he would say *no* rather than explain he didn't have a phone."

"I was about to punch him in the gut just to keep him from making an ass of himself."

"Maybe we should get him a burner so he doesn't tank the whole thing."

"I can hear you," Kofi calls through the wall. Makes me giggle. "You can come in," I holler.

"No, you can't," Chausie counters.

"Don't want to," Kofi says. "There are things I don't need to see."

Chausie chuckles.

"I met a woman when I was dying."

My blunt statement wipes the smile off his face.

"After Frilk sliced me," I say. "She had ears like Larkin, except she was as tall as a normal human. She told me that the purse held a map."

The purse hangs from my neck, and Chausie takes it in his hands to study it. There aren't many people I'd allow this close to my person, but him? Always. He opens the flap to display the beads like arrows pointing to the now empty inside.

"If there was a map," I say, "I guess it fell out."

Chaus sweeps the interior. He even turns it inside out. "I'll ask Dad if he found one. He should be back home by now. A map of what?"

"She didn't say. But she did say that a cursed blade would reveal it."

"Those are the words Robyn used about the blade the crow brought."

"I know. Isn't that weird?"

He fixes upon Leander's claw and stretches across me—in a ridiculous way that flattens me—to procure it from the nightstand. Then he holds it against the purse. When nothing happens, he repositions it. He digs at a few of the beads.

"You're gonna mess it up," I object. "The map isn't just going to appear."

"Why not? Stranger things have happened." Next, he does the last thing I expect. He pulls hard at the seam with both hands.

"Chausie, you're gonna break it."

"What do you want to bet it will come right open if I use the claw as a blade?"

"Nothing. Because I don't want you to rip my bag."

"I'm gonna do it," he says. He takes the purse off of me and searches my eyes.

"Are you asking for permission?"

With a devilish grin, he says, "No," and rips the seam apart. After he peeks in, he says, "You're not gonna believe this," and does the same thing to the other side. Next, he spreads my gutted purse on the bed to expose a square foot of carefully painted hide.

"Chaus," I whisper. "What is this?"

"It's your map."

The endmark seems to be a grave. Chausie traces the route to where a wrapped body is drawn under a mound of earth. The mound is covered in spikey leaves I'm going to guess is sage. Beside the body, some kind of large hide is depicted. "It's like the one hanging at The Vigilance," I say. A part of that hide seems to be the very thing we're holding. It, too, has painted icons in the same shape and placement.

The images are tiny, but I think most of them are birds. There are lions, too. One of them is painted black. In fact, most of the images are painted black, but there are splashes of yellow for the other lions, turquoise for a few of the birds—and shimmering silver that reminds me of the stellar material in Chausie's whip. "Is that Larkin's bird cage?" I ask. "How?"

Chausie points to a silver cup full of red liquid. "I'm gonna go out on a limb and say that's blood. That's you, that cup. Whose grave do you think this is?"

I shake my head. "Why would we need a map to it?"

"Do you really not know?"

"Do you?"

"The Visions of Blood are buried there."

"Are you suggesting we travel to South Dakota to unearth a stranger's grave?"

"We'll be in South Dakota anyway," he says—as if *that's* the part that's the problem.

"We don't even know where the starting point is."

"I do." Chausie traces the route backward to an outcropping of rock where a small blue figure interacts with one woman and three lions, and then further still to where light pours out of an arched entryway that seems to have opened up in the side of a butte.

"It's Laurel's place," I say. "And that's where we met Blue. Chausie, that is me resting on you under the stars before I even knew you were my lion! Our whole journey is depicted here."

"I don't think we've completed our whole journey yet." He looks thrilled. "This may be more of a timeline than a map. What do you think happens to us here?"

Two lions are standing up to a giant—I don't know what—some

kind of lumpy rock monster—while a woman appears to be reading out loud from a large book.

"Tell me that lion doesn't have a mane," Chausie says.

"That lion doesn't have a mane," I say. But it totally does.

Even with all the incredible things we've been through, this feels other-worldly. Who painted this, and when? Why was it buried, and with whom?

"Can we please graduate first?" I ask. "I just want to pretend we're two normal teenagers doing normal teenagery things. Not for long. Just till we graduate." Maybe spring break *is* a real holiday. Or should be treated as such. I suppose even teachers need to rest. I certainly do.

An owl hoots outside the window and is answered by another further away. And then another further still. This is a lower-level room, partially underground, so we stand on the bed to look out the window. "I can't find it, can you?" I ask.

"There." Chausie points to a plump brown owl on a tree limb nearby. It hoots at us.

"It's trying to tell us something," I say. "It's staring at us. Do you think it's Robyn's owl?"

"We don't want to hear it," Chaus calls out.

The sound startles the owl so that it has to flap its wings to maintain balance. "Hoo-hoo-hoooo," it says.

"We're going to graduate first," he insists and closes the window with a thump and a face that says he deserves a medal.

"Thank you, Sweetheart," I say, adopting his pet name. It's old-fashioned. I like it.

"You're welcome, Sweetheart."

The owl continues to stare.

The Leonid meteors shower us every November, some years more prolifically than others. In 1833, the whole world marveled at it. It must have been spectacular. Can you imagine? Without all the light pollution? Some were afraid the End had come.

While researching, I found a book called *The Night the Stars Fell* by Sally Crum, illustrated by Eric Carlson. The pictures, much like the book Beam found in Mauri's library, depict what cultures around the world may have experienced. Native Americans outside their tipis, Sailors on the sea, Australians, Africans, Europeans... Citizens of one world looking up, amazed at something far bigger than themselves. That gives me hope.

President Abraham Lincoln was twenty-four in 1833, a postmaster in Illinois, boarding with a deacon of the Presbyterian church. Later, during the Civil War, when asked if his confidence in the Union was shaken, he said the following:

"One night I was roused from my sleep by a rap at the door, & I heard the Deacon's voice exclaiming 'Arise, Abraham, the day of judgment has come!' I sprang from my bed & rushed to the window, and saw the stars falling in great showers!

"But looking back of them in the heavens I saw all the grand old constellations with which I was so well acquainted, fixed and true in their places. Gentlemen, the world did not come to an end then, nor will the Union now."

WALT WHITMAN, *A LINCOLN REMINISCENCE*

President George Washington called the United States a great experiment. We forget, sometimes, how young it is, how vulnerable. I don't think it can survive the current climate of divisiveness and lies. We must elect leaders who unite us, who love truth, and who respect the rule of law and the separation of powers. Forgive me for pontificating. It's on my heart. Let's do the work to educate ourselves with facts from multiple sources and not be played by argumentative clickbait. I wrote a song called *It Was a Great Experiment.* It's a pledge to humble myself and listen to others in civil discourse. It's pinned on my Instagram page if you want to hear it. @JennDanielsMusic I love this nation. I don't want it to be a big stink to the world. I want it to be a blessing.

Alright, I'm done. Hit me up on socials or email me if you want to chat.

THANK YOUS

To Family Neal (the Seals), who put up with imaginary people renting space in my head. The kids have a friend named Chase, and I have called him Chausie multiple times by accident. I think I'm just gonna let that be his name. My husband, Jeff Neal, made the cover, and my Kate named Mauri. She also suggested calling the kidnappers *snatchers,* which led to the title. My Colin helped me identify things that were *cringe.* A very valuable service to a fifty-one-year-old YA author.

Susan Holland, you are a Godsend to me. Thank you for reading and re-reading and knowing exactly what I needed. Also, Helen Holliday, Anna Joujan, and Jessica Pyper. So many of you have been supportive. I'm looking at you, Jennifer Duran, Jennifer Blake, Mandy Pickett, and Kelly Rhodes.

I am ever so grateful to YOU for reading this, for sharing it, and for leaving reviews. You're the best!

Speaking of which, will you please review Snatcher's Ridge? If you don't know what to write, just throw some stars at it. It helps more than you may know.

ABOUT THE AUTHOR

Jennifer Daniels Neal is a performing songwriter, author, and teaching artist out of Lookout Mountain, Georgia, who has released nine music albums, four novels, a picture book, and two human beings into the world (boy/girl twins now in high school).

FUN FACT: During the summer between writing *The Elixir* and *Snatcher's Ridge,* Jenn was playing a concert when the Humane Society showed up with kittens. She now tours with Frisk, a sweet, gentle, grey cat who shapes and informs her feline characters.

For more information on performances, workshops, author visits, etc... check out https://linktr.ee/jenniferdanielsmusic

 facebook.com/JenniferDanielsMusic

instagram.com/JennDanielsMusic

The Elixir, Book 1 of The Elixir Series, 2023, a paranormal adventure of courage, friendship, and the wisdom of blood

The Locke Box, 2021, a sensual but clean mystery/romance

The Bridge to Isla Sofia, 2022, a genre-bending mystery/romance with Southern gothic flair

The Rucksack, 2020, a short and sweet, feel-good love story

The Soubrette, 2020, the follow-up novella to The Rucksack. Think *Breakfast at Tiffany's* meets crime story drama

Cuckoo Woo Woo, That Chick Can Rock and Roll!, a song turned picture book

Music Albums by Jennifer Daniels include

Dive and Fly (2001), Summer Filled Sky (2004), Come Undone (2009), Live at Red Clay Theater (2013), It's Gonna Be a Good Day! (2018, kids music and movement), Songs from The Locke Box (2021)

Stream them from your favorite music sites.